BREACH
OF
PROMISE

BY PERRI O'SHAUGHNESSY

BREACH
OF
PROMISE

PERRI O'SHAUGHNESSY

Delacorte ▦ **Press**

Published by
Delacorte Press
Bantam Doubleday Dell Publishing Group, Inc.
1540 Broadway
New York, New York 10036

Library of Congress Cataloging in Publication Data
O'Shaughnessy, Perri.
    Breach of promise / by Perri O'Shaughnessy.
      p.   cm.
    ISBN 0-385-31872-3
    I. Title.
  PS3565.S542B74   1998
  813'.54—dc21   98-5519
                                                  CIP

Manufactured in the United States of America
Published simultaneously in Canada

July 1998

10 9 8 7 6 5 4 3 2 1

BVG

TO BRAD

ACKNOWLEDGMENTS

Our deepest thanks to:

Nancy Yost, for her continuing faith and tireless good cheer; Maggie Crawford, for helping us to focus this manuscript and cut to the chase; Patrick O'Shaughnessy, for his keen insights into male behavior; Carole Baron, for her formidable support and enthusiasm.

The Honorable Suzanne N. Kingsbury, Judge of the Superior Court, and the Honorable Jerald Lasarow, Judge of the Municipal Court, and their staffs at the El Dorado County Courthouse in South Lake Tahoe for their kind generosity and time.

Stephen J. Adler, author of *The Jury—Disorder in the Court,* published by Doubleday in 1994, for the real scoop on the American jury machine; Helen Henry Smith, author of *Vikingsholm, Tahoe's Hidden Castle,* published in 1973, for her personal reminiscences of Emerald Bay's fascinating past; Leonore M. Bravo, author of *Rabbit Skin Blanket,* published in 1991, for her unique perspective on this century's Washoe Native Americans; Mark McLaughlin, author of *Sierra Stories,* published by Mic Mac Publishing in 1997, for his folktales of this magnificent region.

A belated thank-you to Pell Osborn for being our first serious critic.

And thanks to Brad Snedecor, for everything.

All errors and liberties of interpretation are our own.

BREACH
OF
PROMISE

PROLOGUE

AT TEN YEARS OLD, OVER a breakfast of tepid oatmeal, I read my first newspaper article, a story designed to grab you, a squib on page two, where they put the sensational stuff. My aunt ripped it out and thrust it in my face. A guy on his way home from the movies fought with a mugger, shot him dead, and died of stab wounds.

All for sixty dollars.

So two fools died for sixty bucks, and two fools killed for it. Sad, wasn't it? My aunt sure thought so. So did I. I knew one of the dead men.

There was a lesson in it for an impressionable ten-year-old, just like there is for you when you read the same story a couple of times a year. Look at that! you say. He's dead, and for what?

Sixty dollars!

Why, that's not even enough to buy a decent meal in a restaurant these days. Not enough to pay rent on a cardboard box. Not enough to die for!

That morning, while my aunt preached in the background, I read the story again and felt like someone in a tree house watching ants marching up the trunk. Young as I was, listening with half an ear to her interpretation, I realized the meaning of what had happened better than she did.

Now I understand it even better.

That mugger didn't take time to question the wisdom of his actions. He was too busy trying to quiet the nerve-wracking din of his body needing things. Like Billie Holiday once said, "You've got to have something to eat and a little love in your life before you can hold still for any damn body's sermon on how to behave."

Sixty was enough for him. Enough to feed him and the family for a couple of days. Enough for a fix. Enough to get somebody else off his back. Enough to make any risk worth it. Enough to strike out at another miserable soul and take his precious life away.

Now that I'm an adult, I see the brief struggle between two ants for a crumb even more clearly. And, like you, I'm everlastingly surprised at the meanness of people's aspirations. I wouldn't risk my life for sixty dollars; I've been sophisticated by my culture. Plus, I have what I need.

Unfortunately, there's a vast, arid wasteland between what I need and what I want. And I've discovered something else.

I have to have what I want.

Now, you're thinking you're above all that. Well, maybe so. But try something for me. Take a moment one dark night. Imagine yourself lying at the center of a mattress stuffed with big bills, how soft that would feel, how secure, how sensual, how gratifying . . . how pleasurable! How cosmopolitan to lie there on money touched by so many hands, that has fallen from the sky to feather your nest at last. All of a sudden, you'd be the luckiest person alive. No more kissing ass for you! Get your own licked for a change.

Sounds like fun, doesn't it.

And indulge yourself in one more sick and twisted daydream. You can have all the money you ever wanted. You don't have to steal it. No, the money is yours for the taking if you'll do this one thing. . . .

You'd grab the chance. Of course you would.

But you wouldn't sell your soul cheap. You'd demand enough to quiet once and for all the silent roaring of your desires. Your number might not be the same as mine, but there is a number.

Admit it. You'd kill for it.

Just like me.

Better to ride in a limo than walk on a street these days. You never know who you'll meet out there. Maybe someone like my father, holding a knife tight in his fist, needing your money. Maybe someone like me. Deadly as I have to be.

Life's hard lessons. You want to be the one who walks away alive . . . and rich.

Rest in peace, Dad.

BOOK ONE
PARTIES

Now look here,
if you were really superior,
really *superior,*
you'd have money,
and you know it.

D. H. Lawrence

1

NINA REILLY OPENED THE WINDOW in her office in the Starlake Building on Highway 50. Warm air smelling of toast and dry grass drifted in to mingle with the brittle cool of air-conditioning. Outside, every shade of rust and gold shimmered in a hot October wind that rustled papers on her desk. In the distance, brightly colored sails waved against the blue backdrop of Lake Tahoe. She could sense a shift in the weather. The sultry air held a tang in it, like the end of something sweet, lemons in sugary tea.

Leaning through the opening to catch a ray of sunshine, Nina watched as a man and a woman in spotless white athletic shoes, plaid shirts tied around their waists, dropped hands so that the woman could stoop and gather some carrot-colored leaves from the ground. She held her little pieces of autumn like a bouquet, dancing a quick step or two in front of the man on the sidewalk. The man continued walking, apparently unwilling to play the game. Giving up, she resumed her place beside him, dropping her leaves one by one as they went on, like Gretel casting off a trail of crumbs.

"Way to keep this place energy efficient," Sandy said, standing in the doorway to Nina's office, hands on her womanly hips. Today she wore a fringed blouse and a shiny silver concha belt that jingled like coins when she moved, khaki pants, and cowboy boots, which made her look like an over-the-hill rodeo rider. Sandy enjoyed dressing for the office but she would never look the part of a legal secretary.

Two years earlier, she had worked as a file clerk at Jeffrey Riesner's law firm, a couple of miles west on Highway 50. In spite of
Riesner's dissatisfaction with her work, her character, her looks, and
her air of superiority, Nina had hired her when she had begun her
solo practice in South Lake Tahoe, one of her more astute moves.

Sandy knew everyone in town and had a titanic strength of
purpose that co-opted or crushed everything in its path. A lawyer
starting up a practice in a new place needed to get clued in fast, and
Sandy had brought in the vital first clients, organized the office, and
installed herself as Nina's keeper. Nina knew law. Sandy knew business, everyone's business.

"What a day," said Nina. "Not that you'd guess it in here."

"High eighties?" Sandy said. "One of the last warm ones this
year. Too nice to be inside."

"That's right. Let's blow this joint. It's four-fifteen and I can't
think anymore."

"Not yet. You have a call on line two." Sandy jiggled her eyebrows significantly.

"Who is it?"

"Lindy Markov's secretary."

"Do I know Lindy Markov?"

"If you don't, you should. She wants to invite you to a party
Mrs. Markov is giving this weekend."

"What kind of party?"

"She does a lot of charity work and hosts a lot of community
get-togethers. This particular shindig is a birthday party for her husband, Mike Markov."

Nina closed the window, turning back to her desk. "Tell her
I'm busy, Sandy. Give her my regrets."

But Sandy, a Washoe Native American whose people had practiced stubborn resistance for hundreds of years, gave no sign that she
had heard. "Lindy and Mike Markov are the biggest employers in
Tahoe. They live up near Emerald Bay. This is a golden opportunity."

"Why? I'm too broke to be an asset to any worthy causes."

Sandy spoke again, her deep voice measured, reminding Nina of Henry Kissinger in his glory years pushing governments around. "And that's exactly what you should be thinking about. We're in business here. And we need more money coming in. You've been tapping into your personal account to pay the office rent, haven't you?"

What could she say? The omnipotent Sandy knew all.

"Maybe they need a lawyer," Sandy said.

"I don't like going to things like that alone," Nina said.

"Paul's coming up this weekend. He called while you were in court this afternoon."

"He's back from Washington? I thought he was going to be gone longer. Anyway, what's that got to do with . . . ?"

Sandy shrugged. "I happened to mention the party. He's up for it."

"I see," said Nina.

"He'll pick you up on Friday at six. Don't be late."

"And if I still say no?"

Sandy heaved a fulsome sigh, her belt jingling slightly with the strain. "Then I'll have to go for you. Someone has to network around here. If you want to pay the rent and the Whitaker bill and Lexis, the new computer, my raise . . ."

"Which raise would that be?"

"I'll be needing a slight raise if I'm going to have to party for you."

"Okay, Sandy. You win. Which line is she on?"

"No need for you to talk to her." She turned to leave. "I'll confirm that you're on the list."

"You already told her I was going?"

"I thought you might. After you had time to think about it."

"Wait. Where is this party?"

"On the lake," said Sandy. "They're chartering the *Dixie Queen*. Taking off from the Ski Run Marina."

———

Paul picked Nina up early that Friday, treating her to a hug that bordered on the obscene. "Three weeks," he said. "God, how I've missed squeezing your cute little bum." While the words were light, she felt his scrutiny. Three weeks was just long enough for them both to feel the distance.

A good eight inches over her five feet four, blond, and forty, with two licks of gray around his temples and two marriages behind him, Paul seemed to have been in her life forever. An ex-homicide detective, he had his own business as an investigator in Carmel. They worked together sometimes. They also slept together sometimes.

She was derailed by other men, sometimes. Just a few months before, she had engaged in an intense flirtation with Collier Hallowell, the associate DA she had always respected. That had ended when Collier's personal hang-ups got in the way. So that left her and Paul, a lousy fit who grated on each other, sometimes.

But every once in a while, when they connected, they went deep down to a place that kept them coming back to each other.

As they drove to the marina, Paul quizzed her about her activities in the past few weeks. Nina talked about the house she and her son Bob had recently bought. "We're making it homey," she said. "It's just that none of us knows exactly what that means. I stockpile paper in every corner. Hitchcock has taken up residence in the ski closet and spreads kibble all over the kitchen floor. Bob rides his skateboard through the downstairs." When she turned the questions on Paul, he was uncharacteristically closemouthed. He couldn't tell her much about the Washington, D.C., job, he claimed. And what was there to say about staying in a hotel?

Paul wasn't teasing her. She sensed his preoccupation and wondered about it. Meanwhile, she could think of many things that might happen with him in a hotel and she spent at least part of the ride to the boat holding that thought, just enjoying his proximity and his big, comforting presence.

At the parking lot for the marina, not too far from Nina's office, Paul pulled his Dodge Ram van in tight beside a creamy-white Jaguar.

"This is something," Nina said, stepping down into a parking lot crammed full of gleaming metal. "Oh, boy. Look over there by the dock. It's like a convention for chauffeurs. Maybe we should have rented a limo."

"You look terrific in that slinky blue stuff," Paul said, coming up beside her. He put a hand on her leg, squeezing gently to punctuate his point. "And if it makes you more comfortable, hell, I'll be your chauffeur. Can't do much about my chariot, but I've got a baseball cap in there somewhere. Anything to make you look less like you're about to jump out of your skin."

She shimmied a little, adjusting her panty hose. "You're right, I'm nervous. I guess I'm just getting into the spirit of things, starting out with my foot in my mouth by insulting your car."

"You've talked with people before. I'm sure I've seen you do that. What are you so worried about?"

"I'm intimidated," she said honestly. "The Markovs are very wealthy. Their business is supposedly huge. They sell health aids of some kind. Mrs. Markov also raises money by the bucketful for the schools and recreation programs here."

Paul took her hand and they walked toward the dock where a white stern-wheeler trimmed in blue rocked gently in the water. From the front of the boat, where Nina and Paul boarded, two black pipes tipped in gold, shaped like medieval crowns, framed a view of the rest of the boat. Silver lights of irregular lengths dangled like icicles from two of the boat's three decks, and at the back an enormous paddle wheel, blades painted red, dripped water. On the bottom level, a wide swath of windows revealed a crowd of partyers already moving *en masse* to a tune Nina could not make out, bobbing between bunches of red helium balloons. The low bumping of bass traveled through the water to rumble up under their feet on the dock.

"Ever been on one of these before?" Paul asked her as they stepped onto the ramp that led to the lower deck of the boat.

"Once. I took a tour from Zephyr Cove with Bob when we first came here. He was only eleven. Very impressed by the glass bottom, even though there's not all that much to see under the lake, just sand and the occasional beer bottle."

"Did you say something about these people wanting to hire you?" he asked as they made their way to the exquisitely decorated party deck. "Because if they do, it looks like your ship has come in."

"I have no idea why we're here. It's one of Sandy's plots. Let's just enjoy ourselves."

They paused before going inside, taking a long look across the lake toward the teals and peaches just beginning to tinge the sky and water. "When I see the lake like this, so beautiful, I think about the Washoe people camping on these shores," Nina said. "It wasn't so long ago, only a hundred years or so."

"I'm sure they'd love the hash we've made of the natural land-scape." Paul gestured toward the casino lights. They had begun to gleam in the fading light, under the evening glow of the mountains towering behind.

"From far away," said Nina, "I think it's pretty."

A striking woman walked toward them, smiling. Several inches taller than Nina, Lindy Markov gave the impression of even greater height. Willowy, with warm coppery hair, she had expressive brown eyes over a prominent nose and jawline. A gold collar-style Egyptian necklace adorned her neckline, dressing up the rust-colored dress she wore over a body as muscular and wiry as an exercise guru's. She might be anywhere over forty. She had reached that certain ageless age.

"Hello, Nina Reilly. I've heard so much about you. I recognize you from the paper, of course. Sarah de Beers and some other friends told me you did good work for them. Thanks for coming to join in the surprise for Mike."

"How are you going to surprise him? I mean, this boat . . ."

"Oh, he doesn't know I filled it up with friends. He just thought we were taking a dinner cruise to celebrate his birthday." She looked around. "He's going to love this. He loves surprises," she said, but she looked unconvinced, even apprehensive. Nina thought, uh-oh. Something is not right.

"I hope everybody gets here on time. Mike's due at seven." She looked anxiously toward the door as another couple arrived, relaxing as she turned her attention back to Paul. "Mr. Van Wagoner." She shook his hand, holding it for a moment before letting go. "So you're a private investigator." Her eyes probed his in the dim light. "Do you dance?"

"Naturally."

She flashed a bright smile. Nina, who knew a stressed-out lady when she saw her, read worry verging on panic in it. "Save one for me." She turned away to look at the door again. More guests, not Mike Markov. She excused herself to meet the next crop.

Nina couldn't imagine how they could stuff more people inside. The decks were full of guests dancing, drinking, and snacking. The usual casual tour boat had been transformed—waiters in black suits dipped and posed with silver trays full of hot treats for the guests; tables with white cloths and real silver for a massive buffet dinner had been set up in the midsection of the center deck.

What must be hundreds of people murmured and milled through the scene, dreamlike in the dusk. Once her eyes adjusted, Nina said hello to a number of them; Judge Milne, who was rumored to be considering retirement, Bill Galway, the new mayor of South Lake Tahoe, and a few former clients. She stayed with the group where the judge was holding forth, and Paul wandered off. Seven o'clock came and went, and the waiters made sure no glass ever emptied, but Mike Markov didn't come and the boat sat at the dock as the lake and sky flickered with the fire of sunset.

By the time the guest of honor finally appeared, everyone, including Nina, had had too much to drink. A lookout gave an advance warning, and a hush fell over the boat.

Nina saw him come aboard. Looking like a man with a lot on his mind, he walked right into Lindy's waiting arms. He was stocky with dark skin, about the same height as Lindy. He embraced her quickly, revealing muscular forearms. "I'm sorry I'm so late," he said. "I was afraid the boat would be long gone." He looked around, puzzled. "Where is everybody?" he asked.

"Surprise!" the crowd shouted. The waiters popped another round of champagne. People poured out of the woodwork to pat him on the back.

For a moment, shock poised over his features like the shadow of Lizzie Borden's ax. Nina had time to think, God, he's having a heart attack. . . .

He shuddered. In that first second he looked only at Lindy, suppressing some unreadable emotion. Then, like magic, as he turned to his guests a cloak of good humor dropped into place. He began to stroll through the crowd accepting genuinely warm congratulations, shaking hands as he greeted people.

"My God, Mikey. Fifty-five. Whoever thought we'd get there?"

"You look damn good for such an old fella!" This said by a bald man leaning heavily on a walker, who had to be teetering toward ninety.

"Great excuse to have a helluva good time, eh, Mike? Like old times."

Lindy trailed behind for a bit, then caught up with him, taking her place by his side. Nina stayed behind as hands thumped him on the back and good wishes floated on the air.

The engine started up. The paddle wheel at the stern began to churn up water, and a mournful, low blast from the horn cut through the sound of revelry, of wind, of evening birds and insects chirping away on land.

Just as the paddle started up and the big boat began to move smoothly away from the dock, Nina saw the final guest arrive.

The young woman came onboard quietly. In her midtwenties, with black hair so long it hung almost to the hem of her dress, the girl wore strappy sandals that crept up her calves like trained ivy. Nina thought someone should say hello and show her the way to the bar. She started toward her, but after a quick glance around, the girl dropped her coat on a chair in the corner, collected champagne from a passing tray, and downed the first half of her drink, edging over to blend into a group of people standing by the door who apparently knew her. "Rachel, honey. Somehow we didn't expect to see you here tonight," a snickering, booze-laden voice called out to her.

Nina wandered off to find Paul, who was watching the great wheel make its waterfall at the back of the boat.

The enclosed main deck, a huge, dark space alive with undulant bodies, still pitched with music from a live band. Far from deflating once the honored guest had eaten his cake and endured a shower of fantastic presents, the party was heating up. Nina dragged Paul to the dance floor, where they danced and danced some more. When a moment of clearheadedness intruded on her whirling brain, she moved outside to get a breath of fresh air, losing Paul somewhere along the way.

At the front of the boat next to the staircase, she leaned un-steadily against the wall of the cabin. They had reached Emerald Bay and the boat was circling Fannette Island, the rocky islet at its center.

In the shadow of the western mountains the water was indigo streaked with green, like shot silk. Fannette rose in solitary splendor out of the bay into a tree-studded granite hill. At the top, the ruin of a rich woman's teahouse presided over the whole sweep of bay.

Nina had always wanted to visit the tiny island. The stone ruin at the top looked inviting under the fading tangerine glow of the sky. She imagined what the teahouse must have been like back in the twenties, a rustic table and chairs for furniture, candlelight, a roaring fire; and Mrs. Knight, coercing friends from the city into the steep climb, long dresses hiked up, waiters with trays and tea sets leading the way.

Someone on the deck above spilled a drink and laughed, then complained about the chill. Whoever was up there went back inside, and the night fell into the shushing of the paddle wheel and the drone of the boat's motor. Nina closed her eyes and sank into a woozy meditation on the high life, and what to do with Paul after the party. Questions swam through her mind as the night's cool air, balmy and soothing, wrapped itself around her.

The door opened and two people stepped out. They didn't see her tucked away beside the stairway. She didn't feel like starting a conversation, so she said nothing. She would be leaving in just a sec, just as soon as she adjusted her shoe around the new blister forming on her heel.

"I thought you were going to wait for me at the marina," a man said quietly. "We would have been back in another hour."

"I just couldn't wait." The voice was a young woman's, and it sounded a little defiant.

"Did you know about this crazy surprise thing?"

"No," said the girl. "Have you told her yet?"

"With all our friends around?"

"You swore!"

"Honey, how can I? I thought we'd be out here with strangers."

"Liar!" the girl said, sounding near tears.

"I will after this is over, later tonight," murmured the man. "I promise I will." The voices stopped. Nina started to rise, then heard whispers. They were embracing, kissing. Oh, great.

Now feeling the cold herself, she waited, hoping they would pack it in soon. Then she heard a cry, and the violent crash of a glass breaking close by them.

Someone new had entered the scene.

"Oh, no. Mike. Oh, my God, no." Nina immediately recognized Lindy Markov's voice. "What is this?"

Oh, no, was right. Nina stayed out of sight behind the stairs, stuck like a fox with its leg in a trap.

"Lindy, listen," Mike said.

The first woman's voice, younger and more high-pitched than Lindy's, interrupted. "Tell her, Mike."

"Rachel?" said Lindy, in a quavering voice.

Nina peered around the corner. No one was looking her way. Markov stood next to the dark-haired girl Nina had noticed arriving late. Lindy stood about four feet away, facing him, her hand over her mouth.

"Oh, Mike. She's got to be thirty years younger than you are," Lindy Markov said.

"Mike and I are in love. Aren't we, Mike?" The girl moved to take his hand but Markov pushed her away.

"Be quiet, Rachel. This isn't the place. . . ."

"We're getting married! You're out, Lindy. We don't want to hurt you. . . ."

"Oh, shit," said Mike. "Shit."

Nina, who for all the attention they were paying to her might as well have been invisible, silently agreed with him.

"Marry you?" Lindy said, her voice shaking. Nina didn't think she had ever heard such fury contained in two words.

"That's right," said Rachel.

"What kind of crap is this? Mike? What's she talking about?"

In a high, triumphant voice, Rachel said, "Look at this. See? A ring! That's right. A big fat diamond. He never gave you a diamond, did he?"

"Get out of here before we both kick you from here to kingdom come," Lindy replied, her voice wobbling.

There was silence. "Lindy, I've tried to tell you," Mike said finally. "You just won't listen. It's over between us."

"Mike, tell her to leave so we can talk," said Lindy.

"I'm not going anywhere!"

"Calm down now, Rachel," Mike said, sounding remarkably composed, Nina thought. "Now, look at me, Lindy," Mike said. "I'm fifty-five years old tonight and I feel every minute of it. But I have a right to choose my own happiness. I didn't plan this. I'm sorry it had to happen this way . . . but maybe it's for the best."

"Five minutes alone with you, Mike. That's my right."

"We don't expect you to understand," said Rachel.

"Who are you to talk to me like this! Mike loves me!"

"Oh, now she's playing that game, where she can't see the nose on her face," Rachel continued, lifting her words over Lindy's. "This is real life, Lindy. Pay attention for once."

"Shut up!" Did only Nina notice the menace in Lindy's voice?

"You had twenty years! Five more minutes won't change anything. Mike, come on. Tell her."

But Mike apparently could think of nothing to add.

"I said shut up!" Lindy rushed toward the girl, knocking her off balance against the railing. The girl fell backward. Nina and Mike both winced at the sound of her cry, then the splash as she hit the lake.

"Lindy!" Mike said. "Jesus Christ!"

Nina searched for a float to throw to the girl. She found one, but a rope was snagged around it. She fumbled to get it loose, her fingers working clumsily at a knot.

Lindy and Mike stood by the railing, their backs to Nina, too deeply engulfed in their own private hell to care what she did. Mike leaned over the side, peering into the darkness. "Rachel can't swim!" he yelled.

"Good!" Lindy said.

"Look what you've gone and done now, Lindy! My God, you just don't think! Now, listen. You keep an eye on her. I need to get help." But before he left, he hurried back and forth along the railing calling to Rachel, reassuring her.

"What I've done?" Lindy said, standing close behind him. Nina recognized that she was beyond reason, out of control. "Look at what I've done?"

The lifesaver suddenly fell into Nina's hands.

"Mike!" Nina said, preparing to toss it the few feet between them. He knew where Rachel might be. She didn't.

Mike turned to face her, putting his arms out to catch.

And Lindy, catching him completely off guard, bent down and took his legs in her hands, heaved mightily and tipped him neatly overboard. "Go get her, then!" she yelled, and the explosion of maledictions that followed was swallowed up by the sound of a second splash.

2

NINA THREW THE LIFESAVER IN after him.

As it turned out, Mike did not save Rachel. Somewhat the worse for the champagne he'd drunk, Nina supposed, he paddled feebly around shouting her name, his voice indistinct, his image a dark blur upon the darker smear of lake.

Not too far from Mike, Nina saw Rachel clinging to the lifesaver. Apparently she could dog-paddle.

Lindy, who had put her hands over her eyes, now pulled them away. "Mike! I'm sorry, Mike!" She shouted into the blackness, into the stars, and finally into the ears of her guests, who heard her cries and flocked to her side.

"Well, what have we here?" said a tall, skinny woman with short, streaked hair, looking amused as she strolled over to the railing and looked out into the night. "Hey, Mikey!" She waved. "How's the water?" She turned to Lindy. "What happened?"

"Oh, Alice. I pushed them in!"

Alice put her arm around Lindy. "Well, well, well. I guess you showed him. Who's the woman? There is a woman?"

"Rachel Pembroke. From the plant. I told you about her."

"Hair to her hips and twenty-five years old. That's so classic," said Alice, nodding.

"Man overboard!" an alarmed man in a silk jacket called. "You okay down there?" he shouted.

"Fine, fine," Mike's strangled voice replied.

"Hang in there, pal!"

A large, handsome man sporting a black tie and long hair jostled for a place along the railing. "Rachel? It's me, Harry. Is that you?"

"Help!" Rachel replied, her voice very faint above the sound of the ship's motor. "Get me out of here before my legs freeze off!"

Leaving Lindy anchored by a couple of concerned guests, Nina ran for help.

But the captain had heard the cries. The paddle wheel slowed to a stop, the engine drone quieted, and the boat halted. A spotlight—hauled out of a musty cupboard and hoisted by Nina and a young man with tattoos—located the wet pair in the black lake not more than a hundred yards away, midway between the boat and Fannette Island.

Before Harry could remove his shoes and jump in after them, the crew lowered a dinghy into the water and rowed swiftly out, first to Mike, who was closer, and finally to Rachel, whose hair stuck to her body and covered her face like tattered black rags.

By the time the dinghy returned to the *Dixie Queen* and the pair was climbing a ladder to safety, Nina had relinquished her beacon to a nearby crewman. She was standing at the front of the crowd with Paul.

Someone wrapped a wool blanket around the shivering girl's shoulders. The music had stopped. The guests bunched together to make room for Rachel and Mike, with the exception of the man named Harry, who glared at Mike as he passed. Lindy stood off to one side like a casual spectator, drawn to the event but uninvolved. Red-eyed, with black mascara streaming down her bloodless cheeks, Rachel walked slowly over to her and stopped.

Nina edged toward Lindy, wondering if Rachel was as angry as she would be under the same circumstances. Taking deep, gulping breaths, the girl just looked the older woman over. "I feel sorry for you," she said finally. Mike came to her side, took her arm, and they walked away together.

Lindy watched them go.

———

Afterward, very late, Nina treated Paul to a drink at the bar at Caesar's and then they went up to bed. Paul was playful and warm, and while her body responded with mindless happiness, she couldn't yank her thoughts entirely away from the evening's events. When she finally tried to untangle herself, explaining that she had to get home to Bob, Paul pulled her back.

"Don't leave yet. There's something I have to tell you," he said.

So here it was at last, whatever had been bothering him all evening. "What?" she asked, positioning herself on the side of the bed while a dozen unpleasant possibilities flashed through her mind. Another woman. A fatal illness. He was broke. He had committed murder. . . .

"They've offered me a job. A permanent job."

"They?" she repeated, as her speculations ground to a screeching standstill.

"A private company. Worldwide Security Agency."

"But . . . you didn't go to D.C. to apply for a job, did you?"

"No. I was hired to consult on the design of some new security systems for a block-long office and shopping complex they're building right outside the city in Maryland. I ran into a friend I worked with years ago back in San Francisco. . . ."

"When you were with the police."

He nodded.

"And . . ."

"We were talking, and this thing came up. At first, I thought, no way. Then I discovered I'm interested."

"I knew there was something."

Paul, who was facing her, pushed a pillow that had gotten between them out of the way and sat up straighter. "They want me to run all the checks, hire all the personnel, and work with the systems designer to eliminate bugs when the complex opens sometime early next summer."

When she didn't say anything, he continued. "It's a long project, big on money, high on hurdles. My kind of thing."

"What about your business?"

"I've hired a guy to learn the ropes while I'm traveling back and forth between D.C. and California for the next six months or so. I plan to keep the business on a small scale."

"Until . . ."

"Until I can come back."

She didn't like the way his answer sidestepped the issue so neatly. "What if you fall in love . . . with Washington? You'd lose everything you've worked for."

"I'm already in love . . . with Washington," he said with a sly grin. "That doesn't mean I won't come back."

"You talk like you've already decided."

"Do I?" He raised his eyebrows. "I'm just giving it serious thought."

"Why now?" asked Nina.

"I wanted to talk to you about it. I could have more free time."

"Free time? For what?"

"There are a few things I'd like to do before they put me out to pasture."

"Such as . . ."

"Never mind."

"No, really. Tell me what you want to do that you aren't doing."

He shrugged. "Climb Everest to the top before I croak?"

"Oh, come on," she said. "You love what you do."

"Sure," he said, "but the job does not make the man, my workaholic friend."

Worried, Nina rubbed his whiskers with her finger. "What about our work here? What about . . . I thought . . . I mean. Don't you want . . ."

"Nina, it's not over. Right now, this job in Washington is still long-term, but temporary."

"What's that mean?"

"I can keep things alive in Carmel, and maybe come back here when you need me."

"That won't last," Nina said. "They'll book you for every minute."

"I need to know how you feel about this." He waited quietly, and only a slight tension at the corner of his lips suggested to her his question was anything but casual.

She got up, reaching for a hotel robe and covering herself. "I don't know what to say." Rummaging under the bed, she located her party dress and underwear.

Paul grabbed for her, taking hold of her wrist. "Oh, no. You're not getting off that easy."

"Okay, Paul," she said, trying not to blow up under the pressure of the moment, afraid to say the wrong thing and damned if she'd beg him to stay. "Imagine yourself working under a jerk, with a lot of other jerks. Imagine how you'll love that after being your own boss for years." Paul had been fired from the police department for insubordination.

"Ah, but I was so much older then," he said, his tone light again.

Why had he bothered to ask her what she thought of his job offer? He would decide whatever he decided, and she had no real say in the matter. She let herself be drawn back to him. Putting her arms around him, she said, "Don't . . ." then paused.

"Don't what, Nina?" he asked. He had his hands around her waist and had moved his head in closer to her neck, where he breathed softly. "Don't go?"

"Nothing," she said. She stayed long enough to leave him happy. Then, slipping back into her clothes, she said good-bye with a kiss to his forehead. She couldn't tell him how to live his life. They were colleagues and friends. He would come and go, and that was the way it had to be. She could not allow this to drag her down. Right now, she needed the strength of a light spirit in order to carry the heavy weight of her own responsibilities.

Early Monday morning, alone in the office, feeling the way a sculptor might on the day a big block of uncut marble was to be delivered, Nina abandoned herself to a feeling of edgy anticipation. A new case was about to materialize. On Sunday, Lindy Markov had left a message that she would be coming in first thing in the morning to see her about an urgent matter that concerned the party on the boat. When Lindy had assaulted Rachel, she had turned a private problem into a public one, and in America, a public problem usually ended with the parties in court.

Setting an armful of pending files down on the credenza, she squirmed around in the chair until it fit, kicked off her shoes, and picked up the recorder. First case: petty theft, a senior citizen caught shoplifting a carton of Camels from Cecil's Market after his Social Security check had run out for the month. An ornery man in his seventies, Fred wanted to go to trial on the matter. The trouble was, he had no defense. Better to go to the deputy DA assigned to the case and coax, barter, ingratiate, and con. Maybe she could get the charge dropped.

But not today. Time to get other things mobilized. "Sandy, please set up an appointment for me with Barbara Banning at the DA's office for tomorrow," she said into the recorder, clicking it off as a soft knock interrupted the silence.

Nina felt a thump inside her chest as her heart responded within her rib cage like an answering knock. Lindy Markov had arrived, announced by the scent of her French perfume.

And because Nina had been waiting for exactly this—this strained face peeking around the door, that fabulously cut vermilion suit, and that sheaf of official-looking papers in a long, manicured right hand—she felt a thrill run right through her, and she thought, God, I love practicing law in spite of everything.

She got up and showed her to a client chair, making pleasant small talk and pouring coffee. Lindy Markov sat down, pulled a finely embroidered handkerchief out of a brown leather handbag, and blew hard into it, collapsing like someone who has just found a safe haven.

A lawyer's chair was about as safe as the copilot's seat in a burning airplane. Still, this spot must be preferable to sitting back in the cabin, choking to death on smoke and not knowing why.

Nina sat across from Lindy at the broad desk. Silence fell. The traffic outside had stopped for a red light, maybe that was the explanation, but the silence between them seemed faintly furtive, as if they had cooked up a scheme to commit illegal trespass and were poised on the verge of it.

"So have you heard anything? Are they all right?" Nina asked at last.

"Rachel and Mike are fine. Nobody's pressing charges."

There was another pause. Lindy didn't seem to know where to start.

"You shouldn't have done that, Mrs. Markov," Nina said matter-of-factly.

"Call me Lindy, please," she said. "And you saw what happened. Don't tell me you can't understand why I did it."

"Yes. I guess I might have pushed them in the drink, too." Nina smiled.

"My temper got the best of me," Lindy said. "I just hate it when I do things like that. But you want to know something worse? It actually made me feel better." She shrugged her shoulders. "And now I pay the price—I just got served with these." She handed over the papers.

"May I see?" Nina asked, reaching for the papers. While Nina jotted quick notes on the material, she heard Sandy arriving, just in time to catch the first batch of Monday morning calls. Good. She could focus entirely on Lindy.

Lindy had been served two sets of papers. First, an Order to Show Cause why Lindy shouldn't be summarily evicted from a residence on Cascade Road. In the accompanying Declaration of Petitioner, Mikhail Markov averred that on or about October 10, a Friday night, during a social event, the Respondent, Lindy Hawkins Markov, had begun acting erratically, had threatened the Petitioner, assaulted another guest, and had caused Petitioner to be placed in such apprehension that he was compelled to vacate his residence, leaving the Respondent in possession thereof.

It was further respectfully declared that Petitioner was the sole owner of the premises, as set forth in the exhibit attached thereto and incorporated therein, consisting of a deed in fee simple for the real property, and it was further declared that Respondent Lindy Markov had no right, title, or interest therein, and had been living there for some time temporarily and solely as a guest and invitee of the Petitioner. . . .

"How long have you lived at the house, Lindy?" Nina asked, not raising her head.

"Nine years—almost ten." Lindy said. Nina flipped to the exhibit. Lindy's name was nowhere mentioned on the deed to the house and property. Strange. She went back to the petition and declaration, which in dense legalese declared that Lindy now, after repeated demands, refused to vacate the premises. The court was asked to render a judgment finding Lindy guilty of forcible detainer of the premises, to order the sheriff's office to secure the premises, and to issue a restraining order forbidding Lindy Markov from approaching within two hundred feet of the premises or the person of Mikhail Markov.

"He's trying to throw you out," Nina said, translating.

Lindy's eyes, an unusual amber color, began to tear up, but she blinked hard and lifted her chin. "You want to know something about me?"

"What?" Nina asked.

"My dad didn't raise me to be a crybaby. We grew up poor, and that makes you strong. We learned how not to lie down and let a truck flatten you when it comes at you full speed."

"Ah," said Nina.

"I am not giving up without a fight," she went on. "But tell me, can he really do this to me?"

"We'll talk about that in a minute," Nina said, skimming the second set of papers. Notice of Termination of Employment, said the top sheet. In accordance with Article XIII and Bylaw 53 of Markov Enterprises, Lindy Hawkins Markov had been terminated from her position as executive vice president by the president of the Corporation, Mikhail Markov. In the same manner, she had been terminated as an executive of two subsidiary corporations.

The next sheets looked a lot like the first. Upon a majority vote of the stockholders of Markov Enterprises and its subsidiaries, Lindy was hereby removed from her position as secretary of the corporations and directed to turn over any books, records, or memoranda in her possession relating to her duties and obligations in the said terminated capacity. Exhibit 1, attached to that set of papers, was the written record of the said majority vote of the said stockholders. "Fast work."

"Mike was in a hurry."

Nina turned the page to look at that exhibit. Sole stockholder of all stock in the parent company: Mike Markov. Sole stockholder of the subsidiary corporations: also Mike Markov. So the voting had been expeditious.

Why wasn't Lindy's name on the stock, too? And the deed? But before Nina could ask, Lindy began to talk.

"I got to the plant this morning at seven, when it opens. A security guard met me," she said. "He took me to my office. Inside, my secretary was putting my stuff into boxes. They wouldn't let me touch anything, and people were trying not to look. Oh, no wait, not everyone. Rachel was right down the hall. She watched me. I took a step toward her just to ask her where Mike was and another security man came running. They marched me right out of there like a criminal. Luckily, George came along to give me a hand with the boxes."

"George?"

"A friend at the plant."

"Is that when they gave you these papers?"

"No. A sheriff's deputy came to the house Sunday morning and served me. I just threw them on the hall table and went running like I always do. When I got back, I saw them there, but I had this fund-raiser at the rec department I'd promised to attend, so I just told myself I'd read them later. I never did. I got up and got dressed this morning thinking now that we'd had time to cool down, I'd talk to

Mike first thing." Lindy took in a ragged lungful of air. "After twenty years, he's dumping me for another woman," she said, "and I never saw it coming."

"The bum," Nina said, unable to hold her tongue.

"Yeah."

"But . . . you still love him?"

"Yeah. Why do you think I'm here? I want you to help me get him back!"

Nina read some more. Something had bothered her during that brief exchange with Lindy. Something about the signatures on the paperwork had begun to register. Casting her eyes down to the signature line on the termination notice she thought, oh, hell, because Mike had naturally gone over the weekend to the biggest law firm in town, and of course had been pincered and gathered into the claws of the greatest bottom feeder at Lake Tahoe, Jeffrey Riesner, the one guy who could spoil all the legal fun she had been anticipating.

Jeffrey Riesner. Just seeing his name on a piece of paper made her eyes itch. Since first meeting him when she'd hired Sandy, Nina had fought a few pitched battles in court against him. Each contest had taken a little more out of her. Always predatory, Riesner was rabid when it came to Nina. He hovered over her like a vulture, watching for the first sign of weakness. Then he pounced.

All she had done was to win a case against him once, and of course, there was that time when she'd sort of stolen his client . . . but those reasons were incidental, only excuses, not motives for the mutual loathing that descended deep down to the molecular level.

Bad luck that he was representing Mike Markov.

Lindy must have been busy organizing her own thoughts, because she burst into passionate speech. "Mike is not himself. His brother died recently. He told me, 'I'm getting old.' He checks his hairbrush every day to see how much hair has fallen out. Fifty-five isn't so old. His health is good. I mean, we don't jog together anymore but that's because he's so busy.

"Then a few months ago he was getting ready to go to work one morning. Counting his wrinkles in the mirror after he shaved.

Mad about all the new moles . . . I asked him if he regretted never having children. He told me he did, sometimes, but he'd always said the business is our baby, and he still felt that way. But before he said all that, he hesitated, you know? Sometimes you can tell people aren't telling the truth."

"What about you, Lindy. Did you want kids?"

"I would have loved it, but Mike never wanted them and I accepted that. He needed me to be right there beside him, working the same hours. And I'm so oriented toward work. I guess children weren't what I'm about. I'm at peace with having none."

"So that morning, what happened?"

"He studied himself in the mirror like he hated what he saw. Then he said, 'I'm not happy.' "

"What did you say?"

"Nothing. You know how, even in a warm room, a draft can hit you? I was blown over by the cold air coming off him. But I thought, this will pass. We had been through so much together. We had everything you could want. How could he be unhappy? Was I ever wrong about that." She inhaled deeply, as if pulling her feelings back inside herself.

"I'm glad you came Friday night," she said finally. "The only lawyers I know handle business for the corporation, and then there's Mike's lawyer. I never needed a personal attorney before." She took a sip of coffee and smiled tentatively. "You can help me, can't you?"

Sandy knocked and entered at this suspiciously propitious moment, carrying a retainer agreement that she placed ceremoniously on Nina's desk. "Forgot to bring this in earlier," she said.

"My secretary, Sandy Whitefeather," Nina said.

"Hi," Lindy said.

"A pleasure," Sandy replied. "I see you have your coffee." She glided out as if on rollerblades.

"Is that the same Sandra Whitefeather who organized the Casino Night for the women's shelter this summer?" Lindy asked, looking after her. "And that protest against logging in the National Forest this spring?"

"The very same."

"That's right. I remember reading about her. She was with the group who met with the vice president about returning Washoe ancestral lands along the lake last July."

"*The* vice president?"

"That's right."

"She was?" Sandy had never mentioned it.

"It's the first hopeful thing that's happened in a long time for the native people. You're so lucky to have her. She's being considered for one of the boards I sit on."

"No doubt." No doubt Sandy would retake all of Lake Tahoe for the Washoe in a decade, but in the meantime Nina forged on. "Before I know what I can do, I have to ask you a few questions, Lindy. First of all, tell me a little more about your relationship with Mike."

"Well, we met in Nevada at a club called the Charley Horse—that would be twenty years ago in December. Mike was a bouncer. I booked talent, or what we called talent back then. Dancers and comedians, mostly.

"I was pretty good at my work. We even got Paul Anka for a weekend engagement, and a one-nighter with Wayne Newton. I had some money socked away, but I was lonely. Mike was lonely, too. Next thing we knew, we were living together. We both wanted out of Ely so after thinking about it for a while, we decided to start up our own business.

"Mike is an ex-boxer. All he knew was boxing. The exercise craze was just starting then. I got the idea of building a boxing ring as part of an exercise studio, to get the guys in. After a short time living in a trailer outside of town, we moved to Texas and rented a warehouse in downtown Lubbock, did a lot of renovating, and then I went around and put up flyers everywhere. Like that," she snapped her fingers, "we were in business. The boxing studio worked so well we opened up another one and then another one."

"Who put up the money to move you and get you started?"

"I did. We used my savings. Plus, a little business loan from the bank."

"Did Mike contribute?"

"No, he was broke. But he sure knew how to box. He could slug a guy down in a knockout, first round, until some problems with injuries forced him to retire from competition. Seven years later, we got crowded out there so we moved our operations to Sacramento. Politicians would leave the State Capitol Building at lunchtime and come down the street to spar a little. They loved it. That was about the time, thirteen years ago, that I thought up the Solo Spa idea."

"What's that?" Nina said.

"A combination hot tub and swimming pool. Shaped like a big tin can, big enough to stand a person up in and let them move around a little, small enough to install inside your house, in the bathroom or the den or the garage. You can soak in it, but the main purpose is for water aerobics and exercises at home."

As she spoke about the business, Lindy became more animated. She obviously loved her work. "Mike built a prototype and applied for the patent, and we took out a big loan. I modeled for the first brochure. Mike made me hang myself all around the spas in a bikini." She laughed a little at the memory. "Pretty old-fashioned, huh? But that was a long time ago, remember."

"Do you still model?" asked Nina.

"I did workout videos to demonstrate the product, but I haven't done that for years. No, I did a lot of the planning but Mike stayed up front. We used to joke that he was the obligatory man. In a big way, that was true. Even now, a lot of people are more comfortable writing large checks to a man."

"Hmmm," said Nina. Maybe that explained the scarcity of big checks awaiting deposit in her own office.

"At first nobody seemed that interested, but then some of the hospitals started recommending it for their patients who couldn't go to public pools for a lot of reasons. The Solo Spas turned out to be great for relieving arthritis, helping with osteoporosis, oh, all kinds of conditions. Clinics all over the world started buying the spas for physical therapy. That's when I dreamed up phase two. We designed the smaller, less heavy-duty model and marketed it to the public.

"That same year, we bought the house. We've been there ever since. Mike renovated the basement to be his workshop and we called it the corporate headquarters. Money started coming in so fast we couldn't count it." She shook her head in disbelief. "We hardly had time to spend it. We both were working so hard to keep up with the demand."

"Mike was the president of the corporation and you were the secretary of the board."

"Right. And Mike was the CEO and I was the executive vice president. Several years ago we formed the two subsidiaries, one for the spa business and one for the exercise studios."

Nina picked up the stock certificate attached to Lindy's removal notice and asked the question that was bothering her. "Why is all the stock in Mike's name? Why don't you have half?"

"Mike hates red tape. He said it would be easier."

"The California Community Property law will protect you on that," Nina said. "Right down the middle, I would think. Now, along the same lines, I don't understand why the house is in Mike's name, too."

"Everything's in his name," Lindy said, wavering in her control. "The apartment in Manhattan, the house in St. Tropez. The only thing I have is my car, which is a Jaguar—very extravagant, leather interior, two phones . . ." She blushed faintly. "My biggest indulgence. Then there's this worthless mining claim my father left me, and my personal bank account, where I put my salary checks—my fun money—"

"Ah. You're paid a salary?"

"Well—up to today I was. Seventy-five thousand a year. Mike took the same amount for himself. Our accountants said we were employees of the corporation."

"Have you lived together all this time?"

"Yes."

"No separations?"

"No. Mike has always been a good man. Faithful. And I've been loyal to him. We love each other. We promised to stand by each other through thick and thin in the eyes of God. And we did. This Rachel thing . . . it's so unlike him."

"You obviously know her."

"Rachel Pembroke. She's our vice president in charge of financial services. She's been sucking up to him for months but it didn't scare me because Mike and I were so tight. This has to be just a crush. Male menopause, like the women's magazines call it." Lindy studied Nina's desk, concentrating hard. "I have to get him back. He's like bread to me. Like air."

"Yes," said Nina.

"I don't like to analyze things too much. My way of dealing with problems is to act. I can't just sit on my hands and do nothing. That's why I need to talk to Mike, Nina. Then he'll come back."

"I hope so," Nina said. "But have you considered the possibility that he won't come back? That it's over between you?"

"I'm considering that now."

"How much do you reckon your companies are worth, Lindy? Do you have any idea?"

"Depends on who you ask. At our last audit, not quite two hundred fifty million dollars for everything, lock, stock, and barrel," Lindy said. "Mike would say more like one hundred with equipment wear and tear, depreciation, all that jazz figured in." Coming from her mouth, the amount sounded as prosaic as pudding.

Nina sat back in her chair. "That's . . . a lot of money."

"It's not like there are piles of it lying around. Mike calls it the lifeblood of our business. We don't personally get to spend it. Well, not usually. So tell me. What do you think? Will you be my lawyer?"

"Let's get to that in a minute. There's something I should tell you first. Mr. Riesner, your husband's attorney, normally is a litigator—his business is to try cases. If your husband has retained him, I think we have to consider the possibility that you and Mike might not reconcile—that this might be the opening salvo of a divorce case. At least I can tell you that we will handle whatever comes. California's law is very clear—all property obtained in the manner you've described, during your marriage is as much yours as his, even if he's splashed his name all over everything."

"No!" Lindy said. "This can't happen. No litigation. I just need to see him. . . ."

"Well, let's take it step by step. You want to talk to Mike. I'll call Mr. Riesner and try to set up a meeting. There's a hearing on this eviction notice set for November first, about two weeks from now. No reason Mike should live there instead of you, is there? It's half yours, no matter what the deed says. It's community property. As far as the termination and your removal from the board, I think it's probably illegal, since you're actually a half owner in the company. I can't understand why you let him do that, put everything in his name."

"He just . . . he was so touchy about it. We're a unit, Nina. You see? What difference did it make?"

"Not much. Since you were married and the law protects you."

Lindy leaned over the desk and stared at Nina with red-streaked eyes.

Nina thought, she has to understand somewhere behind those weary eyes that he is never coming back. But there are things I can do to help her get through all this. I can handle her legal problems. It's a major divorce, and they'll put up a fight, but when it is over, she'll be a very wealthy woman worth millions of dollars. A mountain of millions.

For once, a big, easy case, Riesner notwithstanding. Some good hard work, some hand-holding, a great big fee. An enormous fee, a lawyer's coin in the fountain. Nina observed in herself a feeling she did not welcome, the first faint stirrings of greed.

While she berated herself silently, Lindy spoke.

"Sorry, what did you say?" Nina asked.

"I'm telling you that Mike's a good man. A decent man. He promised me we'd always share everything. He just never wanted to—I never could get him to—"

Riding high on her excitement, Nina felt ready to handle anything. "To what?"

"What I'm trying to tell you is . . ." she paused, her mouth open. She closed it, swallowed and tried again. "Mike and I never got married."

You could have heard a pin drop. Or a telephone receiver, when Sandy, eavesdropping in the outer office, dropped hers. Or a big, easy case dropping right off the winnable spectrum.

3

"EXCUSE ME FOR JUST A moment," Nina said to Lindy. She slipped her shoes on under the desk, pushed her chair back, and walked out the door, past Sandy, who was watching her quizzically, and down the hall to the women's rest room.

"Why, oh, why?" she asked the rest room mirror, which maintained a prudent silence.

Nina threw cold water on her face and dried off with a paper towel. While running the rough paper over her cheeks, she started laughing. For just a nanosecond there in the office, before Lindy had spoken those crushing last words, Nina had thought she was going to have her first deep-pocket client, the kind that can actually afford experts and exhibits, investigators and appeals. And attorney fees. She had been mentally rubbing her hands together thinking of the fees like a greedy old Scrooge.

Instead of deep pockets, she now appeared to be talking to a black-hole client, a cast-off girlfriend who had squandered her rights years before.

"Palimony," she told her reflection. Her reflection grimaced. Her cheeks were burning, and her long, fluffy brown hair had expanded and now threatened to take over the room. She wet her hands and tried to smooth it down.

As usual, the man had been careful and the woman had been in love. Lindy wasn't going to have any proof of an agreement to share everything, just a lot of memories of sweet pillow talk over the years.

Palimony cases were poison and every family lawyer knew it. She had handled a palimony appeal herself while still doing appellate work in San Francisco three years before, and she had lost.

The more she thought about it, standing there at the sink trying to squeeze her hair down, the madder she felt. Lindy didn't yet understand that she had been given a swift kick in the pants and a bounce out the door. She was still talking about how she loved the guy! But how could she possibly understand what was coming?

Mike Markov and Jeff Riesner would crush her, then condescend to a paltry agreement to pension her off if she promised to be a good girl and shut up. If she was lucky, she would end up with enough money to join those other middle-aged women who filled the casinos and tennis clubs, unable to find fruitful employment, shell-shocked survivors who had lost twenty years of work experience as well as the relationship.

She was angry at Lindy for being such an idiot, and at herself for not asking right away about the date of marriage.

The worst thing about the whole situation was Riesner. She couldn't take the case now, even with all the other problems, because she couldn't take on Riesner and the team he would assemble without at least a fifty-fifty chance. He was too smart and too pit-bull ferocious. She wouldn't have the resources or the law on her side. She would lose. She would be humiliated. This would be his chance to drive her law practice right into the ground.

Admit it, Nina, she told herself, you're afraid of him and you don't want to go up against him unless you're pretty sure you can beat him. He's too mean.

The other lawyers in town feared him, too. Lindy wouldn't find a champion at Tahoe; no one would want to take on Riesner. The only lawyer he never fazed was Collier Hallowell, a deputy DA in town, who had referred to Riesner as their "resident dickhead," she remembered. And even if Collier had not taken a leave of absence, as a prosecutor he would be useless to Lindy in this case.

Giving up on the unruly brown mop that blew in all directions around her head, Nina washed her hands, then pumped lotion from a

dispenser and rubbed it in. It was so damn discouraging to see another good woman go down, though. Damn discouraging.

She went back down the hall trying to harden her heart. Lindy,
sitting where she had left her, looked a little better. What had Nina
been saying before she left? Oh, yes. Something along the lines of,
you're well protected, no problemo. Nina fell back into her chair.
"Why didn't you get married?" she asked.

"He had one nasty divorce already. That made him reluctant.
He said we were married in every way that counts."

"And you?"

"I wanted to marry him, and we did go through a ceremony in
a church at the beginning, just privately, without any papers or anything. . . ." Her eyes teared up. "But remember, Mike and I met in
the seventies. Plenty of girls my age were not getting married. And
my own divorce had been painful. At one point years ago, we came
very close to getting married. Mike seemed ready. Then he was
called out of town for two weeks. When he came back, he started
making excuses.

"As time passed, I think the iron wasn't hot enough. There was
no urgent reason to get married. And he told me a million times that
we shared everything, work, home, love. We had nothing to gain
from making it legal."

"You mentioned a ceremony?"

"We just kneeled in a church together, and promised to love
and cherish each other forever. To share our lives."

"No priest or pastor?"

"No."

"But you have the same last name."

"I started using the name Markov within a few months of moving in with Mike. We were trying to start the business in Texas and
dealing with all these bankers. Everyone thought we were . . . you
know. People still do."

"Did he introduce you to other people as his wife?"

"Of course he does. I am his wife."

"Lindy. Listen closely. This is important."

"I'm listening." Lindy's fingers tightened on the desk.

"Forget what I said before. Your situation is a very difficult one."

"He's not himself at the moment. He's acting crazy. This will all blow over," Lindy said.

"Listen to me. Mike's left you. He's fired you, and he's about to throw you out of your home. Do you honestly think it's going to blow over?"

"He won't do that. He can't."

"I think he can," Nina said. "Unless you have a letter, a contract, something in writing, or some very credible witnesses who will swear that Mike told you half of everything was yours." She waited, crossing her fingers mentally.

In vain. Lindy coughed, then adjusted herself in the chair, looking troubled. "I don't have anything like that. But he always called me his wife. We were married in the eyes of—"

"Not in the eyes of the State of California. California doesn't recognize common-law marriages. You have to go through the process and get a marriage certificate."

Something must have penetrated the fog of Lindy's denial. Every jittery line of her body registered alarm. "Do you mean—could I really lose everything?"

"The burden would be on you to prove that you and Mike had such an agreement. It's difficult, because there's a presumption that the assets in his name are his property."

"But Mike wouldn't let that happen."

"I imagine he'll offer you something," Nina said. "What we have here is often called a palimony case, though you won't find that word in any statute. It's not unusual in this country for a woman to live with a man without being married, and it isn't even so unusual anymore for her to go after some assets after termination of the relationship.

"But I can think of a long list of people who have sued the rich and famous and come out of the litigation feeling like Titanic survivors, only poorer. In general, they lose. I happen to have done some work on a similar case awhile back and I still remember some of the defendants in other cases." She named a few of the many that came immediately to mind: Lee Marvin, Rod Stewart, Merv Griffin, Martina Navratilova, Clint Eastwood, William Hurt, Joan Collins, Bob Dylan, Alfred Bloomingdale and Van Cliburn. "Jerry Garcia's estate was sued after he died."

"Do they always lose?"

"Not directly. Most cases end up settling out of court, being dropped, or lost on appeal," said Nina. "The problem is that often the case boils down to her word against his, and that's not enough to meet the burden of proof."

"I've slept with him all these years! I was his wife in every way. Doesn't that mean anything?"

"I hate to sound so blunt, but an agreement to provide money in return for sexual services is not compensable. A relationship like that is called a meretricious relationship."

"But he promised we would share everything. He promised he would marry me someday. I always operated based on that idea. It's a breach of promise!"

"Actually, if you sue Mike, you can't sue for breach of promise."

"But that's exactly what he did. He made promises and broke them."

"Unfortunately, California doesn't permit a lawsuit to be based on a breach of promise of the type you're talking about," Nina said. The last series of questions and answers between her and Lindy had been rapid-fire, as Lindy's distress grew more intense.

"I don't believe any of this is happening," Lindy said. "We have always been so close. To quote John Lennon, which he used to do all the time, 'I am he.' We're practically one person. Anything that separates us is temporary," she said stubbornly.

"What you need to look at," Nina said gently, "is what is happening right now. You may be right about Mike. People do change their minds. Meanwhile, you have to decide what you want to do, if anything."

"I can't just sit back. If that means I have to fight him, I will," she said. "I'll fight for what's right." She looked at Nina. "There's something else I should probably tell you. When I got in to work this morning, one of my friends there took me aside just long enough to tell me he suspects Mike's moving company assets. I didn't believe him, but if you're right about him preparing for a lawsuit . . ."

"That's more evidence that he probably is."

Lindy seemed to make a decision. "Listen. I've got some money. I want you to get going on this. Get an associate. Get whatever you need." She took a checkbook out of her pocket. "How's a hundred grand as a retainer? I know you'll need more as you hire people. Write up an agreement with a schedule of payments, and I'll sign it."

Nina examined the check. A hundred thousand dollars. So much money. "Lindy, I . . ."

"Please, Nina. To tell you the truth, I don't think this thing will go very far before he comes back to me. He needs me. Once he comes to his senses, he'll remember that. But I can't sit back and let his momentary insanity ruin my life. It's not right for him to take everything. It's not right for me to have to beg for crumbs. And remember, this is not just about me. I'll bet there are a lot of women in this boat."

"I'm sorry, Lindy," Nina said as gently as she could. "But this kind of case costs a fortune. And unfortunately, you can't use your old business accounts." She handed the check back.

Lindy's face turned gray. She couldn't just throw her checkbook at Nina and get what she wanted. Everything in her life had changed in an instant.

"Where will you find that kind of money?" Nina asked.

"Hold on," Lindy said, pulling out another checkbook. "I have about twenty thousand in my personal account. Take that."

"I can't do that. You'll need it to live on."

"Please."

"I have to do some research," Nina said, "and some thinking before I can give you a decision." She couldn't take the case, but

Lindy needed some time to adjust herself to her new situation. "I realize you have to respond to these papers right away. I'll call you tonight or at latest tomorrow morning." She stood up, averting her eyes.

Lindy sat there, as deflated as the red party balloons back on the boat must be now. "Okay. If you have to," she said. Reluctant to end an argument she had not entirely won, she took a long time to gather her things and leave. Sandy, who had been hovering at the door, showed her out.

Then Sandy came into Nina's office and sat down in the chair just vacated by Lindy, turning two dark pebble eyes on Nina, her broad face smooth and unwrinkled as Truckee River rock. Today, her single long braid of black hair was laced with a strip of leather. In the outer office the phone rang but she gave no sign of hearing it.

"Well?" she said. "Good party? Does she have some work for us?"

"I knew that party was a mistake," Nina said. "And don't pretend you weren't listening."

A minute stiffening of Sandy's shoulders signaled Nina that she had guessed correctly. "I missed a lot, although I caught the shattering climax," Sandy said. "What happens now? You can't exactly divorce a man you never married."

"Eight letters," said Nina. "Starts with a *p.*"

"Paranoia?"

"You're good. But let's hope not."

"Hmmm. Give me a minute."

"I've got court at ten. I've got to get going."

"I've got it," she announced as Nina put her hand on the doorknob. "Paramour. She takes a lover and shows him what he's missing."

"Well, not exactly what I had in mind, but that's a possibility."

The pebbles flashed with light. "Not palimony."

"Bingo."

"But the plaintiffs never win those cases, do they?" said Sandy.

"Speaking strictly about money, which we don't do often enough, you're on the wrong side."

"Yes, that's true."

"Who's the lucky guy representing Mike Markov?"

"The lucky guy would be Jeffrey Riesner."

Sandy made a sound low in her throat. Her eyes narrowed to a squint.

While she grappled with this latest abominable turn of events, Nina escaped out the door.

That afternoon, Nina hit first the on-line computer resources, and then emptied her pockets of change at the copy machine, collecting everything she could find in a cursory overview at the law library.

Palimony. The word had been coined in the seventies when Michelle Triola sued the movie actor Lee Marvin for a share of his earnings after a relationship without the benefit of marriage. Unfortunately for Ms. Triola, although the jury awarded her some money for "rehabilitation," an appeals court had thrown the decision out. She got nothing, but Marvin v. Marvin had put the concept onto the legal map, and that was almost as good as setting a precedent.

Nina skimmed the cases she already knew and a few she didn't. Liberace's estate had been sued by his lover, a young fellow who felt stiffed, so to speak. It was hard to take some of the cases seriously. There was a border area of frivolous cases in which aggrieved lovers simply felt entitled to something after their partners died or moved on. The cases were full of the ingredients the press loves the most: romance and fame.

And, considering the pot of money involved, how they would love this one.

For some time she lost herself in the suit filed by Kelly Fisher, the model who had been Dodi Fayed's lover before Princess Diana, and who had actually been able to sue for breach of promise in a French court. As Nina had told Lindy, there would be no such luck in hard-nosed California. There had to be some kind of contract to share income and assets, and the contract had to be provable. At least, that was how the issues had been decided in the past.

As she sat at the library conference table straining her eyes on the fine print of opinions, she thought to herself that she had never seen the word "love" in any of the thousands of pages of California laws. "What's love got to do with it," she hummed to herself as she read.

Love was yin, traditionally the province of women, female, subjective. Law was yang, male, objective. She felt uncomfortable about Lindy's position. Show me the hard evidence, the lawyer in her said. Promises of marriage, sex, talk of love, midlife crises, affairs—the legal system had washed its hands of these. She didn't want to be associated with such sloppy emotional matters herself. A woman lawyer had to take special care to be more objective than anybody else.

Yet these matters were now inextricably intertwined with a huge amount of money, and the legal system was being used to keep the money in the hands of Mike Markov. It wasn't right. Her anger worked on her, as it always did, seeking a productive outlet. But what could she do all by herself in a fight against these big boys?

She found herself thumbing through the Civil Code, skimming mindlessly through the sections on marriage. They wouldn't be applicable to unmarried people, but what were Lindy and Mike if not married? Lindy was much more than a girlfriend.

Frustrated, Nina thought, we need more laws to cover this, and caught herself just in time. Her entire wall was covered with the Annotated Codes of the State of California, with so many new ones passed each year that no one could keep up.

All right, make an old law fit, she thought. She went through the statutes again. This time her eye caught on a humble little statute that would probably be repealed as obsolete the first time some modern lawmaker noticed it: Civil Code section 1590 said, *Where either party to a contemplated marriage in this State makes a gift of property to the other on the basis or assumption that the marriage will take place, in the event that the donee refuses to enter into the marriage . . . the donor may recover such gift. . . .*

Nina repeated that to herself. She thought of dowries, of handsome men in high collars, of jilted fiancés.

Suppose Paul gave me a wildly expensive diamond engagement ring, she thought, but I refused to marry him after all. The ring would have to go back, or at least, the jury could give it back to him if he took me to court.

Say she gave him something. I will give you my fortune if you marry me, she said to herself, trying to paraphrase the code into words she easily understood. She still didn't quite get it. She tried again. I promise you something, and in return you marry, or promise to marry, me. Yes. That's what the code said in plain language.

She thought again about her interview with Lindy, about what Lindy had said.

Looking down at her legal pad, which had more doodles than notes, she saw that she had drawn a pair of wedding bells with a ribbon on top. Musical notes made a circle around them.

Certainly bells had begun to ring in her brain.

She planted a big kiss on the homely phrase before copying it down.

At five o'clock she slammed closed her last book of the day, then drove to her brother Matt's to pick up her son. Matt and his wife, Andrea, lived with their two children in a neighborhood known as Tahoe Paradise, only a few blocks from where Nina and her son now lived. Matt ran a parasailing business in the summer and a tow truck business in the winter. Andrea worked at the local women's shelter, a way station through which a steady and burgeoning stream of battered women and their kids flowed.

Tucked into a clearing in the woods in a small wooden house with a stone fireplace that smoked for most of the year, they lived the way people had lived a hundred years ago at Tahoe, the only visible nod to suburbia being the struggling lawn that was now, with all the rain they had been having, a silky-looking iridescent green patch.

She pulled the Bronco up to the house, removed her shoes, and marched across the damp grass. Might as well enjoy it. Winter was just around the corner.

Andrea opened the door before she could knock. "Nina! We expected you for lunch," she said.

"I'm sorry. I just got busy. Is Bob still here?"

"He and Troy are up in Troy's room working on the computer."

Nina reached out to squeeze Andrea's arm. "How's everyone doing? Have they been at it since they got home from school?"

"Pretty much."

"Did Bob do any homework?"

"I doubt it."

"Uh-oh. It's going to be a long night."

"They work awfully hard. He needed to do something besides the usual grind."

"I wish he'd gone outside to play. It's so beautiful this time of year," Nina said, breathing in the pine air, feeling the kiss of a breeze.

"Like mother, like son," said Andrea, leading her into the house. "Put 'em in a dark room with a computer and they're as happy as Bill Gates."

"We're not going to hit you up for dinner. I've got to get him home." Nina went upstairs to get Bob.

Other than the difference in size, Troy and Bob looked identical from the rear in their California boy uniforms, Van's two-toned suede sneakers, emblemed T-shirts, baggy plaid shorts, hair a modified monk style. Troy, a year younger, turned around to say hi when she came in. Bob continued to stare hypnotically at the screen in front of him.

"Hey, Mom. Come and look."

From the time he could talk, Bob had demanded that she witness and convey her blessing upon his every act. She wondered if this was unique to male children. Bob's cousin Brianna, who was younger, seemed more self-contained than either of the boys. Nina applauded the improved Web page, then bribed and threatened him out the front door. "Where's Matt?" she asked Andrea as they stood in the doorway and Bob ran down the path to the car.

"Packing up the last of the parasails, and if I know him, paying a final tribute to summer's end with a little ride around Emerald Bay. Hey, isn't that where you went on the *Dixie Queen* last weekend?"

"Yes, it is." Nina gave her a brief rundown of the party and its grand finale without naming its participants.

"Did you see the little island in the middle, Fannette?"

"Yes."

"I heard the most interesting gossip about that place last week from a woman whose grandfather created some of the handmade wrought iron light fixtures at Vikingsholm."

"That's the Scandinavian-looking mansion on the bay across from the island."

"Right. Built by Lora Knight, who also built the teahouse on the island."

"What gossip?"

"Before the teahouse was built, a sailor built a tomb in the rocks."

"Who for?"

"Himself."

"Is he buried there?"

"Nope. Drowned in the lake. His body was never recovered. You know Lake Tahoe," she said. "It's too cold for bodies to float."

"So what happened to the tomb?"

"She said tourists used to visit it, but that by the time the teahouse was built, nobody knew where it was or what had happened to it."

"You're trying to spook me."

"It's the solemn truth."

"Well, one fine day, let's get Matt to load up the boat and check that place out. Can you go on the island?"

"There's no dock anymore. You have to swim from a boat, or kayak there. Besides, his boat is chronically ailing."

"First chance I get, I'm going."

"You're not going anywhere. I recognize that gleam in your eyes. Something wicked has come your way." Andrea was looking at her appraisingly. "You always look happiest when you've got some horrible problem at work."

"True," Nina said. "Horrible problems are my beat."

Andrea laughed in a girlish treble that went with the curly red hair and the blue jeans and the flannel shirt.

"Andrea, have you ever met Lindy Markov?" Nina asked.

"Of course. She's involved in some charities and nonprofits around town. She gives fund-raisers at her house. Everybody comes, partly because of their curiosity about her home, which she's happy to satisfy in the service of her pet causes."

"Have you been there?"

"Yep. Cost me two hundred bucks, too. A worthy cause, but money we couldn't afford." Andrea made a face. "Oh, Lord, how Matt moaned. A dent in that untouchable college fund for the kids. He practically cried. But sometimes there are more immediate problems that need attending."

"Andrea, you're such a good soul."

"No. I found help when I was desperate." Andrea had weathered a rough relationship with her first husband, the father of her two children, and a shelter like the one she now managed had helped her get free. "This is just another token dime to the dollar."

"Where do the Markovs live? What's the house like?"

"Near Emerald Bay on Cascade Road, on one of the most magnificent estates on the lake, bar none. They must have acres of lakefront property. Mrs. Markov has been generous with the shelter. Wish we had more like her. She propped up a lot of women who needed help."

"I wish I hadn't asked. You make her sound like a saint."

"She's no saint. Just generous."

Nina heard the horn on the Bronco. "I have to go."

"Wait. Is Mrs. Markov in some kind of trouble? Anything to do with that scene on the boat you witnessed?"

"You know I couldn't talk about it if she was."

"Well, I just want to say, please let me know if there's anything I can to do to help her. She's one in a million."

Bob honked the horn of the Bronco again and Nina trotted out to the car and caught sight of him in the driver's seat. His head nearly scraped the ceiling. In three years he would be driving. The thought was appalling.

"Mom, Christmas is coming," he said as they approached the corner of Kulow.

So it was. She hadn't given it much thought, but like most kids, Bob had.

"There's this program I want for the computer. Troy and I can use it on our website to make things three dimensional."

"That sounds nice," she said, swinging the Bronco into their driveway. "You be sure to ask Santa for it." Bob knew the truth about Santa but liked keeping on with the fairy tale, protective of their few family traditions.

"It's kind of expensive."

"Oh?"

"About three hundred dollars."

"Oh."

"I'll just hope Santa can bring it, and if he doesn't, I won't be disappointed."

"Bob, since we bought the house, this year is going to be tight. Isn't there anything else you want?"

"Just one thing. It's what I really, really want."

"What's that?"

"You don't want to know." He got out and slammed the door. Nina could see Hitchcock inside the house, scrabbling at the window and barking a greeting.

"I do. What do you really want?"

"I want to visit my dad." He ran for the door, slipped his fingers under the potted plant to extricate the key, and unlocked the door while she stood on the driveway feeling as if she had been hit with a snowball the size of a snowman.

Bob's father, Kurt, a man she had loved once but never married, now lived in Germany. A ticket to Germany would wipe her out.

So this would be one of those holidays where she would worry that she could not do right by Bob. She worked too hard, she worked long hours, she lived in a little cabin, and she couldn't be both mother and father. And she couldn't afford to give him what he really, really, wanted.

At eight-thirty, while Bob was in the shower, the phone rang.

Sandy, who never called Nina at home, spoke. "I was cruising around the Net," she said, chewing on something. Nina wondered, not for the first time, where Sandy lived. She had never been invited to find out. "I was thinking about that Mrs. Markov."

"What'd you find?"

"A case. I wasn't sure you knew about it. Maglica v. Maglica."

"Doesn't ring a bell."

"Down in Orange County. You ever hear of the Maglite?"

"A little flashlight? I use it to take the dog out for a walk."

"Well, there you go. The guy invented it. And he and his so-called wife built up this huge company. They had a falling-out and she sued him."

"For what?"

"Breach of contract. She asked for half the company. Unlike these other cases in this old brief of yours I've been looking at, this one went to a jury."

"And?"

"The jury gave her eighty-four million dollars, mainly for her services to the company."

"Wow."

"Of course, I'm just a badly paid peon without a brain in her head getting it all wrong."

"Oh, stop it, Sandy. It sounds interesting. Give me the Web address and I'll look it up before I go to bed." Sandy gave it to her.

"Are you taking the case?" Sandy asked.

"I'm still deciding. Most signs pointed to no, but then I got the glimmer of an idea at the law library—too soon to talk about, though. And now this case you've found shows somebody has won at least once in a similar lawsuit."

"Markov's another Maglica," Sandy said.

"What's so special about this case that you're spending your evenings doing research without being asked?"

"Lindy Markov helped some girlfriends of mine a few years ago without putting them through a lot of bureaucratic bilgewater. Now she needs help."

"And here's another thing," Nina said. "She needs a firm in Sacramento or San Francisco, a firm with the resources and capital to carry the case. There's so much money at stake."

"But . . ."

"Think about what your average thug will do for fifty bucks on the street."

"I'd rather not," said Sandy.

"Now multiply that take by a couple of million . . . and consider how far our friend Jeffrey Riesner might be willing to go to mug Lindy Markov."

"That's exactly what I have been thinking," Sandy said. "Now listen. He had a palimony case out of Placerville some time back. And here's what he did." Sandy avoided saying Riesner's name the way some people avoided curse words. "He associated in this dude from L.A. who handles all the Hollywood people. Winston Reynolds. He'll want to do that again for this case."

"Unless we beat him to it," Nina said.

"You see the beauty of it. Slip the big gun away before he even notices your fingers in his pocket."

"Mom!" Bob yelled from the bathroom. "Bring a towel, quick! Bring a bunch of towels!"

"Hang on, Sandy," she said. "What's the matter?" she shouted holding her hand over the mouthpiece.

"Oh, man," he said, "too late. Oh, man, oh, man."

———

An hour later, after the flood in the bathroom had been cleaned up and Bob was finally in bed, Nina threw on a sweater and took the dog out for his last walk. The moonless night blazed with stars, a sight she had forgotten about while living in San Francisco in the days before she became downsized and divorced. She could hardly believe that she was into her second year of solo practice, hanging in there and even developing a reputation.

Hitchcock ran with his nose to the ground, nuzzling at the foot of the tall trees and around the bases of the dark cabins. His black fur blended into the dark. Cassiopeia and Orion splashed across the sky. She gazed up, waiting for a shooting star with the same feeling of anticipation she had been fielding all day. Why was it when you wanted to see one of those silver streaks lighting up the black sky, you never saw it? That kind of thing liked to tickle and tease the corners of your peripheral vision, and never gave any warning.

At the door to her house, she hurried in to catch the phone.

"Nina," Lindy said, "I couldn't wait till morning. A friend gave me your home phone number. I know it's late. I promise I won't talk long."

"A friend, eh?" A flinty-eyed friend built like the Rock of Gibraltar, Nina bet. She had a strict rule about giving out her home number, but Nina was beginning to understand about how it must be for spectacularly successful people like Lindy. The usual rules did not apply to her. She assumed a smooth pathway over obstacles and found one, or threw money down to create it. "What can I do for you?" she asked, trying to insert the brisk professional note back into her voice that a barking dog awaiting his ball had a way of dispelling.

"I borrowed some more money," Lindy said. "Five thousand. Could we start with that? I may be broke, but I still have my friends. Alice Boyd just took out her checkbook and wrote me a check, and some other women have offered to do what they can."

"But Lindy, I'm a sole practitioner. I'm really sorry but that won't be enough." She felt terrible. She really wanted to help Lindy but five thousand wouldn't scratch the surface of the kind of expenses they would incur. Nina didn't see how she could take the case under the circumstances without bankrupting herself.

"I believe I can get my hands on at least another twenty thousand, maybe even thirty before the trial. And then, when we win . . ."

"You mean *if.*"

"When," Lindy said firmly, "we win, I'll pay you ten percent of whatever I'm awarded by the court."

The words rang in Nina's ears. Ten percent. If the court awarded her half the Markov assets, that would be in the realm of ten million dollars. Cut that in half to be realistic, and you still came up with an unbelievable figure.

Her fingers clenched the phone. She was unable to speak. So here it was, streaking across a black sky. Her big chance. A case with a heart to it, and issues that were unresolved in California law. Something that might set a precedent for other women like Lindy, who had worked behind the scenes only to be left with nothing. A case that might make her rich.

A case with one big flaw: a client with no money.

Even if she could somehow scrape together the money to keep them afloat as they prepared for a trial, how could she justify taking such a risk? If Lindy lost, Nina could lose everything.

But an opportunity like this one wouldn't come knocking again. She had lived long enough to know that.

She had some assets left. And there had to be lots of ways to get the money they would need. Maybe she could associate someone else in who would assume some of the risk for a big payoff. . . .

Lindy was talking. "People are so amazing. Everyone's doing what they can for me." She sounded moved. "I treasure my friends."

"I guess they treasure you, too."

"If that's true, I'm lucky," Lindy said. She didn't say anything else. She waited for Nina.

"Meet me at my office at nine tomorrow morning," Nina said. She hung up, pushing away a nasty little feeling that told her she had no business taking this case.

4

FIFTEEN DAYS LATER, NINA STOOD up as Judge Curtis E. Milne of the Superior Court of El Dorado County materialized from the wall behind his dais. Or so it appeared. Actually, a nondescript, burlap-textured partition extended out in front of his personal backdoor to the courtroom, and he merely came out and sat down behind his tall desk, but the effect was that of a magical manifestation. A Baraka chief from the Congo would have appreciated this encouragement of superstitious respect.

Unfortunately, many California judges these days got no respect from the office they held—they had to put up with lawyers who no longer bothered to control their tantrums and defendants who dissed them to their faces.

Judge Milne, an ex–district attorney with fifteen years on the bench, was an exception. His bailiff, Deputy Kimura, had toured the courtroom, meticulously collecting bubble gum and newspaper litter before Milne came in. Any disturbance or other breach of protocol while Milne's court was in session meant expulsion or worse. "The Judge," as he was called by the little community of Tahoe lawyers who appeared before him on a regular basis, was actually a small, balding senior citizen, but in Nina's mind he stood ten feet tall in his black robes and his voice erupted like a volcano.

When the judge came in the courtroom fell silent except for the interminable noise of the ventilation system, and all rose. Although the Order to Show Cause had been taken off the morning Law and

Motion calendar and had been specially scheduled for two o'clock, the place was packed with reporters and other community members. Photographers lounged in the public hallway outside the courtroom, and several TV vans waited outside the courthouse. The Markovs were private people, but they were monstrously rich. Everyone wanted to watch the action in this particular family feud.

At the plaintiff's counsel table, Jeffrey Riesner stood in a thousand-dollar suit with Mike Markov, while Nina had taken her place at the other table with Lindy at her side.

Nina had spent several days after her conversation with Lindy trying to get Riesner on the phone, to set up the meeting Lindy had requested. All she got was Riesner's secretary, who was so sorry, but Mr. Riesner was unavailable.

Markov, barely contained by a charcoal suit stretched tight across the upper arms, hadn't even acknowledged Lindy when she came in. Dressed in a simple burnt-sienna-colored suit over a soft beige blouse, she had tried to talk to him but Riesner had taken his arm and led him firmly to his chair.

It was just as well. Markov had brewed to a boil; his clenched jaw and bulging eyes made that clear. He had been served with Lindy's responsive papers just a few days before. Obviously, he hadn't liked what he had read.

Rachel Pembroke sat in the front row of the audience seats, close enough to Markov to whisper back and forth with him. Her legs in an extremely short skirt were crossed in that very uncomfortable way that makes legs look their best, and she was enjoying the attention of the reporters who took up most of the other seats. A long-haired man nearby had riveted his eyes on Rachel's face.

"That's Harry Anderssen," Lindy told Nina in a low voice, "the model for our new ad campaign. Rachel's old boyfriend."

Nina recognized him as the man on the boat who had called out to Rachel when she went overboard during Mike Markov's party. His hair was shorter and darker than the supermodel Fabio's, but there the differences pretty much ended.

The judge took his seat with a flourish of his robe. As everyone sat down, Nina noticed her hands were trembling; from the extra cup of coffee at lunch, she told herself. Next to her, Lindy stared straight ahead, her posture proud, her hands folded tightly on the table. Making a show of her support in the first row behind Nina's table, Lindy's friend Alice, the one Nina had seen on the boat, turned her thumbs up at them, flashing a smile. Nina stole a look at Riesner. Instantly his eyes swerved to hers, as if programmed to respond to the mildest contact.

He smiled a smile both malicious and somehow smutty. It always made her feel that he had some kind of sexually sadistic feeling for her; that he would enjoy degrading her. At least he couldn't stare through the counsel table at her body right now. "Ugh," she murmured, dragging her eyes back toward Milne.

"Markov versus Markov," Judge Milne said, looking down through his half-glasses at the file on his desk. "Appearances?"

"Jeffrey Riesner of Caplan, Stamp, & Riesner representing Petitioner Mikhail Markov, Your Honor," Riesner said, jumping to his feet. The weighty firm name contributed to the desired illusion that he and his client had an army behind them.

"Nina Reilly, Law Offices of Nina Reilly, representing Mrs. Lindy Markov, the respondent and cross-complainant," Nina said, rising. She had two offices if you included Sandy's.

"Well, let me see what we have here in this blizzard of pleadings," Milne said. "As I understand it, Mr. Markov has filed an action to eject Mrs. Markov from a residence located at Thirteen Cascade Road. He says she is merely a guest and invitee in his home, or at most a tenant at will, and he says she has threatened him. Am I right so far, Mr. Riesner?"

"That's correct, Your Honor. Let me clarify an important point at the outset. This lady who calls herself Mrs. Markov is not now and never has been the wife of my client—"

"In a moment, Counselor. Now, Ms. Reilly. You have filed on behalf of your client a Response to the eviction proceeding, alleging that your client cannot be evicted because she is part owner of the premises. You have filed a rather detailed declaration by your client in support of that contention. I understand that. It also appears that you have filed a cross-complaint in the eviction proceeding which has caused the whole proceeding to be kicked upstairs to the Superior Court."

"That's right, Your Honor. If I may—"

"Now, this cross-complaint rather widens the scope of the issues, if I am reading it correctly. Your client appears to be suing Mr. Markov for wrongful termination, fraud, breach of fiduciary duty, constructive trust, breach of contract, intentional infliction of emotional distress, *quantum meruit,* suit to quiet title, partition for an accounting and appointment of a receiver, declaratory relief . . . is that it? Have I stated all the causes of action?"

"Yes, Your Honor. Of course, the cross-complaint may be amended to add additional causes of action later."

"I would have thought we had plenty," Milne said to a ripple of laughter. He treated the audience to a throat-clearing that continued long and loudly enough to silence them, then said, "I note you allege that the sum of approximately two hundred fifty million dollars is in issue." That instantly curbed the chuckles. All activity in the courtroom momentarily ceased.

Nina let the deferential hush linger for a moment, then spoke. "Markov Enterprises has a current value somewhere in that realm," Nina said, keeping her voice steady. "Our primary contention is that Mrs. Markov is a half owner of all assets the couple has acquired during a twenty-year relationship, including various real property and the assets of Markov Enterprises."

"So it's only about a hundred twenty-five million dollars we're talking about?"

"That's the approximate figure, subject to proof."

"That's a lot of money, Counselor."

"No shit," Mike Markov said audibly from the other counsel table. Milne looked over, and Riesner shushed him.

"If I may, Your Honor," Riesner said.

"Go ahead, Mr. Riesner. Please explain what we can accomplish in the half hour available today."

"It's simple," Riesner said. "I urge the Court not to let the filing of this massive and quite frivolous cross-complaint cause any confusion. What my client needs today is a temporary order of the court, pending any final judgments or orders, that Ms. Markov must leave the residence forthwith. Both of them can't live there anymore, Your Honor, that's clear from our supporting papers, and the house belongs to Mr. Markov.

"Our only other request is that the Court order Ms. Markov to stay a reasonable distance from Mr. Markov and from her former workplace, and that she refrain from contacting Mr. Markov. There's nothing special about this situation, Your Honor. A relationship ends, and one of the people can't let go. That's all it is."

"Ms. Reilly? Do you agree? Are these the issues before the Court today?"

"I agree that some temporary orders are all that's needed at the moment, Your Honor. But those aren't the orders the Court should issue. Mrs. Markov is requesting that she be given sole possession of the parties' residence pending further order of the Court. Also—"

"Let's talk about the house, then. Mr. Riesner?"

Riesner charged into his argument. He granted that it was a long relationship, but all good things must end. Ms. Markov had stubbornly refused to leave the house, and it belonged to Mr. Markov. She had never paid rent, so that was not an issue. Mr. Markov needed immediate relief from the Court because much of his businesses was conducted from an office in the house, as well as in the workshop in which he was working on a new product with a tight production deadline.

Milne nodded his head, following along. These strong, objective reasons expressed quite logically the grounds for putting Lindy out on her rear.

Riesner went on. Mr. Markov, out of the goodness of his heart, had been prepared to pay for Ms. Markov to stay in an apartment or hotel room in town for the next six months, but it was obvious Ms. Markov was out to get Mr. Markov, so that offer was no longer feasible. Mr. Markov was willing to allow Ms. Markov forty-eight hours to remove her personal effects, but due to Ms. Markov's jealous and aggressive state of mind, which had caused her to attack a friend of Mr. Markov's, and Mr. Markov himself, a supplemental order should be issued forbidding her from, well—to be blunt—trashing the house. A security detail from Markov Enterprises could supervise the packing.

In a glib flurry of catchphrases, Riesner constructed his image of the case. The spurned, unpredictable, jealous girlfriend. The important businessman. The clutching, tearful scenes, followed by threats when she realized he was serious. Sloppy female emotions that had no place in a court of law.

"All right," Milne said. "Ms. Reilly? I note that your client does not claim to be married to Mr. Markov. Nor do I see any written evidence in the paperwork to indicate she has any ownership interest in the house. Would you please address those points first?"

"Although the parties never took out a marriage certificate, they did consider themselves married, Your Honor. Mrs. Markov has been Mr. Markov's wife in every sense of the term except the technical legal one for twenty years."

"But the technical legal one is the one we're concerned with, isn't it?"

"Not at all," Nina said. "There is another basis for the claim. Mrs. Markov is half owner of the house because the parties agreed twenty years ago to work together as partners in building Markov Enterprises, and to share the fruit of their labor fifty-fifty. The house was built by the parties together, and Mrs. Markov has lived there just as long as Mr. Markov. She, too, pursues her life and business interests from the house."

Riesner broke in. "Saying it doesn't make it so, Your Honor. She hasn't produced a speck of written evidence that her client had some kind of partnership agreement with Mr. Markov. And, again, I hate to be so blunt, but exactly what business interests does this lady have? Since she no longer works at Markov Enterprises . . ."

"That remains to be seen," Nina said.

"Since she's unemployed at the moment," Riesner said, raising his voice and drowning her out, "exactly what business interests are we talking about, besides the obvious one of soaking Mr. Markov through the good offices of Counsel here—"

"At least I'm not trying to destroy the woman who helped and supported me and made me what I am," Nina said loudly.

"Oh, please. Your Honor, are we going to have some sort of emotional outburst now? Is Counsel going to cry until she gets her way?"

Nina held on to the counsel table so tightly that her knuckles hurt, so choked with anger that she couldn't dislodge a word.

It didn't matter. Milne had already made up his mind. "Counsel," he said in an unusually kind voice to Nina, "all I have in front of me in the way of evidence of ownership is a deed to the real property. A deed has to be accorded great weight. It has to be given precedence over mere words. That's one of the basic tenets of real property law. Clearly, the parties cannot continue to live together. At least until there is a final resolution of the claims you have made in this cross-complaint, one of them must go. The one that stays has to be the one with the deed to the house.

"The Court will grant the petition based on the Order to Show Cause. I'll also grant the restraining orders to keep the peace in what seems to be a rather volatile situation. Now, let's move on. What else have we got?"

Without fanfare, Lindy worked a gold band off of her finger and dropped it into her purse. From the table across the way, Mike Markov watched. Nina said, "We're asking that Mrs. Markov be permitted to continue working at Markov Enterprises pending final resolution of the litigation."

Milne raised a hand to stop her and said, "I don't think we need to spend much time arguing that here, Counsel. I've read your arguments and I find them unpersuasive. If Mrs. Markov was wrongfully terminated, she will have her remedy at law in due course, up to and including back pay."

"Actually, she is not an employee, Your Honor. She's an owner."

"Mr. Riesner? What do you say to that?"

"It's just another appeal to sympathy, Your Honor. The stock certificates are right there in your file. She doesn't own a single share."

"But we're contending that is because Mr. Markov has defrauded her, Your Honor!"

"Well. I understand the contention," Milne said. "Unfortunately, the contention is in dispute. From what I have in front of me today I don't see a clear probability that your client will prevail on this issue. With regard to Respondent's request to continue working or to continue receiving her usual salary *pendente lite,* the request is denied.

"I believe that disposes of the interim matters raised in the Petition, Mr. Riesner. Now, Ms. Reilly. You had requested another set of orders, I believe. Connected with the claim that a partnership exists between the parties. Proceed. Time is running short."

Riesner offered the judge his familiar sycophantic smile. Markov sat back in his seat observing the proceedings, glancing now and then at Lindy as if to read her true purpose. All Nina had left now was the long shot. She took a moment to compose her mind, acutely aware of the round beacons beaming sickly yellow light into the cavelike room with its panels and green-tinged walls and its shifting, silent crowd of watchers.

"All right," she said. "The Court has a deed and some stock certificates, and Mrs. Markov doesn't have much besides her word at this point regarding those issues. But there is another issue that we have become aware of, Your Honor, both urgent and serious."

"Like hell!" Markov said derisively from the counsel table, and once again Riesner leaned over and said, "Keep quiet!" before Milne could.

"Very urgent," Nina repeated. "It's this, Your Honor. Mrs. Markov has learned that Mr. Markov is hiding assets. He's contracted to sell two warehouses and an apartment in New York in the last week, to a holding company based in Manila, which is so new I couldn't even get the S.E.C. paperwork on it, Your Honor. By the time a final hearing occurs on all these matters, he'll have transferred most of the assets of Markov Enterprises overseas at this rate. That'll be the end of Mrs. Markov's right to have these matters decided as part of a judicial process."

Nina went on with her argument. She told Milne that she knew little of these transactions because she knew little about what was going on at Markov Enterprises. They had had no time to investigate what was hidden up Mike Markov's sleeve. After this hearing, Lindy would have no access to the records of the business, except what Nina could extract bit by bit in the discovery process. That information would be censored and abbreviated. Even if the Court issued a restraining order forbidding Markov from moving assets overseas, the vast sums involved ought to be enough to convince the Court that Lindy Markov had a right to have that money protected until her claims were adjudicated.

Openly anticipating his midafternoon break, Milne's eyes glanced at the clock on the wall above the jury box. Nina hated losing her audience.

"We therefore ask the Court to appoint a temporary receiver for Markov Enterprises," she said, making her voice louder than usual, trying to gather back the judge's attention, "a certified public accountant from the list of names we've provided the Court, to make an accounting of the assets and debts of the businesses and to prevent waste of the assets," Nina said.

"Mr. Riesner?" Milne said.

Riesner just smiled, though Mike Markov looked ready to take Nina on bare-fisted. "Well," Riesner said with a wave of his hand, as if swatting off a buzzing fly, "I hardly know how to respond. The request is so utterly capricious, so potentially damaging to the companies, so patently designed to bully and bedevil my client . . ." He knew he had it in the bag, and his voice took on the note of pretentious urbanity that always made Nina want to smash her code book over his head.

Instead she took notes.

Then Mike Markov, who also appeared to think it was in the

bag, interrupted his own lawyer. "This is a load of horse crap," he said over Riesner's voice.

All eyes turned to him. He was shaking with fury.

Riesner froze midsyllable, and Milne said sharply, "What did you say, sir?"

Rachel Pembroke leaned forward and touched Mike's arm in a futile gesture to calm him down. When he moved his arm away with a jerk, she pulled back, startled.

"It's bullshit," Mike said. "That's what it is. Lindy doesn't want my business. She wants to get back at me. I can accept that. But don't think I don't know who's responsible for putting this idea into her head." He glared at Nina, then turned slightly so that he faced the judge and audience equally. "Here's how it is. If I want to trade my company to the king of Siam for an elephant, I'll make the trade. Nobody but nobody else runs my business. I'll see myself bankrupt before I let that happen. That's my response."

Someone in the audience clapped and said "Attaboy." Riesner leaned down, whispering urgently to Mike.

Milne looked at Mike, looked at the audience. Then he slowly stood up from the bench, leaning forward. Nina had never seen him lose his temper.

"So you'll do whatever you want with it?" he said to Mike very deliberately, as if intentionally goading him further.

"You're damn right I will," Mike said, rising out of his chair.

Riesner pushed him down and this time, though still in the grip of a combative frenzy, Mike finally seemed to comprehend that he had made a grave error.

"I want to apologize for Mr. Markov," Riesner began, but Milne cut him off.

"You're going to get that receiver, Mr. Markov," Milne said. "The receiver will assure that no business assets are sold or transferred until further order of the Court. The receiver will perform an accounting of every dime you take in and pay out. Do you hear that, sir?"

"Your Honor, please—this isn't fair—we request—" Riesner pleaded desperately.

"Is that clear, Mr. Markov," Milne asked, without bothering with a question mark.

"Very clear," Riesner replied.

"So ruled. Court is adjourned until two-forty-five." Again, the courtroom rose. His robe billowing behind him like a kite tail, Milne disappeared behind his partition.

A dozen conversations burst out. Riesner sat down. He and Mike Markov looked at each other. Nina grabbed Lindy and said, "Not a word until we're outside." Lindy nodded. The reporters rushed forward and Deputy Kimura motioned his head toward the door by the jury box that led to a private hall and a way out past the clerk's office. Nina and Lindy ran for the door, pursued by at least a dozen people, and once they made it through, the deputy closed the door behind them.

They waited in the hallway visiting with the clerks, then jogged out to the parking lot without interference and got into Nina's Bronco. As they began to drive away, they noticed a commotion on the south side of the lot right near the exit lane.

"What's all that shouting?" Lindy said. "Oh, no! Look!"

Nina craned her neck and saw cars had stopped exiting. All of the television cameras were pointed at one spot, where two men in suits stood facing each other. "It's Mike and Harry, Rachel's ex-boyfriend," Lindy said.

Mike Markov stood absolutely still in a clearing between trees, while Harry yelled into his face.

"Harry looked mad in court today," Lindy said, lowering her window. "What a waste. He must still have feelings for Rachel."

Nina could see Rachel in the crowd that had formed around the two men, looking inconspicuous but engrossed.

"You dumb thug," Harry said to Mike in a voice loaded with contempt. They could hear each word clearly.

"Harry," Mike said, "why don't you shut the fuck up? This is no place to argue."

"Poor Mike," Lindy said. "He'll never understand guys like Harry. To Harry, any camera is an invitation."

"You and your goddamned money," Harry said. "You think you've got it made. You think you can buy her!"

Mike was silent, although Nina and Lindy could observe the heat of his emotions in the redness of the muscles in his neck.

"How much are you giving her, Mike? A million? More? How much are you promising her to play house with you for one whole year? Does she get a bonus for sticking it out for two? Isn't that the way rich old farts do it these days with pretty young things? Buy them?"

"You're making a mistake, Harry."

"No, you're making the mistake. Because, Mike, she loves me. Your money's not going to affect that in the long run. She'll come back to me after she's grown up a little and realizes what she's gotten herself into. But you'll never get it until she leaves, will you? Because you're old, and you're vain, and you've had way too many slugs to the brain to see how it really is."

So fast his arm almost blurred, Mike threw a punch, but before it reached Harry, two uniformed policemen grabbed him. They pulled him back and escorted him away. On the patio in front of the courthouse, they stopped and sat him down on a bench. One took a position in front of him, arms folded, mouth moving. Nina could imagine the lecture he was giving.

"Doesn't look like they're going to arrest anyone," Lindy said with relief.

Another policeman escorted Harry to his bright-yellow car. A few seconds later he flew by Nina and Lindy looking as pretty as the quick, colorful, visual splash of a billboard advertisement.

"What was that all about?" Nina asked.

"Rachel. They were fighting over Rachel. She's the focus now."

"Harry's just lucky Mike didn't land a punch on that faultless jaw of his," Nina said.

"That wouldn't help his modeling career," Lindy said, rallying.

"Doesn't he work at Markov Enterprises?"

"Not anymore. He was my assistant in marketing, but Mike fired him recently. I guess he found out about Harry and Rachel, how close they used to be."

"Didn't you say he modeled for your new ad campaign?"

"Yes. He didn't start as a model with us but it's hard not to notice Harry's looks. One night a few years back, Mike and I brainstormed a way to cut some corners. We started using posed photos of Harry in all our print media. Well, business really picked up. Other businesses saw him and liked him, too. Now, he's really in demand. We finished some ads with him for television right before Mike fired him." Lindy looked in the side mirror. "Let's go. Oh, boy. Here come the television trucks," she said.

"Hold on." Nina pulled into the street and took off down Al Tahoe, watching the rear window. They zigzagged through the shopping center and out another entrance.

"A stimulating day," Lindy said.

"Yes. More than usually dramatic, even in court," said Nina, noting with satisfaction that no one seemed to be following them. Her mind slipped back to the earlier events of the day. Markov and Milne had both lost it. And if she hadn't been thinking about sloppy emotions, she might not have focused in on the anger that had circled like a storm in there, and now that she came to think about it, always did orbit the courtroom. But nobody considered anger sloppy, because anger was so very masculine.

"They do get emotional," said Lindy, "don't they?"

Nina laughed. For the next few blocks, they listened to the radio, while Nina ruminated and Lindy leaned tiredly back against her seat.

"Nobody won in there today," she said, breaking the silence. "I lost my home, and he's losing control of the business."

"That's true."

"Seeing Mike blow up in court shocked me. No wonder he almost broke Harry's face afterward. He's like a stranger, with just glimpses of the old Mike peeking through once in a while. A receiver's going to drive him nuts. He's very hands-on."

"Your interests will be protected," Nina said. "It was the right thing to do."

"Maybe legally. But suddenly, this is not about Mike and Lindy anymore," she said sadly. "It all comes down to money."

Nina didn't have a response, so she concentrated on her driving.

"Nina?" said Lindy.

"Yes?"

"Do I really only have two days to move out?"

"I'm afraid so."

"Then, will you do me a favor?"

"Of course."

"Stop by tomorrow. There's something I'd like to show you."

5

After dropping Lindy off at the parking lot next to her office where she had left her car, Nina drove directly on to her next appointment. For the first time in months she turned on the car heater and shut out the dusty dry scents of autumn by rolling up the windows. Along the parkway between the highway and the lake a steady stream of joggers and skaters cruised along. High cirrus clouds blocked some of the sun and the lake had turned choppy in a rising breeze.

Sandy was waiting for her after lunch along with several clients. She followed Nina into her office and said, "I finally got a call back from Winston Reynolds's assistant. She says he can only meet with you at eight tonight."

"He's here in town?"

"He's in L.A."

"Well, that won't work. The Tahoe airport's closed to commercial planes, even if there were direct flights. Reno's airport is sixty miles of hard driving from here. He can talk to me tomorrow."

"He's in trial. His assistant said he's making a big effort to free up dinner tonight, but you have to get down there."

"I could charter a flight," Nina said. Her normally frugal nature balked at the thought, but this was no time to pinch pennies. "Call the airport and see if I can get a charter." She went into her office, feeling grand, and pulled out her office checking account records, which didn't look grand. How far would twenty-five thousand dollars go? How would she snatch Winston Reynolds away from Riesner without paying a whole lot of money up front?

She needed him. She would think of something.

Sandy buzzed and said, "Six hundred round trip. Six p.m. You'll be there by seven. The pilot will wait at LAX until you're ready to return."

Nina raced to the school to wrest Bob from a street hockey game he was playing with friends on the asphalt field. He didn't want to leave and sulked through the ride home, growling at her when she said he'd be sleeping at Matt and Andrea's that night. "There's no place quiet to do my homework there," he said. "Troy's got way less than me and then him and Bree play around. And I don't even have a desk there. I'm old enough to stay home alone."

"Not overnight, you're not," said Nina automatically. "And I'm sorry to do this to you on a weeknight. But I'll make it up to you on the weekend."

"How?" Bob asked as she pulled up to their house.

"How about a bike ride around the Baldwin Mansion and Pope House?"

"What day? I've got a science project."

"Sunday afternoon. Without fail. Try to finish your project on Saturday."

"Mom, don't make promises you can't keep. What are the chances?"

"Cynic," she said. "But you're right. It's not a promise. I'll just do my best. Don't I always?"

Bob relented then, and together they climbed the steps to the front porch of their house. Throwing her most expensive, new powder-blue suit and matching heels into a suit bag, she helped him stuff his backpack with books, called Andrea, and got Matt instead.

"Matt, I'm embarrassed to ask you this, but I'm in a pickle," she said, without preamble.

"Hi," said Matt. "And how are you?"

"In a rush. Sorry."

"What's up?"

"I need a favor," asked Nina, "just like I always seem to need a favor."

"You sound so guilty."

She felt so guilty. She had never fully expressed her deep gratitude for all that Andrea and Matt had done for her and Bob when they arrived in Tahoe, friendless and practically destitute. They had given the best thing anyone could, a home for the single mom and the confused little boy.

"I wouldn't ask except it's the best place for Bob. I need to go out of town on business tonight."

"You know, when you say you wouldn't ask, you make me feel bad. If we don't want to do something, we'll let you know, I promise. And you need to promise that you'll continue to ask, anytime, for anything, okay?"

Lindy treasured her friends, but Nina treasured her family. "You're the best. Can I drop him at four?"

"Tell him it's taco night. That ought to excite him."

A female pilot, pleasant and polite, had charge of the sporty little two-seater Cessna. Lolling in the leather seat, staring out the window at the lights of Tahoe Valley spread out below twinkling like a bejeweled Indian tapestry, Nina decided she would never fly coach class again. She could get used to living this way. . . .

She felt relaxed when she disembarked at LAX. After a short conversation with the car rental agent, who told her there would be a slight delay, she grabbed a large, caffeinated cola at a bar masquerading as a restaurant. Taking a stool next to the black windows overlooking the airstrips, she watched lonesome-looking business travelers nuzzle their drinks like lovers, and observed as a dozen planes took off and landed without crashing, marveling at the survival of all the fragile little packages of flesh crammed inside.

She stopped at the restroom to change, removing her official travel clothing of soft stretch leggings and a sweater and exchanging them for the snug-fitting suit, stockings, and shoes she had brought.

At the mirror, she liberally applied makeup, including red lipstick. When in the Southland, she would do as the Southlanders do. Anyway, once in a while she enjoyed turning into a glamorous stranger.

Standing in line at the rental car agency, she studied a map of the maze of freeways and streets she needed to memorize if she was going to arrive only fashionably late. The car, a radiant-blue Neon with turquoise trim, was low to the ground and zippy as a sports car. She joined the million other cars flowing through these arteries into the night, another bright corpuscle in L.A.'s lifeblood.

She turned the radio on to a song with a lot of bass and let the music travel through her, all the way down to the toes in her high-heeled shoes. All her life she had climbed a ladder routinely and without thought, slipping more often than she wanted. For the first time, she had glimpsed the top. And there, in that upper region, shiny and bright, was the payoff, a glorious mountain of gold, the Markov money.

A share of that kind of money would set her up for life. She could buy her house outright, or a bigger, better house, and finally create the kind of stable home life Bob needed. She could work less, be more available to him, maybe even be more available to a relationship that would put a man in her life and in Bob's on a more permanent basis. She could buy Bob all the things she couldn't afford now, the fancy athletic shoes he wanted, the computer software that was out of her price range, all the tickets he wanted to visit his father in Europe. She might even turn into the parent she wanted to be, patient, generous, and undistracted.

Pulling up in front of the hotel that housed the Yamashiro Restaurant, she handed her keys to the parking valet.

The maître d' was expecting her. He led her past the regular restaurant, where silverware and glasses clinked and people talked in muted tones, where sounds and colors were as discreet and perfectly balanced as in a Japanese temple, into a private room of bamboo and scrolls.

A black man about six feet four, at least a foot taller than she was, stood up and held out a big hand with a diamond band on his ring finger.

"I appreciate your making time for me," she said.

"You're so very welcome." She got a brief whiff of spice and starch before he stepped away. "It takes my mind off the case in progress. We've been in trial for two weeks. I'd forgotten there was an outside world and beautiful women with propositions for me," he went on, "even if they happen to be the legal kind."

With a deep, compelling voice and a solid, athletic body, Winston Reynolds inspired total confidence. He wore metal-rimmed glasses and a navy-blue suit with a crimson tie, standard trial attire. About forty-five years old, he had hair that receded a little to expose a broad brown forehead. Notes scribbled on his napkin revealed that he had kept himself occupied while waiting for her, no doubt recording things to remember after a long day in court, but he didn't seem as wiped out as she would have expected. In fact, his eyes had caught and held hers as she came through the door. She saw his interest and brushed it aside. He had too many impersonal reasons for turning on the charm with her tonight.

"It's a lovely restaurant," said Nina, adjusting her skirt and setting down the ever-present attaché beside her.

"It is, isn't it? This is a real treat. Please thank your generous client for me." He had already ordered wine. He poured her a glass, studying her openly, approvingly. "Let me say right now how much I appreciate you flying down here just to take me out to dinner tonight." He took a sip of his wine. "My mama would get a kick out this situation, a woman like you wooing me. Dad, too, God rest his woman-loving soul."

A waiter silently arrived before she could respond, and they ordered. The restaurant featured fresh fish of every kind. Nina wanted shrimp but it could get messy, so she ordered beef, figuring she should concentrate on Reynolds, not on whether she was dripping sauce all over her best suit. Reynolds went for the duck.

He leaned back in his chair, swirling his wine in the glass, and looking into its red depths gave a half smile. "Tell me about the Markov case," he said.

"I'll tell you what I can without violating the attorney-client privilege. Lindy Markov lived with Mike Markov as his wife. She worked alongside him for over twenty years, building a business from scratch. Those two crucial facts are undisputed."

"I understand everything is in his name. Your secretary mentioned a few things to my assistant. I hope you don't mind."

"He put everything in his name and she agreed to that, because they had a deal to share everything equally."

"So she says."

"Yes. And so she will testify in court."

"Has she got anything in writing?"

"You must understand we can talk more about her position when you commit to taking the job."

"I see. You want me to get involved without letting me have a chance to evaluate the case?"

"Not at all. Here are the basic pleadings and a summary of the issues and the basic facts about the Markov relationship." She pulled up her case as she spoke, opened it, and passed over a manila folder. Reynolds spent a few minutes looking it over, sipping thoughtfully from his glass from time to time. He was a fast reader.

"You got any rabbits in the hat?" he said when he had finished. "Because you're gonna need lots of magic to win this."

"Well, there is one case that has enough in common with our situation to be potentially useful," Nina said.

"Maglica versus Maglica," said Winston. "That's been news for years around here. We're all waiting to hear how she does on appeal. But I believe the lady in that case was older. She devoted her adult working life to building that business. The relative youth of your client might adversely affect your outcome."

Nina smiled, happy he had passed his first test. "Yes, but Mr. Maglica had already established something of a track record as a businessman. The Maglites venture was his second undertaking. I think

Lindy's primary role in developing this, the Markovs' only successful business, will be easier for us to demonstrate."

"I like the sound of that," said Winston.

"And while we haven't found much in the way of legal precedents to encourage us yet, we're confident Lindy Markov is entitled to a substantial share of Markov Enterprises. We've sent out our first set of Interrogatories and we've already scheduled Mr. Markov's deposition for December."

"Moving right along."

"The Superior Court is very efficient in El Dorado county, Mr. Reynolds. We'll be in trial in six or seven months in spite of the magnitude of this case. Mr. Markov's chafing under the receivership the court ordered, and Mrs. Markov is in financial difficulty."

"You don't think you can settle it?"

"Mr. Markov has hired Jeffrey Riesner. I believe you know him?"

"I do."

"Then you know what we're up against. He's hard-line and uncompromising."

"And that's just the beginning with him." He was teasing.

"He hates to settle. And my client wants something she's not going to get."

"Which is?"

"Mr. Markov. She wants a reconciliation with him, but I don't believe that's a possibility. The lawsuit will drive them further apart."

"So it's a battle. Palimony cases are very difficult to win," Reynolds said, "but you knew that, didn't you, Ms. Reilly?"

"Yeah," Nina said, feeling disappointed. She knew, but she hoped she hadn't blown her evening and a thousand bucks just to hear a final nail being driven into the coffin of her case. "I know it, but I'm going to fight it with or without you, Mr. Reynolds."

He laughed. "Well, at least you don't come down here talking trash. I appreciate that."

"You don't think the case is winnable?"

"I didn't say that. Every case is winnable but only if it gets to the jury. That's the hard part. Get it to the jury and you always have a chance. Actually, a couple of our colleagues, and I won't name names, have been in touch with friends of Mrs. Markov to offer their services to her."

"Really? If her case is so hopeless, why?"

He stared at her as if scrutinizing an idiot for some small hint of intelligence, then shook his head. "Money. All that money up for grabs! Enough money to make a sane man mad with greed. Enough money to get big firms all over the state wondering how to steal your case. You understand?"

She nodded. For the first time since considering the case, she felt the sheer power that so much money exercised. Well, she had felt some of it, too, on the drive over, the tickling of her own desire for money, for what it could buy, for the freedom it represented.

"It's a big case," he said. "Too big for you, but you know that. That's why you're here."

"Well, now," Nina began, but Reynolds wasn't finished.

"So you know what I overheard today at the racquetball club? I heard what Mrs. Markov did when the other guys came knocking," he said. "She told them to go piss up a rope. She said she already has excellent representation." He laughed heartily. "She may be right. You've made a good beginning in court, and you've got a loyal client. I couldn't have done better myself."

Nina lowered her eyes, so he wouldn't see the mingled relief and pleasure she felt. That other lawyers would want this case should not surprise her, but it did. She had actually thought she was doing Lindy a favor. Now she was starting to see the Markov case in a whole new light.

"Have you ever handled a really big piece of litigation, Nina?"

"I've handled jury trials in homicide cases," Nina said. "I doubt that it gets much worse than that."

"Have you ever had a jury trial in a civil case?"

"No," she said.

"I'm not trying to undermine your confidence. I just want to see if you appreciate what I can do for you. I do jury trials in civil cases. Cases a lot like the one you have. That's all I do. You know how they used to call Mel Belli the King of Torts? Well, here they call me the Prince of Palimony."

"I wouldn't be here all dressed up in a restaurant in L.A. when I ought to be home putting my kid to bed if I didn't appreciate what you can do for me," Nina answered.

"Well, then. What do you have in mind?" He ran his thumb absently around the rim of the wineglass, his brown eyes gazing steadily at her. "You want me to handle the trial?"

"No. I want to handle the trial. I want to associate you in as a cocounsel, but I want to have the final say as far as strategy. I realize you don't usually play second chair, Mr. Reynolds, but even second chair could make you a rich man if we win this case. I'm operating on a reduced hourly fee basis with an additional contingency fee of ten percent of the final recovery. I'll give you half the ten percent, plus pay your hourly billings each month at the rate of a hundred dollars an hour."

Reynolds had knit his brows and sunk his chin into his shirt. He usually charged three hundred an hour, she knew, but he didn't usually have such a massively abundant pot of gold waiting for him at the end of the rainbow. Nina let him think about what she had said for a moment, then added, "If we ask for only half of the value of their business, our claim is for over a hundred million."

He was nodding. "Now that's what I call money," he said. "Five million for each of us if we won that much. I could pay all those back taxes the IRS is asking for. I could pay off the place in Bel Air and the alimony. I could take that vacation my doctor's been ordering. But . . ."

"But?"

He spilled a drop of the wine into his plate. "There's many a slip 'twixt the cup and the lip," he said. "Somehow, with all my wins, the amount of money I really need to solve all my problems always seems to hover just out of reach. Have you noticed that? It's like a dark force out there that steps between us and our just deserts, leaving us to salivate and starve and wonder why. Even if we win at trial, appeals take years. And nobody ever comes out with any money on appeal."

"Not this time. Working together, we can make it happen if anyone can. Everyone tells me you're the top attorney in this field."

"Those are kind words," he said. "Thank you. You've probably guessed, I like being flattered, even when it is necessary."

He was mocking her. She refused to be waylaid. "I doubt Jeff Riesner's made an offer as generous," she said.

"Ah. so you've guessed. Yes, Jeff and I worked together on a case last year out of Sacramento. He has called my office several times in the past few days."

"You haven't talked to him?"

"No."

"You knew it was about the Markov case?"

"That's what the message said."

"So . . ."

"I can't abide the guy," Reynolds said, smiling. "Even if he's going to be the one on the winning side."

Now she felt offended. "Mr. Reynolds," Nina said, "Am I wasting my time? Because I get the feeling you're not listening. And if you can't take me seriously, I should probably leave."

"Now, hold on," he answered, "I'm hanging on every word. You're offering me the chance to spend time at Lake Tahoe, which I love, and to take a gamble on big money, which involves a minor weakness of mine, as you may already have surmised. And I think we have something in common. We'd both rather represent the under-dog. I apologize if I've given the wrong impression. It's a bad habit that comes from keeping people off balance as a matter of course. Even playing second fiddle, I'd kill to get on this case." He raised his glass. "A toast," he said, "to you."

Nina raised her glass, too. "You're in?" she asked.

"You betcha."

By the time the food came, presented so artistically on exquisite plates she hated to disturb it, they had finished the wine, started using first names with each other, and hammered out the beginnings of a deal. She offered him an office across the hall, and he said he would come up for a meeting as soon as his trial was over.

"I've got a jury consultant for us that might just be available. Young and the hottest ticket in town. Her name's Genevieve Suchat," he said, as they started on their green tea ice cream.

"I think I've heard of her, but . . ."

"Now, this is no time to scrimp on help. You've got to spend money to make money."

"Winston, I . . ."

"She's got a slight hearing problem, but that doesn't slow her down for a second. Wears a little thing in her ear but you don't strike me as the type who's going to hold that against her."

"Well, of course not!"

"She worked with me on a case down in Long Beach. Just as smooth and cool as this ice cream."

"Did you win?"

"We did. She has won almost every case she's been associated with." He took a sip of water and pushed the ice cream saucer away. He had finally slowed down.

"Jury consultants spend a lot of time on research, don't they? I have to think about keeping our expenses down," Nina said.

"Now, wait a minute here. It doesn't make financial sense to use them in every civil litigation, but with so much money at stake in this case, you'd be nuts not to use one. I've never heard of a case of this size that didn't have jury consultants on both sides. Nina, you want to be a winner, you have to leave no stone unturned. And you know our friend Riesner's going to get the best."

He didn't say "again," although they both thought it. He knew how to play her already, didn't he?

"Why not talk to her?" he went on.

"Fine," she agreed. "I'll talk to her. Maybe we can limit her involvement. . . ."

"Bold strokes," Winston said. "No limits. This case is too big. We go for broke, with Genevieve, with everything. Because that's what real winners do. You know I'm right."

He was right, but the "go for broke" line had chimed louder than everything else he'd said, and continued to ring in her ears. Her dad used to say that all the time, and one day he had woken up flat broke.

"I'll call your office and arrange a meeting right away," he said, then ordered another bottle of wine. He talked about his background, his football scholarship to UCLA, the shock of his teachers and coaches when he walked away from it and immersed himself in academics, his law school studies at Yale, the two ex-wives and the three children he supported. He was full of himself, but maybe he had a right to be. She couldn't help liking him.

The coffee came, and the frightful check. Her watch said eleven o'clock. "Sorry," she said. "I've got a plane waiting. I'll call you tomorrow." She paused, then said, "I'm thrilled to be working with you, Win." She stuck out her hand.

"Cinderella," he said, taking her hand between both of his, "better find both dancing slippers, fast. We've got a long way to go if we're gonna avoid getting stuck with a pumpkin."

6

THE NEXT MORNING, NINA CALLED Sandy to tell her she might
not get into the office until after lunch. Sandy said that Genevieve
Suchat, the jury consultant, was due in the afternoon. Apparently
determined to convince Nina to hire her, Winston had made the
arrangements with impressive efficiency.

After taking two white pills to quiet the pounding in her head,
she drove straight to the Markov house on Cascade Road. Rain
slammed the road outside and her wipers slapped a quick, useless path
through the river flowing down her windshield. An unexpected skid
around a hairpin curve forced her to slow as she wound along a dirt
road that hugged the lake's edge.

Iron gates with gilt-tipped arrows on top stood open, and behind them a massive stone mansion met her eyes, turreted like a
castle, surrounded by grounds so well-groomed the plants looked
manufactured.

She pulled into a spot close to the house, awed at the ostenta-
tion and thinking how very, very much money it would take to build
such a thing in California, on the shore of the state's most desirable
lake.

No umbrella presented itself in the box of emergency items on
the floor of the littered backseat, so she rushed to the front door and
rang the bell, narrowly avoiding a fatal slip off of the slick doorstep.
In the relentless rain, the gigantic house loomed over her like a pile of
boulders ready at any moment to give way in a landslide. Even the

lake, merging its gray into the sky, had a leaden pull to it, as if the heavy gray water exerted more gravity than the rest of the earth.

Lindy answered, looking gaunt in a loose-fitting kimono over a black bodysuit. In spite of her impeccable hair and makeup, Nina could detect signs of the recent travails in her face.

"Thanks for coming," Lindy said. "Let me take your jacket. You can leave the boots there." She pointed to a stone bench under which resided the cleanest-looking shoes Nina had ever seen outside of a store display. Next to the bench were a dozen stacked cardboard boxes.

Lindy led Nina down a hallway, past two octagonal foyers, and through an oak-floored room as big as a ballroom. Above them, fighting to conquer the dismal day, crystal chandeliers lighted the way, swaying slightly in an invisible breeze.

They walked on. With blackened slate over many of the passageway floors, stone walls and rain pouring down the windows, the most brilliant lighting could not entirely exorcise a Gothic creepiness from the house.

In a room with a view of the lake, the sun hidden behind ribbons of clouds, Lindy apologized and asked Nina to wait just a minute.

She left. Nina sat down on a long bench that ran the length of the room, at least a hundred feet long. Some exercise equipment and objects she couldn't identify filled one small alcove. The rest of the space, mirrored on one side, might function as a dance studio. She and Bob lived in a house that would fit into this one room.

Lindy reappeared. "Sorry. I've got our housekeeper, Florencia, helping me with the packing."

"It is a magnificent house," Nina said. "I'm sorry about all this, Lindy."

"You're not responsible. Blame Rachel. That's what I do."

"What's it like," Nina asked suddenly. "I mean, to be rich?"

"What a funny question."

"Forget it. I don't mean to be rude."

"No, it's interesting." They walked across the room. Lindy

stopped when she reached the area full of equipment. "The truth is, maybe because I had so little growing up, I really loved having money. It's addictive as any drug that gets you high. Money blunts all the rough edges, soothes your soul, makes you feel special and powerful. There is nothing in the world as seductive.

"Have a problem? Throw enough money at it and I promise it will go away. Worried about the environment? Fund a cleanup project. Feeling sad? Plan a fabulous vacation. You feel like you can do anything when you have enough money, and there are so many things I still want to do in my life."

"You mentioned power."

"A real high, and easy to buy. People, too."

They were in an area that held a stationary bike, a treadmill, a stand holding up a set of shiny silver free weights, and a number of odd things Nina had noticed while Lindy was talking. The biggest item was a transparent, cylindrical tank nearly as tall as Nina, full of water as clear and beautiful as a glass of turquoise Caribbean seawater.

"So I want my money," Lindy said, sticking her hand over the top to wet her fingers. She took them out, looking satisfied. "And most of the time, I believe I deserve it, too."

"You worked hard for it, Lindy."

"Mike won't see that. Plenty of other people won't either. But money is only one reason for suing Mike. The other reason is that this case will make him face me and make him keep his promises to me."

"No system can force someone who has wronged you to stay with you or love you again," Nina said. "Money is the only compensation available, the objective standard. Your loss has to be quantified somehow. Emotions . . . they can't be quantified."

"I refuse to give it all up on demand. I refuse."

"Lindy," Nina said slowly, making ripples in the water with her fingernails. "What you said before . . . Are you by any chance thinking that you've bought me?"

"Of course not, Nina." Lindy looked hurt. "You know this is about an issue that's important to women, not just to me. And you're doing this because you want to help me personally. Those are all the right reasons. And now we're a team. No, the people you can buy are a whole different type."

"What type?"

"Money is God to those people." Drying her hands on a towel, as if physically expressing that she was done with that unpalatable line of thought, she stepped away from the tank. "Forgot to tell you to bring a swimsuit." She rummaged in a cabinet near the spa.

"Oh, I wanted to mention I've hired one of the best palimony attorneys in the state to help me with your case." Nina described some of Winston's recent wins to Lindy. "Plus I'm interviewing a potential jury consultant this afternoon."

"That sounds great. We're going to win, whatever it takes," Lindy said. She handed Nina a swimsuit. "This is probably about your size. Hop in the tank."

When Nina shook her head Lindy said, "Nina, it means a lot to me that you see what I do. What I'm good at."

Oh, why not, Nina thought. She'd just jump in and out and everybody could go back to work satisfied. She donned the simple black suit Lindy handed her as quickly as she could, imagining what Sandy, back at the office fielding irate inquiries, might say if she could see her now.

Against the wall a set of steps led to the top of the tank. Nina climbed up and stood looking into the water, the skin on her body rough with goose bumps.

"In you go," said Lindy. "Need a push?" Suddenly realizing what she had said, she began to giggle, a nervous laugh tiptoeing along the brink of tears.

Nina slipped in feet first. Warm and supple as velvet, the water embraced her. The tank wasn't wide or deep enough for diving. It hardly contained her up to the neck but she could extend both arms out to their full length. Air began to simmer up from the bottom.

"It's like . . . a vertical spa." She wondered if she would float on the air. The bubbles blew up around her, popping like tiny balloons. She didn't float, but she felt like she weighed about ten pounds.

"That's right." Lindy turned the music down.

The sensation of the air bubbles and water felt fantastic.

"Now get ready," Lindy said. "I'm turning on the surf."

What the hell? Jets of water began to shoot upward. Nina had to struggle to keep her feet down. "Hey!" she said. "Hey, wait a sec here!"

The jets stopped. Lindy, smiled at her from the stairway beside the tank. "Don't you just love it?"

Buoyed by the water and her own improving spirits, Nina had begun to bounce up and down. "It's . . . stupendous. And now am I supposed to do water exercises?"

"That's a big part of it. We've produced a whole series of videos to go along with it. Actually, several series, all new every couple of years. Want to learn a few moves?"

"Lindy," said Nina, then stopped herself. Might as well take advantage of the moment. "Okay, maybe just one."

"This will just take a few seconds more, I promise." Lindy ran her through a few exercises. For one, Nina used only her toes to propel her entire body up, then down, her arms tightly pushed to her sides so that she rocketed smoothly through the water.

"Aqua-dynamics," said Lindy. "You move faster and work those ankles. Now try bouncing on your knees. You'll have to hold your breath and go under to get your knees down to the ground. Then push off as hard as you can. Don't worry about splashing. The tank's designed for that."

The exercises took some getting used to. Nina had to work to get her knees to touch, and to bend at the waist, positioning herself so that she had room to complete the maneuver, but after a few minutes she could see that this was wonderful, vigorous fun.

"Then, of course, you can jog ninety miles or stretch like a prima ballerina. The Solo Spa is also great for getting people that weight-bearing exercise they need without destroying their feet. We have a lot of disabled clients, and people who are trying to thin down."

"You said the exercises are only part of what you can do with this spa."

"That's right. In the past few years, we've been marketing the spa as more than an exercise aid. Water's an ancient healer, and there's nothing more primeval than submerging in this warm womb to mend a broken spirit or stoke the creative fires. People are seeking spiritual solace. What could be better comfort than this blending of the physical and the spiritual? You'll like this." She turned a knob in the tank and the bubbles increased.

Nina felt weightless. She stopped moving and hung in space, supported by the bubbles. "Words like solace, healing, and spiritual usually send me running for the hills, but I can see exactly what you mean. This is a hot bubble bath for the gods."

Lindy looked happy. "I see we have a convert."

"Are they all see-through like this one?"

"No. This is a demo, like the one we use in the videos. Most of the ones we sell are trimmed in wood like a regular outdoor spa."

"Most?"

"Well, a couple of the casinos in Reno have special-ordered a pair with two layers of glass and acrylic, with twinkling lights between layers, for floor shows."

"Good God."

A distant phone rang and Lindy disappeared around a corner.

Nina closed her eyes, basking in the comfort of the warm water. A moment later, she opened them and was so startled to see a sturdy man with round ears peering in at her that she let out a small scream.

She stopped moving and hung there in her transparent bubble. When he didn't say anything she said, "Hello."

"You're Lindy's new lawyer?" he asked. He took his hands out of the pockets of his dirty overalls and placed them on the spa.

"Yes. And you are?"

"A friend," he said, examining her body through the plastic. "I'm glad I caught you here."

She wasn't. Not at all. She debated getting out, and decided climbing a ladder would make her feel even more vulnerable.

"I want you to know something." He spoke slowly, running a finger along the wet condensate on the outside of the tank, tracing a circle with a smaller one inside of it.

Like a target, Nina thought.

"I know you're in it for the money," he said, all motion suddenly halting. His face was so close to the tank, his breath made a fog on it every time he breathed.

"Who did you say you were?" Nina asked, by now very frightened at his tone and the strange look in his dark eyes.

"I know a few things about you lawyers. And I want you to know, if you dump her or hurt her or accept some kinda under-the-table payoff from that slob Mike to drop this case, I'm going to . . ."

Lindy came back into the room. "Oh, George, here you are. That was Alice. She'll be here any second to drop off a set of keys."

All sense of threat fading from him the minute Lindy entered the room, he ambled off toward the door. "I'll get started, then."

"Who's that?" Nina asked.

"George Demetrios. He works at the plant."

"Scary guy," Nina said, beginning to climb a clear acrylic ladder up the side of the tank that led to the steps down.

"What, George?" Lindy laughed. "Yeah, I guess he does come off that way sometimes, but you don't have to worry about him. He's devoted to me. George is really just a lovable lunk. He's helping me move a few boxes over to Alice's house today."

At the bottom of the stairs, Lindy handed her a towel and a white robe. Nina dried off. "Lindy, thanks for the demonstration. This is a fantastic product."

"Only one of many. Our centerpiece. Now, let me show you how we market our spas. It'll just take a minute and it's warm in the showroom." Located down a winding stairway, the showroom turned out not to be the display of pools Nina expected, but an intimate, plushly carpeted space with armchairs for ten, and a five-foot screen.

"This is a quickie selection reel," Lindy said. "The workout videos last longer."

They watched as a series of swimsuited bodies in all shapes and sizes and colors, old and young, took to the pool, running through exercises as light-footed as astronauts at zero gravity, moving rhythmically to jaunty music.

"We used to use only young, pretty girls. It was my idea to get all kinds of people on tape. Real people always come off clunky and fake when you try to use them in advertising, so these are all actors. They look great don't they? Just like real people only just enough better-looking to make you happy to identify with them."

Nina didn't answer. The actors did look great, but businesspeople made Nina nervous when they talked so blithely about the subtle forces they wielded to coerce and manipulate her.

After the tape ended, Nina put her clothes on and gathered up her briefcase.

"Thanks for taking the time," Lindy said. "Before I moved out I wanted to show you a little bit about our business, so you could see that I haven't spent twenty years living off Mike and just twiddling my thumbs."

"You have worked hard," Nina said, "and you obviously know your business."

A tall woman with streaked hair, wearing a short aquamarine sweater dress appeared in the doorway with a gun in her hand. Amused gray eyes peeked out between uneven bangs that swept the curves of her cheeks.

"Oh, Alice," Lindy said. "Have you met my attorney, Nina Reilly? Nina, my best friend, Alice Boyd."

Alice set the gun casually down on a chair and strode rapidly up to Nina, her high heels clicking on the oak floor. She shook her hand. "So Lindy has subjected you to the ritual baptism," she said, gesturing toward Nina's wet hair.

Nina touched her head. "I guess that's true," she said.

"Now you belong to us."

"Don't listen to her," Lindy said comfortably. "She's never been the same since that time she spent in the loony bin."

"That's such a lie. I'm the same, only much more devious about expressing my feelings," Alice said.

"Excuse me," Nina said, "but didn't you just set a gun down over there on that cushion?"

"Almost forgot," Alice said. She walked back and picked up the gun. "This is for you, doll," she said, handing a silver snub-nosed gun to Lindy.

"What for?" Lindy said.

"Meet your new best friend." She held it up for them to admire. "Isn't it something? You can kill someone with this adorable, polished-nickel designer special from thirty feet away. No need to get blood all over yourself. You see someone coming to do you harm, and *bam*. You lay them low." She walked around, taking aim at various items around the room. "Pow," she said. "There goes the mirror from France you're always bragging about. Not to Mike's taste anyway, was it? Pow," she said again, pointing toward a vase. "Down goes the Ming." She stopped and stared at the gun. "What strikes me as strange is that most women have yet to recognize the power of this little equalizer. With guts and a little practice, we have finally been handed just the tool to win that war against our oppressors."

Lindy looked a little embarrassed. "Alice, I don't know what Nina will think. Put the gun away."

"Don't be ridiculous," Alice said. "No, really. Here you are in these gorgeous surroundings for what is probably the last time." She nodded toward the room. "If I were you, I'd grab the moment. Why leave all these nice things for the king of shit and his sleazy little consort to play with? Know how to operate one of these?" She flicked the safety off.

Lindy took the gun away, and pushed the safety back in place. "I don't want it."

"For twenty years you've lived in your fortress. Now you're going to be rubbing shoulders with the peasants. That would be us,"

Alice said to Nina. "Lindy, you don't know how bad us peasants can be. You ought to protect yourself."

"Take it back, Alice. I mean it." Lindy handed the gun carefully to her friend.

Alice shrugged and stuck the gun into her handbag. "Suit yourself." Saying she needed to freshen up, she excused herself.

"Now here we go again. You're going to get the wrong impression of Alice, too," said Lindy. "She's the best person, but I'm afraid this stuff with Mike has reminded her of some bad things in her past. She'll settle down."

Nina wondered if Lindy was one of those rare people who could read souls, or if she was simply a blind fool when it came to picking friends and family.

As they approached the foyer, she became aware again of the rain eddying down gutters, drowning the view from the windows. At the sight of the boxes stacked high by the door, Lindy stopped short. Then she composed herself and said good-bye.

Nina was so late leaving Lindy's that she headed straight to court for the morning criminal calendar without stopping at the office, the Bronco leaking transmission fluid all the way. Her mechanic had already advised her to replace the carburetor. She would need a new truck soon. These thoughts occupied her as she negotiated the puddles at every corner.

Back at the office by lunchtime, she saw that Genevieve Suchat was already waiting.

"Hi," Genevieve said brightly, springing up from a chair across from Sandy's to shake Nina's hand. A Southern lilt made it sound like "Hah."

Sandy's son, Wish, sat in the chair next to Genevieve's. A very tall, gangly nineteen-year-old, he thumbed through his latest fixation, a magazine full of surveillance tricks for spies. He had recently announced his plan to become a detective like Paul, and to that end was taking courses in criminology and photography over at the community college.

Wish was their odd-job man. From the sparkling looks of the place, Sandy must have had him doing some cleanup. He glanced up and nodded hello to Nina, then returned to his apparently absorbing read.

Nina shook Genevieve's hand. Her light, breathy voice reminded Nina of one of the scantily dressed girls sending out suggestive invitations from an on-line website she had recently forbidden her son access to, but her curly, sprayed wheat-colored hair and the tailored black jacket trimmed in burgundy over a long burgundy skirt were quite demure, if fashionably cut.

In one ear, Nina glimpsed the silver hearing aid Winston had mentioned, catching the light behind a pair of small silver earrings. Genevieve looked more like a Genny than a Genevieve—a modern working girl who had just stepped out of a big-city highrise and into the mountains without changing her style a bit—but Winston had warned Nina that she preferred the more formal sound of Genevieve in her work relationships.

Genevieve already knew Sandy, she told Nina, sounding as confident as if she felt she'd been eating at Sandy's dinner table for years. "Sandy and Wish were telling me all about the Washoe Nation," she said. "And they have quite the extended family."

Sandy rarely got personal with visitors. Genevieve must have a way about her.

Because Genevieve requested it, they went to Planet Hollywood, the restaurant at Caesar's, for lunch.

"Casinos aren't known for their fine dining," Nina apologized. The babbling patrons and clamorous kitchen must be hard on someone with a hearing problem. "We do have some nice places."

"But I love it here," said Genevieve, eyeing the movie relics that lined the walls surrounding the faux palm trees. Apparently the din would not be a problem for her. "Is that Darth Vader over there?" she said, getting up from her seat to study the cases.

She returned a moment later. "His suit looks littler than in the movies." The waiter appeared, asking for their orders. She studied her menu. "The blackened shrimp is probably great, but I'll just have a salad. You a gambler?" she asked Nina.

"Um. I confess to a taste for the slots," Nina said, a little put out by the question. They were on what really amounted to an interview, after all.

"Me, too," Genevieve said, handing the waiter her menu. "Also poker, blackjack, roulette . . . I'm a real slut for a quick buck. Maybe we'll have a little time to hit the tables before you have to go back to work."

The waiter turned to Nina. "Pomodoro," Nina told him, glad for the distraction. She was amused by Genevieve's inappropriate candor but not interested in spelling out her own proclivities on that front. Studying the menu, she realized she had worked up an appetite in the spa. "Can you bring extra Parmesan for the table?"

"How wonderful for you to be able to eat like that and stay skinny," said Genevieve when the waiter left. "I could never eat a big, heavy pasta meal in the middle of the day, although during trials I stick to comfort food. Peanut butter sandwiches, chocolate chip cookies, whole milk."

"I order fancy when I eat out because I'm a lazy cook," said Nina. "My son and I live on canned tomato soup."

"Then you both ought to take supplements," Genevieve said disapprovingly. "I take a multivitamin plus extra vitamin E and folic acid and ginseng every day."

"And I suppose you like high doses of vitamin C for colds."

"Yes, I do," said Genevieve.

"And you think I should, too."

"You are under a lot of stress," said Genevieve in a supportive tone, "aren't you?" And the little voice in Nina's head started up, saying, uh-oh, better straighten up, you're being assessed.

Genevieve had a Master's degree in statistics from M.I.T. and a Ph.D. in psychology from Duke. She told Nina she had considered law school. Then, with a decidedly wicked smile, she said she had eventually settled for being the brains behind the brawn.

By overnight courier, along with Genevieve's impressive resume, Winston had sent Nina a copy of her thesis on "crowd psychology," with its special emphasis on the decision-making process of jurors in the American legal system. The whole thing looked mathematical, filled with charts and formulae and statistical gobbledygook that she couldn't follow.

Taking a leaf of lettuce onto her fork and tasting it, Genevieve said, "This morning on the plane I read all the pleadings you sent down to Winston, and I talked to Winston late last night. If he wins his hospital malpractice case, I'm predicting one point seven to one point nine."

"How can you make a guess like that?"

"Went for a split-the-difference jury, then had Winston ask for three point six."

"But the standard jury instruction is that you can't have a compromise verdict. Juries aren't supposed to—"

"You know they do it all the time," Genevieve said. "They just get cagey to avoid trouble. See, they'll go one point seven because one point eight—exactly half of what we asked for—would be too obvious. Problem for him in this case is the judge, plus he got saddled with a couple of wild cards on the jury he couldn't keep off," she said, shrugging, but obviously more than irritated by the thought. "No matter how good you are, there's still some risk."

"Will he take time off after this is over?"

"Not Winston. He's got trials back-to-back. The next one's in San Diego, nonjury." With the discipline of a drill instructor she ate another lettuce leaf, detouring around a nearby crouton. "He said to tell you Sandy faxed him the minute order with the trial date, and he's freed up the two weeks after that. I like May twenty-first, too. I've got a double murder case coming up next July."

"I hope we can go with that date. Both sides want to get this over with. Mike Markov is furious that we've interfered in the business by getting a receiver and an accounting. Lindy Markov is broke for the first time in years. I'm fronting a lot of the costs myself . . ." including two hundred an hour for you, Nina thought. "I can't afford to let it drag on."

"From what I've read and what Winston tells me, this is your big one, Nina," Genevieve said, smiling. "You could hit the jackpot with what I reckon your fee agreement must be. None of my business, of course, except I want to help you make it happen. Can we sit down with Miz Markov real soon? I'd like to ask her a few questions and get a good picture of her fixed in my mind."

The soft voice, which occasionally slipped into a kind of countrified dialect Nina thought she must use for emphasis, coupled with the royal blue eyes, had distracted Nina for a second while she contemplated the extreme contrast between Genevieve's savvy talk and the delicate girl sitting across the table. Genevieve probably made good use of that contrast when it suited her. Good. Maybe her looks would fool Riesner into underestimating her.

Genevieve was saying, "Right off the bat let me tell you women might not necessarily favor Lindy, unless we strike fast and make sure they do. They might think she got what she deserved. She knew what she was getting into. She knew he didn't want to marry her. She knew he kept things in his own name to maintain his ownership. So we'll need to be cunning as the little snake that slips through the grass and zaps the dragonfly before he even knows she's there."

"I understand you and Winston have worked together before."

"Right. On a worker's compensation case against a bank down in Long Beach. Remind me to tell you all about that sometime after I've had a few and we've got some time to burn. He's quite a lawyer. In the beginning, nobody liked our client, but Winston spun their heads around and lined 'em up just the way we wanted by the end. I can't wait to work with him again, and with you for the first time, Nina. I've read about you, which, if you think about it, is remarkable. L.A.'s about a million miles away from Tahoe, psychologically speaking."

"You live in Los Angeles?"

"I grew up in New Orleans. Now I live in Redondo Beach, a half block from the ocean on Catalina Avenue in a little Spanish bungalow."

"Any family?"

"No. My parents are both dead, and I don't seem to have time for a steady guy. Just another lonely gal, lookin' for love," she said. Dimples peeked through her cheeks. "When I first got there, I learned to surf. Had to give it up when I started workin' twenty-hour days."

"You did? So did I. In a wet suit of course. I grew up in Monterey."

"Well, it's warmer in Redondo, but my favorite spot was the wedge in Newport."

They shared some stories. Nina couldn't help liking Genevieve. She wouldn't put it past her to be fibbing about surfing, although she couldn't catch her in an outright lie. But wouldn't it be just like a person with her speciality to research Nina's background, seeking some common ground before showing up for an interview? She enjoyed the conversation and had to admire Genevieve's strategy, if that's what it was.

"I have to tell you, I've never used a jury consultant before. And I have my doubts about it."

"I'm your first," said Genevieve. "I'll take that as a compliment."

"You need to realize that you're coming on as a consultant. I want you to give me the benefit of all of your knowledge, but I reserve the right to make my own decisions."

"You'll listen to me if you plan to win. What exactly do you know about jury consulting?"

"Very little."

"It all started over twenty years ago with the trial of the Harrisburg Seven. That was the first time I know of when some of these techniques were used to help the defense team in selecting jurors."

"Did they win?"

"That case was settled the night before the trial began," said Genevieve. "But since then, social scientists have shown that, when employed by a knowledgeable pro, these techniques can work. Name any recent major trial, and I'll give you five to one odds they used a jury consultant."

"I'm not sure why it makes me uncomfortable," Nina said. "Maybe I just don't like the idea of manipulating a jury . . . but of course that's exactly what I'm trying to do myself every single moment."

"It's war out there, honey. And it's not like you know for sure how people will vote once those doors to the jury room shut behind them."

"You're right. There are always facts to muck up the works."

"Too true," Genevieve said vehemently. "The dominant factor in any trial outcome, no matter how carefully you handpick your people, is still the facts. But what people will come to believe are the facts and how they will react to them, that's where we come in. I'd say it's legal malpractice not to use a jury consultant in a big case these days."

"Funny, Winston said the same thing. I guess that makes me just a little old small-town lawyer committing malpractice left and right," said Nina.

"Yes, just a small-town lawyer. Not much, is it, when you could be a superstar?" Genevieve said without a hint of sarcasm. "You're attractive; that's a big plus for most juries. A little short, but a session with a shoe salesman should cure that. All that long hair"—she shook her short hair disapprovingly—"you might think about cutting. If not, we'll work on style. That leaves your clothes and your . . . um . . . attitude for later."

"Mighty nice of you to hold off."

Genevieve couldn't ignore Nina's irritation this time. She laughed. "You'll get used to me. I'm going to be after you worse than your own mother. Now, what's the word? Are we doing this thing together or not? I'll do a damn good job for you."

"If we can work out the financial details. You're going to have to receive the bulk of your fee at the end of the trial. . . ."

"We'll work those details out later. Meanwhile, just let me tell you what else I'm going to do for you."

Nina pushed her empty plate away and sat back to let the meal settle heavily into her stomach.

"I'll be up here a lot from now on. We'll begin with a tele-phone questionnaire to people in the local venire. That's to get a handle on who lives here, their prejudices, type of work, political leanings, group affiliations, etcetera. From that information, I deter-mine whether the jury list reflects that population. If it's not a favor-able group, we might want to request that the pool be increased. I believe in this county, El Dorado, you can request that the pool be expanded to include jurors from adjacent counties. That might be useful to us. I'll find out."

"What kinds of questions do you ask?" said Nina.

"Questions that will help us determine underlying personality characteristics. Then you and I will get together to analyze the survey results. I do what's called a factor analysis—bottom line, I create a scale of factors predicting juror favorability. That's where we decide what the crucial issues are in this case and what critical set of opin-ions, determinants such as economic status, racial prejudice, distribu-tive equity positions, and so on will end up being deciding factors."

"No graphs, please!"

"I'll hide them in a hole in the wall and never tell you where," Genevieve promised.

"And that last thing you said. Distributive equity?"

"That's an old idea. Aristotle defined it first. You'll be hearing a lot from me about it. The question is, to what degree will a certain prospective juror tolerate inequity in a relationship?"

"Like the one between Mike and Lindy Markov."

"Correct. I'll figure out which types of people are most likely to recommend specific remedies for the particular perceived inequity in this case, a good specific remedy for our client being stacks of leafy-green money." The thought fired her up and she extended her empty hands over an imaginary pile of money.

"I can't knock that," Nina said slowly.

"So the most important part of what I do before the trial is to work with you to develop two juror profiles, one of your friend and one of your enemy. That involves juggling information, using at least two common approaches, multiple regression and automatic interaction detection, to find out what characteristics we need to know and how they can be combined to create our good and bad Frankensteins."

"I'm not sure I know what you're talking about."

"I'm sorry, I've degenerated into jargon. You don't have to worry about that stuff."

"Okay."

"After that, I'll be working with you on your *voir dire* questions. And I'll help you figure out which facts to emphasize and deemphasize in your opening statement. And how to present your evidence. And—"

Nina's mind reeled with the possibilities Genevieve raised at the same time as it mused over the compromise of her own principles. Her way was not Genevieve's way. But she had no choice. She needed Winston, and he insisted on Genevieve, so she would make the most of the situation, taking what served her purposes and discarding the rest. "Can you do all this on your own?"

"I've got two assistants in L.A. who'll conduct the phone interviews and help me collate what we gather. Later, we'll need a private investigator. I can recommend . . ."

"That's okay. I work with someone from Carmel, Paul Van Wagoner."

"If we can get hold of the potential jury list ahead of time, he's going to have to run around and talk to the neighbors and friends to give us some early info. If not, while the judge and attorneys are interviewing candidates during the *voir dire,* he should be out there digging in the trash cans so we can make a more informed decision about your peremptories and challenges for cause."

There actually seemed to be some cockeyed attempt at science behind what Genevieve did. Maybe it actually would work, giving certitude to an area of legal practice that had always been pure hunch. Genevieve was like an army sneaking up on Riesner's flank . . . of course, he'd have a jury consultant, too.

Though she had been ready to dislike and merely tolerate this upstart, she found she enjoyed the grinning Genevieve, who now sat across from her, all attention turned to twirling a fork between fidgety little fingers.

"Maybe I've been missing a bet, not using a consultant before."

"You have indeed, but it's never too late to start doing it right," Genevieve said. "You and me and Winston, we're going to give that rich man a lickin' he won't forget." She patted the napkin to the edges of her lips and said, "Do we have time to play a few slots? I won eleven hundred last time I was here. Three red sevens. Had to have a row of red, white, and blue sevens to win the car. I was so very pissed!"

Genevieve played like a kid with Monopoly cash, tossing a hundred dollars down the progressive slots in the quarter of an hour they stayed. Nina stuck to her regular quarter slot machine and lost twenty. One thing she learned about Genevieve in those fifteen minutes: she could talk about statistics until she had the whole world snowed, but she was a gambler to the bone. The casino brought out that basic personality trait in sharp relief.

And, she thought, that makes it unanimous. Genevieve, Winston, and Nina. Rub-a-dub-dub, three gamblers in a tub.

7

LINDY LAY FACEDOWN IN the cold sand listening to the black water brushing the shore beside her. This strip that ran along the edge of their property belonged to her, and now a judge had ordered her to stay away from it.

Sometime long after midnight her eyes had snapped open in Alice's guest bedroom, after a dream that had left no images, just an urgency. Urgent! Her chest burned with the moment.

This urgency felt like sexual anticipation, potentially explosive, and as her physical cravings had for years, it fixed on Mike. She needed him and the comfort of his arms, as she always did when things got rough. She had to talk to him. So she had gotten out of bed, thrown on her cross-trainers and her jacket, and gone in to the dark dining room to find her keys.

At the gate to the estate, though, her mood had altered. A new sign on the curved iron arrows of the gate said KEEP OUT. Mike had probably put it up for the reporters, but it applied to her now, too, so she walked the perimeter of the fence to the little gate on the far side in the woods and climbed right over it, and walked down toward the water, and lay down near the dock until she could figure out what to do, her chest feeling tighter every moment, as if her heart wanted to rupture. She wished she had pebbles to toss at his window, something that would tell him she was here, waiting. Tell him how angry she was. How hurt.

For a while she lost herself in the rhythmic sound of the wavelets and the cold, grainy feel of the sand. Geese honked above, flying overhead, late for their appointment down south. The breeze moved gently over her back, stirring her hair. She remembered the other times she had awakened in the middle of the night, after her father had died.

When he died he left her with no support. She would lie in her bed looking at the ceiling, imagining death, wondering what it was like to be nothing and nowhere, getting so far into the blackness she could barely claw her way out in the morning.

Aunt Beth, who had often stepped in when times were bad, took her in permanently, and when Lindy was seventeen, helped her find a job at a coffee shop in Henderson and a room in town. Lindy spent only her base salary, saving all her tips in a big pickle jar, an antique her aunt had kept around, God knew why. When she saved enough, she moved on, putting on her suit jacket from the Salvation Army store and applying for a job as a secretary at the Burns Brothers' Car and Truck Stop in Mill City.

After a few years she was booking the acts at a casino in Ely, making enough to rent an apartment and send a hundred dollars to Aunt Beth every month, taking night courses at the business school. She earned a reputation as hardworking, never late, never missing a day, always giving it a hundred fifty percent.

After a brief, disastrous marriage, she had met Mike. He worked as a bouncer in the club, a guy on his way down at thirty-five, ten years older than she was but like a kid in so many ways. He stood the exact same height as she did, five feet eight, and he had a surprised, boyish expression, eyebrows raised high like he still couldn't believe he'd been given a knockout punch. After sixty fights, thirty-two as a pro, he'd cut open his eye one too many times and the Nevada Boxing Commission doctor had said he would lose the eye if he kept fighting.

He didn't care about that, Mike had told her; he still had the other one. He wouldn't accept that his fighting days were over. He came from a family of poor Russian immigrants who had settled in Rochester, New York, in the forties, and they had all the faith in the world he would still someday make it big and send his smart younger brother money for school.

On her way out at five o'clock he would come on duty and stand by the door to say good night to her. Laughing at the stupid jokes he made, she worried about him and finally worked up the nerve to invite him over to her place for dinner.

It was midsummer in the high desert, about a hundred ten degrees in that town, and the air-conditioning had quit on her. She couldn't cook at all, so they ate olives and crackers and cheese and drank cheap Russian vodka with 7UP, sitting out on the shady fire escape above the main street. He didn't even kiss her, but the next day he came by with a new air conditioner and put it into her window for her, and then they did a lot of kissing on the dusty red couch in the living room.

That day had been the happiest day of her life, because she mattered to someone again.

"Dad," Lindy breathed, and rolled over and looked into the California sky. "You out there?" No answer. He was gone, gone somewhere forever where she couldn't follow, leaving behind a tender indentation in her heart. She pulled herself to her feet and started walking up the hill toward the big house.

Sammy, their rottweiler, came rushing toward her, wagging his whole rear end when he recognized her. "Sammy," she whispered, crouching a little to scratch him behind the ears. "What are you doing outside? Your job is to stay in the house. You're supposed to guard Mike," she said, rubbing him on the back. Then she remembered. Rachel didn't like Sammy. She probably didn't want him inside. He followed her silently as she climbed the wide wooden stairs up to the backdoor.

She turned her key in the door, which unlocked without a squeak. Her watch told her it was three-thirty.

In the dark kitchen the only sound was the humming of the refrigerator. How strange to creep around her own house. She opened and closed a few drawers, maybe to reassure herself that this was the place in spite of how alien it felt. Without giving it any thought, she picked up their sharpest knife from one of the drawers, a favorite she used to cut the tips off of carrots. She had bought the knife herself at Williams Sonoma on a trip to the Bay Area. She had used it often, helping the housekeeper with party preparations. This knife definitely belonged to her.

She passed through the dark silence into the hall to the reception room where the great staircase wound upstairs. Her footsteps in the big rooms seemed to echo with the sounds of parties gone by.

The banister felt warm to the touch. She led with her free hand, running it along the smooth surface upstairs, around the curves she had been so proud of when they first had the stairway built. At the landing she paused, waiting for a sign, but there was no sign. The house slept. Tuesday was the housekeeper's night off, and Florencia lived far away in what Mike called the dungeon, a two-bedroom apartment on the basement level that opened out onto sloping gardens at the side of the house.

The heavy Persian rug in the upstairs hallway muffled her progress. She approached the bedroom door. How outlandish everything seemed. She was a foreigner in her own home. On its stand by the door, the big blue Chinese vase was still filled with the same willows and reeds she had arranged three weeks before, dried and dusty now, looking like plants arranged by some other woman's hands, the new woman of this house.

She used the knife to push open the door. In the dusky light, Mike was lying on his back, snoring lightly, asleep. Rachel lay on her stomach beside him, her lower leg and bare foot free of the covers, her right leg looped over his, her beautiful long hair covering her shoulders.

She looked at them for a long time, clutching the knife in her hand, struggling to accept the proof of her eyes so that she might finally allow the umbilicus that still tied her to Mike to disintegrate, feeling the shaky instability that comes when death is very close.

Mike's eyes opened. He had always been a light sleeper, awake at any sound. He didn't move. Neither did she. For a long moment they stared at each other.

Then, while Rachel slept on, he carefully pulled the covers off himself and got out of bed, not taking his eyes from Lindy's. In the dimness his bulky nakedness shifted like a shadow among shadows. Bending down, he picked up his old wool robe from the floor, pulled it on, tied the belt. He stepped into slippers. Lindy watched, hypnotized.

He came to her and touched her. That corporeality of his touch, the blanket-warmed fingers, shocked her out of her reverie.

"Mike?" she said softly.

"Who else?" he whispered, and she wondered if he was smiling. She took in the familiar smell of his body.

He nodded toward the door. Then, holding on to one of her wrists, he drew her out of the room. In ghostly procession they drifted down the stairs, back through the kitchen, out the backdoor. Sammy picked them up at the door and followed close behind.

Out on the path, where they could hear the lapping of the lake, Mike looked at the knife, then at her face. Standing across from him she saw again how well they fitted together. It was as if their bodies had been molded exactly in reverse, so that her curves disappeared to accommodate the knobs and slopes of his physique. After a moment, while the breeze hushed and the sounds of the lake receded, she reveled in their mutual awareness. Breathing deeply a few times, she thought about the knife in her hand, not wanting to give it up.

"What's the plan here?" Mike asked, sounding so much like his old self, she almost melted.

"No plan."

"All action, no talk," said Mike, teasing gently. "The knife, Lindy. Give me the knife."

"No."

"Lindy, if you don't give me the knife, you're going to have to use it. You don't want to hurt me, do you?"

She didn't know what to say to that. He stood there patiently, fearlessly, the breeze ruffling his robe, looking the same as he did in the ring years ago, not a care in the world in spite of the tough punk across the way wanting to rip his heart out. Deciding, she lifted the knife from her side and raised it so that the tip just brushed his stomach. He didn't move, didn't even blink. This was the Mike she knew. She turned it around so that he could take it by the hilt.

He dropped it into a low bush beside the path. She buried her head in the scratchy wool, and his hand came up to stroke her hair.

"I'm having a hard time, Mike," she said. "I love you."

"I love you, too, Lindy," Mike answered, like in the old days when they had just met. They went down to the beach, clear of the forest, while he half-supported her, and they crumpled to the sand together.

"I'm sorry," he said. "So sorry. I think I was dreaming about you."

"Won't you—will you please—"

"It isn't right—"

But her hand was pulling at the tie around his waist and the robe fell open.

"Please," she said.

"Oh, Lindy."

She put her arm around his neck and drew him onto her, and after lying there with her for what felt like a long time, his hands tugged at the zipper on her pants, then pulled them down to her shoes. He lay on top of her for a moment, his heavy weight lulling and comforting her.

Then he gave her his love, like he always had.

Afterward, when they were dressed again, sitting together and supporting each other, looking out at the lake, he said, "I'm ashamed. I should have known better."

"Is there—any chance—"

"I'm marrying Rachel." He spoke without malice, sounding almost as confounded by his own words as she felt.

"She's so young."

"It's a fresh start. I looked around one day, and everything looked different. It was like another man was living my life, doing all the usual things, paying bills, making love, on the phone, and I was outside looking in through a window at him, mixed-up as hell. I couldn't hear the words anymore. I didn't like what I saw there, this old face and these wrinkled-up paws of mine." He held his fists up. They both inspected them in the dark, until he dropped them again. "They were . . ." He thought, but couldn't come up with the word he wanted.

"Beautiful, Mike." She had told him that many times.

"You remember? Like bowling balls, smooth to the touch, cruising down the alleyways . . . fast."

"Oh, I remember."

"Now, see that?" He tried to flex. "I can barely bend the fingers. I got arthritis in them, I think. I'm just so tired. . . ."

"Of what? Of me? The business?"

"I don't know. I don't feel the same as I used to about anything."

"I just can't believe it."

"I still care for you."

"You have such an odd way of showing it."

"Don't leave yet, Lindy. We may never get to talk like this again. It'll always be the lawyers, the reporters . . ."

"The money," Lindy said.

"I'll take care of you like I always have."

"Was it you taking care of me, Mike? Or me taking care of you?"

He shrugged.

"We worked so hard. Remember when we started up the first exercise studio in Lubbock? I called everybody in town to find somebody, anybody for you to instruct. I got that phone slammed down in my ear so many times I still don't hear right."

"We put everything we had into it."

"Why didn't you ever marry me, Mike? I proposed to you lots of times."

"I don't know." He lifted a handful of sand and let the granules sift through his fingers. "Were you going to kill me with that knife?"

"I don't know."

"Well, thank you. That you didn't kill me." They both laughed a little. "You're such a wild thing, Lindy. Remember what you did to Gil before the divorce, when you two broke up? Sixty-two stitches. I know I haven't forgotten."

"Don't remind me. But he really had it coming. That shitheel married me for the sole purpose of getting his hands on my savings. He plotted to rob and humiliate me. Anyway, who knew that vase would break all over the place like that?" Lindy said.

"I guess that's your biggest fault, and maybe the cutest thing about you, too. You're just reckless, and I never knew anyone else that could blow a gasket like you do."

"I do have a temper, but I'm not mad now. I've been thinking about the first year we were in the black. Now that was a Christmas. You in your Santa Claus suit, making love to me on the dining room table. You can be so funny."

"You think I'm happy about what I did to you? And what you're doing to me? Ah, Lindy. Things took a turn."

"So you're getting married." Lindy blew into her hands to warm them. "You stupid bastard. I doubt she cares about you. She sees the money. She's following the dollar signs."

"She says she loves me. Maybe there will be a baby."

"I gave you the business. That was our baby."

"It was my business. I started it. My fists and my hands made everything happen."

"My brains and my words. Both of us made it happen, and you know it." She wanted to go on objecting but something held her back, some unquenchable faith in the future that told her not to say anything unforgivable. "What a waste, us talking like this." she said. "It's not going to change anything. It doesn't mean anything. Might as well listen to Sammy bark."

"I don't want to string you along. You and me . . . we're finished. Let me take care of you. I'll send you a check every month."

"Thanks for the offer. But I don't want your charity. I want you to remember the two of us, what it was all about. Love for each other. Respect. A generous spirit. What has happened to you? Have you forgotten everything?"

"Speaking about that, Lindy, I need you to do something for me."

"What?"

"Get your lawyer off my back and get that receiver out of my company. You know how we've always done business at Markov. Our deals are based on trust, and we need to be flexible to take advantage of our markets. A receiver will kill us."

"Nina explained that to me. He's just there to oversee—"

"He'll oversee us right out of business!"

"You won't let that happen, Mike."

"Please don't let it come to that, Lindy. Think about what I'm saying." He looked back toward the house. "I've got to go in before she wakes up," he said, lifting Lindy's chin with two fingers, his mood shifting as quickly as day had begun to break. "Isn't it unbelievable," he said, "us coming to this." He didn't point to the knife, but she knew they both had it on their minds. "Isn't it crazy?"

"Crazy," Lindy agreed. They stood across from each other, a matched pair of champagne glasses, bookends, socks. Two that belonged together.

He brushed his hand along her cheek with all the old tenderness, and for that instant Lindy remembered what a great couple they made.

Then, in the gray light, Rachel appeared, running toward them in a satin robe, her long black hair flying behind her like the wings of a raven. "What's going on?" she cried, pulling up beside Mike, panting.

"Nothing. Lindy and I had to talk."

"At this hour?"

"No," Lindy said. "He's not telling the truth. He's trying to protect you. But you have a right to know," she said. "Mike and I just made love, right there in that spot where you're standing. And it was fantastic, Rachel. Better than ever."

"What?" Rachel said, stepping back. "No. You're lying. Mike?"

"Let's go back inside," he said, taking her arm and casting a furious look back at Lindy. "We'll talk there." He tugged her arm but she shook him off.

"No, we'll talk now," Rachel said. "Is it true?"

"Yes, it's true."

Mike had been standing almost exactly between the two women, but now stepped up to stand closer to Rachel. At the same moment, Sammy took his place beside Lindy. She put a hand down to pet him, but even Sammy's warm fur was no solace. She watched Mike with Rachel. She saw by the way he looked at Rachel he was lost to her, enchanted.

Mike took Rachel's hand. "Rachel, for as long as we're together, I swear I'll never touch another woman. This was . . ." His mouth moved, but he couldn't articulate whatever it was he was thinking.

During the pause that followed, Rachel seemed to calm down. She appeared to be thinking. "I know what it was," she said finally, breaking into a terrible smile. "A consolation prize, right, Mike? It's only fair to offer a cheap consolation prize to the pathetic loser."

"Now, Rachel, let's just go. Don't start something," Mike said calmly, trying to pull her up the path to the house.

"He loves me," Lindy said. "He has always loved me."

"If he loves you so much," Rachel said, "what's he doing over here with me? No, wait. Don't say anything. Let me answer that for you.

"He's over here with me because he knows we're just about to climb right back into that big bed upstairs for the kind of really hot sex you're too worn out to give him these days. Yeah," she said looking hard at Lindy. "My suggestion is you stick to dark beaches and rooms without lamps from here on out. The light is not your friend."

"Don't speak to me like that! Mike?"

But Mike had no control over Rachel. "Oh, come on," she

said. "I'm not saying anything you don't notice every morning when you look in the mirror at those icky crowfeet and run for the makeup bag."

"Stop this!" Mike tugged hard on Rachel's arm, but she did not budge.

"If Mike didn't have money you'd be out of here so fast we wouldn't even have to smell the stink of your exhaust fumes!" Lindy said.

"Temper, temper, Lindy. I understand you get . . . kind of crazy when you're upset. Mike warned me about you," Rachel said.

"I . . ." Lindy said, unable to frame a sentence, the anger in her welling up so high and so deep it threatened to drown her.

"I have an idea!" Rachel said excitedly. "Let's be friends. Let bygones be bygones. That's the civilized way to go about this, isn't it? And as a token of our new relationship, I'm gonna invite you up to the house right now. Isn't that a good idea, Mike?" she said eagerly. "Don't you think that would be just lovely?"

"Well . . ." Mike said. He shuffled his feet clumsily on the ground as if he were trying to establish a foothold in quicksand.

"Really, how about that for fair?" She took Mike's arm. "C'mon Mike. Let's invite her right upstairs with us. Remind the old sow how it's done."

Lindy ran toward her and wrenched her away from Mike. "You wouldn't know love if it bit you right in your bony ass!" She pummeled Rachel with her fists all too briefly before Mike flew up behind her, pinning her arms to her side.

"Sammy, get her!" she shouted, fighting frantically to free herself from Mike's iron clench.

Sammy jumped. Rachel screamed as he knocked her flat to the ground.

"Get her!" Lindy cried.

Rachel continued to scream.

"Sammy, down! Down boy!" Mike roared at the same moment.

"Go Sammy! Bite her face off! Tear her eyes out! Sammy, go!" Mike's hands gripped her. "Ow! Mike, that hurts!"

"Down, Sammy!" Mike commanded.

The dog, who had listened to this garble of incoherent commands with increasing agitation, looked at them. Confounded into paralysis, he stepped slowly off Rachel.

Rachel scrambled up. Bursting into hysterical tears she ran for the house. Sammy walked up to Mike and Lindy, wagging his tail tentatively. "Good boy," Mike said. "What a good boy."

He held on to Lindy until Rachel had made it back inside, then he dropped his hands from Lindy's arms. "Don't come around again," he said. "Next time, we'll press charges."

"Mike," she said. "Wait. Talk to me."

Without another word, he turned and followed Rachel up to the house.

"He won't marry her," Lindy said to herself, brushing the sand off of her clothes and watching his back as he melted into the bright background of morning's first sun. "One day he'll wake up, and the devil that's holding him will let go. He'll feel his power again. And then he'll want me back."

BOOK TWO
DISCOVERIES

A wonderful fact to reflect upon,
that every human creature is
constituted to be that profound secret
and mystery to every other.

Charles Dickens

8

ON NOVEMBER 12, A WEEK and a half before Thanksgiving, Nina woke to a cold house. Bob was stirring downstairs. During the night, Hitchcock had evidently decided against the hooked rug on the frigid floor and joined her in bed. She was spooning with her dog! Was this the fate of a single woman?

Shoving the dog to one side, she jumped out of bed, ran downstairs, turned on the heater, then ran back up and pulled the feather bed around herself while the heater roared to life. While she lay there in delicious comfort she thought of Paul, missing him. Other than a few brief telephoned hellos, she hadn't heard much from him since the Markov party.

She never seemed to find the time to call him. She needed him to help her come up with a detailed and impartial history of Markov Enterprises and to carry out preliminary interviews with anyone Lindy might suggest could be a favorable witness.

She needed him in her bed.

The house warmed up and soon she saw Bob's head peeking around the bedroom door. Seeing that her eyes were open, he ran to the window and pulled the curtain, saying, "It's snowing! Mom, you have to see this."

Outside the air had turned white and wispy. The snow was so heavy she could barely see out, but the whiteness moved, drifting downward.

Pulling aside the covers, she threw on her robe and accompanied Bob downstairs. "Get your clothes on, Bob. I'll drive you to school. We missed the bus."

"Hey, maybe they'll call a snow day!"

"I'll find out." While Bob started up their new CD of African ska music, she got the coffee going and laid out bowls for the oatmeal, then called the school to find out that, thank God, they hadn't canceled the school day.

Bob sat down at the kitchen table to wolf down a couple of bowls of oatmeal, and Nina headed back upstairs to put on her warmest wool suit. To keep her hair dry under her hat, she knotted it, pinning it to the back of her head. "Bob! Don't forget to put your lunch in the pack!"

Overnight, fall had given way to winter. Nina felt a rush of exhilaration bundling up in the parka and gloves and boots and pushing open the door to a foot of fresh snow. Transfigured overnight, the neighbors' old junk car next door had become an ice sculpture, and the trees were festooned with white. Not a breath of wind blew to stir the airy, cool flakes melting on her cheeks.

They got into the Bronco and she put it into four-wheel-drive, hoping they wouldn't have to get out again and shovel the hilly driveway, but it trundled up without a problem.

"What's the big rush, Mom?" Bob asked as they skidded slightly on a curve.

She slowed down. "We're trying to get going on the Markov depositions, but we're having trouble with Mike Markov's lawyer."

"Deposition. That's where you interview the people in the case and it's all written down, right? And then later you trip them up when they say something different during the trial."

"How did you know that?"

He shrugged. "I think from TV."

At Bob's school, trucks and SUVs and Subarus jammed the parking lot. She kissed him good-bye and watched him disappear into the white, running in spite of the slipperiness and his heavy backpack.

———

Through the rest of November and into December, Nina continued to fight with Riesner over what documents would be produced at the depositions, which had to be postponed twice so they could go before the Hearing Examiner and obtain rulings. Riesner refused all her calls and she had to fax every communication.

Professional courtesy in this case consisted of faxing motions at five o'clock on Friday so the other guy got them on Monday and lost three days of prep time, informal press conferences in which the object was to influence the entire jury pool, and stonewalling on each and every interrogatory.

She had known how it would go and she paid back each trick, even adding a few of her own. She became friendly with Barbet Schroeder of the *Tahoe Mirror* and fed her tasty tidbits once a week until Barbet was following her around with her tongue hanging out. The producer of a show on Court TV called and asked what she thought about televising the trial. This kept her up a few nights, until the producer finally called back and said it wasn't going to happen as there was a juicy sex murder going at the same time in Indianapolis that they had chosen to televise instead.

Lindy called almost every day, demanding detailed progress reports.

"But this case is going very quickly," Nina reminded her.

"Being broke sure got old fast. Whenever I come into town, Alice has to pay for everything. I hate it. I feel like I owe everyone something all of a sudden. I want this thing resolved. I want to see the look on Rachel's face when Mike loses. I want my money."

Nina knew how she felt.

Lindy was spending a fair amount of her time raising hell at the casinos with Alice. A few oblique references in the paper gave way to full-blown mentions on the gossip page of the San Francisco paper after one incident, when they were both thrown out of Prize's Club.

During one of Lindy's late night calls to Nina's house, Nina asked Lindy about it.

"They blow every little thing I do out of proportion," Lindy said. "Except for that one night. The night before going to Prize's, I saw Mike. I'm not going to go into that. It was bad. Alice and I went out the next evening to play craps. I guess I had more than my share to drink. She hardly ever drinks but she kept me company. Then we got on to the topic of her divorce and that really set her off. Well, you saw how she gets. She pulled out that stupid gun. Took a few pot-shots at the craps table."

"My God!" Nina said. "Did she hit anyone?"

"She hit the table," Lindy said. By now, she was laughing. "She's such a nut. I don't know if she did it out of anger or just to cheer me up because I was losing. I doubt she could tell you, either."

"Were you arrested?"

"She knew the pit boss so they didn't call the police. They just tossed us out of there like sacks of rotten potatoes."

"Lindy, this is serious. No matter how bad you feel, you need to keep a low profile. All of the jurors in your case will come from this area. You don't want them reading about your wild, drunken exploits right before they decide whether to give you money for being such a hardworking businesswoman, now do you?"

"You're right, Nina. I'm sorry."

"And another thing. Your friend should not have a gun."

"She doesn't anymore. I took it away from her right then and there."

"Where is the gun, now?"

"I hid it in my suitcase. She won't find it there, because she's a privacy freak."

After calling Paul's number in Carmel for weeks and not reaching him, she called his office ten days before Christmas and got a new number for him in Washington. "Run, run as fast as you can," she teased when he answered. "I will still catch you."

"I could swear I left my new number on your machine one lonely evening when you were out carousing with another man," Paul said.

"More like having a late meeting."

"Uh-huh," he said, but he didn't sound worried.

"Anyway, I'm sorry I haven't been able to call more often. I'm really swamped. Why did you change hotels?"

"They moved me to an apartment at the Watergate. It's more comfortable than a hotel room."

"More of a long-term place," she said.

"Well, yes. I couldn't spend all my time in a hotel. That's no life."

"No," she agreed, actually preferring to think he had no life there.

"Nina, you would love it out here," he said, changing the subject. "Talk about being in the thick of it! Guess who I ran into in an elevator of an office building on K Street. Ralph Nader. Almost knocked him down. And then I saw Henry Kissinger in a corner grocery store in Georgetown one day. It's so different from California. The history here—well, it's out walking around the town, buying Twinkies."

"Wow," said Nina. "Sounds like you are enjoying yourself."

He assured her he was not, that he missed her and all the other mountain folk, keeping it light, asking after Bob, and Andrea and Matt's family. They talked for a while, catching up. Then Nina asked the question uppermost in her mind. "When can you come back?"

"Not until late January. I'm stuck here over Christmas," he said.

"Oh, no," said Nina. "You can take a few days, can't you? I thought we might sneak in some skiing over the holidays. I don't have much time, but I thought maybe we could swing a weekend up at the lodge at Squaw Valley."

"There's the alternative."

"What's that?"

"Wrap yourself up in a pretty bow, put yourself on a plane, and appear on my doorstep."

"You want me to come to Washington?"

" 'Want' is weak. I long for it. I desire it."

"Paul, I'm busy, too. Even though Bob and I will celebrate

Christmas over at Matt's, I still have to buy presents, decorate the tree, do the whole number. I just can't take any time away."

"If that's the way you want it," said Paul, sounding pissed.

"That's just the way it is," she said, "same for me as it is for you."

Eventually, he cheered up. In the end, he agreed to call the minute he had some time to help with the Markov case.

He left her with the suggestion that he couldn't wait to show her something new he had thought up, something involving the four tall bedposts of her new pine bed.

The holidays came and went in a blur of green and red and family visits. Bob seemed happy with the new software she'd scrimped and saved to buy him and did not ask again about seeing his father. She knew he hadn't forgotten. He just didn't want to hurt her.

In order to keep Winston informed about developments in the case, and therefore involved, Nina continued to send him copies of all the written battles and arguments. He called regularly with encouraging words and some excellent strategic advice, but he always seemed too tied up to come up to Tahoe. In this way, without it ever being plainly expressed, she learned that famous trial lawyers don't sully their hands with the dirty little processes of pretrial discovery.

Genevieve stayed in Tahoe long enough to observe Nina a few times and to attend a short civil trial in another matter in which Riesner was the plaintiff's attorney to, as she put it, "search for the soft underbelly." Before she left, she and Nina set up a conference call with Winston, who agreed with Genevieve that Riesner would appeal to underdeveloped personalities who didn't like to make their own decisions, and stronger conservative types looking to harden their positions.

They followed up with a discussion of Mike's potential witnesses. Nina told them that, aside from Mike, his girlfriend would pose the biggest threat to them at trial if she could shake off her credibility issues with the jury. Rachel Pembroke had a long history at Markov Enterprises, a responsible position there and a personal view of the Markov relationship that would undoubtedly bolster Mike's position.

Then at Genevieve's suggestion, they brainstormed what she called the "mantra" for their case.

"Let's get it all down to five words or less," she insisted. "Look for an inspiration as we keep draggin' our nets through the facts."

"We'll know it when we see it," Nina said, "as Justice Potter Stewart said."

" 'It's trophy-wife time,' " Winston said.

"Ooh, that's good," said Genevieve.

"She made him rich, then he dumped her," Nina said.

"Too long," said Genevieve. "We need something catchy like 'Where's the beef?' Or like Paula Jones and the President's 'distinguishing marks.' That was the mantra for that case."

Winston laughed.

"We sound so cynical." Nina soft-balled the criticism by including herself as a target. "There are important questions in this case. Things like, what is a marriage? What actually is a family? You know?"

"I like it," Winston said, rolling happily over her objection with his enthusiasm. " 'What is a family?' Only it doesn't cover the business aspect."

They ended up with something Lindy had told Nina: the business was their child. That summed up Lindy's position. Nina liked it because it seemed to reach for a deeper truth, an emotional truth she hoped a jury would embrace.

Outside, the snow deepened along the roads and in the woods. The landscape turned from dusty olive, tan, and blue to blinding white and blue, while Squaw Valley, Heavenly, Sierra Ski Ranch, and the other resorts hustled to get the maximum number of lifts operating. The town filled up again after its autumn lull. The winter season had begun.

Depositions began on the first Tuesday in January. Nina beat Sandy to the office and spent an hour going over notes before she arrived.

At ten o'clock, the parties assembled in Nina's cramped conference room. After one memorable pitched battle the Hearing Examiner had decreed that Mike Markov would have the honor of being deposed first. Special rules had been devised to limit the number of hours per day, and Nina would have only two days with him. He sat across from her now.

After commenting on the lamentably disheveled state of Nina's conference room and the generally inelegant surroundings, Riesner was suspiciously calm and quiet. He had the chair on the left. At the end of the table the stenographic reporter, Madeleine Smith, tried to lighten things up by chatting about the fantastic weather. Wearing beige pants tucked into boots and a knit sweater that covered her almost to the knees, Lindy fidgeted, appearing uncomfortable. In a week, it would be her turn.

"Swear the witness." Mike raised his right hand and the reporter made him promise to tell it like it was. He wore a tweed sports coat over an open-throated golf shirt. His thin black hair was brushed neatly back, and his soft suntanned face shone slightly from soap and water. He had an odd expression on his face. Nina couldn't quite identify it. Shame? Guilt?

Her goal for his deposition was quite simple. She would be trying to scare up anything she could use against him. She would listen for inconsistencies and she would gather details in enough bulk to trip him up during the trial.

From three feet away, he didn't look like the evil despot Nina had tried to make him in her mind; but Riesner did. He wore the Stanford ring, his personal fetish, on the manicured hand resting on top of the pile of papers they would be going through. His lips curled, but she couldn't say they formed a smile.

Nina placed her new leather attaché, a gift from her dad, directly in front of her, making sure Riesner noticed, feeling rather petty. When he had entered her offices for the first time months ago, she felt he had seen at a glance exactly what she was, a shoestring practitioner with shallow pockets. She couldn't compete at this level, but by God, she would show off what she had.

"Okay," she said. "Mr. Markov. On November first you were served with Requests for Production of Documents numbered one through thirty-five. It has been subsequently ordered that you bring all documents in response to this deposition at this time."

"He has complied with the Requests except as modified in subsequent hearings," Riesner said. "Here are the responses, numbered from one to thirty-five."

"Thank you. Let's get these marked as exhibits." While stickers were placed on the exhibits, not a word was said. Lindy looked at Mike; Mike glared at her. Riesner sighed, sat back, crossed his legs. The room felt too hot. Nina sketched abstracts on her legal pad. Outside, cars mushed through the barely plowed street.

"All right. Cross-Complainant's Exhibit One. All records, memoranda, notes, written memorializations, and any other document of any sort whatsoever tending to support Cross-Defendant's claim that the parties agreed that the businesses and other property in issue were to be and remain the separate property of Mikhail Markov," Nina read.

"For the record," Riesner began, "Cross-Defendant continues to object to this Request on grounds that it is overbroad, calls for a conclusion, is vague, ambiguous, and unintelligible, and all the other grounds set forth in our opposition thereto last week."

"Noted," Nina said briefly. Riesner could object until he gave himself a sore throat, but he still had to turn the documents over. Mike still hadn't opened his mouth. Riesner passed over a manila file stuffed with papers, and Nina began picking them up one by one, identifying them for the record, and having Mike authenticate them. Before the day was over, Sandy would copy them. There were originals of the corporate documents she had already seen, Articles of Incorporation, Bylaws, registration documents, Profit-and-loss Statements, and so on. The next group included the deeds to the Markov homes, several titles to vehicles, and other titles to property, all in Mike's name.

Then came the tax returns, both corporate and personal. After Mike had stated for the record what they were, Nina put these aside for copying. She would go over them with the accountant down the hall from her office this evening so she could ask intelligent questions about them tomorrow.

The next group seemed to be a series of interoffice memos and correspondence with suppliers and customers in which Mike made various policy and executive decisions. So what? She wasn't impressed. Lindy had a similar pile of documents lying in wait for Mike. Each note and memo had to be identified for the record. Nina was very careful, very formal as she described the documents for the reporter.

Exhibit 1 was the most important of the lot. If Mike didn't have some kind of smoking gun here, they'd be all right. They'd have a good chance.

Mike kept on, polite, unfaltering, answering each question after a short pause, sometimes consulting for a moment in a low voice with Riesner. As the morning wore on, the tediousness of the process settled them all down.

Unwritten rule of legal practice number 13: If you dread it, it will come. It came just before noon. Riesner had put it at the bottom of the stack just to raise a little more hell with her.

A sheet of lined notebook paper like the kind Bob used in school, the document in question was crumpled, stained, and had been drafted on a manual typewriter that needed a new ribbon. SEPARATE PROPERTY AGREEMENT was typed in capital letters at the top.

Mikhail Markov's apparent signature at the bottom was followed by Lindy's.

Lindy, who had her eyes on the document, too, scratched her arm, the only reaction she showed. Her silence at this moment was a worrisome omen.

"What's this, Mr. Markov?" Nina said sharply.

"That is a separate property agreement between Lindy and me," Mike answered, keeping his face impassive. But Riesner couldn't resist. Victory flashed across his long face, and his false smile turned real before Nina's eyes.

You son of a bitch, she thought, shaking her head, her mind boggled by this blow.

She began asking narrow questions about the exhibit, and Mike answered everything in an unhesitating, well-rehearsed voice.

He and Lindy had agreed that if they ever split up, they would keep each other's property separate. The business was in his name and she understood that only he would continue to run it on that basis. They had sat down and talked about it the day they moved to California, thirteen years before, on October 12, and Lindy had typed their agreement up on their old Underwood. They had both signed it. Mike spoke in a flat voice, just spitting out the facts, keeping his eyes off Lindy.

"Let's take the lunch break," Nina said. "We'll start again at one."

"Oh, let's," Riesner said. He and Mike got up, two wealthy, successful men without a care in the world, and walked out, leaving the exhibits to fester on the table. Nina left, too, and went back into her office. Sandy laid out box lunches for both of them on Nina's desk while Lindy visited the bathroom.

Nina hadn't moved by the time Lindy returned. Lindy sat down heavily beside her. "Well?" Nina said.

"Well what?"

"Why didn't you tell me?" She let her anger show.

"There's nothing to tell. I do remember, during the time he's talking about, we were in the red. Mike was feeling very insecure. Things were rocky between us. We were arguing a lot. You argue a lot when money is low, it's natural."

"So you signed an agreement that you have never once mentioned to me."

"I never saw that piece of paper before in my life," Lindy said, shaking her head. "It's a forgery. Or a joke."

"Look at it again."

Lindy picked it up and studied it. "Looks like our old Underwood," she said. "That's strange, because I gave that typewriter to Goodwill years ago. Maybe he took it out and hid it somewhere. Or I suppose it's possible he typed the agreement way back before I donated the machine." She said the right words but her tone was wrong, all wrong.

"Lindy?" Nina said. "You see this paper? If it sticks, it means we'll probably lose. Both of us." She got up and leaned her arms on the table, moving in close to extend the full force of her enraged gaze onto Lindy. "Don't lie to me."

"I've never seen it before."

Nina shook her head, incredulous.

"Anyone can forge a signature," Lindy was saying. She held the paper at arm's length, squinting at it. "I'd even swear it was mine if I didn't know better."

"You need reading glasses, Lindy," Nina said, leaving the room.

Riesner and Mike came in a little late and took their places, the cool air and clean scents of the outdoors trailing behind them.

The load of wet concrete Riesner had dumped on Nina was drying now, tightening, weighing heavier and heavier, suffocating in its implications.

She didn't believe Lindy. If real, that piece of paper might be worth a hundred million dollars to Mike. If a fraud . . . but it wasn't. Riesner would never take a risk like that. He had to know Nina would discover a fraud, and that the jury would reward Lindy accordingly.

Could Mike be lying to Riesner? No. Riesner would already have had the thing looked at by professionals, because he never trusted his clients.

Why would Lindy keep the knowledge of this devastating evidence from her own lawyer?

Stupid question. Denial, fear that Nina would bow out, hope that Mike had lost it . . .

What now? Walk barefoot over a bed of burning coals all afternoon. The joy of law.

"Let the record show we are gathered here again and all parties are present," Nina said to the grinning, smirking red devils behind the polite faces of the men across the table from her. Madeleine's fingers began working her reporting machine.

Nina walked the hot coals all afternoon without even giving her opponents the pleasure of an ouch. Mike claimed he kept the agreement in his fishing tackle box, where he also kept his Social Security card. He insisted that Lindy signed the agreement of her own free will after a calm discussion. He said his divorce back in the sixties had cost him everything he had, and that at the time the agreement was signed he had feared that Lindy, too, would leave him and take the little that he had struggled to build. He readily admitted that he had initiated the discussion, but he said Lindy had typed it up. He kept looking at Lindy, who seemed to have zoned out.

At about three o'clock he said, "Can we please go off the record?" Nina nodded, and the reporter shut down her machine, stretching her hands.

"Lindy," Mike said. He held up his big hands. "Quit while you're ahead."

"Leave me alone."

"I'll give you a million dollars to walk away from this."

"Keep quiet, Mike," Riesner said, raising his voice. He took hold of Mike's arm. "Let's go in the other room and talk." Mike shook himself free, his eyes never wavering from Lindy.

"You can't win. You're wasting our time. You're ruining the business."

"Me?" Lindy was outraged. "I'm not even involved."

"The longer you force me to screw around with this shit," Mike said, "the quicker things fall apart at work. Hector, Rachel, they're running the show, but nobody's making the big decisions because of that receiver your lawyer put there. We're not meeting the orders."

"So get over there and make things right."

He continued as Lindy spoke, as if deaf to her. "MarDel is suing us. Understand? We'll go broke if I don't get back to work, and as long as the receiver's coming in and sitting in my office, I'm not setting foot in there."

"I can't do anything about that."

"But you can. Use your head," Mike said. "Let's make a deal."

"Don't say anything," Nina said to Lindy. "Mr. Riesner, please instruct your client that he is not to address my client directly, or the deposition is over, and I'll ask for sanctions."

"Come on, Mike. Other room." Riesner jerked his head.

"Lindy, take the deal," Mike said.

"Now you listen," Lindy said. "You can't buy me off with half a percent of what the company's worth. You want me out? Offer me fifty percent or keep your big mouth shut."

"A million. That's my offer," Mike said. "My only offer. I'll see you in hell before I'll ask again." He let out a laugh. "You thought I'd forgotten it, or lost it, didn't you?" He allowed himself to be stood up and marched into Nina's office. The door slammed, and they could hear the voices next door, but not the words. Madeleine said, "I think I'll go chat with Sandy for a minute." She closed the conference room door behind her.

Nina turned to Lindy. "He didn't forget it. He didn't lose it. What do you say to that?"

"I say he's sinking mighty low. He won't get away with this."

"Lindy, that paper changes everything."

Lindy said nothing.

"I can try for two million, if you want, but at this point, it's my opinion you won't do any better. You can put it away, buy a house. You'll have interest income."

"No."

"It may be the best I can do for you, considering."

"Considering what? This crummy old thing?" Before Nina could prevent it, Lindy reached over, picked up the piece of paper, and tore it into jagged halves. Nina lunged at her, calling, "Sandy!"

They struggled. Lindy's fists had locked fast. Sandy came running in, followed by Riesner and Markov. And then Lindy stopped. Looking as if suddenly all the electricity had failed, leaving her in the dark, her grip loosened. Nina took the pieces out of her hands and gave them back to Riesner.

"How can you humiliate me like this, Mike?" Lindy said calmly. But the calm after the storm held more portent than the actual thunder that had preceded it. "Rachel put you up to this, didn't she? She's the one who's pushing you until you're like somebody I never met and wouldn't want to know if I did. This has all gone too far." She was raving but Nina couldn't figure out how to stop her. She tried to break in, but was shoved aside and ignored. "I'm going to do what I should have done already and put all of us out of our misery right now. Kill her!"

"Sandy. Take Mrs. Markov out of here," Nina commanded.

"Well, now," Riesner said. "Death threats, destruction of evidence. Nice client control, Counselor. I think we'll be going."

"But . . ." Mike said. Lindy had begun to breathe in hiccuping gasps, one way of not crying, Nina suspected. For a moment, Nina thought Mike was going to take her hand.

"Yes, indeed. The deposition is over," Riesner said. "I'm afraid I have to take this exhibit back with me to ensure it is not destroyed." Firmly, he edged Mike into the outer office.

The outer door slammed.

"Did you get a copy of that thing, Sandy?" Nina said.

"Right after you broke for lunch," Sandy answered.

Madeleine, who had been hovering in the doorway, said, "Are we adjourned?"

"Oh, yes," Nina answered. They were as adjourned as they could be without being stone cold dead.

9

SCHOOL STARTED AT THE UNGODLY hour of seven-thirty, so the next morning when Nina let herself into the office after dropping Bob off, she knew she would have some time alone. Avoiding the answering machine with its winking light, she went into her office and pulled up the blinds. Snow everywhere, covering up all the dirty tricks and poverty and lies, making everything look so pretty. Turning on the lamp at her desk, she pulled out her checkbooks. Forced-air heating labored valiantly through the grate in the ceiling, the only sound.

She scratched quite a few numbers on her yellow pad and called a couple of credit card automated lines. Fifteen minutes later, she knew everything there was to know. Unlike Markov Enterprises, she didn't need an expert to figure out which way the wind blew.

Assets: the house on Kulow, equity thirty thousand, mortgage payment fifteen hundred a month. She had sunk all the money left after the divorce into it.

The cottage on Pine Street in Pacific Grove her aunt had left her, value about two hundred thousand. She owned it free and clear. The two students renting it barely covered the property taxes and upkeep.

The Bronco. Value, maybe two thousand considering the rapidity of its disintegration. Her jewelry, clothes, and furniture, another couple of thousand. The office furnishings and equipment, the same.

Accounts receivable. Closely balanced to the accounts payable. Monthly operating expense, including Sandy, about ten thousand.

Credit card debt, for the washer-dryer and the new fridge, fifteen hundred. Not bad at all. That was it, Reilly Enterprises, both sides of the register.

Now she looked at the page on which she had estimated the costs of getting through the Markov trial. She had started out with twenty thousand from Lindy, and only a month later she was down to five thousand, thanks to signing up Paul, Genevieve, and especially Winston.

She had counted on Winston to put up half the costs of the litigation, not to take money out, but Winston had managed to come onboard without putting up anything. In fact, he had taken a ten thousand dollar retainer for himself. He had explained that the IRS was causing him a lot of grief right now, plus his current case had tapped him out. He had made vague promises to come through in the crunch.

Now Winston, her much-vaunted cocounsel, had just lost that major case and probably could not contribute a dime to the costs in advance of trial. And her client had probably lied to her about signing a separate property agreement, which left their case looking weaker than ever. And Lindy had very little more to give.

That left Nina to scrape up enough money to make a major motion picture out of an anemic plot with mediocre box-office potential.

She pushed aside the ominous feelings in her gut. You have to spend money to make money, she said to herself. She leaned back in her chair and put her stockinged feet up on the desk. The heat was making her drowsy. She'd get up and make some coffee . . . instead she drifted into a reverie.

On the last warm weekend in October, she and Bob had ridden their bikes down the pathways by the Baldwin Mansion. After wearing themselves out, they had stopped and climbed on a rocky pier to check out the lake. Not far away, off to their right she noticed a long white cabin cruiser with the name *The Felony* written in italics on its impeccable side. At the helm, in a white captain's hat, the wind whipping his hair so that the bald spot showed, Jeffrey Riesner had stood. He noticed her at the same time and turned so that the wake of his cruiser practically drenched them.

Jeffrey Riesner owned a house on the water at the Keys. His wife stayed home with their toddler. Nina sometimes caught sight of her in her little red running shorts jogging by the office, pushing the stroller, so buff that nary a ripple jiggled even in the most sensitive places.

Riesner was the same age she was. Where did he get the money to live like that? And Winston had told her all about his Ferrari and the place in Bel Air he had managed to "scavenge," as he put it, from his second wife. Even Genevieve's studiously nonchalant wardrobe suggested she made more money than Nina did.

She would have a million dollars in the bank at least, post-taxes and debts, if she won the Markov case. Then she would live a whole different life. Move up in the world. Travel, first class all the way. She and Bob, at the Pyramids, cruising the Greek Isles . . . even Jeffrey Riesner would be forced to rethink his automatic contempt for her, wouldn't he, impressed by the only thing that impressed anybody: money, money, almighty money . . .

Of which she needed a lot right now.

She called the bank. Requested the paperwork to arrange for an equity loan on the cottage and a second mortgage on the house on Kulow. Dictated a letter informing the students in Pacific Grove of a rent hike. Applied for another credit card with a fat credit line. Canceled her appointment to have the Bronco fixed. She'd limp around in it until the trial in May.

By the time she was done, she had hocked everything. You had to spend money to make money.

Several more days went by without communication on either side, but that didn't mean Riesner wasn't working behind the scenes. Nina, too, kept herself busy. Friday, she called Lindy at Alice Boyd's house. She wanted Lindy to tell her the truth.

"Ms. Reilly!" Alice answered in a delighted voice. "I understand from Lindy that all is very hunky-dory on the lawsuit front."

"Well, I'm glad to hear she thinks so," said Nina.

"Don't you? Is something wrong?"

"Ms. Boyd, may I speak with her?"

"Call me Alice and I'll call you Nina, okay? When in Rome, or Tahoe for that matter . . ." she said with a laugh. "Anyway, she's out. I don't expect her for a couple of hours. She's helping to pack food boxes for some holiday thing."

"Could you ask her to call me?"

"Sure. Mind if I ask what this is about?"

"I just need to talk to her."

"Don't stonewall me, Nina. Lindy and I go way back. I loaned her the money to get this show on the road, you know!"

"Yes, she told me that. I know she's very grateful for your help."

"Well, to be honest, she's been a good friend to me, and I'd sure love to see her get that gorilla Mike off her back permanently. Oh, and that's something I want to ask you about."

"Ask me?"

"Yes, you. Do you know much about me?"

"Very little." She remembered Lindy's laughing reference to the loony bin, though.

"Yeah, that's Lindy. Weak on the gossip front, always has been. If you need the dirt on anyone, you give me a call, Nina. You just skip right over here. Will you do that?"

"Okay," said Nina, melting into the surrealism of this conversation like one of Dali's clocks.

"Now, let's get back to me. Here's the cheat sheet, abbreviated version of my saga: I had a world-class nervous breakdown when my husband dumped me four years ago. I did a few things . . . let's save those details for the rumor mill. They come out a lot funnier that way. Then I spent a year locked up. Not in jail. In a place worse than jail. You may remember hearing about that."

"Uh-huh," said Nina, trying to sound only mildly interested, and curious to know what reaction Miss Manners recommended under similar circumstances.

"But that's all in the past, okay? My life's back on track. I haven't had too much to do with the law—just my divorce and the commitment. But my experiences really got me hooked into the local resources, you might say. I know people from all walks of life, people who will jump through hoops for me and mine. And here's something else you should know. I want Lindy to win this lawsuit. I'm prepared to do whatever it takes. So we come back around to my question. What do you want me to do?"

Nina was silent.

"You heard me, didn't you?"

"I heard you," Nina said. "Alice, the most important thing you can do right now for Lindy is just . . . continue to be her friend."

There was silence on the other end of the line.

"Alice?"

"And to think I actually recommended you," Alice said, and hung up the phone.

On Sunday afternoon, under a blanket on the back deck, looking out at the snowy forest, Nina curled up with a cell phone instead of the proverbial cat. Through the picture window she could see that Bob and his cousin Troy had abandoned the computer to lounge on the rug in front of the fire and eat popcorn.

"Winston?" Giving up on having her calls answered at his office, she had called his house in Bel Air.

"Nina! I've been trying to get back to you. Great ski weather up there, I hear. It's almost beach weather here in L.A. The smog's cleared so we get our yearly look at the mountains."

"Yeah. I saw you on the news. Too bad about your case."

"Yes, what a disappointment."

"You seemed pretty sure you'd wipe the floor with them when we talked."

"I would have, if the judge had let me and if I'd had a little more leeway with the jury selection. The clients are going to appeal, naturally," Winston said. "The judge just shut us out. We couldn't get half the good stuff into play. I turned them on to a good appellate lawyer, but meantime I've got a fortune tied up in costs I've advanced. But no problem. There's still your case. Lose one, you gotta believe the next one's going to be a win for sure and you're gonna work twice as hard."

"Really? You've read the pleadings, had dinner with me, haven't even heard about the discovery, and you're so sure?"

"Sure I'm sure. Look at the talent we have onboard. It's just another jury." But he had heard the strain in her voice because he immediately added, "Right. What happened?"

"Riesner pulled out a written separate property agreement," Nina said, "signed by our client. Our client claims she's never seen it before, but she has said the signature bears a remarkable resemblance to hers."

A deep sigh came from the other end of the phone.

"Yeah," she said again. The slate-gray sky seemed to be darkening by the minute. A stray cinder from the chimney drifted down to the deck.

"She never even gave you a hint there might be something lying around?"

"I had no idea."

"Tell me about it," Winston said in his warm, reassuring voice, and she went over the day of Markov's deposition with him, trying to be as precise as she could about Lindy's reaction to the document.

"The way you tell it, she's lying," Winston said when she was done.

"Maybe she is. I'm not psychic. But then, some people look like terrible liars when they're telling the truth. I know I want to believe her but she sure makes it hard."

"Depressed, are you?"

"Deeply."

"Hmmm. So what now?"

"I call you, the famous trial lawyer, for advice. Isn't that why you're on the case?"

"You want my advice? Here it is. First, find out whether there's anything we can use to show duress. Press her for details about the scene on the day that she signed and I guarantee, there will be dirt for you to sift through. Second, assume the document is a fraud. Prove it by getting an expert to swear the signature is forged, or busting Markov's chops during cross-examination. Third, stonewall. Don't let Riesner get it admitted as evidence."

"Piece of cake," she said. "Anything else?"

"Did you think you were gonna bring down a few million in legal fees without having to sweat for it? You're gonna sweat. Hear what I'm saying? You should have expected something like this. You don't like surprises, you're in the wrong business."

"True enough," said Nina, but she felt disappointed. Somewhere deep in her irrational heart, she had hoped Winston, her high-priced talent, might instantly solve all her problems.

"Now let's get crackin'. I'm coming up to help you finish the depos. I'll bring Genevieve. She'd like to see the witnesses and get started organizing a shadow jury. We just moved into the hardball phase. We're going to bring it home, Nina. You hear?"

"I hear."

"You hear and you believe?"

"Winston, I'll believe it when I see it."

He laughed. "I'll be up Thursday. Let's finish Markov that day. Then Friday, let's get the little gal who caused all this trouble—Pembroke. On Monday, let's do anybody else that's important. Can you set that up?"

"I'll do my best. I ought to be able to drag Riesner back before the Examiner by Tuesday. I know Markov doesn't have any big obligations. He's refusing to work at the company and he won't let Lindy go back. I'd say he's pouting, but I guess you're not supposed to say that about CEO's."

"So who's minding the store?"

"The second-tier executives, Rachel Pembroke and this Hector guy. Hector Galka, the Executive Vice President of Financial Strategies and Accounts, and an old friend of Mike Markov. I'll try to line them up for Friday and Monday."

"Okay. Help's on the way. Now. What else are we going to do?"

"Get a forensic handwriting analyst," Nina said. "Get the signature on the agreement analyzed. I suppose there's a remote chance it is a forgery, though I can't believe they'd be so idiotic."

"Everybody's idiotic around this much money. But here's a thought. Let's skip that step. Don't get a handwriting analyst. Call Lindy and tell her you're going to hire one, and tell her it'll be expensive and a hassle and is she sure she can't remember signing that thing. Get me?"

"You think that'll smoke her out."

"Exactly."

"Oh, for Pete's sake. She lies and I pull tricks on her. What a way to do business."

"It's for her own good."

"Speaking of things being expensive, how much is this shadow jury of Genevieve's going to cost?"

"You ought to check with her, but the last one she did for me—oh, between forty and fifty thousand. Hire the people, Genevieve's time, all that."

"What? That's impossible! We just don't have that kind of money, Winston."

"Okay, look, I'll talk with Genevieve. We'll work with you on that, see how we can minimize our costs. And then you'll have to find the money. Just keep thinking about your piece of the pie, and what a small investment it is against your return. I do wish I could help more with the finances," Winston said. "This is an expensive business. It sure is. I'll try to kick in something later on."

"Lindy said something about being able to come up with some more money at some point. . . ."

"See! You're getting the hang of this business already. If you need money, you get money."

"I'm still very—concerned."

"Go ahead, sweat," Winston said. "We'll come up and sweat with you. We're workin' it, that's why you're sweating. That's just how it goes. We're getting started. We're with you. You hear?"

"I hear."

"Yes. You hear. But do you hear and believe?"

"I'm working on that," she said, her heart a little lighter.

Lindy returned Nina's call on Monday night. "Alice said you called me. I'm not sure why she waited so long to mention it except that she's mad about something. Anyway, I wanted to tell you I've decided I'm not going to be attending the rest of the depositions. Is that a problem?"

"No, but why not?"

"I have to get out of this place," she said. "This whole situation is making me crazy. Some days I know we'll win and I'm going to walk away with my fair share, and other days, I see myself five years from now, spritzing flowers all day long, working for Alice at the shop I helped her buy. Or maybe even living with her, like Joan Crawford and Bette Davis in a horror movie. I'd play the former hotshot, now faded and out of my mind, wallowing in a glorious past. Alice would be crippled, having shot that gun one too many times, and we'd live out our poverty-stricken lives in a ramshackle old place in black and white, all the color having left with Mike and my money."

"Don't worry so much. You'll be all right."

"I hope that's true. But the big reason I'm not coming is I don't think I can stand to hear Mike's version of what went on between us until I have to, during the trial."

"What will you do?" Nina envisioned some other friend's house, or maybe Lindy would move to a suite at Caesar's.

"I got a form in the mail from the Nevada Mining Commission. My dad used to go out to this canyon out in the Carson range and visit this claim we had," Lindy said.

"A mining claim?"

"Yes, he thought he'd find a vein of pure silver the Comstock lode miners missed. He was always looking for a fast buck. A real dreamer. He never had the patience to work the mine properly, but I'd go out there with him and we'd dig around and stay in an old trailer he'd found somewhere. You have to work the claim every year and file some paperwork or you lose it, but if you do that, you can keep it indefinitely. The claim and the trailer were all he left me."

Nina said, "You're not thinking of doing what I'm thinking you're thinking of doing, are you?"

"Well, the trailer's got a radio and propane and a generator. There's a water tank out back. Don't worry, I'll be back when it's my turn to get on the grill."

"But why? Why would you do that?"

"I'm broke," Lindy said. "Now there's a big difference between broke and poor. Broke is a temporary thing. Poor is different. I've been poor, and I know the difference. I've got prospects. I've got a place to live. By God, that's one thing that's not in Mike's name. It's warmer down there, only three thousand feet altitude, no snow. I can do some riding and some thinking."

"Riding?"

"My horse, Comanche. Mike doesn't own Comanche either. I looked at what I have right here and you know what? I've been worse off."

"You don't have to live like that," Nina said.

"Look, Nina, this is temporary. I know you're putting out a lot for me and I know you can't do it all. I've been able to scrape together a few thousand, and that goes to you today. You get every penny I can find right now to win this case."

Grateful she did not have to ask again for money, Nina wondered, not for the first time, why a woman who had worked for so long could have so little left. "But how will I reach you?"

"Don't worry. It's only a little more than an hour away by car. And there's a gas station and a little store where the highway meets the dirt road into the mountains. There's a phone there. I know the couple that run the place."

"I don't know, Lindy. I—"

"What business is it of yours?" Lindy said testily. "I'm a grown woman. I'll take care of myself. I grew up like this, Nina. What'd you think, I'm just some soft society matron who can't tie her own shoes?"

"It's not right," Nina said. "I don't feel I'm taking good care of you. You shouldn't have this kind of hardship."

"I'll be all right."

"Lindy," Nina said. "I want to ask you again about that agreement."

"I signed it."

"You did sign it?"

"I was lying, and you knew it. Don't pretend."

"Why did you lie, Lindy?"

"I'd almost forgotten all about it until I saw his lawyer waving it around. To me, it meant nothing at the time, just a piece of paper talking about money we might never have. But you were so grim-looking when you saw it. I got scared."

"Who prepared it?"

"I typed it up. Mike asked me to. He wanted me to sign it, so I did. So now we'll just have to deal with it."

"Did you mean to sign away any rights you might have in the company, Lindy?" Nina said, her voice shaking a little from the magnitude of the question.

"I was willing to do that, since it was the main obstacle to our getting married," Lindy explained. "He told me—he promised—that if I signed the paper we'd get married. And that's, I swear to God, exactly how it went."

"And then?"

"And then, like I said before, he had to go out of town. When he came back, I said if we didn't get married, I'd leave him. And he sweet-talked me. He didn't want me to leave. In other words, live with it. And I stayed, because I loved him. That's the whole story, Nina."

Nina put aside the melange of thoughts Lindy stirred up, concentrating instead on writing as much as she could of the story on the legal pad in front of her.

"So, he didn't hold a gun to my head," Lindy went on, "or try to punch me out."

"But he promised he'd marry you if you signed it."

Lindy said bitterly, "That's right. And I remember what you told me. I know there's no legal help for somebody breaking their promise to marry you."

"No, there are no breach-of-promise suits," Nina said in a vague tone. "But a gift made on the assumption that a marriage will take place may be recovered."

"What does that mean?" Lindy said.

"It refers to a seldom-used statute that harks back to the days of buggies and girls in crinolines you just reminded me about. But I think—I'll get back to you about that."

"How are we doing now, Nina? Have I wrecked everything?"

"This agreement isn't good news, Lindy. You already know that. But I do have our two associates coming up to help us out soon." She didn't know exactly why she wanted to cheer Lindy up, since she was the one who really needed the cheering. "They are going to give our side a real boost."

Lindy sounded subdued. "I'm sorry about lying. It's not that I don't trust you, it's just that you have to remember, I'm used to being the boss. I'm used to making strategy decisions without consulting anyone, except maybe Mike. And he wasn't exactly available to set me straight this time around."

"Apology accepted."

"Listen, I'll call your office from the gas station and give Sandy the number. She can leave messages there. Meanwhile, gotta go."

"You're leaving now?"

"I've got to run some errands over the next couple days, then I'm packin' up my saddlebags and strappin' on my spurs, so to speak. Good luck. Keep me posted."

"You be careful," Nina said, and a vision sprang into her mind of Lindy on a big white horse wearing that gold Egyptian necklace she had worn to the party trotting up Highway 50 past the casinos, heading for the foothills of Nevada. "Please."

On the following Thursday, Winston and Genevieve arrived. Genevieve looked animated and ready for action. Sporting fresh bags under his eyes, Winston had a strangely hangdog expression on his face.

While they waited in the conference room for Mike Markov to arrive so that they could finish deposing him, Nina took Winston aside.

"Are you all right?" she asked.

"I ended up working red at the roulette table on my way to bed last night. I swear, that wheel is the Jim Jones of gambling. It lures you with a few inspirational wins so you get cocky. You start betting numbers. You win some more. People are clapping and shouting, all riled up, watching the chips stack up in front of you. Then suddenly the room goes cold. The balls slips into a zero and then a double zero. The croupier rakes it all in."

"I know what you mean."

"Really? I lost ten—over two thousand dollars."

Had she heard right? Nina felt steamed. She could have used some of that money. "Two hundred's about my limit, even when I'm on a real bender."

"Worst part is, I'd do it again."

"It's a good thing you don't live up here."

"Doesn't matter where I am," Winston said, "I'm having a ball and taking too damn many risks."

Mike Markov walked in with Jeff Riesner, immediately making it clear his whole attitude had hardened. Nina explained that Lindy had decided not to attend any further depositions, and he said, "Good." Then he said his prepared piece, that any offer of settlement was withdrawn.

These preliminaries settled, they hunkered down to the task of looking at the other thirty-four exhibits, the business records, and miscellaneous notes that came from a twenty-year relationship. After

Winston greeted his old pal Riesner with a hearty show of chumminess that came close to making Nina feel uncomfortable, he settled down next to Nina, politely ignoring him. Genevieve lurked so inconspicuously in her corner Nina frequently forgot she was there.

As soon as she could, Nina got back to the agreement. "Okay. It says here that the parties hereby agree to keep their separate property separate."

"Right."

"So you would get the business, which was in your name. And all the other substantial assets like the mansion, which came later, went into your name."

"Yes."

"And what did she get? What was her side?"

"Her salary. Whatever she accumulated in her name, that was hers."

"What was her salary at the time you signed Exhibit One?"

Mike thinned his lips. "I can't remember."

"Well, according to Exhibit Twenty, the business lost money thirteen years ago, the year this was signed. Does that refresh your recollection?"

"Probably wasn't much of a salary that year. But it got a lot better," Mike said.

"Yes, but that year she signed the agreement, Mr. Markov, what was she getting out of it? What did you exchange for her giving up her right to any ownership interest in the company?"

"The company wasn't worth anything, either. Nothing for nothing. That's about what we exchanged."

"The company was in the red, but it wasn't worthless. You still had the name and some equipment, and you opened a gym in Sacramento that year, didn't you?"

"Yeah."

"So what did Mrs. Markov get out of the deal?"

Winston leaned over and whispered, "You know what you're doing?"

"Tell you later," Nina whispered back. Riesner's ears had

pricked up, but he seemed as in the dark as Winston about where she was going.

"Whatever she had was hers," Markov said.

"Isn't it true that you promised that if she gave up her rights to the business, you would marry her?" Nina said.

Riesner stirred, but sat back, apparently unable to justify in his own mind any objection to this line of questioning.

"No," Markov said. "She may have hoped I would, but it's not the same thing as me saying the words like that."

"So you never said the words?"

"Never did." Markov looked very uncomfortable.

"You just led her to believe you would?"

"She believed what she wanted."

"Do you consider yourself an honest man, Mr. Markov?"

"Wait a minute—" Riesner said, but Markov was already saying, "That I am."

"Then I ask you to tell me this, after careful reflection if you need it: did you know that she believed that in exchange for signing this agreement you would marry her?"

"I don't follow."

"Read the question back," Nina told the reporter.

The reporter repeated the question.

"She said, 'Now we can get married,' " Markov answered. "I never said it to her. She said it to me."

"Before or after she signed?"

"I don't know. Before, I think."

"This line of questioning is going nowhere," Riesner interrupted. "There's no cause of action for breach of promise to marry. Even if he did promise to marry her, so what?"

"That's true," Nina said. She looked at the stenographer, who was doing her job, moved on with her questions, and left that interchange with Markov sitting in the deposition transcript like a charge of plastique in a Belfast trash can.

10

ALICE BEGGED LINDY TO STAY on and see things through from the comfort of her cantaloupe-colored guest room, and Lindy calmed her down with the promise of a return visit during the trial. She couldn't wait to leave. Everywhere she looked she saw reminders of what she was losing. Even the lake lurking around every corner, running alongside the roads, a hidden presence, seemed tainted by her memories.

On Friday, she located a clothing store willing to sell her used designer clothes on consignment and a jewelry store that offered her two thousand for her twenty thousand dollar watch. She took it.

Back at Alice's, she threw the dazzling array of fashion she had acquired for all the charity functions and fancy dress parties into four fluff-filled boxes.

Alice came into the room to watch her pack. She had her hands in her pockets, and her chin-length blond-streaked hair framed the tense expression on her face. She dressed as well as she could on a very limited income as a florist. Today she wore a plum-colored blouse with a shawl-length scarf thrown around her shoulders and looked like a million bucks.

"Where are you taking those boxes?" Alice asked. "Not out to the dump site?"

"It's not a dump, it's a trailer, a perfectly nice one. I'm storing these . . . in a shed on the property," Lindy lied. She didn't want to admit she was selling them. Alice would be too upset and might just go off into one of her tirades about Mike.

"Why don't you stay with me? It's the least I can do for you after all you've done for me."

"Stop talking about that. I didn't do anything."

"Oh, no. You didn't do anything," Alice said, crossing her arms and snorting. "That night I was lying in the bathtub with a razor at my wrist and a bad attitude, you didn't break in the door and pour Ipecac down my throat until I threw up the pills. You never dragged me out of that party when I knocked out that Italian guy with a bottle of Bushmills, before he woke up enough to kill me. You didn't pay my rent until I could get a job or help me buy my business. And you had nothing to do with the down payment on this house 'cause you're just a parasite on society, a real rich bitch, aren't you?"

"Quit it, Alice. You know I appreciate the offer but right now, I'm so angry and hurt I really need to get out of town before I do something awful. I have these fantasies. . . ." Lindy's thoughts weren't good. She had been having nightmares. She thought that out there in the canyon, maybe all that earth and sky would leach the badness out of her like rain washing the dirt. "I'm afraid of myself, sometimes."

"You're not going to do something stupid, are you?" Alice asked. "Don't go and hurt yourself."

"No, not myself. Actually, that would be better than what I'm thinking."

"Oh, you're stuck in the murder and maim mode that comes right after he makes his announcement about the babe."

"I guess I am."

"I used to think of all the ways to kill him, lingering lovingly over the details. How I'd pluck his eyes out and squish them. What I'd do to his you-know-what. How I'd repair that undescended brain of his with a hammer. I'd be worried about you if you weren't having those thoughts. Mike's a bastard. My advice is, you go for it, sister. You take out that gun of mine from where you have it hidden and you blow his head off."

"Alice . . ."

"Crime of passion. You might serve two, three years, and it's so worth it. Maybe you'd get lucky like I did and end up in a hospital, supposedly correcting the error of your ways but instead medicated into a state of zombiedom." She took a scarf off the bed and removed her shawl to try it on, looking at herself in the mirror. "That was pretty restful. No cooking, no cleaning. Hardly any sex." Removing it, she tossed it into a box. "But you won't because you are basically a civilized person."

Lindy did not hate Mike. She hated Rachel. Alice wouldn't understand that. Alice blamed everything on men. She had recently made friends with her ex-husband Stan's girlfriend.

"Well, I'm glad you think I'm so civilized," Lindy said. "And I'm going to work on maintaining that reputation in spite of the baseness of my instincts."

She dropped the boxes at the cleaners, who agreed to deliver them to the consignment store in a few days. Then, dressed in her oldest, warmest parka, she drove her beautiful black Jag to the top of the Emerald Bay overlook, playing her favorite compact disc, driving slowly, enjoying the ride and wistful at the same time, knowing something beautiful in her life was over and it was too early to be thinking about new beginnings.

Once at the pull-out, she parked, got out, and stepped across the wet granite rocks to Tahoe's most famous view.

She couldn't see their house, which was located about a half mile south of the big green bay along the main body of the lake, but every boat that was willing to brave the cold that day she examined, as she had for the past months, looking for Mike. She climbed up the boulders for the highest perch, then stood in a cold wind, until her wet boots nearly froze to the rock.

Back in the car, she drove the Jaguar to a car dealer at the "Y" where the two local highways intersected. He offered twenty-five grand for her sixty thousand dollar car, and threw in an old Jeep in trade. She had very little to move from the Jag to the Jeep, just her battered leather suitcase.

She was close to the plant. Before she left town, she would take one more look at the place that had been her second home for the past dozen years. Turning on the noisy heater of the Jeep, and throwing it groaningly into gear, she drove up Tucker from the "Y" until their factory came into view. If he was telling the truth about abandoning the business, Mike wouldn't be there today, so she didn't have to steel herself for a chance encounter for a change.

She parked at the far end of the lot next to the building. Looking smaller than she remembered, their first factory stood on a low hill abutting a stand of fir trees. Its corrugated metal roof and red painted sides made it look more like a barn full of animals than a business, but the second story had windows on each end. The marketing group—three people—and the bookkeeper had offices up there. Mike and Lindy had worked up there occasionally.

Time sure got away from you, she thought, rolling her window down to examine the building for signs of neglect. But the place looked spiffy as ever, and she could hear the hum of a saw, probably doing up a redwood frame for a spa. Business as usual.

They had set the wheels efficiently in motion. She shouldn't be surprised to see that these wheels continued to turn without them, but she was. All the machinery should halt, shouldn't it, without her and Mike, the heart, soul, and guts of that business?

Dressed in slacks and a sweater, the petite figure of a woman appeared in the doorway. Rachel Pembroke. That's right. Rachel and Hector were running things now, weren't they? What a laugh. Rachel couldn't count her change from a movie ticket purchase, and worse, had no interest in anything smaller than a hundred dollar bill. Hector was a nice guy who knew his numbers but had the imagination of a stuffed duck.

Wrapping herself up in a sealskin coat, Rachel jumped into her company car, a golden-brown Volvo sedan, and turned left, heading downhill toward town.

Strange how things turned out. Lindy hadn't even thought about finding Rachel here. But here she was, dumped in Lindy's lap, just as if Lindy had studied a timetable and plotted logistics. Why

Lindy wasn't even driving her usual car. Nobody would ever suspect Lindy Markov would be caught dead in this rattletrap. She was anonymous. And she couldn't control the jealousy that rose up so powerfully in her she almost choked.

Lindy gunned the Jeep and followed.

Knowing she shouldn't, Lindy continued to follow Rachel's sedan, her stomach churning with emotion.

They had gone about a mile when the strangest thing happened. Rachel's car started to weave across the center line.

Rachel must realize there was a car behind her, but she couldn't possibly recognize Lindy behind the wheel in her wool scarf and sunglasses. Meandering down the road with the windows wide open to the cold, Rachel drove on, about two hundred feet ahead of Lindy, probably daydreaming about that day not long from now when she would have everything that belonged—that should still belong—to Lindy.

Lindy didn't know and didn't care why she was mindlessly following Rachel, but at a certain point it did occur to her to wonder what came next. She decided to make Rachel pull over. They would have a long-overdue talk. She would say, go back to Harry before it's too late, before things get really ugly and you get hurt. Rachel might listen. And if she didn't, Lindy didn't know what she'd do then. Alice's gun, tucked into her suitcase on the seat beside her, gave her little comfort. Pushing the case open, she took the gun out, just in case things got crazy.

But suddenly the roving that had appeared merely aberrant gave way to insanity as Rachel veered crazily back and forth along the frozen road. Her car, out of control, sped up, then slowed down, then made a sharp right over an embankment. Like a wasp zooming after a bit of meat, it flew purposefully through the air and vanished.

Lindy slammed her foot on the brake sending her own skidding car straight down the road toward the point where Rachel's car had vanished over the edge. She knew enough to stop braking and steer into the skid. For a few moments she fought to slow and stop the Jeep. She then sat very still, stunned.

The lonely mountain road stretched ahead in the eerie silence, the snow piled high on both sides in some places. Rachel must have plowed right through a drift and over the side. Lindy, whose heart was pounding so hard she thought she could feel it beating through her sweater, spotted the other car in a ditch off the side of the road, its rear end sticking up into the air, the exhaust pipe spewing fumes.

Stupid, stupid girl! What was with her? She could have killed herself, and Lindy, too! Lindy pulled up about fifty feet from Rachel's car and sat for a minute more, shaking, giving herself a second to restore her breathing to normal, then jumped out, her mind blank, just moving to keep ahead of the action that had almost overtaken them both.

She got out of the car, forgetting the gun, trying to figure out what to do next, when, out of the dim twilight of forest and trees, Rachel appeared. She was climbing quickly, clumsily up the snowy slope, heading straight for Lindy.

She must have seen Lindy following her, Lindy realized as she moved from one cold foot to the other. So here it came, the dreaded, hoped-for confrontation. And now, something strange. As the figure came closer, she got the distinct impression of a much larger person than Rachel. That must be her own fear blowing Rachel up. In the dimming light, Rachel looked immense, and so dark, dressed in bulky black clothes like a Ninja. And where was her face?

An instant later, Rachel, who had never slowed in her amazingly swift ascent uphill, knocked Lindy down. But Lindy had seen it coming, so she toppled softly into a snowbank. She leaped up, ready for a real round, if that was what Rachel wanted. And that was when another very strange thing happened. Rachel pushed right by her without stopping and ran down the road, faster than Lindy had ever seen the indolent Rachel do anything.

Nonplussed, covered with snow, Lindy stared after the girl until she disappeared around the bend. A few hundred more feet and the idiot would reach Highway 89. There she could flag someone down

easily. Maybe she had a concussion or some other brain injury. Or
. . . could she be afraid just at the sight of Lindy? Even though she
knew it was disgraceful, Lindy enjoyed a delicious moment of pleasure at the thought.

What now? Get back in the Jeep and chase after her? But Lindy
realized Rachel would blame her for the accident. The smart thing
for her to do was to leave. Yes, time to go, pretend this had never
happened. How humiliating it would be, having to admit she had
been trailing Rachel, and she was sure Rachel would blow it up into
a lot more. Maybe she just wouldn't admit it. Truth had its limits.

A keening sound like the cry of an injured animal interrupted
her thoughts. She ran over to see what could make a noise so terrible.

The front of the car appeared to be stuck in a snowbank. Rubbing away the snow on the window Lindy saw the strangest thing of
all. There was a woman inside in the driver's seat. Utterly confused at
the sight, she stepped back. The woman stirred and she heard that
awful sound again.

Lindy tried the handle. The door fell open, and Rachel tumbled
out into the snow onto her back, still wearing her sealskin coat. She
was semiconscious. Her eyes fluttered. Blood began to flow from
somewhere.

Her eyes opened. When they landed on Lindy, she screamed
and scrabbled at the snow, trying to use one arm to drag herself
backward.

"Let me help you," Lindy said, but Rachel's eyes bulged out
and she tried to shriek again and then her eyes closed and she stopped
moving. Had she fainted? Was she dead? Lindy bent closer to find
out.

A big black Ford Ranger came down the road from the direction of the plant, and Lindy recognized the driver as George Demetrios. Within seconds George came running. "What happened?" he
asked, panting.

"I don't know," Lindy said. "Do you have a phone in the
truck?" While George ran back to call an ambulance, Lindy sat in the

snow beside Rachel. She wanted to do something, so she lifted Rachel's head very gently off the snow and put it in her lap.

She had a dizzy, disoriented feeling. The sun shot bright ice picks through her sunglasses. Her scarf and one mitten had fallen off and the snow burned her hand. A few feet away, the forest turned dark and mysterious again. Rachel's face seemed to shine in its ghostly sleep, so young and pretty, almost virginal-looking in its freshness.

A thought struck her. Here was Rachel in her arms. So who was the other one? The Rachel who ran?

Had Lindy run Rachel off the road? Maybe Rachel had recognized her car, felt Lindy's fury behind her, and in her own fear had run her own car over the edge after all.

The figure running up the hill must have been a passerby, nothing more.

She heard a siren. George appeared on the side of the road. "Get the hell out of here, Lindy," he shouted. "This doesn't look so good. Let me take care of things from here."

Propping Rachel's head over a soft part of the sealskin coat, Lindy grabbed her scarf and mittens and ran all the way up the hill to her Jeep, pulling away just as the ambulance arrived.

11

AT TEN MONDAY MORNING, ON a threatening day with clouds billowing over the western mountains, Rachel Pembroke entered Nina's conference room looking as if she'd stepped off the runway at a New York fashion show. The dress was Isaac Mizrahi, the shoes Manolo Blahnik. The perfume made you want to lean in and breathe deep. Her long black hair gleamed like an oil strike, geysering down the front of her dress. A diamond on her left hand flashed prisms of expensive light. She was young, beautiful, and about to be very, very rich.

Everyone had heard about her trip to the emergency room on Friday afternoon, and that she had told the police she was convinced that Lindy was involved in some plot to harm her, but the only obvious sign of her troubles was a long scratch on one cheek. Apparently, Nina thought, Rachel was the kind of person who came out fighting.

Genevieve followed her to the conference table, looking understated in a sensible wool suit with a rose-colored blouse. She laid her notepads and pens out neatly on the table in front of her. Winston was a no-show. He and Genevieve must have decided to alternate on the depositions. Riesner had called to say he was running late.

"Oh, hi," said Rachel to Genevieve, peering at herself in a silver-backed mirror, obviously mistaking the woman at her side for a secretary. "I'm dying for some coffee. Think you could get me some?"

Nina paused at the door to see how Genevieve would respond. Up came the curly head. "How do you take it?" Genevieve asked sweetly. "In your lap or on your head?"

Rachel snapped her compact shut. "Excuse me?"

Genevieve laughed lightly. She held out her hand, which Rachel shook, looking confused. "Forgive me for not introducing myself to you right away. I'm Genevieve Suchat, jury consultant for the other side."

She held on, and apparently pressed a little hard, because Rachel gave out a teeny squeal and pulled sharply away. "Well, I certainly didn't mean to offend you," Rachel said, massaging her hand.

"Oh, God, no. I'm sure you didn't," Genevieve said, with a false smile.

Genevieve put her vexation with Rachel into one word during the lunch hour, as they walked down the snowy path that led from the office into the Truckee marsh now piling with snow. "Flaunting," she said, her Southern accent very pronounced. She seemed most Southern when she was most upset. "Don't you just hate flaunting?" She kicked at a loose clod of hardened snow. "Must drive Lindy Markov insane, seeing Rachel dolled up like that in clothes only Mike could afford."

"She's going to be tough for us," Nina said. "I already told you I think she's very convincing. According to her, Mike makes every major decision."

"Naturally, she says that. She's his girlfriend."

"But she sounds so reasonable," Nina said. "She's full of facts and figures. She remembers specifics the rest of them have forgotten all about. She's very personable and very professional, once she starts testifying. And she also comes across as being so understanding of Lindy's situation. I hated the way she so magnanimously excused Lindy for attacking her the night of Mike's party."

"She ought to get that plane ticket early."

"Plane ticket? For what?"

"The Oscars," said Genevieve, and they both laughed. "She's got a lock on Best Actress for next year."

"Her believability makes our job harder."

"I'm watchin' her," Genevieve said. "I'm studyin' every eyelash on that gal. I'm going to help you prepare for her testimony at trial, And when we get done, Miss Rachel's going to look like a ten dollar hooker at the Tailhook convention."

"Well," Nina said. "I don't know. That kind of approach might backfire. I don't feel comfortable with all these stereotypes. Like— Mike's the man, so he ran the company and Lindy helped. Or Lindy's the greedy, cast-off mistress. Let Riesner rely on those old stereotypes. I don't want to sink to that."

Genevieve rolled her eyes. "Nina, I know it's a temptation. I've seen it a thousand times. The lawyer wants to state the logical, honest truth of the matter. But that's all head stuff. You don't win the heart of the jury appealing to their reason. And if you don't win the heart of the jury, you go home with a hole in your pocket."

This statement made Nina stop and turn to face Genevieve. "That's all I know how to do, Genevieve. I don't want the jury to decide based on sentiment. I want them to decide based on the—"

"Oh, honey, you have so much to learn. You want to make that big fee or not?"

"Of course I do. I just—"

"Well, I'm going to make sure you do. Now let's go back to that primped-up thing and wipe the fifty dollar lipstick off that smart mouth of hers."

Over the weekend, Lindy had holed up in her trailer, tying up personal business, paying bills, lying on the couch, and gazing out the window at the cloudless sky. She expected Rachel to accuse her. She expected to be arrested.

Tuesday afternoon, when no one had come, she broke down and rode Comanche to the little store. There, she changed a few bills for quarters and went to the phone to call George Demetrios at the plant. He wasn't there anymore, a coworker told her, but she had a number at home which Lindy tried.

She hated having to call George. He had a crush on her, and she didn't like to encourage him. Still, it was lucky George had come along when he did out there on the snowy hillside. Or had it been luck?

"Hey, Lindy. How are you?" George asked with real concern.

"Fine, George. But why aren't you at work?"

"You don't know?"

"Know what?"

"I got canned."

"What? You've been with us for five years! Mike has lost his marbles. How can they fire you?"

"Oh, he had nothing to do with it. It was Pembroke got me fired."

"But . . . she doesn't have a lot to do with manufacturing directly, does she?"

"I don't know what she does. I just know she talked with my boss, and the next thing I knew I was out on my . . . fired."

Picturing his thick lips and olive skin, she thought for a moment. "You think they did this because of what happened on the road?"

She could almost hear his brain chugging around the idea. "Maybe, so," he said.

"How is Rachel?"

"She's okay."

"George, how is it you happened along when you did? Were you following me?"

"I guess I was," he said.

"Why?"

There was a long silence. "I saw you at the plant," he said. "I saw you take off after Rachel."

"Oh."

"I just didn't want you to get into any stupid kind of trouble."

Although the scene had been the cause of several sleepless nights, the idea of her following Rachel and George following her up the snowy road suddenly struck her as terribly comical. She stifled an urge to laugh. You just never knew what people were going to do, did you? "What happened after I left?"

"They hauled her off to the hospital. She had a few cuts and bruises, nothing big. Then the police came to interview me because she said you were stalking her."

"She did? Wow." Could just one time be called stalking?

"She starts in on this story that you were in the car with her and told her to pull over. That you pulled a knife on her."

"In the car with her? But I wasn't!"

"Yeah. Said she drove off the road because she was scared to death and hit her head on the steering wheel. But she looked okay."

"What did you tell them?"

"I set them straight, told them I saw it happen and there wasn't no one there but her."

"Oh, George."

"Everyone knows things aren't so hot between you and her. I didn't want anyone getting the wrong idea. I knew it wasn't you. You left in that Jeep you were driving. How could you have been in the car with her?"

"You lied for me, George. You shouldn't have done that. What do the police think?"

"They didn't believe her. She's got her picture in the newspaper all the time. They thought maybe she just wanted to get back in the paper and wanted to make you look bad. Anyhow, that's how I got fired."

"I'm so sorry," said Lindy.

"The place is a mess without you and Mike running things, anyway. Maybe it was time for me to move on. But I should tell you . . . people've been saying things. You know how they are. They don't mean you any harm."

Lindy felt touched. You could never buy George's kind of loyalty.

"But I did hear one guy swearing he saw you in the parking lot by the plant," George went on, "just sitting there like you was waiting for someone to come out. So I fixed that."

"You didn't hurt him?"

"Lindy, I don't do that anymore since you got me into that program," he said, pained. "I just talk to people, like the counselor taught us to do. I told him he must be dreaming and made sure he believed me. You got better things to do than come round here harassing somebody."

"George . . . thank you. I'm so sorry about your job."

"Oh, I'm working with my brother at his cabinet shop, learning a few things, having a pretty good time."

"I'm glad."

"Say, maybe you and I could . . . I don't know. Hit the slots one night? Go ice-skating? Would you like that?"

"You're so nice, trying to buck me up. But, no, George."

"I thought it might be that way," he said. "Well, I hope somehow things work out with you and Mike. Meanwhile, you just let me know if you need anything, 'cause I'm your man."

"Promise me you won't follow me anymore, not even for my own good. I don't need a protector."

"If you say so."

She could tell from the tone of his voice he didn't believe her. What a sweetheart.

A mechanical voice came on the line, demanding more coins. Lindy searched her pockets, but before she could insert another quarter, she heard George hanging up.

As she climbed into the saddle and steered Comanche up the slushy road, she recalled meeting George. One windy day after he'd first been hired, he'd thrown a punch at the foreman, Bill Henderson. Henderson wanted him fired, and the resulting in-house investigation turned up a record on George. He had served two years for assaulting his sister's husband.

When confronted, he admitted the conviction, but said that his sister's husband had been beating her. "I tried talking to him," George had said when she asked him about it. "He's just not the type who listens so good."

Lindy had involved him in a transition group for ex-offenders, calmed Henderson down with a little money under the table, and won George's allegiance forever.

Easing off her horse, she walked Comanche to his quarters next to the trailer, breathing in the dry air and feeling invigorated from the exercise she was getting. Casting a pleased glance toward the palette of brown and purple in the distant mountains, she began brushing Comanche, starting with the front of his head and working her way across his velvety shoulders, wondering, who had attacked Rachel? That had been no publicity stunt.

At least the cops weren't going to show up at the trailer. But George's comments about the business had worried her, and that got her thinking about the trial.

As she brushed, she had a wild idea. Alice. That gave her a good laugh. Alice the avenger, dressed in black, minus the high heels. Hard to believe, she thought.

But if not Alice—who?

12

ON A SOLID GRAY DAY in February, almost three months before their trial date, Nina convened the shadow jury of six women and six men in the extra-large conference room down the hall from the offices that she had rented especially for the event. This cross-section of the community would help them to determine who to look for in the jury selection for the real trial.

First went Winston, who launched into the opening statement that he and Nina had spent the past week drafting. This process alone had been valuable for Nina as they honed the enormous collection of facts and legal points in order to make the opening statement work. They wanted pith, or the jury would lose sight of the forest. They wanted to anticipate Riesner's opening statement. They wanted to awaken sympathy and respect for Lindy.

They had finally decided that Winston would make two points and two points only: that Lindy had an equal part in building and running the business, and that the separate property agreement was invalid because Lindy had given property on the basis or assumption that a marriage would take place.

The witness parade for the shadow jury, which proceeded much more quickly than in a real trial, began midmorning. The mock Lindy and mock Mike performed admirably, trying to give the dry words on paper in front of them some kind of truth without hamming it up.

"It's goin' great, isn't it Nina?" Genevieve asked during the lunch break, as they walked across the street to the deli.

"Mmm," said Nina, who had watched the morning's proceeding with a growing mixture of confusion, fascination, and abhorrence. Rehearsals and theater had never been her thing. Why couldn't they just go for a conscientious jury and let the strength of the facts carry the day? Why all this showbiz?

Because she wanted to win.

Still, in her view, the name "shadow jury" was the closest thing to accurate so far this morning. These witnesses had no substance. The shadow trial bore only a remote resemblance to a real trial. Where was Lindy's forlorn disappointment? Where was Mike's anger? Where was the place where all their plans went awry because someone lied or changed his story and the lawyers scrambled madly to regain control of the uncontrollable?

"You're not buying this yet," Genevieve observed. "Fine. Just wait until you see my recommendations."

"Maybe I'm just a little nervous about my performance in the summation this afternoon. I'm going through my usual freak-out at the thought of a trial, even a fake one."

They found a place at the counter and Genevieve insisted on ordering strangely named rye sandwiches. While Nina looked over her script, Genevieve chatted with the waitress, who agreed to put on a fresh pot of coffee, and the two reminisced about growing up in New Orleans and eating beignet, with Genevieve sounding relaxed and happy.

"Eat." Genevieve intruded suddenly on Nina's thoughts, pushing a ruffled-lettuce-rimmed sandwich toward Nina. "You're going to love this."

Smoked turkey with pickles and mustard. Nina ate it anyway.

"I almost forgot," Nina said as they paid and stepped across the street through a frigid breeze. "Lindy Markov wants to meet with you again."

"Yes, I already heard. She's been pesterin' me. Wants to know

all about the jury selection process. We're meeting tonight for dinner.
You come, too."

"Sorry. She's not an easy client. She gets too involved," Nina
said. "But I can't make it. I've got plans. It'd be better if you don't
talk about specifics, okay, Genevieve?" Meanwhile Nina would be
slipping into a bath, a meditation, a moment with Bob, and then over
to a meeting with someone she hadn't seen for far too long.

"You don't want me to talk about the case with her?"

"I realize it's probably protected by the attorney-client privilege
even if I'm not there. But I don't want to take a chance. I've had
trouble with that kind of thing before."

"You're in charge." Genevieve sounded slightly exasperated. It
had to be hard for her, Nina thought, with her personality, to consult
instead of lead. She had the same confidence in her abilities, the same
close involvement in the case as Nina herself, but she wasn't a lawyer.
Genevieve drifted in and out of one of those tangential quasi-legal
consultant positions that hadn't existed a few years ago. Cutting-
edge, yes, but not anchored by tradition or much experience, either.

When they reached the conference room door, dozens of curious eyes watched them enter. Genevieve fielded smiles all around.
Nina caught a few nods of wary respect.

She needed to smile more, like Genevieve.

After dinner Nina helped Bob set up his school books on the
kitchen table. Setting the sound on the disc player strictly to low
volume, she drove back to the office to meet Paul. By now she felt
beat and wished they had put it off until the next day, but she had
promised. And she did want to see him.

A week before, Paul had called her. After rehashing his disappointment that she had not been able to join him in Washington over
the holidays, he told her he was on hiatus from his work there while
some unexpected construction glitches got resolved, and had tied up
some Carmel business, so he could make himself available. He had
driven up that afternoon in his van and checked into his second
home at Caesar's to look into Mike Markov's business and back-

ground and locate witnesses who would testify that Mike had presented Lindy publicly and on numerous private occasions as his wife.

Nina had missed him, but didn't like thinking about that. Did she love him? She asked herself now and then. She had been in love twice, with Bob's father years ago, a feeling now over and only dimly resonant, and with Jack McIntyre, whom she had married. But five years later she and Jack had decided to call it quits. Her recent divorce from Jack still hurt a lot. She wanted to live quietly with Bob and build her practice here, until all emotional pain floated away down the Truckee River.

On the other hand, she was a young healthy female who got lonely at times. She wanted something, just not that crazy fool emotion that sends the rest of life spinning into outer space. Paul had his faults. He could be an overbearing jerk, actually, but then he could be a strong shoulder to lean on and a buoyant heart when things looked bleak.

The evenings spent in her four-poster bed or in Paul's various hotel rooms always held the hint of adventure, an unpredictability, a romantic sheen. She imagined he could now see the advantages of their relationship, too. Even though he had his consulting work in Washington, D.C., he was still available to her and didn't talk much about the future. He had quit pressing her on the point of marriage and settled into this trysting thing rather well, she thought.

In the small library–conference room next to her office, Paul was waiting, drinking a cup of coffee. "Hey, lovely lawyer-woman," Paul said. He set his cup down and put his arms around her.

"Hi, Paul," she said, allowing herself to disappear for just a moment into his chest and let his heat surround her. "How have things been in Washington?"

"Almost as cold as they have been up here," he said, playing with her earring. "It's been slow. Lots of delays because of the weather."

"You know what? I'm really happy to see you!" she said.

"Ditto," Paul said, smiling at her.

"I missed you."

"Me, too."

"You missed yourself?" she asked.

"Don't be cute."

She stepped back from him. "We need to get right down to it tonight."

"Good idea!" he said. "Let's entirely dispense with the preliminaries. Where will it be this time, the floor, this big wide chair, or hey, here's this nice long, comfy table . . ." He patted it, pushing files over to one side. "A little scratchy. But you've got a tough little rear end . . ."

"Do me a favor."

"Anything, as long as it involves those delectably painted toes of yours."

"Can you please disperse that fog of lust you hang around in long enough to tell me what you've found out?"

"It's more entertaining than you think in here."

"Come on, now."

He planted a final kiss on her nose and took a chair. Nina sat opposite.

"Oh, before we start, I forgot to ask." Nina messed with the papers on the table in front of her and tried to keep her tone casual. "Have you made up your mind about the job yet? I mean, it sounds like a great opportunity." She had spent more than a few long nights pondering the job he had been offered on the East Coast, finally deciding she should encourage him to do what was best for him. That was the right way to care for a good friend like Paul. "You'd probably be a fool to turn it down. You're in the prime of life, at the height of your profession . . ."

"Wait a minute. Last time we talked, I'd be selling my soul to take that job." He sounded more than a little annoyed.

"Well, you would be," she said lightly. "I'm just trying to say the right thing here, Paul. I don't want to be selfish and hold you back. On the other hand, I want you to make the decision that is right for you."

"I see," he said, looking at her with an expression she could not interpret. "Well, I'm playing it cool. I haven't said one way or another."

"You haven't turned it down?"

"No."

"I was just wondering," Nina said.

"I'll let you know when I decide," he said.

"Oh, good."

There was a short pause. Nina looked for something in her briefcase and Paul looked at her. "So how did the pseudo-trial go today?" he asked finally.

"Alarming. Provocative," Nina said quickly, eager to move on in the conversation. "Not that our substitute Riesner looks or acts anything like Jeff Riesner at all. He's an attorney friend of mine named Rufus who can talk the same talk, but has an entirely different effect on me. He sounds darned reasonable. I can't speak for the pseudo-jury."

Paul grinned. "That dirty rat Riesner. Just your luck to get him on the other side."

"But who better to represent Mike Markov? In court, he's pure, scorched-earth aggressiveness. He's going to have the jury believing they have to strike down this evil, predatory female. 'She can't let go.' Something like that will be his pitch. Oh, if it was only someone besides him. Someone decent like Rufus. I win, I take him out to lunch. With Riesner, I win, I watch my back."

"So who won the case today?"

"Well, you have to understand. First, this shadow trial is a pretty pale rendering of the real thing. It lacked several real elements. Drama. Passion. Tedium. Andrea was Lindy. She laughed a few times in the wrong places, and Winston had a handkerchief hanging out of his back pocket like a fluffy little tail for the longest time that nobody even noticed except the jury. I guarantee that won't happen at trial."

"Where was your notoriously clever jury consultant during this kinky event?"

"Quietly running the show from the sidelines. Generating these statistical models she likes so much. I reminded her she promised to protect me from that stuff, so now we skip to the generalizations. Anyway, we started by running through the testimony, at least the way they think the testimony will be presented at this point. As I figured, the stickiest mess was the one relating to that separate property agreement Lindy supposedly signed one fine evening, Rufus's favorite toy and probably Riesner's when the real time comes."

"And?"

"In our first opening and closing arguments, we emphasized the promises made verbally, that unofficial wedding ceremony they went through years ago, the assumptions and expectations of the parties."

"How'd your jury like that?"

"They didn't. We lost. We ran through another version, where we stressed Lindy's role at the company and kept up the attack on the agreement. That one seemed to ring the right bell. Our second approach proved more persuasive. We won, sort of. They awarded her twenty-five percent of the net worth of the stock."

"Surprised?"

"Not really. I felt all along that Lindy's work would make or break her case. That's a visible thing. We can point to real evidence of her contributions, evidence of Mike's reliance on her, evidence of her regular participation in big business decisions, evidence that directly links her efforts to the success of the corporation."

Paul nodded.

"After it was all over, before collapsing into a heap, Winston, Genevieve, and I did a quickie analysis and discovered things were exactly as Genevieve had predicted based on her preliminary research, questionnaires, and statistical models. We had a sexual Armageddon on our hands. The men initially sided with Mike, the women with Lindy. Of course, that picture changed as we got into our arguments, and that's another place Genevieve comes in. She needs some time now to go over the results along with some questionnaires and interviews she'll be conducting over the next couple of days. Then she'll write up specific recommendations."

"So is any of this going to help you win?"

"Yes. I think so."

"Do you believe in this, Nina? Shouldn't you just put your best case on, and hope the unpredictable crowd somehow fumbles its way to justice? People aren't cattle. You can't presume to predict which cereal they'll choose on a given day."

"Rice Krispies for Andrea, Raisin Bran for Matt, Lucky Charms for Bob, and Grape Nuts for me, pretty much every day except Sunday. So don't be so sure, Paul." Nina found a fresh piece of paper and poised a pen above it. "Now, let's go over where you are."

His notes neatly arrayed on the side opposite hers, Paul ran a hand through hair that looked blonder than ever and longer than Nina remembered. He had accumulated an extensive file on Mike Markov, which held a lot of detail about his long friendship with Galka and recent indiscretions with Rachel. He was also working with a woman in the marketing department at Markov Enterprises who thought she remembered a video from a sales show made a few years before that might help them nail Mike in a lie at trial.

"And here's something you might not know. Rachel is still friendly with her ex-beau Harry Anderssen. Sees him once in a while for dinner, without Markov."

"The male model?"

"That's right. She lived with him for years and picked up most of the tab because his income has always been erratic, except during the time he worked at Markov. I'd say their financial involvement goes way back."

"Harry Anderssen," Nina said, nodding. She told him what she had witnessed between Harry and Mike outside of the courthouse the day of the hearing.

"Not a surprise that he's pissed she's leaving him for Mike."

"We already figured he'd be on our side. My God, Paul. You think she'll go back to him?"

"At the moment, she seems determined to stick it out with Markov. But apparently Harry's no stranger to violence. Sounds like he restrained himself out there with Mike. Before he took up modeling and cleaned up his image, he was a bodybuilder who specialized in street fights. Maybe Harry's putting on a show for Rachel, hoping he can tap into the gravy train even after she marries Markov. Was she there to see the argument?"

"Yes."

"Interesting."

They spent almost another hour looking through what he had and discussing the list of chores Nina had put together for him.

When they were finally finished, it was past nine. They had drunk all the Cokes and it was snowing again. She needed to get back to Bob, who was alone at home. Paul also looked ready to call it a day. He had begun a tap-tap-tapping with his foot that suddenly sounded very loud.

"What's the matter, Paul?" She pointed down.

"Huh?" Noticing, he stopped his foot. "It's just—never mind."

"No, come on. Tell me."

"Okay," he said, reluctantly. "Keep in mind, you asked. Now here we have a woman who has enjoyed the pampered existence for years because of this man's success with his business. Pools, castles, servants, the whole bit."

"She had a big hand in the business."

"Yes, that's right. And, according to you, she was paid a salary for her work. Now, let's try to look at this objectively. They lived together without being married, in spite of her frequently expressed interest in marriage, *ergo,* she had to know he never wanted to marry her. She agreed to the deal."

That last sentence sounded like an awfully good mantra for Jeff Riesner. Nina hoped he'd never think of it.

"But she claims that he held out marriage as bait several times, most crucially when he forced her to sign that paper," Nina said.

"So your strategy is going to be that she's a poor victim of this bully? I mean, this guy is obviously just trying to protect his assets. Maybe he gets a scent of what's coming, and he wants to reassert the deal they had all along, that they would keep their assets separate. And she signs it. He doesn't hold a whip on her, he asks her to do it and she does it. He puts it away in a drawer. Because he never intended to marry her, simple as that."

Paul went on, his face reddening slightly. "Does she run to a lawyer to protest this forcible signing of a contract? No, she does not. Now, years later, she says she's forgotten all about signing it but that if she did, he must have promised he'd marry her in return. It's too convenient. If he said that, I'll eat my shorts."

"You have no idea what he said. The things that go on between two people are complicated," Nina said. "How can you begin to know what the dynamics were that night?"

"Okay, let's go even further back. From the start she knew damn good and well what she was getting in Mike Markov. A person who refused legal ties with her. A man who was very up-front about his feelings."

Nina shook her head. "What she knew is not the issue. What she anticipated or hoped for isn't either. The question is, what are her rights under the law? Did they have a contract? Did she agree to forfeit her rights to their business in return for a promise of marriage? These are fine legal points. She operated as his wife for many years, working with him, building up a company, sharing everything with him."

"Except that for all those years they were together, the bottom line is that they never married. The man put his assets in his own name and she agreed to it."

"That may be true, but . . ."

"Lady love, it is so true."

Nina hadn't even noticed how angry she was getting, but she knew it now. "I'd better make a note for Genevieve. You're exactly the guy we don't want on the jury. A man with two ex-wives and a gripe."

"Hey, my sweet-faced petunia, my wives never took me to the cleaners."

"If your prejudices and your professional attitude are clashing too much, let me know so I can hire less-troubled help. Oh, and please. Call me Nina. Even 'boss' is beginning to sound good."

"It's obvious what's happening here. She can't have him any-more, so she wants plenty of the next best thing, hard cash," said Paul with an obstinate look in his eye. "And so do you."

Nina threw her files into a case and snapped it shut. "I'm damn tired. I've had a long day. I'm going home."

"Hey, wait a minute. You're not going to let a little disagree-ment ruin the evening? Come out and have a nightcap." He tried to catch her by the arm, but she twisted away. "Look, I'm sorry. I had a long drive—"

"Paul," she said, walking out the door, "quit attacking my mo-tives. I'm an advocate for this woman in a legal case. She has every right to decent, thoughtful representation. She has every right to present her claim in court."

"Decent and thoughtful, huh?" he said, stomping after her to the front door. He followed her all the way out to the parking lot. "If that's the way you see yourself, why are you so touchy the instant I disagree with you? Huh? Tell me that. You're usually so levelheaded."

She climbed into the Bronco and turned on the headlights and wipers. Snow began to settle on his hair. "Okay, then I'll tell you why," he said. "There's too much money here. It's twisting you up. It's coming between us. You're being a hypocrite, and you're letting all those dollar bills blow over your eyes and make you blind."

"I'll talk to you tomorrow," she said. As she drove away, she watched him in her rearview mirror, standing with his hands in his pockets, letting the snow pile onto his shoulders, still as a snowman.

Later, buried in the warm nest of her down comforter, her anger dissipated and her humor returned. Why, I'll be damned, she thought. She and Paul were no different than the shadow jurors. Their emotional loyalty lay with their own sex, and that was that. She didn't like the thought that followed, that Genevieve could easily have predicted their argument, right down to Paul's descent into name-calling there at the end.

13

"LOTS OF LAWYERS HAVE INTUITIVE theories about jury selection," Genevieve said. She had organized a meeting to discuss the shadow jury's recommendations. It was late Saturday morning, and after changing the timetable to suit him, even Winston agreed to attend. They had so much to do before May that they had begun keeping long hours at the office. He let everyone know that one thing he would not do was neglect his exercise. Here he was in Tahoe and he intended to enjoy it, get out there and run in the morning even in the dead of winter, and when the weather nicened up, do some boating and swimming.

Beyond the picture window in the office across from Nina's where Winston and Genevieve had moved in, the winter sun glared off wet new snow. Icicles twinkled on treetops, melting.

Winston smothered a yawn, and looked at his watch. "I don't mean to be rude, but can we speed things up here? I've got a few things to do today." He wore sweats, and his pet radio, a compact, enigmatic-looking black box the size of a thick wallet, lay on the table in front of him. His hair glistened, still dewy from the shower he had taken after his run.

"As I was saying. Clarence Darrow thought about culture and religions when he looked for friendly jurors. For example, he liked the Irish for the defense, and excused Scandinavians whenever he could. He thought they had altogether too much admiration for the law. The San Francisco attorney Mel Belli had a whole system worked out for himself. He divided people up by their occupations. For the defense, he'd pick a waiter over a salesperson, or a doctor over a secretary."

"But not us," Winston said. "We don't do intuitive anymore."

Genevieve went on as if he hadn't spoken. Gone today was the country-fried humor and the ole girl persona. Though the Southern accent didn't change, when she talked about her area of expertise, it toned down considerably. Genevieve even looked a little nervous. Today was her day to show she was worth the money Nina had been paying her. At two hundred an hour, her billings this month had been horrendous.

"Of course, everyone's got funny ideas about race," Genevieve went on. "Conventional wisdom has always held that African Americans will vote for the plaintiff if it's a civil case, and vote for the defendant if it's criminal. Asian Americans are said to be easily persuaded by the majority on a jury, and Hispanics tend to be passive."

"Not everyone," said Winston. "I know better."

"Will you kindly let me finish?" asked Genevieve.

"C'mon, Winston, quit teasing. Give her a break," Nina said. Winston folded his arms in front of him and leaned back in his chair.

"Males favor women, females favor handsome young men. Females tend not to look kindly upon other females," Genevieve continued firmly. "Conventional wisdom."

"Bosh," said Winston. "Fairy tales. You know what Alexander Pope said about your precious jurors? 'Witches hang that jurymen may dine.' Now that's the truth. That's the reality."

"I agree," said Genevieve.

"You agree?" asked Winston.

"We have to forget about conventional wisdom. People today are going to be influenced by culture, religion, TV, current events, and yes, even the state of their stomachs—our lives aren't as narrow as they used to be. We'll need to make our choices based on very pragmatic considerations. For example, here's a simple recommendation for you from our panel, Nina. Lighten up."

"You're not the first to recommend it, but what exactly do you mean?" asked Nina.

"I'm talking about the color and style of your clothing. The big shoulders, the severe suits make you look authoritative, but they'd rather you persuaded them more softly. Go for something quite neutral with a hint of warmth. A taupey-peach. Pastels mixed with beiges. You need to emphasize the feminine in this trial. This is a case about a woman, don't forget, and it's classic in the sense that it's a woman who's getting shafted by a man."

"Taupey-peach? You've got to be kidding," Nina said.

"Other impressions were fairly uniform. They thought you seemed quite professional. They liked your manner, except that they find you too reserved."

More smiling, Nina reminded herself, practicing.

Winston said, "What about me?"

"You know you're good, Win. You started off well. They liked the simple statements of fact, and they liked it that you didn't raise your voice or get emotional on them. But once you got past the essentials, I'm afraid you wandered too far afield and lost them."

"Oh?"

"They didn't want to hear in dollars and cents how much Lindy made, how much she should have made, how much they made when they started out, their current per annum income before taxes. What's at stake is so ungodly huge, it doesn't compute compared to ordinary experience. So we don't talk about specific amounts. We just say, she ought to get half."

"Don't want them thinking about how much each one of the Markovs blows on car wax each month," said Winston.

"That's right," said Genevieve, snapping open her briefcase. She handed out to each of them a report fastened inside transparent binding. "These are all my suggestions, based on telephone interviews, the demographics, the shadow jury comments, the focus groups, and so on." At twenty-five pages long, it barely fit inside its binding. Winston picked it up and let his arm drop to his side heavily, pretending he couldn't even hold it up.

"I've spoken with Lindy and told her to lose the beautiful clothes, let some of the gray show in her hair and not to be afraid to show her feelings on the stand," Genevieve said. "This is no time for discretion."

"She doesn't strike me as someone who's going to have a problem with discretion. The opposite, maybe," said Winston.

"She needs to be warned about appearing bitter or vengeful. These are qualities our jurors derided. Andrea, playing Lindy, got a little too angry when she talked about Mike. The right mood seems to be wistful and sad for Lindy, whereas we need to be very matter-of-fact. We should be perceived as advocates who are just stating the bald facts, not too pushy, just cognizant of the weight of evidence we have that proves our case.

"Nina, when you talk with Lindy about her testimony, be sure you go over that with her. Make sure she knows how important it is to be consistent in the exact language about what was said, and make sure she uses the phrase 'expressly promised me,' especially when it comes to that promise made in consideration stuff.

"Go over her deposition with her until she knows better than to contradict it. Our shadow felt that there were some contradictions in what Andrea said. I've made notes on those statements, and I know you'll want to look them over with Lindy, so that we can be perfectly clear this time around.

"Oh, and I'm afraid the 'wedding vows' they exchanged in lieu of a legal marriage made a poor impression. On the whole, our shadows didn't feel it was important. We can't ignore the fact that a religious juror might find it significant, but we should probably only touch on this event.

"Now, regarding the statement from Lindy that he repeatedly made her all those promises. The men found that humorous and pitiful, I'm sorry to say."

"What about the women?" Nina asked.

"With the right approach, barring a hard-sell leader from the opposition, the women can be persuaded to stick with our side. One problem we're left with is not to antagonize the men. We'll talk more about that before the trial. Oh, and here's another point suggested by one of the shadow jurors: We might hint that maybe Mike would have failed without Lindy. After all, before he met her, he wasn't doing well at all."

Nina said, "That's good. I hadn't thought of that. You've done a nice job, Genevieve. Let's talk more after I get a chance to read the whole thing."

"I second that motion. Hey, Genny," Winston said. "We finished here for now? Want to see what's lucky today at the craps table back at the hotel?" He said over his shoulder to Nina, "Can't even get close on weekend nights. Too many people."

Genevieve said, "Give me ten minutes. I have to find something I stuck away somewhere under all the garbage on my desk."

"I'll wait, then."

"You brought me over this morning. You better wait." She went to her desk in the corner and sifted through the disorder.

"Well, I'd better go now if I'm going to catch Bob's basketball game over at the school," Nina said, checking her watch. "Bye." She went out to the parking lot of the empty building and started feeling around in her purse. No keys. She must have left them on her desk. She walked rapidly back and down the long dark hallway to her office and found them. Now that she was here, she decided she might as well pick up Lindy's deposition to take with her, but after a cursory search, she couldn't find it. Maybe Winston had a copy she could borrow.

Without knocking on the door to his office, she opened it and looked inside. Letting out a yelp, she jumped backward.

Winston had Genevieve on the ground, her body pressed down on the rug below him. Her arms looped around his neck, and her skirt had worked its way up to the top of her thighs.

It was some kiss.

14

NINA WATCHED BOB'S BASKETBALL GAME without seeing much. Her mind's eye was stuck on the image of Winston and Genevieve on the rug. They had jumped up when she came in, offering a weak apology that had done nothing to ease the jolt they had given her. She hadn't realized they were involved with each other—in that way. They weren't kids! They should have known not to carry on at the office.

Blanching at the the piercing sound of squeaking shoes, she sat in the bleachers beside the other parents in the gym, shouting, whistling, and stomping when the others did. She had brought the team snack, and after they won their third victory in a row, the boys ran for her and she slapped the fruit drinks and miniature bagels she had picked up on the way into their clammy hands.

At home, Bob showered and changed. Nina picked up a friend of his and dropped them at the movies, then headed for Caesar's and the long elevator ride to Paul's digs on the tenth floor.

She knocked three times before getting an answer.

"Well, look who's here," said Paul.

No smile. No embrace.

He opened the door wide. He wore gray athletic shorts and he was drying his hair with a towel. Humid air from the shower floated into the hall.

"Can I come in?"

He stepped aside, beckoning. "Take a seat," he said. "What can I get you to drink?"

"Whatever you're having."

"That would be straight whiskey, then."

"Fine."

He poured her a glass from the pint bottle on the table and handed it over, then sat down across from her, wrapping the towel around his shoulders so he looked like a model in a men's wear ad, right down to his trendily surly expression. He must have been working out on the Nautilus machines in the health club several floors down.

"I'm sorry," said Nina.

"Are you," said Paul.

"I don't know why I've been in such a mood. In my own defense, I can only say I was insane."

"The insanity defense never works in California. You'll have to do better than that."

"You have a right to your opinion of the case. I know you'll do a good job for me either way."

Paul took a longer drink than usual. She took that to mean he needed fortifying. He hadn't forgiven her yet. "What's bothering you?"

"Right now, your shirtless self. The smell of soap wafting off of your body. The tan line where your socks usually stop."

The shadow of a smile flickered on his face. "Don't stop there."

"Can we start over, please?"

Paul gave his hair a final thoughtful ruffling with the towel, and she thought she could see satisfaction in his eyes. He was enjoying this uncustomarily abject attitude of hers.

Well, fine. He had a right. "I need you," she said. "Not just for the investigation, but to talk to, Paul."

"I ought to tape this," Paul said, throwing his towel on the floor, and she could see from the diminished tension in his body he had eased up. "Then I'll play it back next time you get going on me. You get so self-righteous. Because you're invested in a cause, everybody close to you has to rally around to your side. Well, that's not always going to happen. Some of us prefer to maintain some detachment."

"I wouldn't exactly call you detached."

"Ah ah ah," Paul said, wagging his finger at her. "Don't blow it now. Tell me some more about my tan line." He looked down at his ankles and laid a dopey grin on her. She laughed.

"I've made my speech."

"Okay, then," Paul said. He got up and sat down beside her, on the bed. "Fill me in. How's it going?"

"Well, I saw something this afternoon. Winston and Genevieve kissing in my offices."

"Ah. You didn't like that."

"I have to question their judgment, that's for sure."

"Those kids."

"Exactly. They aren't kids. This isn't hormones, it's folly. Now, I know things get intense when you work closely with people. I don't object to their fling. Just . . ."

"You'd prefer they play in their own backyard."

"Exactly. And it doesn't help that we had a meeting today where I finally saw the clashing between our styles clearly. Winston and Genevieve are only interested in tactics. Maybe they're too big-city for me. They're taking over, and I don't like their—their cynicism. I feel ganged up on sometimes."

"They're not hard to understand. They're in it for the money. Just like you, right?"

"No, I'm not," she said. "It's an important legal case with important issues."

"And important money," Paul said.

She kept her mouth shut to stave off any further talk on the matter. Kneeling down in front of her, he slipped her shoes off and began massaging her stockinged foot. "Listen, Nina. If you don't like the way things are going, fire Romeo and Juliet. You're the boss. Go it alone."

"Not possible at this point. With the trial just around the corner, I need them. Besides, they do seem to know more than I do about this whole jury business. It makes me mistrust my own judgment. . . ." His hands kneading her feet sent radiant heat coursing up her legs.

"Ah, who cares what they do on the rug after-hours," she said. Her voice trailed off.

Paul got up and stood behind her. Taking a long strand of her hair, he curled it around his finger. His hands pulled gently at her jacket, and took it off. Immediately his thumbs pressed deeply into her shoulders as he began working the tight muscles around her neck. She sighed as her tension melted away at his touch. Her head drooped forward.

Paul took the drink from her hand and put it on the table.

"I find . . ." he said, continuing a mesmerizing circling motion at the center of her shoulder blades, "it's always a good idea . . ." His fingers moved inside the top of her blouse. "When things look a little bleak . . ." They began a slow, gentle journey from the back of her neck. "I need to forget my troubles . . ." Settling in to explore the vicinity in front. "Lie down for a little while. Now, doesn't that sound like a fine idea?" The hazy twilight had faded, and his hands appeared to ignite as they touched her skin, his tan against her pale.

"Excellent . . ." Nina said.

He turned her around, backing her onto the bed.

". . . suggestion." The light went off, but her eyes had closed anyway; there was only Paul's clean-scented body beside her, burning.

Book Three
Trials

*You don't approach a case with
the philosophy of applying abstract justice.
You go in to win.*

Percy Foreman

15

"Mrs. Lim fits. Age fifty-four, close to Lindy's. Realtor, two grown kids, husband with heart problems. Member of the American Association of University Women. Her parents are both dead. Her questionnaire says she doesn't have a problem with people shacking up. Equality in a relationship—she says it's important." Genevieve said rapidly. She reached for her jacket pocket and whispered, "Hang on. I'm getting beeped. It's Paul."

She left the courtroom for a moment to call him. Paul had ferreted out the fifty-five names in the jury pool, and was finding out what he could about the candidates to help Lindy's team make more informed selections.

Nina stalled Susan Lim with a few more questions.

The jury box was against the left wall of the cavelike courtroom, closely attended by the bailiff. Nina's station, the table on the left reserved for the side bringing the main action, was closest to the box and about ten feet from the court reporter and the witness box in front.

Milne's roost occupied the right front corner. Over at the long table to Nina's right, Riesner and his new associate, Rebecca Casey, put their heads so closely together, Nina could swear they touched. If he had done that to her—come to think of it, he *had* done that to her a couple of times—she would be cringing the same way she would from a scorpion in her shoe. In their encounters, Riesner usually edged up close, getting in her face, trying to intimidate.

Rebecca, pleasant-faced and professional-looking, was Riesner's match for Winston Reynolds. Educated at Stanford, she was younger than Winston, somewhere in her late thirties. Her confident air and no-nonsense attitude must be helpful when negotiating the testoster-one-laden halls of Caplan Stamp etcetera. She nodded at something Riesner was saying and passed a quick note behind Riesner to Mike, who also sat at their table in a spiffy suit he had surely never worn before, his thick neck bulging out of the collar.

In that suit, Mike didn't look honest. Was it the perspiration dotting his forehead and the bashed-up nose? His jaw worked as he gritted and relaxed his teeth. The yellow-tinged lights in the ceiling of the paneled courtroom shone down on him without mercy. He looked unwell, the flesh on his face sagging more than Nina remembered from his deposition a few months ago.

Obviously he felt the pressure of the judgment facing him up front as well as the judgment behind him, which consisted of the corps of reporters and other media types jamming the courtroom. Lindy, who sat on Nina's left, closest to the jury box, had been leaning over frequently to look at him, not a wise idea. Winston, who had handled the *voir dire* the day before, loafed in his seat next to her. He was relying completely on Genevieve, but Nina couldn't do that.

Nina turned back to Mrs. Lim and asked a few more polite questions. Aside from the fact that she fit Genevieve's profile of a "friendly" juror, Nina liked Mrs. Lim's earnestness and the thought she put into her answers. She looked successful and smart in the tweed suit, like someone who would listen carefully to the judge's instructions and think through the issues.

Genevieve returned in the nick of time, sliding in next to Nina, and said breathlessly, "Paul just found out that she filed an employment discrimination complaint with the Office for Civil Rights twenty-two years ago, when she was just getting started in the business world. Don't look at me! We've got to have her. Look bored." She yawned and opened her notebook. Nina looked at the clock above the jury seats. Eleven-eighteen, already well into the fifth day of jury selection.

"Thank you, Mrs. Lim," Nina said. Using the prospective juror's name was another of Genevieve's innovations and an indubitable improvement. The more you acknowledged a person's identity, as she put it, the more loyalty you won. The grocery clerks where Nina shopped used the same technique after she handed them a check. "Thank you, Mrs. Reilly," they would say, and she'd think almost subliminally, exactly as intended, aw, they noticed me.

Milne announced, "Mr. Riesner? I believe you have the next challenge." Riesner could now exercise one of his six peremptory challenges on any of the twelve nervous people sitting up there, some nervous because they wanted to be excused, some interested enough in the process and free enough of commitments to want to stay there.

"The cross-defendants will thank and excuse Mr. Melrose," Riesner said, offering Mr. Melrose the consolation prize of a simpering smile that said, nothing personal, I'm sure. He had chosen well. Nina had decided that Melrose, a Lutheran widower with a sad look in his eyes, would be kindhearted about the situation, a reaction that could only help Lindy. Poor Mr. Melrose edged his way awkwardly from the jury box and disappeared forever from the case.

Mrs. Lim remained. She wore her gleaming black hair short, tucked behind her ears, neat and businesslike. She would remain a sitting duck until—

"How many more peremptories do we have?" Nina whispered to Genevieve.

"Last one," Genevieve scribbled. Nina bit her lip and searched the faces in the jury box. None of them looked back.

Lindy also scrutinized each person. Now and then during the selection process she had written a vehement NO! or YES! as various jurors were called to the jury seats and questioned. Most of the time Nina had agreed with Lindy's assessments. And she had to admit that so far she also agreed more or less with Genevieve. The primary difference seemed to be that Nina never felt sure of anybody, while

Genevieve watched, consulted her notes and profiles, and judged without doubt.

So far, their disagreements had been minor and resolvable. Of the eleven people seated in the box this morning, besides Mrs. Lim Nina liked four, had doubts about four, and feared two. Riesner's team had unseated her strongest choices over the past few days, and she in turn had thanked and excused the ones he had to love, the ones who fit Genevieve's other profile, the negative one. *Avoid:* her report read, *Conservatives. No higher education. Divorced men. Hunters, fishers. Young married women. Republicans*—since political and religious affiliations had been nosed out by Paul—*follower types, wealthy types.* There were many more such guidelines, graded by degree of hazard.

"Now this next one, Clifford Wright. What do we know about him?" Nina said from behind her hand as a light-haired, boyish-looking man with an engaging smile made his way to the chair still warm from poor Mr.—what had been his name?

Genevieve slid over the chart she had whipped together on Wright when they had received a list of jury pool members the week before. "Thirty-nine years old," she said. "He scored high on his questionnaire. Currently campaign manager for our congressman. Skis, plays racquetball, rides a bike. After a number of casual girl-friends he recently married. Mother divorced from father after twenty-three years, which could be excellent; she continued to re-ceive alimony from his father until her death last year. Loves ice cream, Chinese food, vegetables. Won't eat strawberries, apples, or peanuts because of allergies. Self-described feminist. His wife works, not with him, but they pool their money and have accumulated enough for a down payment on a house. Paul didn't get far with him . . . he just moved to Tahoe from Southern California. He was a state assemblyman there and is active in politics here. His voting record showed a definite liberal bent. Leader type. He smokes. Good on paper. Let's see how he fares with your questions."

"Mr. Wright, my client, Lindy Markov," Nina said, gesturing toward Lindy. Wright turned his smile on Lindy.

"You've lived in Tahoe how long?" Nina began.

"Just a year."

"And before that?"

"In the suburbs of L.A. Yorba Linda."

She went on, asking him some neutral questions to give him time to get accustomed to the pricking of many eyes and the reporter tapping out his every word.

"The town you grew up in. It's in Orange County?"

"Yes."

"Birthplace of Richard Nixon?"

"Infamous for it."

"People in other part of the state would probably say Orange County is one of our most conservative counties. Would you agree with that?"

"Yes, it's conservative."

"How is it conservative?"

"It's a place that has probably seen more change in terms of growth in the past three decades, my whole lifetime, than anywhere else in the world. People are struggling to hold on to old-fashioned values, like family and religion. They feel a little under siege, I guess, so they are pretty noisy about it."

Articulate s. o. b., Genevieve scrawled for Nina to see.

"Would you say you share the conservative attitudes Orange County is famous for?"

"I would have to say that I couldn't wait to leave."

"You don't have old-fashioned values?"

"I got tired of the paranoia, the bigots, and the rigidity. I got tired of the traffic and pollution. I got tired of not being allowed to walk on people's lawns."

Nina wasn't satisfied. He sounded so candid. Too candid. Under the candor and the smile he seemed quite nervous. She veered back into neutral territory. After a few minutes, he had let up his guard only slightly. "Is this your first experience with the criminal justice system?" Nina asked.

"Yes, it is."

"Nervous? People usually are."

" 'Fraid so." He laughed.

"It's not an easy place to spend a morning, is it, Mr. Wright? Bet you'd rather be out," she pretended to consult her notes, "riding your bike up the path near Emerald Bay on a glorious day like this?"

"You bet I would."

Nina smiled and let the audience have their laugh. The tension in the room lifted enough so that Clifford Wright finally lost the tightness around his mouth.

"Unfortunately, we're all here doing our duties today," said Nina. "We're here to decide some very serious issues. This is a case that some have described as a palimony case. Are you familiar with that term?"

"Sure. Clint Eastwood was sued for palimony, wasn't he? Also Bob Dylan. Even Martina Navratilova, I think."

"What did you think about those cases?"

"Well," he said slowly. "I didn't follow the details, you understand. But from what I heard, Bob Dylan's girlfriend lived with him for a long time, even had and raised his kids. She probably ought to get something. The Martina thing, that was iffier."

"So, as a fair-minded person, you think you could try to look at these things on an individual basis."

"That's right," he said. He gave her a frank open smile. "Mrs. Reilly," he added.

"Do you understand what a contract is?" Nina asked.

"I think so."

"How would you define it?"

"An agreement."

"Do you know that in law, there are different kinds of contracts, both oral and written?"

"Yes."

"Do you know that, in law, an oral contract has the same validity as a written contract?"

"Yes, I knew that."

"Do you think they should?"

"As long as you know what the agreement was, I have no problem with that."

"Would you agree that it's easier to prove an agreement in writing, Mr. Wright?"

"Well, of course."

"But not every writing is an agreement, is it?"

"No. Even if it says it's an agreement, it might not be a—you know—legal agreement. I would guess it has to meet certain standards."

Nina glanced back at Genevieve, who looked pleased. And at Winston, whose eyes had narrowed. The answer was too good, and he had noticed.

"Any time you have two people, you can have two interpretations of the same situation, wouldn't you agree?"

"You can."

"From the very little the judge has told you in introducing this case a few days ago, do you have any thoughts as to which of the parties is probably right in this case?"

Wright raised his eyebrows. He looked almost offended. "I would have to listen to the whole story to know that," he said, shaking his head. "I just don't know at this point, Mrs. Reilly."

"Could you find in favor of Mrs. Markov if it is proved beyond a preponderance of the evidence that she and Mr. Markov had an oral contract, an agreement, to share all their assets, regardless of the size of those assets, regardless of the fact that they never put it in writing?"

"Yes."

Several times during the questioning, Nina could feel Riesner behind her, wishing to object. He didn't want to sit while she interpreted law to suit her purposes. On the other hand, lawyers tried not to interrupt during *voir dire*. It usually backfired. He would be taking his turn again soon enough, and she, too, would be resisting the impulse.

She continued to question Clifford Wright for another ten minutes.

You kept him up there a while, commented Genevieve's note when she finally sat down. *Longer than the others.*

He's too earnest, Nina wrote back, watching Riesner begin his round of questioning, flipping to a fresh page in her notebook so that she could take notes on anything that might need follow-up or close scrutiny. Riesner hadn't quite finished when Judge Milne called for the lunch break, but Nina didn't need to hear more to know what she thought.

Managing to avoid the reporters, the three of them—Nina, Genevieve, and Winston—walked outside to an area between the two long, low stone buildings where pale sunlight and a breeze awaited. Lindy had walked out to her car. "We're missing spring again," said Nina. "Here comes and goes another season while we rot inside."

"Think of the money we're saving on sunscreen," Genevieve said. "You're quiet today, Winston."

"Quiet doesn't mean asleep."

"How do you like Mr. Wright?"

"I'm still thinking," Winston said. He wore Vuarnet sunglasses, reminding Nina of another case that had come and gone quickly and dramatically in her life a few months before. Each case seemed to last an eternity, but once it ended, she blinked once and moved on.

"He's perfect," said Genevieve, not able to wait any longer to let them know her opinion.

"Too perfect," said Nina.

"No, really," said Genevieve.

"He played us like a harp. I felt managed," said Nina.

"The perfect juror comes our way, and you suspect him because he looks too good?" Genevieve persisted.

"He's slick."

"Are you nuts? He comes off great. He comes off honest. And he comes off fair."

"I don't care how he comes off. I want him gone," Nina said, raising her voice slightly, not looking at Genevieve.

"Need I remind you we only have one peremptory left? What

about Ignacio Ybarra? He's a Catholic, very conservative. A disaster. Or Sonny Ball? Paul thinks he's a dope dealer. He's totally unpredictable. Because we knew we needed to save as many peremptories as we could for the disaster waiting in the wings, they've both made the cut. Surely you wouldn't keep them and waste a peremptory on Wright." When she saw her logic did not seem potent enough to budge Nina, Genevieve turned for support to Winston, who had wandered off onto the grass. "What did you think of him?"

"I'm inclined to agree with Nina that he's not showing all his true colors," Winston said. "But then again, who does? That doesn't mean he's not on our side. What does matter is, he seems sincere."

"You call that sincere? What about when I asked about his wife and his eyes got misty?"

"He's sensitive," said Genevieve.

"He's full of it."

"Where do you get this, Nina?" Genevieve asked. "Not from his questionnaire. Not from his answers up there. This is your own prejudice talking. I warned you, you're goin' to project stuff. Maybe you're a little attracted to him, and you're reacting against that."

"He doesn't like me," said Nina, stymied by the vigor with which Genevieve and Winston defended Wright. It seemed obvious to her that he was a bad fit with their case. She felt him trying to charm her. She didn't like the feeling that he wanted to be on the jury. He should be dragged, like everyone else, into doing his duty. He should take no pleasure in it, but should be willing. A juror should never be eager, and she felt he had somehow betrayed his eagerness, adopting an unreal, evenhanded style that somehow didn't suit the personality on the paper, the go-getter with a new job and better ways to spend his time.

"You don't think he likes you," Genevieve said. "That's irrational, and Nina, what we are about is logic. Trust me, Nina. Let me do the job you hired me to do. I won't let you down."

Nina turned to Winston. "Well, Winston?"

He took his time. "Let's say you're right and he's a problem," he said. They had come to the parking area and stood beside the blue

Oldsmobile Winston had rented for the duration. "I'm handling a lot of the trial work. Maybe I can counterbalance that initial prejudice. I think we can work with him. You can win him over. As far as him being such an eager beaver, I don't have a problem with that. I think he expects to learn something about the very rich. I think he's interested in the money angle. That's not bad in itself."

"I told you in the beginning," Genevieve said. "I can only give you my advice and you're free not to take it, but we need to save that challenge. Don't throw it away on Wright. This is what you need me for," she argued, "to help you with those distinctions that don't come natural. He's gonna come around. I'm telling you."

They were right about needing that last challenge in case of an emergency. Nina went over in her mind where in the process she could have saved another peremptory, so that she could spend one on Wright. She came up empty-handed.

"Okay. If Riesner doesn't challenge, he's in." When they returned to the courtroom, Nina sat back in her chair, closing her eyes, hoping for help from her enemy when her friends deserted. Maybe Riesner would hate Wright.

No such luck. Riesner didn't challenge.

Rather than brave the lightning storm of photographers in the public hallway, Nina slipped through the door by the jury box and into the private hall that led to the judge's chambers, past a number of clerks offices. She intended to hang there for a couple of minutes until the group dispersed, then head out the locked door to the main hall a few feet away from the regular courtroom exits. She didn't want her picture taken today.

She waited in the short part of the L-shaped area for a few minutes, until she judged the coast to be mostly clear, then headed down the longer stretch toward the door to the exit. Almost instantly, she spotted Winston, who had apparently had the same idea.

She could only see him from the back. He had stepped inside one of the clerk's offices and was leaning over the desk, talking cheerfully with a frizzy-haired, vivacious redhead Paul always seemed to notice, too.

"He's after her body," a voice drawled. Genevieve had come up behind her. "Spends all his spare time down here lately. Guess it's time to collect him. C'mon." In spite of her cool manner, jealousy glittered in the corner of her eye.

Nina went along to help drag him away.

"This is it," Nina said, watching wearily late Thursday afternoon as another pack of people were herded into the crowded courtroom and the clerk began to speak. "The home stretch."

"Do you, and each of you, understand and agree that you will accurately and truthfully answer, under penalty of perjury, all questions propounded to you concerning your qualifications and competency to serve as a trial juror in the matter pending before this court; and that failure to do so may subject you to criminal prosecution?" droned the clerk for the sixth time.

"I do," answered the new pack, while the insecure faces in the jury box looked on.

"We're going to finish today," Winston whispered as the people took their seats and some more paper-shuffling started the last round. "I feel it."

"Alan Reed," called out the clerk. Genevieve didn't have to show her the report on him; they had been talking about him the day before and praying he wouldn't be called to the box.

An openly conservative man of fifty-seven, he was divorced and still harboring grudges about it, according to Paul. He spent his weekends hunting and fishing with his buddies. At the top of his report, Genevieve had drawn a skull and crossbones.

After a few questions it was obvious to Nina that Reed was precisely the kind of juror they couldn't have. Genevieve gave a thumbs-down signal under the table and Winston couldn't help shaking his head at one or two of the answers.

"Ms. Reilly. I believe this is the last peremptory challenge," Milne said, waiting.

Nina asked for a moment, then went over the jury chart of their selections so far and Genevieve's thumbnail summaries one more time. Mrs. Lim, they all agreed on. The five other women: a divorcée in her fifties who was the caretaker for her disabled adult child, a student, a mountain climber, a clerk and a housewife—they would stay. The two men, a biologist and a history teacher, did not excite her, but might be open to their arguments. Clifford Wright, they disputed, but Genevieve and Winston had won the day on him. He was definitely in. She zeroed in on the candidates who troubled her most.

"Ignacio Ybarra, age twenty-three, telephone lineman, very quiet, has a little girl but is having trouble keeping contact with her because of some bad feelings between him and her grandmother. Close to his parents and a large extended family. Likes hiking, college degree. Very religious, goes to church twice a week." Not great.

"Kevin Dowd. Retired, early sixties, plays golf, made a fortune in investments, drinks too much, likes women too much, looking for a party." Yuck.

"Sonny Ball, late twenties, tattoos, earrings, mostly inaudible responses, looking for work for the past three years, a couple of brushes with the law. His parents live in Oregon. They're estranged. Paul suspects he was a dope dealer." Horrible, but others who had taken the stand had been even worse for different reasons, and they only had six peremptories in all.

Altogether, thirteen people. One had to go. But who?

She studied the four faces, searching for clues, feeling nervous. The men looked back, offering nothing definitive. Ignacio Ybarra looked resigned. Kevin Dowd smiled, sure he was in. Sonny Ball wet his lips with his tongue and gave her a slit-eyed look that hovered somewhere between a wink and a leer.

Reed stared at her, chin tipped up, arrogant. He expected to be cut, and so disguised none of the disdain he felt for her and her client.

Let him have his wish.

"The cross-complainants will thank and excuse Mr. Reed," Nina said. Genevieve fidgeted unhappily. She had pushed to use the last peremptory on Sonny Ball. Winston bowed his head. A sigh stretched across the courtroom. Several jurors sat back in their chairs, finally relaxing.

It took only another two hours to select two alternate jurors who would listen to the testimony but deliberate and vote only if another juror became incapacitated. Patti Zobel would be fine. She was another divorcée. Couldn't anybody stay married up here? Was it the air or something? And Damian Peck, the other alternate, a pit boss at Harvey's whose dentist wife made more than he did, also seemed a decent bet.

"Swear the jury," Milne said finally, and the fourteen people in whose hands Lindy would find triumph or misfortune stood up and held up their right hands.

16

On a sun-bleached Monday in May, seven months after Mike Markov's fateful birthday party, the time for opening statements arrived.

Hoping to avoid the media, Nina had left home early but found herself pulling into a courthouse lot already jammed with television news trucks and people swinging video cameras. Up above, in the pine trees ringing the lot, a flock of small brown birds kept up a chorus of cheeping to rival the noisy excess of the mob below. In all the cacophony and confusion, she forgot her briefcase and had to return to her car to retrieve it.

Feeling oddly flimsy in a white blouse under a muted peach suit, she spotted Lindy and Alice across the parking lot just pulling up in Alice's old Taurus. She walked over quickly and joined them. Together they headed across the lot, storming firmly through the throng that massed around the entrance to the courthouse. Right before she reached the door, Nina had to shove a particularly long, nasty-looking microphone out of her face to avoid swallowing it.

Inside the building, Deputy Kimura had just opened the courtroom doors. A long line of people who'd been waiting dashed inside, jostling for seats. Before closing the doors for good, he allowed in a few stragglers. These lucky late-birds squeezed into the back and stood leaning against the drab paneling.

Nina saw that Rachel, surrounded by a phalanx of Markov Enterprises employees, had taken a place directly behind Mike. Harry

Anderssen, her ex-boyfriend, had taken the seat directly behind her. He glared at her back as she leaned forward and squeezed Mike's hand. She had her long hair tied back and looked modest in a dark dress topped by a dark yellow jacket. Mike was the quintessential businessman in a granite-colored suit and a green tie so dark it was almost black. When Riesner dropped an arm lightly over his shoulder and began talking with him in a low voice, Rachel moved demurely back.

Riesner wore his usual blue suit and smirk.

Looking uncharacteristically indifferent to fashion, Lindy was wearing a long skirt below a matching dove-colored sweater set, her only concession to vanity a pair of pearl earrings. As they took their places, she pointed out to Nina some people she knew. Meanwhile, Alice, sitting right behind them, talked nonstop, jiggling the high-heeled mule on her crossed leg in a silent, frenzied rhythm.

A few seats away from Alice, Nina saw the disturbing dark-haired man who'd threatened her when she'd been in the Solo Spa. He stood up to wave at Lindy as she turned to say something to Alice.

"Oh, look," Alice said. "There's George, Lindy's puppy dog. She just gives a tug on the leash and he comes."

"Alice," said Lindy, with a nervous look around the overstuffed courtroom. "Leave George alone."

"No, really. I think every woman needs a guy like George in the background to do her dirty work."

"Dirty work?" Nina started, but was interrupted by the clerk.

"Superior Court for the State of California is now in session, the Honorable Curtis E. Milne presiding."

They all rose as the judge entered the room. One feminist publication had brought out a noisy contingent of rabble-rousers who sat near Riesner, trying to engage him in dialog, but Judge Milne imposed silence in his court with a slight raising of the eyebrow. How he managed it, Nina did not know, but all the power of the institution of justice came to life in those sparse hairs.

Once he was satisfied his courtroom had come to order, the

judge rustled in his chair, studying the documents before him, adjusting his glasses and running a hand over his bald pate. He directed himself to the jury.

"The moment is at hand, ladies and gentlemen. We will begin by hearing opening statements of the attorneys. That is all we will be able to get through by noon, which is the time the court has allotted for this matter today. We'll reconvene again tomorrow at nine o'clock sharp.

"The attorneys tell me that they expect to take no more than six court days to present their evidence. They have agreed that I may read you this very brief introduction to the matter you will be deciding.

"The primary question in this case is whether or not these two people, Mikhail and Lindy Markov, had a written, oral, or implied agreement to share ownership in a business known as Markov Enterprises. If you decide that there was such an agreement, you will be asked to determine exactly what form any such agreement took. If you decide that the agreement provided that Lindy Markov was a part owner of the business, you will need to decide the worth of that business, and how to divide any assets and debts that came from the business, including several residences used by both parties. You will also be asked to determine some facts in dispute regarding a certain piece of paper which will be presented to you as Exhibit One."

He moved into a general discussion of juror protocol: no discussion of the evidence until they retired to decide the case, no reading about the case or watching TV news for the duration, no independent research, keep an open mind until the time came to decide, don't be prejudiced against the party because you don't like anything about his or her attorney.

The jurors, in the box to the left of Nina, looked suitably impressed with the gravity of their responsibility, except for Sonny Ball, the tattooed warm body in the back row.

"Ms. Reilly, are you ready to proceed?"

"We are, Your Honor."

"Do you wish to make an opening statement?"

"We do." Nina rose, leaving her notes on the table. Her pastel suit glowed warmly under the lights. Her heels were a compromise between comfort and height, and her usually unconquerable long brown hair had surrendered to the ministrations of a local hairdresser who had smoothed and sprayed until it lay down and played dead.

But on her way up toward the podium from which she would speak to the jury, she put these and other such trivial concerns aside.

Standing the three feet from the jury box Genevieve insisted upon, Nina let her gaze sweep over each of the jurors in turn.

"The story you are about to hear is an old one. You've heard this before. We all have. A man and a woman meet, fall in love, and build a life. They share a warm and loving home. They create a business together. For twenty years, twenty satisfying years, they live together. Then, a sad thing happens. One of them falls out of love."

Nina paused for emphasis, breaking her concentration long enough to see that the jurors were responding to her with the desired level of engrossed attention.

"It's devastating to the one left behind. We can all imagine it, can't we? All those years, those habits of a lifetime, the morning coffee together, the shared double bed, the welcoming hugs, the kisses good-bye . . . suddenly there are great big gaping holes. But these things happen. Good people get hurt. Nobody is to blame when love dies. Nobody is responsible for the terrible emptiness of that double bed."

She lowered her head and put her hands behind her back Perry Mason–style, pacing a few steps before raising her eyes back to the jury box.

"No, no one is responsible for the loss of that loving relationship. Lindy Markov has suffered that loss, true. It is true that Mike Markov is engaged to a young woman who once worked for Lindy. But that is *not* why we are here in court today. Let's be clear on that point. We aren't here to talk about love. We're here to talk about business. Business between lovers, maybe. A business both of them nurtured as another couple might nurture their child. But we're talking about business, the kind of business that is based on a *legally enforceable partnership agreement.*

"In the testimony you will hear, you will learn that again and again, over twenty years, Lindy and Mike Markov said to each other, we're in this business together. We're in this for life. We share the good times and bad times. Whatever we have, we *share.* Whatever we owe, we share in that, too."

"They made mutual promises, ladies and gentlemen. Promises made, but not kept by one of them. The promises relating to their love—those can be broken, and never come before a jury. The law doesn't protect that kind of promise.

"But, as you will hear, the law does protect a partner in a business enterprise when the other partner breaks his promise. Two people build a business with their sweat and their talent. They both put everything they have into it. They run it together for many years, with increasing success. And when the partnership ends, *they each take their share.* That's what they do. It's the only fair thing to do. Right? They each take their share.

"That's how it's supposed to be. That's how it is under the law of the State of California.

"Yet in the case you're about to hear, that's not how it happened.

"What you'll hear from several witnesses, including both Lindy and Mike Markov, is that one of the partners *took it all.* Every square foot, every dime, every stick of furniture, all of it.

"Mike Markov did that. He took it all, the whole shebang, and he left Lindy with nothing. He even threw her out of the home she had lived in for years, leaving her with a horse and an old trailer out in the mountains.

"He kept—well, he kept quite a bit. Quite a bit. There will be several estimates of how much Mike and Lindy's company, Markov Enterprises, was worth at the time they separated. Let me tell you a conservative figure as to what the business was worth.

"He kept around two hundred million dollars."

She had built up to it well. Even the audience, to whom this was old news, heaved a collective gasp. Most of the jurors must have told the truth about not reading about the case in the papers because their mouths hung open. Juror Bob Binkley, the whipped-looking history teacher, straightened up from his slump and gripped the front rail. Nina looked straight at him and nodded. That's right, Mr. Binkley, she tried to tell him with her eyes. This is big, this is huge. You're doing something important here.

On the other hand, early on, Sonny Ball's eyes had fixed on a spot somewhere between Nina and the jury box, and there his focus remained. Either he was mighty dense, didn't care, or already knew about it.

"I know all of us—the lawyers, the clients, the courtroom personnel—appreciate your willingness to take time from your busy lives to render judgment in this case. It will be up to you to decide the ultimate facts. We'll be asking you to decide, does Mike Markov take everything, the house on the lake, the business, the cars, the boat, the entire fruit of their very productive years together, while Lindy Markov doesn't get brush, comb, toothpaste, or bobby pin?

"You'll hear from the witnesses the whole story of the business, how Mike and Lindy started from nothing and how Markov Enterprises became a great success. You'll hear that Lindy, while not formally married to Mike—"

Another look of astonishment from the jurors. Nina moved on, having broken that bad news as casually as she could.

"—was in every respect Mike's equal partner in terms of responsibility and workload in the business for twenty years. This isn't a story about a woman who supports a man from the home. This woman was at the office, at the plant, out there finding clients. We'll show you that Lindy had as many ideas for new products as he did, and that she was as important to the company's success as he was. She didn't stay home and raise the children and give dinner parties. *The business was their child.*"

Nina paused so that the words would reverberate through the jurors' minds.

"So what's the problem? What issues make it necessary to bring this case to you? Well, there are two of them. First of all, Mr. Markov says that it all should belong to him now, because he put his name on everything. That's what the testimony will show. He put his name on the company stock, on the home they lived in, on every major asset. *Her name got left off.* How did Mr. Markov explain that to Lindy?" Nina raised her eyebrows, looked expectantly at the jury. They didn't seem to have a clue.

"He told her he wanted to avoid the red tape. He told her it didn't matter whose name was on the certificates and the titles, because it was all half hers. He held title for both of them.

"Watch Mr. Markov when he testifies. You'll see he's a proud, old-fashioned man. He wanted to be the president, so that left her with the executive vice presidency. She wanted what he wanted. Nothing new there." Nina gave juror Mrs. Grzegorek, the attractive older woman who worked at Mikasa, a tiny smile. Mrs. Grzegorek didn't smile back.

"He wanted his name on the stock, and she went along with that, too. As she'll testify, she never dreamed this would be used to try to take her share of the company.

"And there's one other event in their long history together that you will hear about. You'll learn that thirteen years ago Lindy signed a piece of paper that Mike asked her to sign. He had her label it: Separate Property Agreement."

The expression on Cliff Wright's face never changed, but his hands shifted in his lap. He knew exactly what that meant.

"Lindy signed it. She'll tell you why. And I have to tell you, this is the one place in this case where love does enter in. She signed it because Mike said that if she signed it he'd marry her. The business was going down at that time and they were going through a difficult period in their personal lives.

"Lindy agreed. She signed the paper, carrying out her side of the deal. And Mike—well, you'll hear that Mike went on a business trip. He didn't marry her, didn't carry out his side of the deal. And that piece of paper disappeared for thirteen years, until now. Lindy never got a copy. She assumed it had long since been discarded or destroyed.

"The judge will instruct you on the law regarding this type of agreement. You will be instructed that a gift or property given on the assumption that marriage will take place can be recovered by the giver if there is no marriage. That may not make much sense now, but it will. The testimony will make it clear that Mike didn't marry Lindy. So when that piece of paper is discussed, I hope you'll ask yourselves these questions: Did she promise to give Mike everything in consideration for his promise to marry her? Did he keep his promise? If not, then *what did she get in return?*"

"Objection!"

She went to the bench with Riesner and accepted a scolding from Milne for arguing the law in her opening statement.

Then, calm within herself and trying to inject the same calm certainty into her words, Nina added a few more important points and brought her opening statement to a close. "And now, ladies and gentlemen, it's up to you. I have talked with you, listened to you, and I believe you will be fair. Thank you."

She could swear that, as she walked back toward her table, she caught the ever-so-slightest nod of approval from Milne. She decided she must have imagined it. She tried and failed to feel the jury's vibes behind her.

Back at the table, Genevieve squeezed her arm, murmuring, "Excellent," and Winston gave her an under-the-table, double thumbs-up.

Lindy looked at Mike, who looked pointedly away from her.

Looking debonair and confident, without a hair out of place, wearing his trademark half-grin, Jeff Riesner took the podium. With all the heavy baggage removed from his character, Nina realized a stranger might actually consider him attractive. He looked innocuous and cool up there, like a man without a bone to pick. That shiny polish on the surface was exactly what made him so successful in his profession. More than in almost any other profession, success in law depended on the right look, and Jeffrey Riesner had spent years cultivating it. The jurors waited to hear an opposite take on the same situation, and he basked in their attention.

"Let's talk about the evidence," he said. "In this case, we will have testimony from people, each with a point of view, each with a stake. Your job is to judge their credibility and weigh the value of what they say. You might feel from listening to all the witnesses that this is a complicated or confusing case. There is a lot of money involved, and this may make the case seem more complicated.

"But it's not complicated. This case is simple, and comes simply down to black and white.

"Because there is also another kind of evidence. With this kind of evidence, there's no point of view, there's no stake, there's no credibility problem. That evidence, ladies and gentlemen, consists of writings. We ask you to pay close attention to the written exhibits in this case, because they were prepared before there was any stake, any point of view. The writings we will introduce will tell you a very clear and straightforward story.

"First, you will learn that there is one written document that does not exist. That written document is a marriage certificate between Mike Markov and Lindy Markov. The two parties in this litigation never married. There is no community property, no automatic share because of the relationship. No alimony. No sympathy money. There's no marriage here. No one will show you a marriage certificate. Lindy Markov was Mike Markov's girlfriend. They broke up. That's what happened in their personal life.

"Second, we will show you a set of writings that prove that Lindy Markov was an employee of Markov Enterprises. You won't just hear people talk about it. It's simpler than that. You're going to see her personnel file, the salary record, her job description. You'll see she was paid fairly, she was given regular raises, she had an expense account. She was an executive with the company, and she had an agreement with the company that she would do certain work and in return she would be compensated. You'll see it in writing, ladies and gentlemen, plain and clear.

"Third, you will see, in writing, who owns Markov Enterprises and a home here in Tahoe that is in issue in this case. It's just as plain and just as clear. You'll see the deed to the house, and you'll see the owner's name, Mike Markov. You'll see the stock certificates that are accepted the world over as evidence of ownership. The name on the certificates is Mike Markov. No mystery, no complication.

"And fourth, last and most important of all, you will see another written document that reinforces and confirms the other written documents. That document is called a separate property agreement. You will be able to read it for yourselves and see the plain language of this agreement. You will see that the agreement states that Lindy Markov has no claim to Mike Markov's property, and he has no claim to hers. It's right there. In writing, as simple as can be. What it does not state"—he paused for emphasis, chopping the air with his hand—"is that Mike agreed to marry Lindy. That's just not there.

"So why are you here in court today, taking precious time from your lives to act as a jury? Let me try to frame what Lindy Markov is claiming she will show. Besides the hugs and the kisses and the obfusc—"

"Your Honor," Nina said, jumping up.

"Approach." They went up to the bench, leaned their heads in close. "Save the argument, Counsel," Milne said in a low voice.

"Sorry, I got carried away."

"Carried away? He was reading from his notes," Nina said.

"Counsel?" Milne said. "No argument in the opening statement or I'll cut you off at the knees. Tell 'em what you intend to prove and sit back down."

"I understand. Won't happen again." As they walked back, Nina caught a glimpse of juror Bob Binkley's notepad. Mixed in with what looked like scientific notation, he had carefully listed Riesner's points. Nina groaned inwardly.

"Four simple points," Riesner continued, "in writing."

In writing. Riesner had hacked his trial mantra down to two words.

"What else will you hear? You may hear that Lindy Markov was with the company for a long time, and was a valuable employee. You may hear that Lindy always wanted to get married. You will certainly hear that Lindy wants half the company, now that Mike has left her." Riesner raised his eyebrows.

"Mike's been very successful, ladies and gentlemen. You will definitely hear that. He has done so well that you may feel you want to take this chance to spread some of his money around. But you can't do that. There are contract laws, marriage laws in this state, and the judge will tell you what those laws are, and that you have to follow them. I know you will follow the judge's instructions.

"And I know that during this trial you will keep in mind these four simple facts that we will ensure are brought to you as evidence: that the parties never married; that Lindy Markov was an employee of Markov Enterprises; that Mike Markov's name is on all the written evidences of ownership; and that the parties expressly agreed that Mr. Markov's property was not subject to a claim by Lindy Markov.

"Plain and simple. Black and white. In writing. Ladies and gentlemen, follow the law. I know you will do that. Mr. Markov trusts you to do that.

"Thank you." He smiled and nodded.

Wow, Genevieve scribbled on her pad, passing it to Nina and Winston as Riesner sat down. *He's no schmuck.*

Nina had taken notes. In writing.

Mike's defense would be very strong.

Damn.

Winston, Genevieve, Nina, and Paul met for lunch in the cafeteria while Lindy left for a better lunch with Alice. Winston and Genevieve sped through the line and took seats at a table. Nina, a few people in front of Paul in line, loaded her plate, and still a little shaky as she came down from her tightly orchestrated performance of the morning, knocked heavily into the man ahead of her, spilling some lettuce on the floor.

"Oh, I'm so sorry," said Nina.

"Well, if it isn't Miz Reilly, coming after me," said Jeffrey Ries-

ner, jumping back, scrutinizing her as if seeking something in particular; an insight, cooties, a pearl-handed pistol? Nina didn't know
what. He set his tray down with a bang, smoothing his clothes,
twisting around to make sure no salad dressing marred his suit. Unfortunately, there were two distinct oily spots at the back of the left
leg of his trousers. "Look what you've done," he said, pointing.
"You did it on purpose, didn't you?"

"Sorry," she mumbled again.

"You're as clumsy at getting your food as you are in court."

Suddenly, she had no more apologies left. "Can we move on,
here? There are people behind us."

"Do you have any idea what this suit cost?"

"Send me the dry-cleaning bill. Now, please step aside and let
me pass."

"You'd like that, wouldn't you?" And he smiled what Paul
called his death's-head grin, as cold as a face without skin. "But I
don't think I will. I like it right here. You're the one who ought to
be slinking out of this town, and it shouldn't be long now before you
do just that."

Not wanting to engage in a free-for-all with him in the cafeteria
out from under Milne's steady eye, Nina waited silently, feeling her
neck redden, while he painstakingly reassembled his tray, taking his
time to align crooked utensils precisely beside his plate, deliberately
drawing out the task. He finally finished and set the tray down at a
table near the window at a decent distance from Nina's crew, then
headed for the men's room out in the hall, brushing at his trousers
and casting her one more black look.

"Whoops," said Genevieve, smiling sympathetically as Nina sat
down. "Next time, consider skipping the salad. He's obviously a
steak and potatoes man."

"Just my luck," said Nina, pulling out a large dinner napkin and
tucking it into the front collar of her new blouse. She wasn't about to
mess up her clothes or lose her temper. She looked around but didn't
see Paul.

"Save your response for the courtroom," advised Winston,

spooning tomato soup. "He acted the same way with the male lawyer opposite him in the case we did together. It's just posturing. Anything to knock you off balance."

"He can't really believe I did that on purpose. It just happened. The personal stuff—it's all on his side," Nina said, disingenuously. She dribbled warm Italian dressing over the white iceberg lettuce and began to eat.

Genevieve started telling Nina what she had done well and what she might work on "just a little." Nina listened without comment, experiencing a rerun of her resistance to Genevieve's stage-managing. She had to watch herself. Sometimes she felt ornery enough to do the exact opposite of what Genevieve advised just because Genevieve advised it, even if Genevieve was right.

"You know, there's research showing that some jurors actually make their final decision based on the opening statements. How did you think they took yours?" Genevieve said. Apparently sticking close to her in-trial, comfort-food diet, having finished her sandwich and Winston's leftovers, she bit into a chocolate chip cookie, putting her plate on a nearby table and pulling out her notebook.

Nina tried to give her impressions. Clifford Wright had appeared to listen to every word of her opening. Such conscientious observation made her uneasy. Having no rational basis for her feelings didn't stop her from distrusting him. All of his responses in the *voir dire* held him up as the ideal juror.

Still she couldn't help thinking how much he reminded her of a boy she'd known in high school who slicked his hair back and became president of the student council by talking up the virtues of honesty and a drug-free life. Only on Saturday nights did he revert to what he remained at core, a lying pothead. She could only hope any such reversions by Clifford Wright would happen outside of the jury room.

Nina had almost finished her salad when Paul appeared at the head of the table, a steaming cup of coffee in hand.

"Is there room for one more?" he asked.

"Coming right up," said Genevieve, scooting over to make room for him.

He sat down beside her, across from Nina. "I caught some of the show this morning. Some nice touches."

"Thanks," Nina said, happy to see that he really did look pleased.

"I didn't get a chance to thank you for your contribution to our jury selection, Paul. I think you saved us from making at least two fatal mistakes," said Genevieve.

"You got the jury you wanted?" asked Paul.

"You never get everybody you want. But we got a lot," said Genevieve.

"We slugged our way there," the incorrigible Winston said.

"Glad to hear it," said Paul, sipping his coffee.

"The climber, Diane Miklos, sure acted receptive," Winston said. "I like that lady."

"She's probably got tattoos bigger than Sonny Ball's hidden under those army surplus clothes of hers," Genevieve teased. "She's exactly your—" she began. She looked toward the door. Her eyes widened.

Jeffrey Riesner shot back into the lunchroom from the hall a changed man, coatless, his fly undone, a terrific bruise starting to purple on his cheek, his hair sopping wet. "Call the police!" he roared at the astonished elderly man at the cash register. "Someone attacked me!"

"You need help, sir?" asked the cashier.

"Look at me! Look at me! Call the police!" He went over to the corner and sat down, pulling out a handkerchief and drying his face.

The cashier spoke rapidly into the phone.

"Have you called yet?" Riesner asked. "What did they say?"

"Yes, sir," said the cashier. "The bailiff will be right down."

"Forget the bailiff. Get the police over here. Now!"

Deputy Kimura came running in, hand ready at his holster. "What happened?"

"Someone came after me. . . ."

"What did he do?"

"What does it look like? I was attacked! He assaulted me. Isn't that obvious?" Riesner rubbed his face.

"How'd you get all wet like that?"

"Washing the blood off! How do you think?"

"What did he look like?"

"Big guy, very strong."

"Where did this happen?"

Riesner cast a furious look at Nina's group, then pointed at Nina with a shaking finger. "You!" he said. "You're behind this."

"Where did it happen, Mr. Riesner?"

"He's not there anymore. And if you stand here gibbering for one more second he'll get away!" Riesner shrilled. "Why don't you go after him?"

"Where did the confrontation take place?" Kimura asked stubbornly. "I don't even know where to start."

"In the goddamned toilet downstairs by the Muni Court office!" Riesner said. "And no, I didn't see his face. Just look for a big . . . I don't know. Now, why don't you just do your job and go get that bastard!"

Kimura ran from the room.

Nina looked at Paul. He, like the rest of them, stared at the dripping, gesticulating lawyer in complete amazement.

Or did he?

What was that in his face, rollicking around the corners of his eyes? Could it be . . .

Amusement?

17

THE NEXT MORNING BEFORE COURT, Nina met Paul at Heidi's for breakfast.

"I'm just having juice," said Paul. "Gotta keep that Malibu look."

"Coffee, poached egg, wheat toast," said Nina to the waitress, who at six-thirty in the morning looked like she'd been up all night.

"Changed my mind," added Paul. "Two sides of sausage." The waitress scurried away on her two-inch-thick-soled white foam shoes. "You talked me into it," he said with a smile to Nina. "By the way, where were you last night? You got away before I could make a plan to ravish you. And then later, nobody was home, not even Bob."

"I turned the phone off."

"Did you now?" he said. "You going to tell me what's so urgent we have to talk while I'm still half asleep?"

"You know very well. You did something to Jeff Riesner in that bathroom yesterday."

"I never," said Paul. "Nobody can prove a thing. How's he doing?"

"He's on the rampage. He's been humiliated in front of me. He'll never forget that everyone saw him like that. He asked the judge for a one-day continuance, but all he got was a bruise and some shaking up, so Milne said no."

The waitress brought their food, and sighing deeply, as though it was all too much for her, poured more coffee. "Anything else?" she asked.

"We're fine," said Nina.

After she left, Paul said, "Don't you just hate it when the waitress looks so pooped you want to bundle her off and send her home to bed? I feel like I should jump up to help her."

"Paul, you'd better tell me what you did."

He took another bite of sausage. "Mmm. This is what I call sausage. I might just have to have a teeny bit more."

"You attacked him in the washroom, didn't you?"

Paul continued eating until every bite was gone.

Nina knew him well enough to know he was deciding what to tell her. She tried to choke down some egg but put her fork down when she realized her seething stomach couldn't take it. "Jesus, Paul. This is serious."

Paul drank his coffee. "All right. I was behind the two of you in the cafeteria line. I saw the whole thing. You know, he positioned himself so that you pretty much had to run into him. Why do you let him treat you like that?"

"Believe me, he does it without any encouragement from me," said Nina. "But Paul, you can't sink to his level."

"Oh, but I can. He made my blood boil. I set my tray down. The food didn't look too good right then, so I took a little walk down the hall to the washroom to take a couple of deep breaths and calm down."

"Oh, no."

"It was foreordained. I walked in, and the bastard happened to be standing in one of the stalls, door wide open, back to me, taking a whiz, whistling to himself. Off-key. Just smug as hell, hitting low notes where there should be high ones. The kind of spineless whistling that really grates on me."

"No."

"Yes. The hair on the back of his head grated on me. His expensive shoes grated on me. I found myself perturbed. There's no other word for it."

Nina lowered her head and put her hand over her eyes.

"I wanted to turn him around and coldcock him. But for your sake, I didn't want him to know who did it to him." He waited for a reply, and, not getting one, went on, "So I pulled a little trick I learned from an old con named Dickie Mars, a guy I busted when I was still on the Force. Dickie learned it at San Quentin. You rush the guy, push hard at the shoulder so he loses his balance, and trip him at the same time. You guide him as he's falling so his head's above the toilet, and you—you wash his hair for him. That's what Dickie called it. The Shampoo. When you let go, all the guy cares about is sucking in some air and wiping his eyes. You're long gone."

"You're getting a kick out of telling me this, aren't you?" Nina asked.

"You don't have to be Irish to appreciate a good story," said Paul.

A long silence ensued. The waitress appeared. "More coffee?" Neither of them answered, and she went away.

"I'm sorry. I am. I lost my temper," Paul said. "He had it coming, but I shouldn't have done it. It's this damn case. It's the money, money, money. It's making everyone nuts, all that money floating out there, up for grabs. Haven't you noticed? The lawyers, the reporters, the crowds of people following this case, eating it up. It's mass hysteria. It's greed so gargantuan, it should make any sensible person flinch at the sight of it. I'm afraid it's going to ruin us, and I let the pressure get to me."

Nina was shaking her head.

"Look, let's forget about it. He's all right. I'll watch myself."

Nina said slowly, "Paul, you're fired. You're off the Markov case."

"What? It was just a prank."

"I—I—you're fired, Paul. Send me a bill. We'll have to get along without you. I have to do it, as Lindy's attorney. You assaulted the attorney I'm arguing a case against. You jeopardized my whole case!"

"You're firing me?"

"That's right."

"For protecting you."

"For losing your temper and doing crazy things."

"By now you should expect the unexpected. That's who I am."

She searched her bag and threw a five-dollar bill on the table.

"Nina, friends forgive friends," Paul said.

"You don't even understand why I'm so upset, do you? You never liked this case or this cause, and now you're trying to sabotage me. You didn't dunk Riesner to protect me. You indulged yourself in a little tribal dancing, a minor war over territory. It had everything to do with you, and nothing to do with me. But Paul, if I lose this case . . ." She stopped and stood up.

"The world comes to an end?" Paul asked. "Look, Nina. Aren't you forgetting what's really important?"

"And that would be you?"

"Us, Nina."

But she barely heard him. She was already out the door.

"Call Lindy Markov to the stand," Nina said.

With a glance toward Mike, who did not return her look, Lindy stepped forward. Dressed in a subdued blue skirt and jacket, Lindy showed her real age to be somewhere in her midforties. Under the direction of Genevieve she had quit coloring her hair, and beneath new gray strands her healthy face looked wan.

The clerk swore her in. She took her seat.

"Hello, Mrs. Markov," said Nina.

"Objection. Lindy Markov is not a married woman," said Jeffrey Riesner, getting an early start.

"She's been called Mrs. Markov for many years. It's the name she uses."

"Overruled. The jury is instructed that the use of a title like Mrs. doesn't constitute evidence of marriage in this case," Milne said curtly, as if he had already thought the matter through.

"You call yourself Lindy Markov and have for many years, yet you are not married to Mike Markov, is that right?"

"That's right," said Lindy.

"When did you meet?"

"In 1976." Nina took Lindy though the circumstances of that meeting in Ely and the first months of their relationship.

"When did you begin using the name Markov?"

"On April 22, 1977."

"And has that been an important date in your twenty-year relationship?"

"Yes."

"You celebrated it?"

"Every year for twenty years. That was the anniversary of our permanent commitment to each other. That night we vowed to love each other and honor each other for the rest of our lives."

"Was there a formal occasion?"

"Mike and I went to the Catholic Church in Lubbock. We walked in, and nobody else was there. Mike took me up to the altar. He got down on one knee and promised before God to love me and do everything in his power to make me happy for the rest of my life." At these words, Lindy closed her eyes, as if temporarily incapacitated by emotion. She had been saving up emotionally for this moment for so long, Nina was concerned that she would break down.

Slumped between Jeffrey Riesner and his female associate Rebecca Casey, Mike Markov studied the table in front of him.

Nina gave Lindy a moment to compose herself.

"You considered this your wedding," Nina said.

"Yes," said Lindy.

"You knew this was not a legal marriage in the State of Nevada, in that you had not taken out a marriage license and in that the wedding was not officiated over by a priest or other designated official."

"Yes."

"Once you divorced your first husband, why didn't you just run down to city hall and get a license?"

"By then, we were settled together," she said slowly. She paused, looking around the courtroom. "We had moved in together, found a house, and gotten the business going. Mike always said we didn't need a piece of paper to prove our love. He said, 'Lindy, we are man and wife.' Our lives were living proof we belonged together. He told me he was with me because we loved each other, not because the state decreed it. We had both been married briefly before. His breakup had been bitter."

"Did you want to get married legally?"

"It came up several times during our relationship. I'd start thinking about it. But I never doubted him when he assured me we were together for life, in it for good and bad, forever." She looked weepy again. "He thought formal marriage was for people who didn't know what a real marriage was. I think it might have been more decent to be married. I felt ashamed that we weren't officially married, but I wanted to believe him when he promised it would never make a difference. I loved him. I trusted him."

Now Nina, using simple questions, took Lindy through the beginnings of Markov Enterprises, the early years when the Markovs had lived on a financial edge and moved to Texas, where the business had failed.

"You continued to use the name Markov in all business and personal dealings?"

"Yes."

"Your clients assumed you were married?"

"Yes."

"Did Mike introduce you as his wife on social occasions?"

"Yes."

"Were you introduced as his wife at business functions?"

"Yes."

"Over the years, have many acquaintances, both personal and business, assumed you and Mike were married?"

"I believe everyone thought we were. I never talked about it, and neither did he."

"So when it suited his convenience to be married, Mike Markov was a married man, and when it no longer suited him, he wasn't?"

"Objection, Your Honor. Leading the witness," Riesner said without rising from his seat.

"Sustained."

"Did you and Mike ever have any children?" Nina asked.

"The business took the place of a child for us. We gave birth to it. We nurtured it. It grew—"

Riesner snorted audibly. Genevieve had coached Lindy on that answer, and it sounded coached.

Well, they had brought in the mantra.

In the afternoon, Winston handled the questions. For the first time in the past few years, Nina had the opportunity to sit at the counsel table and watch the jury while someone else carried the questioning.

One thing she noticed immediately. Cliff Wright perked up and paid attention when Winston talked. He laughed appropriately. He did not pick his nails. Wright liked Winston, preferred him to her. She wondered why.

And how did Winston appear so fresh? While the rest of the court wilted in the late afternoon, Winston's warm, copper-colored face looked invigorated and ready to go. He was relaxed and utterly in control of the courtroom. During the days of depos and trial prep, Winston had kept such a low profile that Nina had begun to wonder if she had made a mistake in hiring him, that he had been grossly overrated. Now, seeing him in action, she understood his success. You couldn't dislike him.

"Mrs. Markov," he said to Lindy. "You said this morning that you worked alongside Mike Markov for many years at the company you both began."

"That's right. Literally alongside. We even shared an office."

Winston strolled over to a stand next to the table. "Your Honor, we would like to submit to the court's attention photographs taken of Lindy and Mike Markov in happier times."

Riesner turned immediately to Rebecca with a whisper to

show his complete disinterest. They had fought over showing the photos at a pretrial hearing and Riesner had lost.

The first board, a stiff, dry-mounted picture blown up to the size of a large poster, showed two desks, side by side. Behind one desk, Mike Markov beamed. Behind the other, Lindy beamed. Across the gap in the desks, they held hands.

"Will you describe this picture for me?" asked Winston.

"Objection, Your Honor. A picture is worth a thousand words," said Riesner. "It speaks for itself."

"Even a thousand words may not explain the circumstances in which the picture was taken, I'm afraid," said Milne. "Proceed."

"That's . . . that was our office at Markov Enterprises. The office at our first manufacturing plant."

"Located here in town?"

Lindy nodded. "On the hill going up from the 'Y' intersection. We have offices there, plus a production facility."

"For how many years did you and Mike share an office?"

Lindy said, "Always. The whole time. We liked being close to each other. We consulted with each other constantly."

"What does that sign on your desk read?"

"Executive vice president."

"Now, during the years Markov Enterprises has had its principal place of business at Lake Tahoe, what exactly has been your job description?"

"There wasn't one. I did whatever needed doing, as I always had before. Marketing strategies, advertising campaigns, production timetables. I oversaw the day-to-day operating expenses. I helped develop long-term financial plans along with Mike and our accounting service. I trained our sales force and organized our employee benefits package. I hired and fired and promoted and dealt with the unions. As the business grew, my responsibilities grew. And I kept trying to think of new products like the Solo Spa."

Winston seemed to need to study the pictures for a long time. Hands behind his back, he stood far enough away so that the jury had a straight shot at them. "What was Mike Markov's title?"

"President."

"You had desks the same size?"

"Yes."

"If someone came in from the factory, for example, needing something, who would that person speak with first?"

"Whoever happened to be in, Mike or me."

"Would you say when anything important came across your desk, it usually found its way to Mr. Markov's desk?"

"Yes."

"And if anything important landed on his desk, he rolled it over to you at some point?"

"Oh, yes."

Winston took a marker pen out of his pocket, stared at it for a moment as if surprised to find it there, walked up to the picture, and playfully drew a circle around the two people and two desks. Turning back to Lindy he said, "Though you were two people, as far as your clients, your employees, and your business problems were concerned, the two of you operated as one unit, would that be correct to say?"

The linking of hands in the photograph served to emphasize the image he was suggesting.

"Objection!" said Riesner. "Vague. Leading."

"Sustained. Leading."

"Did you work together as a unit?"

"Yes. Like parents raising a family."

"You shared equally in decision-making?"

"Nothing major happened in our business without my consultation and approval."

"You dealt directly with clients?"

"Yes."

"When someone called, say, a new shop interested in carrying your products, who talked to the client?"

"We both did."

"How did you do that?"

"Any important phone calls that came in, Mike would signal

me to pick up. Afterward, we discussed the deal and made a decision together."

"Did employees at the business think you ran it together?"

"Objection," said Riesner. "Calls for speculation."

"Sustained."

"Right," Winston said. "We'll get into that later."

And, with Winston leading Riesner on a merry chase through the labyrinthian legal subtleties of testimony, eventually he did, taking Lindy through a description of a conference she had planned and run while Mike recuperated from exhaustion in Las Vegas.

She came off well, Nina thought as Winston wound things up with Lindy. You had to like someone who worked so very hard, who took responsibility, who loved her job and her man so loyally.

Didn't you?

18

"WHERE'S PAUL?" GENEVIEVE WHISPERED THE next morning as Judge Milne took his place. "I would have thought he'd want to see some of this."

"We don't need him anymore," said Nina, ignoring Genevieve's perplexed look.

The trial started off with Winston, who wanted to unman the defense's biggest weapon right up front. "I have here a copy of a document entitled 'Separate Property Agreement' that appears to be signed by you. Have you ever seen this before?" he asked Lindy.

Nina, taking notes next to Genevieve at their table, continued to marvel at the transformation Genevieve and Lindy had brought about in Lindy's appearance. Her simple clothing, lack of makeup, and graying hair made an utter contrast to the glamorous woman who had greeted Nina at the Markov party. She looked worn out, and therefore more vulnerable. She looked thin rather than muscular, and therefore weaker.

Taking the exhibit, Nina looked it over. Meantime, Winston waited quietly at the podium, directing the courtroom's attention to Lindy.

"Yes," she finally answered, looking at Mike. "A copy of it at my deposition. And before that, thirteen years ago."

"How close can you come to a date?"

"Sometime in the mideighties, I'm not sure when; right after we came to California, Mike had me type up a paper and sign it. It was a one-page document."

"What did you think you were signing?"

"It started off with saying something about how much we trusted each other. Then it talked about separating our assets."

"Did you consult an attorney before signing this paper?"

"No."

"Did Mike suggest you might do that?"

Lindy smiled slightly. "At that time, Mike didn't like attorneys. He just asked me to sign it. He wrote it in the motel room in Sacramento where we lived when we came out from Texas."

"What was happening at that time in your relationship?"

Lindy was looking at Mike again. Mike tried to look indifferent and failed. Rachel leaned forward from her seat behind him and whispered something.

"We were broke. We had liquidated our business in Texas. I've never seen Mike in such a bad state. Until now."

"Move to strike the last two words as nonresponsive," Rebecca said from next to Mike.

"The jury will disregard the last two words."

"When you say 'bad state,' what do you mean?"

Lindy said carefully, "Mike had failed before. He was angry. I think he felt helpless. He talked a lot about his ex-wife, how she had taken everything he had saved during his years in the ring. He thought our business troubles were a direct result of starting out with no money, and he blamed her.

"Every day, we got dunning letters. Creditors made phone calls. Our agent there was trying to sell off the assets and salvage something for us. We were living in a motel in Sacramento run by a gloomy man who called every morning at eight o'clock and said, 'Your rent is due,' like we were criminals climbing out the back window. That little room was so hot. Cockroaches ran in the kitchen all night and the back balcony looked out over a sewage ditch. It was August and over a hundred degrees day after day. I'd sit at the dressing table all day and make calls and write letters, trying to get some money in, and Mike would just lie on the bed. Mike started—he got angry at me."

"Why?" Winston's soft, sympathetic voice.

"I was handy," Lindy said. "He's a proud and stubborn man. He started imagining that I was going to leave him as soon as the agent sent our check, take the money and get as far from him as I could. Then he said he was going to disappear one day and I'd be better off. He was having such a hard time, I didn't know what he would do."

"And what was your response to that?"

She had everyone's attention. Nina saw a few unconvinced looks, and hoped Winston's next few questions would erase those.

"I told him he could have all the money when it came, and put it in a bank account just in his name, if it would make him feel better. I wouldn't take anything. That way he wouldn't have to worry anymore that I would leave him or something."

"You offered to give him your share of the check?"

"It made no difference to me, as long as we were together."

"If you made yourself penniless, a pauper, made yourself completely powerless, gave up everything, he would feel better? Then you couldn't leave him? He needed you to sacrifice all you had to shore up his bruised ego?"

Lindy pushed herself up. "I never said that!"

At the same time, Riesner jumped up from his chair and began objecting.

And at the same time, Winston calmly said, "Withdrawn."

Milne called Winston and Riesner to the bench. Leaning away from the jury so he wouldn't be heard, Milne hissed a few words to Winston that had Winston nodding his head and promising he'd never do it again. Winston had sprung that inspired cruelty on Lindy; it had certainly never been rehearsed in the office conference room. Nina was sure it was spontaneous; he hadn't prepared that outburst of eloquent questions that had forced Lindy into a protective stance and made the real relationship spring to life for the jury.

Now, as Winston received his dressing-down, the jury had

plenty of time to sit there and think about Mike and Lindy, about a man's irrational and sour fears when he hits bottom for the second time, and a woman's willingness to give too much to help him.

Nina knew she couldn't have done that to Lindy. She would feel too much compunction. Also, she felt Lindy's mortification at having these things stated so baldly. Lindy looked shamefaced, like a wife admitting to but excusing a husband that beats her every Friday night.

Dynamite, Genevieve scribbled on her pad for Nina's benefit.

"What happened then?" Winston now said. The lawyers had returned to their places. Lindy sat very straight and stared straight ahead. She no longer trusted Winston.

"I had found a space we could use to set up a boxing ring and a supplier who would set us up on credit. That week a check came from the agent. All we had from seven years of hard work. Twelve thousand five hundred dollars. That night, Mike asked me to type up and sign this exhibit."

"Referring to Cross-Complainant's Exhibit One. And you have already testified that you signed it."

"Yes."

"Now, let me ask you this, Lindy." Winston's voice dropped, and everybody leaned in closer so as not to miss a word. "Let me ask you this simple but important question."

"Yes?" Lindy was all but vibrating, knowing what was coming.

"Why did you sign this document?"

In the silence that followed Nina heard Mike's stentorian breathing.

"Because Mike said we would get married if I signed it. We'd get married and try to gut it out."

A mass exhalation. Several jurors wrote that statement down.

"He promised to marry you?"

"Yes. You know, legally."

"So long as all the money and power were kept completely in his hands?"

"I wouldn't put it that way. So long as—his property was kept separate. He needed that. It was important to him, and it didn't matter to me, don't you see?"

Winston started to comment on her reply, then thought better of it. He thought for a moment, tapping his hand on his chin, and Nina saw again how he used pauses to suck in all the wandering attention. She was learning from him.

He said eventually, compassionately, "But you didn't get married."

Lindy explained again how Mike pocketed the agreement and left for Texas to sign the final paperwork terminating their business there. Winston let her talk.

"When he got back, I kept saying to Mike, let's do it, it's so simple, just go to a justice of the peace and make it official. But"— she held her palms up and shrugged—"we just never did."

"You opened a checking account to deposit the check?"

"Mike did, yes."

"Was your name on it?"

A wary shake of the head. "No."

"Did you move?"

"Oh, yes. Within a week. To an apartment near Howe Avenue."

"Was your name on the lease?"

"No."

"Did you lease the exercise facility and sign some contracts for services and equipment?"

"No."

"Mike did?"

"Yes."

"Did the business begin making money?"

"It took off, and we never looked back," said Lindy with whatever pride Winston had left her.

"Did the business eventually incorporate as Markov Enterprises and were stock certificates issued in that name?"

"Yes," she said, and in a voice Nina could barely hear, she added, "and my name wasn't on them."

"Did you protest to Mike?"

"No. I just asked him again—this was about ten years ago. Could we—let's get married, I said. Like you promised. And he said when the time was right. And I let it go."

"You relied on his promise?"

"I relied on Mike. I always have. I always gave him my complete trust." Her voice sounded surprised, as if only now, in front of the jury that would judge her actions, could she acknowledge that she had been foolish.

"You subsequently established your primary manufacturing facility for exercise equipment here in Tahoe—"

"Yes."

"And . . ."

"And, yes, my name wasn't on anything."

"Then you bought that beautiful house up on Cascade Road. That wonderful mansion," Winston said sadly. "Who found the house and dealt with the realtor?"

"Mike was busy, so I . . ."

"Who put in the flowerbeds and bought the furniture and oversaw extensive remodeling—"

"That was me."

"And who lived there for ten years, only to be thrown out of it like a dog because your name wasn't anywhere to be found on the ownership papers?"

"Oh, stop, please!" Lindy said, tears flowing down her thin cheeks.

Winston had made her cry.

"Court's adjourned until one-thirty. Mr. Reynolds. Get your— get up here."

On cross examination after lunch, to no one's surprise Riesner focused on Exhibit 1. Nina took on the job of making the objections from Lindy's table. Lindy now sat at her right, Winston and Genevieve on her left. The jury filed in, Mrs. Lim, looking stern in her checkered suit, in the lead.

Riesner was in fine form, with a bright, new silk tie in gold and red, buffed from his nose to his toes. The bruise on his cheek gave him a slightly reckless look. His air of false sympathy for Lindy had the exact impact he must have hoped for, casting doubt upon her sincerity.

Then he got to play with visuals, dreamed up during some midnight meetings to engage those media junkie, Generation X jurors, Nina presumed. Tacking a large piece of blank paper over an easel standing at the front of the room, he took a marker pen. "Agreement," he said, while he wrote at the top, "between Lindy and Mike. Lindy gets half of everything, including the business. And here's a space at the bottom for you and Mike to sign. Did you ever give Mike a paper like that to sign?"

"No."

"Did Mike ever give one to you?"

"No."

"Why didn't you ever do that?"

"We had our agreement," she said somewhat plaintively. "A promise between us to live as husband and wife, and share everything. Mike told me that was enough."

"Isn't it a fact, Ms. Markov, that the reason you didn't get him to sign a paper stating that you owned half of anything was that this wasn't your deal, but that the separate property agreement was?"

"No, it wasn't because Mike never carried out his part of the agreement. He promised to marry me in exchange for my signing."

"Ms. Markov, tell me this. The day you signed Exhibit One, if Mike Markov and you went to a justice of the peace that very day, would you have married him?"

"Of course I would have!"

Riesner sailed over to the clerk, flipping a piece of paper toward her and giving it an exhibit number.

"What's this?" he asked Lindy.

She looked at the certificate, looked back at Riesner, and looked at Nina. "It's a marriage certificate."

"Between you and a man named Gilbert Schaefer? Indicating you were married before you met Mike?"

"Yes." Why did her voice keep getting shakier and shakier? She hadn't made a secret of the fact that she had been married before.

"And your divorce became final when?"

Lindy didn't answer. She was looking at Mike again. Her face turned waxen.

"Objection, Your Honor. This is beyond the scope of cross-examination," said Nina, suddenly scared. "Counsel can't question the witness about a piece of paper I haven't seen."

"This is not beyond the scope, Judge," Riesner piped up. "She opened this line of questioning when she brought up the issue of marriage. I did overlook showing this to Counsel. My mistake. I apologize." He walked over and handed Nina the paper with a flourish.

"I'm overruling the objection," Milne said.

"My divorce became final . . ." Lindy started, then stopped. She looked at Nina again for help, but Nina's attention was riveted to the piece of paper she held between a rigid thumb and finger.

"Where did you obtain that divorce?" Riesner asked, seeming to let Lindy off the hook.

"In Mexico. Juarez."

"Now, I'm going to ask you this question again, Ms. Markov, and please give it your careful attention. When did that marriage terminate?"

"Last year," Lindy said. Some of the jurors did a double take. The audience shifted and murmured.

"What the hell?" Winston whispered, and Nina passed him the divorce decree, dated the previous year.

"Quiet," Deputy Kimura said sternly to the audience.

"In spite of your frequently stated wish to marry Mr. Markov, you were not free to marry, isn't that so?" Riesner asked.

"Let me explain! I thought I was divorced the year before I met Mike. I didn't know there was a problem with my divorce until very recently. Originally, I had flown to Juarez and taken care of it quickly."

"You flew to Juarez for a quickie divorce without caring whether it was legal and binding in the U.S.?"

"Of course I thought it was legal! Otherwise, I wouldn't have bothered."

"That's just another lie, isn't it? Where's this famous Juarez divorce decree?" Riesner knew from Lindy's deposition that she had lost it years ago. "Well, where is it?" he repeated impatiently, his voice loaded with condemnation.

"I lost it."

"Lost it?" He strolled around, sighing, practically rolling his eyes. "You're telling us you obtained an invalid divorce decree, lost the evidence of that, and didn't know until last year that it was invalid? Come on, Lindy . . ."

"Objection!"

The lawyers wrangled for a few minutes with Milne out of the jury's hearing, but Nina knew she could do nothing to attenuate the damage done to their case. The jury could not ignore the evidence. Lindy hadn't been divorced, therefore there could be no marriage to Mike.

"When did you find out you were still married to Gilbert Schaefer?"

"My ex-husband called me a little over a year ago. He said he wanted to remarry, but he thought he ought to get a divorce here. He had checked and found out the first one might not be any good."

"So any marriage to Mr. Markov would have been bigamous. And invalid."

"Objection," said Nina. "Calls for a legal conclusion. It's argumentative and speculative and—"

"Sustained."

"So during all those years with Mike Markov, you were still married to another man?" asked Riesner.

"I was married to Mike," Lindy said firmly, "in every way except City Hall's."

The statement sounded moonstruck and flighty under the circumstances.

"Oh, by the way. Did you explain any of this to Mike last
year?"

Lindy shook her head dumbly.

"You have to speak up," Riesner said.

"No. I didn't want him to know."

"Why not?"

"Where are we going with this, Your Honor?" Nina said. She
marched up to the judge with Riesner. Milne leaned over, careful to
whisper, and said, "Jeff. Now, what's this all about?"

"It's about her secrets and lies, Judge. Her poor little wife act.
Her total trust and reliance on Mr. Markov. Not only that. It's her
whole case. She signed that Separate Property Agreement based on a
mutual promise to keep their assets separate. She knew her divorce
was no good. A broken promise to marry—phew! Stinks to high
heaven, and I just proved that."

Milne said to Riesner, "Okay. But you've gone far enough
with this line of questioning. I'm not going to let this last question
in."

"But—"

But nothing. They were dismissed.

As they both swiftly walked the short distance to the counsel
tables, past the jury box, Nina suddenly felt a pressure on her shoe.
Riesner had stepped on her heel.

Over she went, straight forward, in an ungainly leaping motion.
She crashed into the trial table directly in front of an astounded
Winston, and clutched at the table for support, but her hands slid off
and she banged onto the table legs and hit the ground. A stabbing
pain shot down her left ankle.

Deputy Kimura's hands were there, lifting her up, and Genevieve rushed around the table to help her smooth her skirt.

"Court is adjourned until nine o'clock tomorrow morning,"
Milne announced, and the commotion increased. "Are you all

right?" Milne said, coming around the dais in his robes. "That was a nasty fall." The jury filed out, some turning their heads back to see.

Nina tested her weight on her foot. "Nothing seems to be broken," she managed to say. She wouldn't let the tears of pain force themselves through her lids, not with that son of a bitch Riesner watching.

"How extremely clumsy of me," Riesner said. He touched the bruise on his cheek, unobtrusively. "My foot—it just somehow caught the edge of your shoe."

Nina turned away. "Just get me out of here," she said to Winston through gritted teeth. He pulled her arm over his shoulder and hauled her to the elevator and out the door through the barrage of cameras. Genevieve trotted behind with the briefcases.

Nina spent the evening with her foot propped up, trying to keep down the swelling, trying to think rationally about what had happened in court just before Riesner tripped her.

For once, Lindy didn't call, so Nina called Lindy. "I'm killing myself to win this case for you," she said, the extremity of her discomfort making it easy for her to forgo the usual pleasantries. "Why the hell didn't you tell me you weren't officially divorced from Gilbert Schaefer until last year?"

"I thought Gil would stay gone and never come back," Lindy said. "And I thought giving him a hundred thousand would guarantee it."

"He blackmailed you?" Nina asked.

"Not really. I offered. I gave him some of the money I had saved from all those years of salary, and the severance pay I got when I lost my job . . ." She hesitated. "Then I agreed to pay him more after I won if he'd stay out of the case."

That explained why a woman who had made a living wage for twenty years and spent not a dime on her support had so little money to offer Nina up front. Nina stifled the urge to hang up on her. "You really believe throwing money at a problem makes it go away, don't you?" Nina asked.

"That's not my only method. It's just the one that usually works best," said Lindy.

Lindy sure hadn't thrown money at Nina, who was sliding head over heels into debt. Seething, Nina said good-bye. Bob came in, took one look at her, and set about clearing the table and loading the dishwasher.

She caught him on the arm as he walked by. "Bob, without you . . ."

"C'mon, Mom," he said, accepting a squeeze and then deftly pulling away. "I want to finish this before my show comes on." He carried a load to the counter. "Want me to fix up a cold bucket for your foot?"

She didn't answer. He felt around under a cabinet and emerged with a brown plastic pail. "Remember that time I twisted my ankle playing hockey and you told me it would really help and I said it wouldn't and you bet me and you won the bet?"

Massaging her foot, she listened and watched as he foraged in the freezer for ice. Without him . . .

Morning came, and court. Pulling panty hose over her swollen ankle hurt, but the rush of getting out the door made her forget it until she was sitting at the table at the front of the courtroom, where it resumed its throbbing.

"Call Harry Anderssen to the stand," said Winston, giving Nina a tap on the shoulder as he rose, and the jury a benevolent smile.

The show had to go on. Nina could only hope a magician would appear soon to work the magic they needed. While the next witness was sworn in by the clerk, Nina took a moment to study him. Harry Anderssen had been Lindy's assistant in marketing for three years. He wore a turtleneck under a dark green sports coat that matched his large dark eyes and had brushed his long brown hair straight back. Nina had seen some photographs in which he had modeled. In brochures and videos he usually wore shorts and went bare-chested, the better to show off an unusually well-developed physique.

Winston took him through his background and history with the company.

"You held a fairly responsible position?"

"I would say so. The Markovs, then Rachel and Hector, the vice presidents. I was the next layer down, but I worked directly for Lindy."

"How would you characterize your former relationship with Ms. Markov?"

"Employer-employee."

"And how did you perceive her role in the company?"

"Objection," said Riesner. "Calls for the witness to speculate."

"Overruled," said Milne. "Please answer."

"She and Mike ran the company."

"Together?"

"Pretty much."

"Did you observe them working together on a regular basis?"

"Oh, yes. They had desks right next to each other."

"Did you get the impression that one or the other was more important when it came to making decisions?"

"Objection," said Riesner, now showing a little carefully calculated anger. "Lack of foundation. Calls for a conclusion on the part of the witness."

"Overruled," said Milne. "He's asking for the witness's impressions, not for conclusions of fact." For once, Nina felt, the rulings were going their way. She had figured out that Milne tended to let in somewhat more than he had to under the strict rules of evidence. This diminished the number of appellate issues and got closer to the truth. For the thousandth time, she sent up a prayer of thanks that Tahoe had such a fine judge.

"You may answer," Milne told the witness.

"No. I had the impression they were equally important," said Harry. He looked around the courtroom, smiling. Harry seem to like his smile. He used it whenever he could.

"Who did you think owned the company?"

"I saw it as a family business, owned and operated by the Markovs."

"Putting aside Mr. Markov, did anyone else have a greater involvement in the running of the business besides Lindy Markov?"

"No."

"Did you get the impression that Lindy was some kind of assistant to Mr. Markov?"

He laughed slightly, which gave him another opportunity to expose his perfect white teeth. "No. They had plenty of arguments, and Lindy often came out the winner."

"Did the subject of their marital status ever come up?"

"Well, Mr. and Mrs. Markov, that's who they were. Of course we all assumed they were married."

"What about ownership of the company? Did you ever examine any of the corporate documents?"

"No. Why would I? I started out as Lindy's assistant and now I'm just the pinup boy." He stuck his chin out engagingly, and in the jury box Maribel Grzegorek licked her lips. Rachel smiled at him.

"Who did you believe up to the time that the Markovs separated—who did you believe owned the company?"

"Oh, the two of them together." He cast a glance at Mike. "We kidded around at work, called them Mom and Pop. That's what it was like, a family thing, the corner store, a mom and pop operation."

"Mom and Pop," Winston repeated. It made an excellent variation on their mantra.

In her chair beside Nina, Lindy stirred. "He's got a nasty streak. Mike's not going to like this," she whispered to Nina.

"He's saying exactly what we need him to say, Lindy."

"And in conversations with clients, did you you frequently refer to Lindy Markov as an owner?" Winston continued.

"Yes."

"Did Mr. Markov ever do anything or say anything to give you the impression that he owned and ran the company entirely on his own?"

"No. He always said 'we.' *We're* going to introduce a new product line. *We* want to open a Solo Spas outlet in London. Which is not to say they didn't have different areas of responsibility in the company. Mike's orientation is the hands-on side. Lindy is the planner."

Riesner moved in fast.

"You know your testimony will help Ms. Markov, don't you, Mr. Anderssen?" he said.

"The chips must fall where they may." Another fabulous smile. Nina thought, he's going to be a star tomorrow, after the news pictures get taken today.

"Speaking of chips falling, you've got a big one on your shoulder, don't you?"

"Sorry?"

"You don't want Mr. Markov to win, do you?"

"I feel obligated to tell the truth even though Mike was my employer," he said.

"And the man who's about to marry the woman you love— how about that for a little problem?" said Riesner. He didn't turn to look back at Mike, and Nina knew why. Mike's turn to receive an unpleasant surprise from his own lawyer had come. Mike's eyes burned, but he managed to keep his mouth shut. Clearly, in spite of the public scene between him and Harry, he had told Riesner not to use this information because of the embarrassment it would cause both him and Rachel. But Riesner hadn't been able to resist this easy method of showing bias. Nina could practically hear the buzz of the reporters' busy little brains in the back rows, planning how to report this fine whiff of sex.

"I don't know how you mean," Harry said.

"Sure you do, Harry. You and Ms. Pembroke, Mr. Markov's fiancée, were lovers until about six months ago. Now that's true, isn't it?"

"Yes. But—"

"You still care for her."

"I don't deny that. But—"

"You wish she were marrying you, don't you?"

"Whatever," Harry said, and for the first time, his green eyes flashed with anger. "She made the smart choice. I don't really hold it against her. She went for the money."

Even Deputy Kimura couldn't still the courtroom now. Riesner's head jerked back, anger rampaging over his face, as uncontrollable as weather.

"Move to strike the last two sentences as nonresponsive!" he shouted quickly over the hubbub, forcing his face back into the grimace that passed for normal with him.

Winston leaned over to Nina. "You hear that?" he muttered. "The jury's got it all figured out now."

"Sustained. The jury will disregard the last two statements from the witness and they will be stricken from the record. Order!" Milne's gavel came down and the noise subsided.

Nina watched Mike, who had half risen. Rebecca was talking fast to him, her head close to his. While Nina couldn't catch any words, she caught the soothing tone. Rebecca was trying to keep Mike from compounding the mistake Riesner had made.

And whatever she said worked. Mike fell heavily back into his seat. Riesner wiped his brow with his silk handkerchief and spent considerable time leading Harry through more innocuous topics, defusing the bomb. Winston continued his examination after lunch, then Harry was excused. When the afternoon break was called, the reporters and photographers stampeded him, but Harry was in no hurry to get away. He graciously consented to pose for any number of snapshots.

Nina almost felt sorry for Riesner, who had made a fool out of his client and seen his effort backfire. It almost made up for the day before, but not quite.

19

BOB WOKE UP WITH A fever Friday morning. Andrea had to work. Matt had to work. Nina had to work. Matt promised to pop in a few times during the day to see how he was doing. That left Nina with the single mom's alternative: dose him with medicine and prop him in front of the television with a six pack of uncola and crackers, out of Hitchcock's range. She left him with his head lying over Hitchcock's back, looking like hell. "Page me in an emergency," she told him, feeling like an idiot. What kind of a mother would leave a sick child just to go to work?

She would make it up to him when this trial was over.

She arrived at court extremely late. Milne had just called the midmorning break. Fortunately, Winston had jumped into her place. "You owe me," he whispered, passing the torch the minute she dropped her briefcase on her chair.

"Winston. A word." Nina caught him by the coat sleeve just as he got up from the counsel table. He followed her into the cubbyhole next to the law library. Nina shut the door. He filled her in on what she had missed in court. In case he had somehow missed it, she filled him in on what was happening out there in the world.

The stories in the papers had begun by trying to state both sides of the Markov case, but then the commentators had gotten hold of it. For the first few days of the trial Lindy was the poster child. A well known Boston area feminist wrote in her syndicated national column about how the Markov case symbolized the fact that women hadn't come nearly as far as they thought. Lindy turned down all interview requests, which allowed the media free rein to paint her personality and the story in accordance with the particular slant desired.

But now Riesner had turned up a husband, at least a husband who technically had been her lawfully wedded partner for much longer than Lindy had led everyone to believe. As a result, Lindy had been hastily decommissioned as poster child and Mike had now been tacked up.

But the media was only echoing the change of tone that had transpired in the courtroom. Before Lindy started a freefall in front of the jury, one she wouldn't survive, Nina and Winston needed to do immediate damage control on Lindy's image.

"Call Florencia Morales to the stand."

A fit young Latina woman stood in the witness box, her interpreter beside her, and was sworn in.

"You're Mike Markov's housekeeper?" asked Nina. Mrs. Morales listened to the translation and answered. She spoke English fairly well. The translator was just there to make sure the questions were interpreted accurately.

"That's right," she said.

"And you've been employed for the past seven years at the Markov estate?"

"Yes."

"Now, Mrs. Morales, as caretaker you must see a lot of things that happen at the Markov house."

"Yes."

"How many days a week do you work?"

"I'm there every day. I live there. Most days, I work."

"So you were there, on March twenty-eighth of last year, when Gilbert Schaefer came to tell Lindy Markov that they were still married?"

"Objection," Riesner said. "Leading, speculative, irrelevant, lack of foundation—"

"Sustained."

"On that date about a year ago, did you observe the arrival of a man called Gilbert Schaefer?"

"I opened the door to him. He introduced himself."

"What happened then?"

"I called upstairs for Lin . . . Mrs. Markov. She came down."

"And what was her reaction upon seeing Mr. Schaefer?"

"Hearsay, Your Honor," said Riesner. "We object."

"Sustained."

"Tell us, if you will, only what you observed, nothing that you overheard of any conversation."

"Okay," said Mrs. Morales. "She came down the stairs. When she saw him, she turned kind of white, then kind of gray. She wanted to know what he was doing, showing up after such a long time."

"And why had he come?"

"He said . . ."

"Same objection," said Riesner.

"Sustained."

"He told her why he had come?"

"Yes. He just came right out with it, boom."

"And can you characterize his mood at the time?"

"He was clowning around like it was all a big joke."

"What was her reaction when he told her why he had come?"

"She listened. At first she didn't believe him, but he showed her some papers to prove what he said was true. Then, like she was whacked with an ax, she sat down hard on the couch. She was very surprised at whatever he told her."

Nina paced quietly around in front of the jury, hands behind her back, head lowered, as if pondering the scene. She was giving everyone plenty of time to get it, that Lindy had been horrified to learn she was not divorced from this man. She looked at the jury. Mrs. Lim took her notes. Kris Schmidt looked twitchy. Cliff Wright was hard to read. "Now on another topic," said Nina. "Are you aware that Mr. Markov has a niece, age seventeen, who lives in Ely?"

"Yes. I have met her several times."

"When she comes to the Markov house?"

"That's right."

"And when she comes to the Markov house, what does she call Mr. Markov?"

"Uncle Mike."

"And what about Lindy Markov?"

"Aunt Lindy."

Following the afternoon break, Nina took over for Winston, who had already begun with Mike Markov. She was attempting to show the jury that Mike had had all the benefits of marriage with Lindy without accepting the legal obligations, but Riesner had prepared his client well. For the last three hours of the day, stoic and impervious to provocation, Markov asserted that Lindy played only a minor role in the business. He alone had invented the Solo Spa. He had never referred to her as his wife in public or private.

Then it was Nina's turn to play with pictures. She asked for the lights to be dimmed and inserted a video Paul had extracted from someone in the marketing department at Markov Enterprises.

Mike spoke from behind a podium. "Ladies and gentlemen, coworkers and friends. It gives me great pleasure to introduce my companion, my partner, my muse, my wife, Mrs. Lindy Markov!"

The screen went blank.

A sound escaped from beside Genevieve. Nina didn't turn to look at Lindy, seated there.

"Does this refresh your memory?" she asked Mike Markov.

Before giving the rattled defendant a chance to recover from being shown up as a liar in court, she moved in for a strike, getting him to make the crucial admission that Lindy had said "Now we can get married" when she signed the separate property agreement.

At the end of the day, she canceled Friday night's dinner meeting with Genevieve and Winston. They would have to haggle about the day's work without her or wait until Saturday. In spite of their reasonably effective showing that day, she didn't feel good. She couldn't remember ever being in a case before where her actions in court, both good and bad, were so zealously analyzed afterward that she sometimes felt pulverized under the sheer weight of opinion.

Calling Sandy on her cell phone to fill her in and give her what advice she could about keeping things going at her poor, neglected practice, she drove home to Bob and managed to get a dollop of soup stuffed between his puffy, fevered lips before he conked out again at about seven-thirty.

When the phone rang, she didn't answer. She was afraid it would be Lindy calling and she just couldn't reassure her properly at the moment. She couldn't even reassure herself.

This trial had an edginess she couldn't remember feeling before. Everyone jumped at the slightest mistake. Every revelation rated frenzied scribbling in a reporter's notebook.

She put on her nightgown and crawled into bed. Outside the wind blew. She tried to sleep as branches broke off and thumped against the roof, sounding to her groggy mind as heavy and ominous as bodies falling.

20

OVER THE WEEKEND, BOB'S FEVER receded enough for him to take up his station at the computer, where he was lovingly creating a website with his cousin Troy based on their mutual loathing of phony people and love of Boogie-boarding. So, late on Saturday morning, Nina went into the office, straight from a glaring May sunshine into the waiting glare of Sandy.

"I can run this place alone," she said, "but your other fifty-nine clients might not be so sure."

"Sandy, I'm really sorry. But you know I've got trial, and Bob's been sick. . . ."

"Yeah. He called here while you were at court yesterday."

"Was he okay?"

"Sounded low."

"What did he say?"

"Not much. So, I told him about the shaman near Woodfords in my mother's time. A healer. He used to smoke first, a plant that would help him see what was wrong. Then he had two methods for healing. He would sing. Sometimes that worked."

"And then?" asked Nina, intrigued. Sandy must get lonely here all day. . . .

"He sucked the sick person's flesh to get rid of the 'Pain.' "

"What did Bob think about that?"

"Said maybe he'd try listening to the radio first." Sandy looked so serious, Nina squelched any desire to giggle.

Genevieve threw open the door to the office. "Hi, Sandy, Nina. Man, it's been one helluva month, hasn't it?" Her arms spilling files, she breezed her way through to the conference room. "Vanilla bean coffee! Sandy, you're the best!"

Sandy and Nina watched as she whirled from here to there, bringing them both fresh cups and watering Sandy's plants as she passed.

"You would never know she's got that hearing problem," said Sandy as the door closed behind her. "Isn't it great to see a disabled person doing so well?"

Nina, still breathing in the clean air and optimism Genevieve always seemed to carry with her, agreed, wishing she felt half as optimistic. Where would she find the money to get her through this trial? What could she do about her clients?

"You know what I wish?" she asked. "I wish Bob and I could go somewhere right now, tonight, and sleep late every morning and get brown and spend the entire day in the water."

"If you're going to wish," Sandy said, "wish for something useful. Wish for a million bucks, why don't you?"

Winston showed up later bearing cold, roasted chicken and salad, which they ate while they talked.

For a few minutes, they indulged themselves in a discussion of all the places at Tahoe they hadn't been and couldn't wait to go to once they were out of the incarceration they imposed on themselves during any trial. Since they couldn't actually do anything fun, they had fun imagining themselves having fun. Sandy sat with them through the first part of this discussion, then left to tap away on her computer.

Nina led off with her latest plan: to take Bob and Matt's family to a picnic on Fannette Island. That intrigued Winston, who loved to kayak. He decided that would be his first stop, once they finished the trial. Then he wanted to spend at least a long weekend hiking. Then two days lying on the beach. Then he might take a swim up at the

Squaw Valley pool and hike all the way back down the mountain from there.

Genevieve said she hadn't spent enough time alone with a slot machine lately to claim more than a passing acquaintanceship. The trial was cutting into her gambling time.

"Okay, you're waiting to hear from me," she said once they had finished eating, with that charming confidence that a snide person might mistake for arrogance.

"We are?" said Winston, but he was joking.

"Analysis of how we're doing in one word: fanfuckingtastic."

"Is that like those bumper stickers people used to put on VW's, 'fukengruven'?" asked Winston. "Because not too many of those old Bugs were in any shape to brag, you know."

"I don't think we have too much to brag about yet, either," Nina said.

"Well, that's fine. We don't want you two getting smug." Genevieve picked up a yellow sheet and read, then set it down. "So let's start with the bad stuff. The Gilbert Schaefer thing hurt. Some of the jurors stopped listening to Lindy. Most of them frowned at some point during that testimony. I think we're losing Kris Schmidt, and probably Ignacio Ybarra."

"It hurt, all right. I felt like I was having one of those operations in China where they use hypnosis instead of anesthesia, only I wasn't hypnotized," Winston said. They all smiled bleakly at that, and Nina for once felt a certain amount of comfort in sharing her woes with her colleagues. No wonder lawyers banded together into firms.

"The good news is that the mountain climber, Diane Miklos, and Mrs. Lim are solid in the Lindy camp. They don't like Mike; it sticks out all over their faces. Nina, you really got them going in your opening; we've already talked some about that," Genevieve continued. "In terms of the questioning, well, everything I heard about you is true. You're hard-hitting and effective. Eye contact is the only area you need to work on, although you did a job on Markov, that extended-play staring thing at the end. Very good. And smile more, sugar, pul-lease.

"Now, here's something else you should know. We've got troubles. Before he disappeared on us, Paul turned up some late-breaking information that is going to hurt us. Wright's been having marital woes. Too late for us to use our peremptory, unfortunately."

"I heard," said Winston. "And I have something to say about that."

"Go ahead," said Genevieve graciously.

A touch of annoyance at her giving him permission passed over his features. "I think we should recognize that Nina's instincts were right about him. I think she deserves that, and we owe her that."

"Oh, Nina doesn't need my approval like some people. And we can attract him back. Highlight the traditional female role that Lindy played at home. By all reports, other than being a political shark, he likes his women traditional."

"You can't ignore the rest of the jury to win over this one guy," said Winston. "We don't want to lose them once we've got them."

"Nobody's saying ignore them. It's a subtle matter of perspective, which I'm sure Nina can handle, can't you?"

"Uh," said Nina. "No. I won't do that. Besides the bad taste it leaves in my mouth, we've all said many times that Lindy's trump card is that she was an equal partner in the business. Once we get around the Separate Property Agreement, I've always intended to clinch our argument with the fact that she's been vital since the beginning to making their business the success it is today."

Winston nodded his head. "You know I hate popping your bubble, Genevieve," he said, "but Nina's right. I don't think we should change our strategy to win him over. It won't help."

Genevieve said, "What's the matter with you two? You're talkin' like losers! We are not going to let one asshole juror ruin our game! We need nine jurors on our side, and we're gonna get them. You have my personal guarantee."

Nina said, "Genevieve, I've seen a case turn before on the leadership abilities of one angry man. . . ."

"This one won't. We're smarter than he is." Genevieve

slammed a notebook shut as if to put an end to all further discussion on the topic. "Now, moving right along . . ."

They spent most of the afternoon and evening chewing peppermints and nuts going over what had happened, with very little time to plan for the next week, where Riesner would take the reins and redirect the case. And whenever she had a moment to stop and think, the mistake of allowing Clifford Wright to sit up there came back to Nina like a hard plastic tag in her clothing, rubbing at her until her skin hurt.

Sunday, Andrea and Matt invited Nina and Bob along for a day at the beach. Nina said no at first, wanting to sleep late, study her notes, and give Bob a chance to get over his bug, but Andrea came up the stairs to her room, pulled the quilt off of her, and set Hitchcock on her. Packing up her paperwork into her briefcase, Nina agreed to come if they would just sit her at the table with her work. Well, hadn't she just spent a lunch hour in her office sitting around with the others, commiserating about how they never got out?

At Pope Beach, where Lake Tahoe spread a frothy navy-blue all the way to the horizon, they laid out towels in the warm May sunshine. Nina stripped off her layers of clothes right down to her suit. Putting her head on her briefcase, she promptly fell asleep.

Next thing she knew, something cold and wet had landed on her back and seemed to be snaking its way down. Leaping up, she screamed.

"It's just a wet ball, Mom, geez," said Bob, picking up what looked like an exploded rubber star.

She touched her back. "Was that Hitchcock slobber on that ball or lake water?" she asked.

"A little of both,"

So she had to clean herself off, didn't she? In she went, plunging headfirst into the icy cold snowmelt, followed by Hitchcock, Bob, and his cousins Troy and Brianna. They had a water fight until Bree's lips turned blue, then warmed themselves at a fire Matt had built in a grate. After that, there were hot dogs to eat, and a quick chess game against Matt, which Nina lost with poor grace. Laughing, tired, sand stuck to every pore, they piled into their cars and waved good-bye.

Bob made faces at his cousins until the two cars finally parted ways around Pioneer Trail.

"I know I'm not supposed to leave it all until Sunday night," Bob confessed, "but I've got a lot of make-up homework I didn't finish yesterday." He leaned across the seat to put his head on Nina's shoulder.

"You're not the only one," said Nina.

Bob fell asleep before they got home, and Nina watched the lights of the town coming up along Highway 50, one by one, color by color. To distract herself from falling back into the tired groove of worrying about the trial, she tried to drift off into her greedy little fantasy in which she would plunk down a million for her own personal castle. There she would sip brandy and enjoy a view of the glitzy casinos burning like candles across the lake.

But the fantasy made her anxious. What was happening? Why did she have the feeling things were spinning out of control, when on the surface they were doing well enough?

Paul was right. They were all being affected by the Markov money. Riesner, Winston, Genevieve, even Nina were behaving like wild kids at a birthday party. The first blows had been struck on the piñata. They had glimpsed the prize through cracks in the cardboard, and it was making everyone flail and thrash against each other willy-nilly. God, it was a wonder nobody had been killed yet.

21

Winston's cross-examination of Mike Markov took up most of Monday. He hit all the high points and all the low points, and only a few times did he sound impatient. Nina watched him and continued to learn from him.

She saw, for instance, how this sophisticated African-American lawyer from L.A. managed to persuade the white, mostly working-class jury to identify with him. He would drop in little personal references, that he was middle-aged, that he had a bad back, that he liked tea first thing in the morning instead of coffee, that his mother was ailing and in a nursing home. The references were so fleet that Riesner never had a chance to object, but the jurors were affected. Gradually they began to see their father, their uncle, their brother. They warmed to Winston. They wanted him to do well.

Winston had another ability she admired. He took his time. The topic at hand would be fully explored, and Winston didn't seem to care if a juror was fidgeting or if the subject was tedious. Nina was always running through the testimony at breakneck speed, trying to keep the jurors interested. Watching Winston, she realized she needed to slow down and she saw that her problem was a lack of confidence.

He underplayed all the way through the testimony, almost to the end, a strategy Genevieve had suggested that would keep sympathy for Mike at a minimum. Only once did Winston allow himself to show negative emotion.

"Mr. Markov, are you telling us that you used no threats to get this woman you had lived with for years to sign away all her rights?" he said late in the afternoon, allowing frustration to enter his voice.

"I never threatened her."

"She was afraid you would leave her if she didn't sign, wasn't she?"

"I don't remember anything like that."

"You never said you were going to walk out and she would never see you again if she didn't sign?"

"No."

"You didn't say words to the effect that, 'Sign this now, and I promise you, we'll get married soon'?"

"No, I didn't."

"Then why draw it up in the first place? If it wasn't because the two of you were talking about marriage in some way, why?"

"Because I wanted the lines drawn between her and me. Things weren't going so well between us. But I never said I was leaving."

"Seven years you had been together at that point. Do you think you had to tell her? She could tell it from your frown, from the way you touched her, from your voice, couldn't she?"

"Objection."

"Sustained."

"Now all this happened thirteen years ago. How much had the business appreciated in value in those thirteen years between the time she signed the agreement and the time you separated, would you say?"

"Objection. Irrelevant." Rebecca was on duty today.

"Overruled."

Mike shook his head, smiling. "Well, since we were down to a few thousand dollars, I'd say it's appreciated quite a bit."

"You think she would have signed the agreement if she'd had any idea in thirteen years it would be used to cheat her out of a hundred million—"

"Objection! Argumentative."

"Withdrawn," said Winston. "Let me put it this way. It's fair to say, isn't it, that she thought she was signing away a claim to a few thousand dollars?"

"At that time, yes."

"She continued to live with you on the same basis, and continued to work with you in the business?"

"As I've said."

"Why didn't you give her a copy of the agreement?"

A shrug. "She never asked for one."

"Why didn't you folks go to an attorney so she would know she was signing away her future?"

"Objection."

"Sustained."

"Why," Winston asked, his voice rising, "did you never talk with her about it again?"

"It just never came up."

"You knew she thought it had been thrown out long ago, didn't you?"

"Not at all."

"You knew she depended on you, relied on you, to be fair with her?"

"I was fair."

"Fair! You really think you have the right to use that word?" asked Winston, coming as close to rolling his eyes out of sight of the judge but in full view of the jury as he could manage.

"Object to the form of the question!" said Rebecca.

"Sustained."

Looking ready to excuse Mike, Winston flipped quickly through his notes. "Oh, by the way," he said.

Mike, who was practically out of his chair with eagerness to be done, sat back and waited.

"About the Solo Spa, the most successful product your company created. During your direct examination by Mr. Riesner last week, you showed us a drawing of it you made."

"Yes."

"That was the first drawing?"

"Yes."

"Isn't it true that Lindy Markov caused you to make that first drawing?"

" 'Caused' me to make it? No."

"She told you her idea and you made a sketch?"

"No."

"She even made a little sketch herself, which you copied?"

"No. That sketch I made with the red pen I always use—that's the first."

Winston got out the drawing and showed it to the jury. While he did this, Nina set up an overhead projector. Deputy Kimura placed a projection stand and screen to one side of the court reporter.

"Let's just get a little better look at that drawing of yours," Winston said. At his signal, the lights in the courtroom went down. There on the screen, hugely magnified, was Mike's sketch in red pen. Winston pointed beside one of the red marks with a pencil tip. "Hmmm. What's this?"

"What?" Mike leaned forward.

"These little lines here," he tapped his pencil against the screen, "and here? Looks like pencil to me. Does it look like pencil to you, Mr. Markov?"

Mike's mouth opened and closed. The marks were faint but clear.

"Does it?"

"It appears to be pencil. Yes, I must have done it that way first."

"But you always use your red pen to draw, isn't that what you testified?"

"Obviously, I didn't here."

"Obviously, you didn't. Now, let me direct your attention to the date in red ink at the bottom of the page. See these marks here?"

"Not to read, no."

"No? Let's magnify that just a little more." The date sprang up, filling the bottom edge of the screen, and along with it, underneath it, in pencil, some letters.

"Let me further direct your attention to the letters at the bottom of this page. What do those letters say, Mr. Markov?"

"I don't know."

"Really? You can't see they say 'LM'?"

Anyone could see they did except Mike, who said, "I don't see it."

"You can't read those letters, in writing, in black and white, plain and simple up there on the screen?"

Mike didn't respond. The jury members looked across the courtroom from the letters to Mike.

"He has testified he can't read those scribbles. Objection. Asked and answered," Riesner sputtered.

They had done it. *Yes!* wrote Genevieve. Winston had been first to blow up the sketch and identify the initials. Even Lindy hadn't remembered at first sketching the spa in pencil. They had hidden their surprise right under Riesner's nose.

" 'LM.' Isn't that how Lindy Markov always signed her memos, Mr. Markov?" Winston asked, waving a sheaf of them to discourage Mike from putting up a fight about it.

Mike swallowed and admitted it.

"We have nothing further, Your Honor," said Winston, shrugging to show his utter indifference to the man sitting on the stand behind him, who got slowly up from his chair and stepped down. For the first time since his testimony had begun, he turned his unhappy eyes to Lindy.

The next morning, Jeffrey Riesner was back in command, calling Hector Galka, Executive Vice President of Financial Strategies and Accounts. Hector looked tidy today, with his brushy mustache neatly clipped and trim body outfitted in a well-tailored suit. Nina liked his beautiful hazel eyes.

As he took the stand, he avoided looking at Lindy.

Based on his deposition, they already knew what he would say, and he didn't disappoint. He hemmed and hawed, but in the end, for

Hector, there was only one boss at Markov Enterprises: Mike Markov.

During cross-examination, Winston emphasized the bias in Hector's perspective. "By the way, how much do you make per year as a base salary for Markov Enterprises in your capacity as executive vice president," he asked, "not counting year-end bonuses, health plans, that sort of thing?"

"Um. One-sixty."

"One hundred and sixty thousand dollars a year?" Winston repeated, drawing out the words for maximum effect. "And how much did Lindy Markov make at the time she was removed from her position?"

Much more slowly, as if he'd never thought about it before, Hector answered, "Seventy-five thousand a year."

Winston had slipped that by Hector so fast, Hector hadn't had time to do anything but answer the question. It hadn't come up at the deposition, and Hector hadn't been prepared.

And now Winston stood back and said absolutely nothing.

The jury, the other lawyers, the parties, the audience waited, but he bent down to tie his shoe. So they thought about the last question and answer.

A new mood dawned in the courtroom. Agitated whispers came from behind Nina, and she thought, they're getting it, they're getting it, we're going to be all right in spite of everything. Why would Lindy be paid so relatively poorly for what Hector had just testified was similar work? She clenched her hands into fists under the table, willing Winston to grab this chance and run away with the trial with it.

"Why was Lindy Markov paid less than you?" Winston said when he was good and ready and they were all waiting for him to say it.

"Because—because—" Hector stammered.

Winston leaned on the podium, perfectly patient and ready to wait forever. "You're the chief financial officer, Mr. Galka. If anyone knows, it's you. Why?"

Hector's left index finger moved up, slowly, slowly, to his mustache. He combed it gently. "I suppose—you see, she lived with Mike, she had no expenses . . ."

"Because she was a woman, and Mike didn't feel the need to pay her fairly?"

"No, of course not."

"Because the pay was just fun money for one of the owners? How much did Mike get paid?"

Hector answered, "The same as Lindy."

"So, since he got a salary, that made him an employee, too?"

"No . . . You know."

"Yes, I know, Mr. Galka. We all know. Do you remember stating in your deposition that Mike became president and Lindy became vice president because the man always gets to be president? Remember this question from page thirty-three, lines ten to twenty-two of your deposition: 'Is it a big male ego kind of thing?' And your answer was, 'Yes, that kind of thing. He was the man.' "

"I was just—I was just—"

"Telling the truth?"

"Objection," said Rebecca.

Milne called Rebecca and Winston up for a conference. Nina drew stars all over her legal pad while she waited. After some whispered discussion, Rebecca took her seat and Winston resumed the podium.

"Now, you've known Mike for more than twenty years, and you've seen Mike and Lindy at every stage in their life together. So let me ask you, Mr. Galka, and please tell us the unvarnished truth. Wasn't it very important to Mike that he appear to be the boss in the relationship and in the business, no matter what the real responsibilities were?"

"Well . . . I suppose," Hector said almost inaudibly. He looked at Mike, who looked confused, as if he wasn't sure what the problem was. Nina thought Mrs. Lim noted Mike's reaction, as well as several of the other women.

If this didn't win them some of the women jurors, nothing would.

Over the next several days, Riesner and Rebecca paraded the group Genevieve derided outside of court as "the lackeys and shills" of Markov Enterprises. They worked hard to contradict the team image Nina and Winston had carefully built of Mike and Lindy's management style. On cross-examination, Nina and Winston worked to rebuild it.

The last significant witness for the defense, Rachel Pembroke, was scheduled to testify at the end of the week. All through the trial Rachel had sat just behind Mike, looking terrific, holding his hand from time to time, leaving with him. Nina knew Rachel's deposition by heart and knew, because Rachel was engaged to Mike, that her testimony might seem prejudiced to the jury. Nonetheless, she dreaded Rachel's personable, professional demeanor. She was grateful that the incident at Mike's birthday party had already been ruled off-limits by Milne during pretrial motions, and the so-called attack on her everyone had gossiped about for weeks had never even entered the proceedings. Her injuries had been minor, and the event, if it had really happened at all, had been deemed irrelevant.

Rachel had spent months telling reporters about the sweetness of her romance with Mike and how hard they had fought their passion, and the tale that spilled out of her on the stand came with an engaging wistfulness born of practice. By the time she was done testifying, she had somehow shifted many minds around to considering that she, not Lindy, had suffered most in this sad love story.

"Call your next witness," Milne said when she had finished and Riesner stayed seated.

Riesner stood up, saying, "Your Honor, we have decided not to call the final witnesses on the list."

And, just like that, abrupt as a puff of air blowing out a candle, the defense rested its case. Sometimes it happened like that, catching everybody by surprise.

Without missing a beat, Milne turned to Nina and asked, "Will there be any rebuttal?" She had a quick whispered conference with Winston and Genevieve at the counsel table. "No, Your Honor."

"The cross-complainants rest?" Milne said with a wide smile. He must be happy as hell at this sudden termination.

"That's correct, Your Honor. Subject to admission of the exhibits marked for identification."

"All right." He turned to the jury and said, "The evidence portion of the trial is over. We are going to excuse you a bit early this afternoon, ladies and gentlemen. I'm sure you won't mind. Tomorrow we will return for closing arguments." He repeated his daily cautions that they not talk to each other or anyone else about the case. Broad smiles and nods. Deputy Kimura led them out.

Another half hour of getting the exhibits admitted and ordered, and the court day was over.

"We got killed at the end, but overall made some points, Nina," said Winston, as they left the building that afternoon. He stopped to grin for a flashbulb. "My God, I can't believe it's finally coming to an end."

"You were great, Winston, just great," said Nina, meaning it. He had done a beautiful job with his witnesses.

"Do you realize we'll have a verdict soon? Incredible," Winston went on, still hyped from his day in court.

"I think we've got at least five definites on the jury," said Genevieve, trotting alongside as they headed for the cars. "If you want, I'll go over everything with you and explain why. At least two of those are potential leaders . . . that's one thing we didn't really push hard enough during the *voir dire*. We didn't really cultivate a leader."

"Don't fret, Genevieve. And if you don't mind, I think we'll skip the analysis. I need to get home and soak my ankle and fix dinner for Bob."

"But when are we going to work on Winston's closing arguments?" Genevieve asked. "Tonight?"

"That won't be necessary," said Nina. "We've gone over it. And I've made a decision. I'm doing the summation."

They had stopped by Winston's rental car. "Now wait a minute, we had this whole thing worked out," Winston said. "I thought we all agreed I should close."

"I know. I'm sorry." What could she tell him now to sweeten such a bitter pill? She had talked to him about making the closing argument because she had been intimidated. But she was the lead counsel. Ultimately, the responsibility rested on her shoulders. Lindy had given her the case. Nina had to be the ultimate word. She had to be the one to blow it, if that's what was going to happen. Not that she would tell him that.

"You're not taking this away from me," Winston said, starting to look angry.

"I think Winston's on a roll," Genevieve said. "He's got the experience."

"I'm sorry," Nina repeated. "What matters is my case."

Winston slammed his briefcase down on the hood. "Our case!" he roared. "Ours! We sweat equal buckets of blood over this. You're not going to step in here and ruin everything now!"

"You don't think I can handle it?" asked Nina. The two attorneys stood face-to-face, unconsciously squaring off like fighters in the ring.

"It's arrogant!" said Winston. "You think you can get up there, flip your long hair, put a tear in your eye and convince that jury to hand Lindy millions of dollars? How many cases like this have you won? Zero! I've done dozens and won dozens! I can argue circles around you. . . ."

Genevieve stepped smoothly in front of Winston.

"Listen. You're going to have to compromise on this," she said to Nina. "He's right. He's at his peak. He knows what will sway that jury. He has a better chance to crack . . . the hard nuts, if there are any."

"No," said Nina. And this time, she didn't say she was sorry. What would be the point?

"How about if he does half the argument, and you finish it off?"

"Finish it off is right!" said Winston.

"Milne won't let us trade off in the final argument," said Nina.

Winston turned and stalked around the car. He opened the door and sat staring straight ahead, furious.

"Let's talk some more tonight. I'll call you," Genevieve said, putting her hand on Nina's arm.

"I have to work on this my own way."

"You act like you've lost all faith in us," said Genevieve. "Have you?"

"Not at all. I'm sorry to make this change at such a late date. It's nothing against Winston. It's just . . . I'm the lead counsel. I can prepare better alone." In her backyard, where she could address the trees without manipulating, sentimentalizing, influencing . . . the final argument would be hers.

"Nina, be careful about getting stuck with a decision you might regret. Shouldn't you think this over?"

"Okay, say what's on your mind, Genevieve," Nina said. "Don't you think I can do it? Is Winston smarter, or a better lawyer? Is that what you're thinking?" She said it loud so Winston could hear. A few cars over, several people had angled their ears her way.

Genevieve studied her for a moment, then relented, apparently deciding this was one argument she could not win. "I know you won't fuck up, Nina," Genevieve said. "I just know you won't. None of us can afford that." Unintentionally leaving a sharp air of doubt behind to erode Nina's confidence, she got into the car and Winston pulled out.

22

IN THE COURTROOM HUSH, NINA could almost pretend she was in her backyard where she had practiced her summation yesterday afternoon, face-to-face with the dark bark of a tree. All those moon faces out there were pinecones. Better to think of things that way than the other way, which was to admit the hundred judges to her performance. The only ones that counted were the faces of her jury, and those she smiled at before addressing.

She began at the beginning. She laid it out the way she saw it, and a couple of the jurors never started listening, but most of them made the valiant effort to follow. She felt intimate with them. She had wanted only one thing in the last weeks, and that was to connect to each one of them. They weren't friends; they were closer than that now, and she believed some of them felt the same proprietary interest in her. She hoped so.

"And then Mike moved on." Nina paced once across the front of the jury box, and then back to the other end, with her head lowered. She didn't have the art to convey the devastation encapsulated in those words, all she could do was offer this silent prayerful moment to honor Lindy's suffering.

"But Lindy had nothing to worry about, isn't that so?" she continued, lifting her head to search the jurors, one by one. Mrs. Lim's head was cocked her way.

"Right here in court, we all heard him, Mike said she had nothing to worry about. He would 'take care' of Lindy for life.

"He said that. He felt some duty to take care of her, protect her, for the rest of her life. And how did he do that? You heard. He evicted her, fired her, and made sure his name was on every stick of property. Then he flung in her face a thirteen-year-old agreement that she'd signed when the business was worthless on the premise that he would marry her."

She paused. "The judge will read you a legal instruction, because it may be applicable in this case. It sounds so simple. And it is simple. A promise, in this case, made in writing by Lindy to give it all away—in consideration of marriage—in this case, in return for Mike's finally marrying her—is invalidated when there is no marriage.

"And that makes the so-called separate property agreement invalid!"

She looked directly at Cliff Wright. He yawned.

"Yes, it was in writing. But that piece of paper she signed without full knowledge of its contents was not notarized. No lawyer discussed or explained it to her at the time. That grotesque and unfair document did not come about through agreement. No reasonable person can think that under those circumstances she made an informed decision. It's bogus, made in bad faith, and doesn't meet reasonable requirements to be legally binding. You should disregard it."

She went on to Lindy's strong area, the implied contract argument, Lindy's twenty years of working alongside Mike. She knew her summation so well that, in the pauses between sentences, she found time to reflect: on the faces of the jurors, intent, bored, tired, eager; on the long days of testimony that had brought them to this point; and on Lindy herself.

She was recounting Lindy's life, trying to make the jury fully appreciate the loving dedication of this thin, wan woman on whom they must pass judgment. She spoke of the children Mike and Lindy never had, and said that the business, like a child, had belonged to both of them, but unlike a child could be split down the middle. And Lindy deserved half.

"It's in your hands," she said finally. "Thank you."

Nina sat down, feeling drained. She had given Lindy her best.

Riesner, smiling and confident, matter-of-fact, kept his summation even more succinct, introducing Mike's position with the plainest possible language to give the jury the impression that the decision they were faced with was easy.

"This is a simple situation," he said, as he came to the finish. "Lindy and Mike break up. But Lindy's now stuck with this agreement they made years ago. She's got a real incentive to 'forget' about it, or dispute its contents. There's money there for the taking, she figures, and by golly, she wants some of it. She's got to do something, so she hires a team of fancy lawyers to tell you it's not a legitimate agreement.

"But it's right here in writing, ladies and gentlemen. They agreed not to commingle assets. They agreed to keep separate accounts. The business, the properties, those stayed in Mike's name because they belonged entirely to him. That was the expectation, the agreement. Just so that there would be no misunderstanding, they had a document drafted to make sure they agreed, which they both signed.

"That was the deal. The deal," he repeated. "Plain and simple. Black and white. In writing. Read the exhibits. And don't let greed win out this time."

His last words sat there, gathering energy. Nina heard the shuffling and whispering start up behind her. Wanting to do something to soften the bite of these words, she touched Lindy's wrist, even though she knew it wouldn't help.

Only two things remained: to instruct the jury, and to set them loose.

The American jury system suffered from one indefensible flaw—the jury had to sit through the whole trial without knowing the legal framework on which the facts were supposed to hang. How they could, in the end, set aside whatever impromptu conceptual framework they had been using to adopt a new one, no one knew.

Worse, the legal instructions were tedious, contradictory, and sometimes even mysterious.

To Nina, the instructions sounded laughably simplistic. Thousands of subtle distinctions, derived from thousands of cases over hundreds of years, flowed from each statement Milne made now, and the jury would hear only the one-syllable version.

The jury looked at Judge Milne, who adjusted his reading glasses. They seemed like a whole different group from the tentative individuals who had been sworn in at the beginning; a new collective had been born. They even dressed more homogeneously. Mrs. Lim's stiff jackets had disappeared sometime during the trial, along with Kevin Dowd's knit golf shirts and Maribel Grzegorek's hair spray.

Today they had dressed up. They seemed self-conscious, dignified, impressive. Nina wondered if her impression was the result of the exaggerated part they played in her life right now. But no, she had seen it in other trials in which she had sat in the audience, this reassuring aura of decency that came upon the people about to render a verdict. They represented the American public, and they knew it.

In the jury room, would they remain as impassive, as decent? She sat straight-backed with Lindy, Winston, and Genevieve at her table, and she tried to project that same decent aura.

Milne took a sip of water and wet his lips. In a measured tone, he said, "It is now my duty to instruct you on the law that applies to this case. It is your duty to follow the law."

He cleared his throat before resuming. "As jurors it is your duty to determine the effect and value of the evidence and to decide all questions of fact. You must not be influenced by sympathy, prejudice, or passion."

He went on, explaining that the burden of proof was upon Lindy as the party bringing the action. He advised the jury that they must find that a preponderance of the evidence supported one side or the other.

During all this, he read from form jury instructions as modified in his conferences with the lawyers. Not one unplanned word could be spoken, or the verdict might be overturned on appeal. The instructions were written in the plainest English possible, but many of the words and concepts were still new to the jurors and looks of incomprehension flitted across their faces as Milne went on in a voice that never varied and never emphasized one instruction over another.

"In an implied-in-law contract, or quasi-contract as it is sometimes called, a duty or obligation is created by law for reasons of fairness or justice. Such duty or obligation is not based upon the express or apparent intention of the parties.

"A contract may be oral. An oral contract is as valid and enforceable as a written contract."

And now Milne came to a couple of special instructions. Riesner had fought for the first one, a civil statute which could be interpreted to mean that Lindy couldn't recover anything just because Mike had promised to marry her and broken that promise:

"No cause of action arises for breach of promise of marriage," Milne went on with his evenhanded delivery.

Would the jurors think Lindy's whole case revolved around that? They might. Nina shuddered and glanced at them, reading nothing from their expressions.

Then it was Lindy's turn. Milne moved along to the hoary old statute Nina had dug up and worked hard to get into the instructions, section 1590 of the Civil Code. It had been enacted in courtlier times, to assure the return of marital dowries after broken engagements. Milne had seen that it could apply and overruled Riesner's outraged objections.

"Where either party to a contemplated marriage in this state makes a gift of money or property to the other on the basis or assumption that the marriage will take place, in the event that the donee refuses to enter into the marriage as contemplated or that it is given up by mutual consent, the donor may recover such gift."

Now Riesner was wincing. Again, the jury would have to believe Lindy, not Mike or the written language of the separate property agreement. But if they felt Mike had dangled the carrot of marriage to get her to sign the agreement, then she had the right to take back her "dowry," namely the company and any other asset they shared.

Was the jury utterly mystified by all this talk of donees and donors? Were these people smart enough to reason their way through this?

Milne droned on about contracts at prodigious length before moving to the concluding instructions. "Each of you must decide the case for yourself, but should do so only after considering the views of each juror. You should not hesitate to change an opinion if you are convinced it is wrong. However, you should not be influenced to decide any question in a particular way simply because a majority of the jurors, or any of them, favor such a decision.

". . . Remember that you are not partisans or advocates in this matter. . . ."

Milne took a healthy swig of water this time. His vocabulary for ten days had consisted mainly of "overruled" and "sustained," so this lengthy speech was putting a strain on his vocal cords. Luckily, he was close to the end.

"When you retire, you shall select one of your number to act as foreperson. As soon as any nine or more jurors have agreed upon a verdict, have the verdict and answers signed and dated by your foreperson and return with them to this room."

Milne paused. The courtroom shook itself from its swoon. He put down the last paper, and said in a benign voice at odds with the robotic delivery of the previous two hours, "It being late in the day, you will return to court tomorrow at nine a. m. to begin your deliberations."

With nary a rustle, the twelve people chosen to shape the future of a number of other people in the courtroom filed out the door behind them, followed by the two alternates.

Nina put her arm around Lindy. "This is it," Genevieve said, her face pale.

The wait had begun.

BOOK FOUR
VERDICTS

The first perversion of the truth effected by one of the individuals of the gathering is the starting point of the contagious suggestion.

Gustave le Bon

23

>CLICK<

Jury, Day One, Morning:

The seven men and seven women find seats, with the two alternates sitting away from the table. For about twenty minutes, they dither over a foreperson. Mrs. Lim gets strong backing from half. Clifford Wright emerges as the other possible leader. By the second vote, someone switches to Wright.

Cliff: You all know why we're here. We've listened to testimony for nearly ten days now, and we've had more than enough time to think, right?

A titter of agreement.

Cliff: And during our breaks, without doing anything the judge didn't want us to do, I know a few of us have felt each other out, just to get an idea of where we stand. This hasn't been easy, and I know a couple of times tempers have flared.

Man: I'll say.

Cliff: But we're in the home stretch, folks. Let's be smooth and focused. I think it's a good idea to take a straw vote right off the bat, see if by some miracle we're already in agreement.

Some murmurs of assent.

Man: The judge said we should talk about this first.

Woman: Yes, what if we get a verdict on the first vote? I don't think that's the way to do the job right.

Man: Why waste time if we don't have to? I knew how I would vote the minute those lawyers finished their opening statements.

Cliff: Even if we do have a majority this is not a vote that will count. We each get to have our say first, like the judge said.

They vote on slips of paper, anonymously. Clifford Wright reads off the answers one by one. Eight think Lindy Markov should win. Four oppose her claim.

Wright: Well, now, we've almost got a majority. You all remember, we only need nine on this civil case.

Man: So the gals went with hearts, not brains.

Woman: And most of the men were too stupid to use either one.

Wright: Let's not bicker, folks.

Man: It's more fun to think of this as the war between men and women. It kind of encapsulates all the issues. Romantic fancies and the greed of a woman . . .

Woman: Betrayal, power, and the ego of a man. Only this time, the women are winning for a change!

Wright: Let's organize ourselves. Our next step seems to be to go around the room, give people a chance to say a little about who they are and why they're thinking a certain way. We'll go clockwise for discussions. That puts you first, Mr. Binkley. Is everyone okay with first names? I'm terrible with names.

Most agree to first names.

Bob Binkley: I'm a history teacher over at the college. Thirty-two years old and feel every minute of it. Not married and nobody in the picture at the moment. Don't get too worked up if you notice I have trouble breathing sometimes. That's just a touch of asthma.

Anyway, I've had about all I can take of this case. These two, they're greedheads, and the money they are fighting over is obscene. A life spent accumulating wealth for its own sake is wasted.

Man: I never got the idea money was their goal. It just came with their success.

Bob: Nobody on earth should have that kind of money and not spread it around.

Woman: Lindy Markov was involved in charity work. I've seen her name in the papers pushing various causes.

Bob: Good for her. But, considering there's still two hundred odd million being put back into manufacturing yet another device that pays homage to our cultural obsession with staying thin, I'm not impressed. These two fat cats could have settled this out of court so easily without wasting all our time.

Cliff: Can you tell us how you voted and why?

Bob: Oh, I don't think the woman should get anything. They weren't married. I picked Mike because the law's on his side, but I've got an even better idea. I think we ought to take their money and divide it between ourselves. Now that would be fair. Bet we'd make better use of it, too.

Several others get off on his idea and fantasize on the topic until Cliff Wright intervenes.

Cliff: Ignacio?

Ignacio Ybarra: I'm twenty-three and I work for the telephone company as a lineman. My wife died two years ago. I have a son who is three, and for my recreation, I do community theater.

When we talked at lunch the other day, I already said what I think. I think she should get something.

Cliff: So you think she's got a legitimate claim? Remember this is a legal case.

Ignacio: That's not so simple to say. I agree the law should guide us to do the right thing but if it doesn't give you a clear direction, you must look into your heart for what is right. I voted for Lindy.

Cliff: Care to say why?

Ignacio: I'm ready to hear the other people first.

Cliff: Okay. How about you, Maribel?

Maribel Grzegorek: I've lived up here twenty-two years. Came here to ski, and never left. I'm over forty and under seventy, not that that's anybody's beeswax. Used to work as a dealer in the casino. Now I cashier at the Mikasa outlet store.

My biggest problem with this case is that I just can't stomach Riesner.

He reminds me of this old cat I had, the meanest animal you

ever met. You know Mike Markov loses points in my book just for picking a lawyer like that. And that day Reilly tripped? I'd swear that lawyer put his foot in her way on purpose!

Man: Well, if he did she was asking for it.

Others interested in this line of discussion chime in. Speculations continue for a long time, then . . . .

Cliff: You know, Maribel, I didn't like that lawyer either. And it's so easy to be influenced by those feelings, isn't it? But I know when it comes time to decide, I've got to put that feeling aside, and really use my head. Now, I can tell you're a smart woman who can tell the difference between what you feel and real evidence. . . .

Woman: You know what struck me about Reilly? She looked funny wearing all those pale colors, kind of unprofessional. . . .

Man: Don't you remember all the noise when Marcia Clark wore a light-colored suit during the Simpson criminal trial? They do it so we'll like them better.

Woman: (laughing) What baloney!

They discuss the lawyers' clothes.

Cliff: Let's go back to Maribel, okay? What about Lindy's claim?

Maribel: You know, I'm thinking about the real evidence, don't you worry. But I have to say, where do you think Mike Markov would be today without Lindy? Coaching kids at the YMCA, if he was lucky. She had all the imagination and drive. He's an old fighter, a loser by the time she met him. He was rollin' downhill. Now, here she came along with all this perked-up energy to pull him up with her. She was his ticket to a better life. But, let's face it. The law's not always fair. I remember once this gal I knew—

Cliff: So you think the law doesn't really support her claim; but you feel she should get something.

Maribel: Well, I do feel that, on the other hand, we do have to think about the law.

Cliff: Sonny?

Sonny Ball: Pass.

Cliff: *(pause)* Okay, Sonny. We'll move on for now. But at some point, I hope you'll want to share your thoughts with us. Courtney?

Courtney Poole: Wait, I want to say some more about that lawyer, Ms. Reilly. Can I do that?

Cliff: Let's try to stay on the point. . . .

Mrs. Lim: I think Courtney should say what she wants to say . . .

Courtney: Because I thought she really made sense when she said, why should Mrs. Markov come away with nothing, not even a toothbrush? I mean, probably she took her toothbrush, but it sounded to me like she's the one who picked everything in that house. He had no interest. And then, he turned around and kicked her out.

Bob: Well, but remember, they were not legally married. Legally, the house was in his name.

Cliff: Could we hold off on discussion until we finish going around the room? We're almost done here. What are your thoughts, Kevin?

Courtney: Excuse me, but I'm not finished.

Cliff: Sorry. Please go on.

Courtney: It's not like she's going to go out and get a job easy. She's really old. Also, did you notice how she always defended him? She still loves him, even after all he's done to her. I guess he owes her something probably.

On the other hand, does she have any legal rights? How can we judge what they agreed on? We don't get to go in the bedroom, or the church with them. We saw them in court, where they both fibbed and forgot things. You can never really know what goes on between two people. So I have a lot of doubts.

By the way, I'm twenty-two and I'm living with my mom at the Keys while I go to the University in Reno. I'm a psychology major and boy, I am learning a lot here already.

Bob: Yeah, here you are in a locked room with a buncha loonies!

Maribel: Hey, people! Remember that! Bob Binkley openly admits to being loony.

Laughter. They adjourn for a fifteen minute break. Takes them several minutes to get back to their chairs.

Cliff: Kevin, I believe you're next.

Kevin Dowd: I have to say something about what Bob said first because I think we have a basic difference. In my opinion, Lindy and Mike Markov owe the world nothing. It's every man for himself out there, and you have to work to survive. If you fall and you can't get up, tough. They earned what they have. They should decide how to spend it without being under constant attack by spineless punks.

Now, I know something about this situation. Not to put too fine a point on it, I'm a wealthy man. And I'll never say a thing against the ladies, God bless 'em. Where would we be without them? She helped him in a lot of ways, no doubt about that.

But the fact is, and here's where I do agree with Bob, she was an employee of the corporation. She received a salary. And the fact is, she was Mike Markov's lover. But that doesn't make her his wife. And it doesn't entitle her to any of his hard-earned money.

Cliff: What about you, Kris? What do you say?

Kris Schmidt: I'm a housewife with two kids, and I should be at home right now. My kids need me, especially in the afternoon to help them with their homework. These people's problems are pretty darn far-removed from Joe's and mine. He repairs boats, and does dry-dock work at the marina. We scrape by. What's amazing to us is that there are people like the Markovs—I mean, their biggest worry has to be which yacht to take out today.

I just wish I could say I knew the right thing to do so we could all get out of here. Some of the legal stuff really goes over my head. The other night Joe and I were talking . . . we didn't talk about the case, of course. I know what the judge said. But we did talk about this kind of situation in general. Joe says that women almost never get any money out of these palimony cases. I thought that was strange, I mean why not, if there's plenty to go around.

Then I remembered how hard it is for me to wring a dime out

of Joe for clothes for the kids, a night at the movies, anything. I think men are fighting a losing battle to keep women under their thumbs.

By the way, you know where that expression came from? A man used to be able to whip his wife with a stick no thicker than his thumb. That was perfectly legal.

I guess there's no reason she should go off poor when Mike Markov could buy all of us, except maybe Kevin here, a few hundred times over. You notice the way he said he'd take care of her? He'd like that. He'd like her to come begging to him for the rest of her life. That's pretty pathetic.

Cliff: Grace?

Grace Whipple: I'm fifty-four, divorced and taking care of a grown child who has some disabilities. Like Kevin, I also think I know something about this situation, but in my case it's not because I'm rolling in the dough.

It takes a helluva lot of character to stick by someone who needs you. It's an underrated virtue to be loyal. Not that she should be rewarded for her love, but maybe she should have some kind of compensation for giving so much of herself, so much of her life, to these enterprises that totally benefited Mike Markov. She really built something out of not much.

She's close to my age. I like to think I've got a lot of years left to live. If she goes away broke, she's got to start all over. Just imagine a woman like her out there applying for jobs. Nobody's gonna want her. It's not like it's going to be a hardship for him to give up a few of those millions.

Cliff: Frank.

Frank Lister: I'm a retired biologist. I've been involved lately in organizing an organic food co-op. In my opinion, you have to reduce the issues here to basics. What Mike Markov is doing is simple mating behavior, finding a younger mate now that his partner is past childbearing age. Our purpose here is to procreate. We have that in common with almost any animal.

Cliff: Frank, what about your vote?

Frank: The most rational approach is to look to the law. In this

case, I don't think there's any question. She shouldn't get anything.
The law doesn't support it.

Cliff: Um, Diane?

Diane Miklos: I'm thirty-nine and I'm a professional climber.
And I . . .

Bob: Somebody pays you to climb?

Diane: I raise money from sponsors, like outdoor clothing
stores, camping gear manufacturers. Then I take the gear with me
and photograph it while I'm climbing. They use the photos in their
ads. I do slide shows and get people to contribute. My goal is to be
the oldest woman to climb the seven summits, which are the seven
highest peaks. So far, I've done three.

Woman: (very softly) Better move fast Di, because if you're
thirty-nine I'm the queen of Sheba.

Diane: What we have here is a typical situation. Like that black
lawyer, Reynolds, kept saying, "He's a chiseler." That bastard Mike
oppressed Lindy Markov for years. First, he chained her to him.
Then, when he got what he wanted out of her, he dumped her.

She should have protected herself better. She counted on him to
take care of her and that was her big mistake. That leaves us to go in
and even things up for her.

Cliff: Susan?

Mrs. Lim: Please, If you don't mind, I prefer Mrs. Lim.

Cliff: Go ahead, Mrs. Lim.

Mrs. Lim: My business is selling houses. I'm a real-estate broker
in addition to a realtor. Married to Mr. Lim for twenty-three years,
and I have two grown children.

I voted for Lindy Markov. You know, when you're listening
carefully, you can't help noticing how people feel up there when they
are testifying. I saw her cry. I saw Mike Markov suffering, too. But
what we need to look at in a case like this is very simple. We examine
the evidence. The judge told us to figure out the "effect and value of
the evidence," and to decide questions of fact, so that's what we
should do.

Bob: If you look at the evidence, how can you in good conscience vote in her favor? What about the agreement?

Mrs. Lim: That's a good example. Not all the evidence can be taken at face value. Remember in the instructions that a valid contract requires a lawful objective and sufficient consideration. The consideration must have some value. They had no money, nothing, then. She was given nothing in return for signing away all her rights for eternity.

Diane: Why would she sign a paper like that anyway unless he forced her somehow or promised her something? It doesn't make sense.

Frank: She felt he was losing interest in her. She held on as hard as she could. See a woman alone in this society is going to suffer. They're going to be poorer. They lose all prestige. Doesn't mean he forced her.

Diane: That's just ridiculous and insulting. She may have been stupid to sign, but let me remind you, she said he promised to marry her if she signed. Since he didn't marry her, its unenforceable. Guess that means she deserves at least some of their company.

Kevin: Even if you believe she told the truth, and even if you believe that agreement wasn't valid, it laid out the terms for both to see. How can she claim she didn't know that was their understanding if she signed that paper?

Diane: She signed to help him deal with his insecurities. Just like every good woman since time began, she bent over backward to support someone weaker. She never took it seriously. Why should she? There was no money involved at that point.

Cliff: Sonny? Got anything to add?

Sonny: No. Let's just get this over with.

Cliff: Okay, then. That's all of us. I'll keep my spiel short, so we can move on to discussion. I'm forty-five. Married for twelve years, very recently separated, unfortunately. I consider myself to be a feminist. Most of you already know, I served in the state assembly a couple of years back. I'm campaign manager for a congressman at the moment, but I'm thinking about running again this November. I spent a few years in my twenties in law school, then worked as a paralegal and decided to go into politics instead and dropped out.

Bob: Everyone knows you don't need an education for that.

Everyone laughs.

Cliff: That's right. So believe me, I don't think I know more than anyone else here. We all heard the same evidence.

Like several of you, I found the arguments for Lindy's claim very persuasive. And I agree, there does seem to be plenty of money. If we were only interested in fairness, she should get something, for sure. I support a lot of liberal causes, including equal pay for women, and even poor old affirmative action.

But here, our focus has to be the law as it stands today, not how we want it to stand. And nowhere in California law is there financial provision for a woman who is not legally married to a man. There isn't even a reference to so-called palimony. The only exception might be on a local level, where what they call domestic partners are covered by insurers in San Francisco, and maybe some other cities.

Frank: How do you know that?

Cliff: I just knew, but to verify it, I checked some of my old books.

Mrs. Lim: Didn't the judge say not to do any research on our own?

Cliff: I looked it up before he gave us his instructions. And anyway, as I've said, I didn't find anything at all about palimony, which should tell you something about how off-the-wall her claim is.

Based on the law, in my opinion, we can't give her anything. I wish I could say different. But you know, Mike Markov said he would take care of her. He doesn't have to, under the law. But I believe he will.

Diane: What happens five years down the line when he's got a passel of kids and Lindy is just a grim memory?

Cliff: Well, you can hate men and never trust them. But I think most people try to live up to their obligations.

Diane: That's just bullshit! He'll toss a few coins at her and feel he's done his duty. No, it's up to us to force him to do the right thing.

Maribel: Well, you know Cliff's got a point there, and I have to admit I liked what Kevin said, too. We're supposed to follow the law. And just because the man has money, doesn't necessarily mean she should get some.

Diane: I don't believe this. You're going to pull a switcheroo, aren't you? Two minutes listening to the men, and you change your mind.

Maribel: I have a right to change my opinion after listening to other people speak. The judge said so.

Diane: Some women will do and say anything for a lick of male attention.

Maribel: Oh, what would you know about male attention? Didn't your mother ever tip you off about the connection between too much sun and wrinkles?

Cliff: Please, ladies, ladies.

Diane: Please, men, men. Quit calling us ladies.

Cliff: What would you prefer?

Maribel: "Lady" fits some of us here.

Cliff: Enough, people. Let's get back to work. I guess the next step is to work through the testimony and see if we can firm up our opinions, and do this quickly as possible. I know everyone is eager to do the parties in this case justice, and get out of here!

Now, before we move on, just to remind you all, our two alternate jurors are Patti Zobel and Damian Peck. They'll be listening in on our discussion here, but they don't participate. So let's give them a lot to think about.

Kevin: I got something on my mind right now.

Cliff: What's that, Kevin?

Kevin: How do they handle lunch around here? I'm starving.
>Click<

24

>CLICK<

Jury, Day One, Afternoon:

Wright: Let's get to work. Now who wants to go first?

Kevin: Who decided on lunch? Fast food gives me indigestion.

Bob: You certainly gave a good imitation of a man enjoying his meal.

Kevin: Look who's talkin'.

Maribel: You never eat anything, Cliff. We're all snacking like crazy here, then we scarf lunch. Wish I had your self-control.

Cliff: It's nothing to do with discipline. I just have some strict dietary requirements.

Frank: A vegetarian? That's the only way to go. Wish I could stick to it.

Cliff: Well, yes. Also, I have bad allergies.

Courtney: I can't eat garlic. Or if I do, you all better take ten steps back!

Cliff: This is more severe.

Courtney: What can't you eat?

Cliff: Fresh apples, if you can believe that. Now, here's something strange. That particular food allergy can be seasonal.

Frank: Are you serious? I've never heard of that.

Cliff: I've done a lot of research, believe me. When I eat uncooked apples my throat swells. I can't breathe. It could kill me.

Diane: Now there's a fluky way to go. Choked to death on an apple.

Frank: How about the normal allergies? Strawberries, peanuts, that kind of thing.

Cliff: Yeah, they are both on my list of no-nos.

Courtney: Is this like those people who die from bee stings?

Cliff: Same thing, yeah. I'm going to tell whoever it is that arranges our lunches about a good lunch place that uses lots of fresh food and vegetables, if we get stuck here for much longer. Everyone like Chinese?

Some grumble. Most do.

Frank: Are you kidding? Those places load the food with msg, all kinds of weird additives.

Cliff: Not this place. Trust me. Now, let's get back to the issues. I'll start off the discussion with a few thoughts, and you all just jump in when you're ready.

Diane: *(low)* Yeah, tell us what to think about it, Cliff.

Cliff: Oh, and let me remind everyone, let's focus on the case. Let's not get personal. We've just got to look at the facts and come to a good decision here. Maybe today!

In spite of my telling you all how I voted on the first ballot, I see my role here as your leader as impartial. I know a lot of us support Lindy's claims. For the first time in her life, she's going to have to go it on her own. Her lover of many years has left her. Her job is over. There's a lot there to pity. So I really understand how so many of us have taken her side. But maybe before we throw millions of dollars her way, we should be sure we know who she is and why she is suing Mike Markov.

Here we have, in my view, a very competent woman, very on the ball. She's not going to lie down in a ditch and start living out of shopping carts. She's got rich friends, a well-established network. So it's not like we're going to leave the woman destitute if we decide her claim is not legitimate.

Also, while she's suing this guy, she defends him at every turn.

Why? She still loves him. Now, here's another way to think about that. Isn't it possible this lawsuit is not really about money, it's about revenge?

Frank: Pretty likely. We're all victims to the whims of our emotions. She's mad and she's getting even.

Cliff: Also, there's her testimony. Let's look at that. How did you all feel about that? We've been told that an oral contract is as good as a written one. Was she telling the truth when she said they agreed to share everything?

Bob: She lies through her teeth. She lies like a rug.

Frank: As my first wife would say, she lies like a bandit. That suits the occasion.

Cliff: You say she lied. How? Ladies? Pardon me, Diane. Anyone else agree?

Maribel: Well, I think she fibbed when she said she wanted to be married to Mike Markov all along. She never even checked to see if her divorce was final. That's pretty basic.

Grace: She may have twisted the truth a little when she said she thought he would marry her. He never said he would. She knew what the deal was going in, and she accepted his terms because she had no choice.

Kevin: She lied about the property agreement. Said he promised to marry her then. I don't buy that. Here was a guy who had a bitter divorce that ruined him once. By God, he was not getting into that situation again. She lied about her divorce.

Bob: She lied to get the money, that's what it comes down to.

Cliff: She went for the money.

Kevin: That's obvious. As long as Lindy lived with Mike Markov, she lived the high life. She's lost her man but she's damned if she'll lose all the good things she's used to.

Maribel: Hey, you can't blame her for trying.

Bob: But she knew the score going in. Even you've got to see that, Diane, unless you think she's a total idiot.

Diane: Much as it gripes me, I have to admit to a sneaky suspicion she knew goddamned good and well he would never marry her. The minute he showed up with that paper, she should have said "Bye-bye, you stingy cheapskate."

Grace: But she never expected this! She never expected him to dump her for a younger woman!

Maribel: Then she is a total idiot.

Grace: What I mean is, she really didn't see things the same as him. You know what I mean? When he said they were in it together, for life, she believed him. He just said it to get what he wanted out of her, but she never saw that.

Ignacio: He made promises, I believe that.

Cliff: But is a promise the same thing as a legal contract?

Bob: Bingo. It's not.

Mrs. Lim: I think we all take being on a jury very seriously. We want to do the right thing. The real problem is, our quest is so abstract. Put a dollar figure on all the promises someone has made you. That's hard to do.

Diane: This system is really fucked. This woman has a right to something from him, but what she really deserves is his loyalty and his love and nothing we do is going to give her that.

Kevin: You sound like that sassy, sly little thing, her lawyer. The next thing you'll say is, the money is meaningless. Therefore, let's toss a few mil her way.

Diane: Not at all. But let's put this in perspective. He's got dough to blow, and he owes her.

Kevin: That kind of thinking really steams me. Just because there's plenty, she should get some? That's so specious. Why, that makes us no better than a common mugger on the street.

Bob: Our job is to put a stop to these crazy claims the system is doling out. I'm not gonna be one of those jurors who forks over millions to someone just because there's money out there.

Diane: Here's something else everyone should consider. Those lawyers presenting the case. They are the hired help. They will say anything they can get away with to get you to believe them.

Discussion follows about the lawyers being in it for the money.

Wright: Let's move back to the issues. Anyone?

Frank: Back to the ersatz marriage in the church. Remember, at that point they had barely met. They were heavy into the courtship phase. So he got down on bended knee with her. Like kids, they played at getting married. He was wooing her.

Ignacio: Yes, but why do it? Why make this kind of spiritual promise at all?

Frank: That's simple. He did it to get her into his bed. Actions speak louder than words, you know. Let's get this through our thick skulls. He never married her. End of discussion.

Cliff: So we're agreed she's a liar, and . . .

Mrs. Lim: You know, that's awfully harsh, calling her that. And I wonder if it isn't a deliberate attempt to make us forget the evidence in this case, using inflammatory words that make us dislike her.

Cliff: I apologize for using the word if it offends. And flattered you imply I'm such a master manipulator I can make anybody do anything. But point taken. We'll watch how we characterize the plaintiff. . . .

Diane: *(very quietly)* Cliffy, I think you know a whole lot about manipulating people, don't you?

Kevin: I don't recall any evidence in her favor. What I remember were the four points of evidence his attorney made. They weren't married. She was employed by the company. All the paperwork supports his claim that he's sole owner of the business. And she agreed in writing to keep their property separate.

Courtney: He wanted a wife but I think he was afraid of the responsibility.

For a few moments, there's silence.

Cliff: You're awfully quiet over there. Sonny, do you have anything to contribute to this discussion?

Sonny: It's almost five. Let's vote.

They vote again. It's seven to five in favor of Lindy Markov. Movement, as the chairs are pushed back. Sounds of people milling around.

Diane: You did it, didn't you? Changed your vote.

Maribel: Diane, have a heart. I don't have any sponsors. I have a job. And seven bucks a day for jury duty is not going to keep me in panty hose.

Diane: Your employer should pay you for the days you miss.

Maribel: Oh, they will. But you know what? Out of sight, out of mind. I don't want my replacement to become a permanent fixture.

Diane: What about Lindy? You must have thought she had a case. You voted for her once.

Maribel: I like her. I wish her well. But she lied up there, and I can't read her mind. I don't know what the facts are in this case, but I do know, I feel like I'm on a catamaran, jumping from one side to the other. It was that way all through the trial. I've totally lost my balance. I don't know what to think.

Diane: This process is supposed to help you come to your own conclusions. . . .

Maribel: I guess it has. I've concluded it's not going to get any clearer, even if I listen to a hundred people arguing.

Diane: We can help you think this through. Just give us a chance. Keep an open mind. . . .

Maribel: Let's console ourselves with the idea that, in the end, if she loses, like Kris said, she's still riding around in a better boat than me.

Courtney: *(whispering)* Kevin! Get your hand off my knee. I mean it. Right now.

Kevin: *(also whispering)* I've seen the way you look at me.

Ignacio: You okay, Courtney?

Courtney: I . . . I am now.

Ignacio: Would you mind changing seats? Bob won't mind.

Courtney: Good idea.

Movement.

Bob: Heard you were hard up for company, Kev. Or maybe it's your deodorant.

Kevin: So the young buck's got some spirit in him after all.

A few more comments, a few complaints about having to return for another day, and they adjourn.

>Click<

25

>CLICK<

Jury, Day Two, Morning:

Mrs. Lim: I thought a lot last night. It seems to me we talked all day yesterday about the superficial evidence. What about the deep thing that kept this couple celebrating anniversaries for twenty years?

Bob: And off we go for another grand tour on the *Love Boat*.

Mrs. Lim: They shared family. Remember his niece called her 'aunt.' They had a home, a life, a business together. They relied on each other to make big decisions. They presented themselves as husband and wife.

Maribel: Which is more than you can say for some married people.

Mrs. Lim: So why wouldn't she believe what he told her and follow his advice? Why shouldn't she compromise sometimes, bend to him. She loved him, thought they would be together for life, and in an old-fashioned manner, showed her respect for him as a man by letting him have things his way.

Papers shuffle.

These two people were very close on every level. They understood each other very well. After all those years living together as though they were legally bound, we now know she was lulled into a false sense of security, yes. But even he said he always promised her he would take care of her. Because she loved and trusted him, she believed him. I believe he meant those words when he spoke them, too. You see? They had agreements, and they were very explicit agreements, mutually understood.

Grace: They understood each other, that's right.

Courtney: You're saying they really had a marriage of true minds.

Mrs. Lim: Yes.

Ignacio: That looks on tempests and is never shaken.

Courtney: You like Shakespeare?

Ignacio: It was my mother's favorite sonnet.

Kris: Hello? *(She raps on the table.)* Can we save the romance for Saturday night?

Mrs. Lim: And how about this? See, it says right here. "The law protects a partner in business against someone who breaks his word. They should each take their share." She was an equal partner. They had desks right by each other. He broke many promises. The law should protect her.

Cliff: What's that you're reading?

Mrs. Lim: My notes from the trial.

Cliff: I don't think that was testimony, was it? That sounds like one of those lawyers during the arguments.

Bob: And I thought we agreed the lawyers are as full of self-interest as the parties in this conflict, so beware.

Cliff: I believe we are supposed to ask the judge to have anything read back from the transcript.

Kris: Oh, let's not do that. Then we go back into the court, and come back here. That'll take forever.

Cliff: We should not rely on our memories if we're not sure about something.

Mrs. Lim: Listen, Mr. Wright, my notes are accurate! Are you saying I made this up?

Cliff: Mrs. Lim, no need to get so emotional. Of course your notes are not intentionally wrong. Anyway, we've gotten way off the track here. Where's the piece of paper that shows they had a marriage? They didn't, and all the talk about how they lived is beside the point.

Mrs. Lim: I completely disagree.

Cliff: Well, if you insist, I'll call the bailiff. Let's see if the reporter can read that part of the statement back to us. Oh, and while we're at it, let's ask for a little clarification on mutual consent. Mrs. Lim said she wasn't sure they were agreeing to the same thing. . . .

Mrs. Lim: No, Mr. Wright. I said I was sure they *were* agreeing.

Bob: You know, Mrs. Lim, it strikes me you are taking all of this very hard. Why beat yourself up about Lindy Markov? What's in it for you?

Mrs. Lim: That kind of comment doesn't merit an answer.
Shuffling noises.

Kris: Do we have to go do this? Can't we just vote again?
They leave the room for a half hour. Before they return, they break.

Cliff: I'm sure we all feel clearer now that we've heard the transcript read back.

Diane: As if it's suddenly clearer the second time!

Cliff: Apparently, what Mrs. Lim was reading came from Nina Reilly's opening statement, and her words were almost, but not entirely accurate, so I'm glad we got that figured out. Now, let's remember the judge said that things said by the lawyers are not evidence unless they are supported by other evidence. We can't just assume they can prove what they say. . . .

Mrs. Lim: There was plenty of proof. Plenty. He made promises. He broke them. He pretends to forget about them. Isn't that convenient? You think he doesn't remember getting down on his bended knee and promising to love her forever in that church? You think he doesn't remember they started off sharing everything or that he introduced her as his wife a million times? He's ashamed of himself, but he's set the wheels in motion and now he's too stubborn to backtrack.

Diane: It's true. He really wiggled up there.

Grace: He looks bad in general. Did you see the picture in the papers this morning of him outside the courthouse?

Diane: It's hard to believe he ever punched his way out of a paper bag.

Cliff: I have to remind you, we're not supposed to be reading the papers. The judge said . . .

Grace: We just looked at the pictures, right Diane?

Diane: Who has time to read that drivel? I've got better things to do. I'm in training for Mt. McKinley. Three hours a day on the stair-climber, two on a bike, running . . .

Grace: I think he has a lot to hide. He knows he done her wrong. He must just hate himself.

Courtney: I didn't trust him. All those years he introduced her as his wife. Every time it was a lie, and that's according to his own viewpoint!

They talk about the video in court that showed him doing just that, and how Mike Markov did not seem surprised to see it.

Ignacio: I believe he knew in his heart he was a married man. But the business—well, the lawyer referred to it as 'their child.' It's like a custody battle. He'll say anything to stay in control of that.

Kevin: All of that's completely beside the point. Doesn't matter if he lied. Doesn't matter if he's a cad. We're here because Lindy Markov wants his money. And I have yet to hear the reason we ought to give it to her, besides that he gave her kisses and hugs and said a few things over the years he didn't mean and has lived to regret.

Bob: I resent all this valuable time spent over an issue that's just . . . frivolous! Has anyone considered how much both of those rich people are paying all those lawyers? Why, there were times during this trial when there were four or five people sitting at the table on each side. How much do lawyers make? A couple hundred thousand a year? That's practically a million bucks right there, because it probably took them minimum a year to prepare for this trial. Plus, there's the judge, the reporter, the court clerk . . . we pay for them out of our taxes!

Maribel: And let us not forget the little people.

Bob: That's right. We're putting in a whole lot of sweat equity here. And what are we getting out of it?

Kevin: Why, Bob. We have the sweet satisfaction of being an integral part of justice in America.

They laugh.

Cliff: Let's get back to our earlier discussion. We spent a lot of time discussing Mike Markov's testimony. But whether he lied is not the issue. The issue is, does Lindy have a leg to stand on?

Diane: You know, I just can't let this go by. Every time you refer to Mike, you call him Mike Markov. Every time you refer to her, you just call her Lindy. Has everyone else noticed that?

Bob: What difference does it make?

Diane: He sounds more important.

Cliff: I'm sorry, Diane. I really am. If I did that, it was unconscious.

Diane: The worst part of it is, I believe you. You are so unaware of the way you are stampeding this woman, and many of the women here right into dust.

Maribel: Will you please quit being my champion, Diane? I do not feel stampeded. You have such a nerve.

Kevin: Ladies, and Diane, I can see this is hard for you. You see a man who has tossed off a good woman. But where, oh, where is it written that he should pay for that for the rest of his life? They had a good run. Now it's over.

Frank: She needs to forget about him and move on.

Bob: I say we help her along by giving her a kick in the rear end.

Kris: You know what? I'd like to vote again.

Diane: You're giving up.

Kris: She's got her rich friends to bail her out. I need to get back to my kids, and in terms of the universe, who cares whether she walks away rich or poor. She'll toil along like the rest of us.

Diane: Is this the way it works? Somebody wants to go home, so we let Lindy Markov down?

Kris: Diane, I wish I was holier than thou. But I'm not. I'm just a person, trying to scrape by. And I do not have time for this.

Diane: You know what? Up to now I had a shred of faith in the jury system. People would ask me, shouldn't a smart judge be the one to decide? Why waste everyone's time? And I'd say, well, a jury of your peers is what stands between you and a bigot, or an ass-kissing politician, or a hard-line Gestapo judge, or . . .

Maribel: Well, that's a terrible thing to say about Judge Milne. . . .

Diane: God, this is just what I mean! I'm not talking about Judge Milne. I'm talking about a system that is as fair as it's possible to have. There isn't one better. And yet, here we are, letting these guys flirt and cajole and bully us into changing our position.

Maribel: Who's flirting? You just insult people left and right!

Kris: I don't let men bully me. I make up my own mind. You have a hard time accepting that another woman might not think the same way you do, Diane. But we all have life experience and brains, too.

And, put this in your pipe. He said he'd take care of her. He's got such a guilty conscience, that's obvious. So I believe he will. Like I said before, I'd rather she didn't have to beg, but I can see which way the wind is blowing here, and I'm willing to go with the flow because however it turns out, she's going to get something out of him, probably more than I'll ever see in my life. And if she has to beg, well, welcome to the real world, baby.

Diane: Kris, please. You said at the beginning she deserved something. Give this some more thought.

Kris: Didn't you hear me? I don't have any more time to spend on this woman's problems. I have my own. She's not going to jail for a crime she didn't commit or anything! This is just about money. This is not life or death.

Diane: I'm just asking you to take your time before deciding to change your vote.

Kris: Courtney's not the only one who knows something about psychology. I know a few things about your type.

Diane: Huh?

Kris: Yeah, the mountain climber mentality. These are people who are happiest when they are in extreme situations that demand all their attention. They're lousy at living every day lives. That's too boring. I think you'd like to drag this thing out. I think you're enjoying this. You need to get a life.

Diane: That's so unfair. I know how to make beds and do dishes, just like you!

Kris: Unlike Lindy. Can we please vote, now?

Cliff: It's almost lunchtime.

Kris: This shouldn't take long.

Frank: Chinese today?

Cliff: No, they had something else planned. But if we're here tomorrow . . .

Kris: Christ, I hope not.

Cliff: Okay, let's see where we stand.

Mrs. Lim: I would like to say something.

Cliff: And we all want to hear it. After we break for lunch. We've just got time for a vote.

They vote. It's split down the middle, six to six.

>Click<

26

>Click<

Jury, Day Two, Afternoon:

Cliff: I want to start off this afternoon saying I've considered what Diane said earlier, about my referring to Mike more deferentially. That's exactly the kind of thing that drives me nuts about other people, so it really hurt. So I really thought hard about ways I am influenced by own biases.

You know, I mentioned that I am recently separated. And I've searched my heart to see if that has had some impact on how strongly, since the beginning, I have favored Mike's case. I have to be honest with you: it does. I took that idea, that the business was their child, very much to heart.

I have a child, and I foresee that my wife and I will be engaged in a bitter battle for custody. I see that child will be hurt, no matter what I do, but I can't give her up. I will fight to the death for her. Just like Mike is fighting for his company. So I guess I understand. I see Lindy's ownership, in a way, but it can't be cut in half or it will be destroyed, you know, like in the Bible story where the real mother won't have the child cut into two pieces, but the false mother will. Their company will be terribly harmed, maybe irreparably, if Lindy is given a big chunk of their assets. He'll have to cut off an arm, and maybe a leg, and . . .

Diane: Oh, please! He might sell a bunch of buildings and machinery, if it comes to that. Since when does metal bleed?

Grace: Can you let him finish? I want to hear the rest.

Cliff: Thank you, Grace. Anyway, I guess what I'm saying is, it's right to remove yourself from personal considerations, even if it seems impossible. So I went through my whole chain of reasoning one more time . . .

Diane: Let me guess. Mike still wins!

Cliff: Well, yes. There just is not one iota of evidence to support Lindy's claim.

Diane: Figures.

Cliff: No written promises, no marriage certificate, no witnesses to direct promises. It just comes down to her word against his, as to an oral contract. How could Mike have made it any clearer that he did not wish to be married? I mean, they were together twenty years. Should he have written it in blood?

No, on the contrary, what I see is that she signed her name to an agreement that said they should separate their property. There were innuendoes made by Lindy's lawyers that he forced her to do that, using some nasty psychological pressure, but you know, he strikes me as a pretty straightforward person. What she saw was exactly what she got.

Mrs. Lim: Really? What about the fact that for most of those years, he presented her to the world as his wife, and then claimed he didn't? Doesn't that prove he's deceitful?

Frank: He did that out of consideration for her feelings. He wanted to keep her without compromising his own wishes. And as for saying he didn't recall, well, it's possible he forgot . . .

Diane: It's possible I'm a ring-tailed lemur, but I don't look like one or act like one. But then some people prefer their delusions . . .

Frank: Or his very normal sense of self-preservation kicked in.

Cliff: Anyway, I'm hoping we're all trying to vote the law, and not self-interest. Let's make sure in our minds we're being fair to the evidence. And in spite of how we mock the poor lawyers, they provide a necessary service. They must plow through a lot of garbage to pull out the stuff we need to hear to decide. I think they all presented good cases. It's just that Mike's was inherently, objectively better.

Courtney: How can you say that? Lindy's lawyers made as much sense as they did. Also, to me, Mr. Riesner and Ms. Casey had a little attitude, like, the decision's so obvious. Well, I don't think it's so obvious.

Diane: "Smug" is only one of many good words that describe those two.

Courtney: After all, it's up to us.

Grace: Cliff, going back to what you were saying, you got me thinking. I'm a very emotional person. I got all wrapped up in Lindy's problems, because that's the kind of person I am. I just can't leave a dead dog in the road, you know? I'm out of my car, finding a sack, burying the poor thing somewhere . . .

Cliff: You have a big heart, Grace. I'm sure we've all noticed that.

He asks about her child, and she talks for a long time about what it's like to be the sole caretaker for a handicapped adult. Many people sympathize with her. You can feel her relaxing, feeling better just to have some recognition for her difficulties. He suggests that after the trial is over, she call his office. He knows of some social service agencies that might be able to find relief for her. There's a fifteen minute break, and during the break, many people share their worries about how long they've been gone from their jobs and daily lives. Everyone except Frank drinks lots of coffee, and many are nibbling on snacks.

Cliff: Like Grace here, it's clear we all have so many important obligations that are falling by the wayside while we try to decide this thing. So let's try to be efficient. Let's try to come to some agreement here. The tide does seem to be moving toward Mike. I'm wondering what the rest of you die-hard Lindy fans need to be convinced.

Diane: *(laughing)* Well, well, well. No more beating around the bush. You think you've got it in the bag. You know, I have to admire you, Cliff. Here you are, and almost singlehandedly, with just the occasional, bumbling help of your male compadres, you're turning this group around to your point of view. I sure see why you've been successful in politics. Here's how it works, right? You target the weakest links and then you whittle away. . . .

Grace: Weakest link?

Diane: I have to wonder about this child of yours, Cliff, that came out of the blue this morning. You never once mentioned her before. Is she real or rhetorical?

Cliff: I've been experiencing a lot of personal pain, Diane. I don't enjoy talking about it. I'm sure you can understand that.

Diane: You didn't answer the question.

Grace: You see me as a weak link, Diane? Talk about a piece of work. You think a person has to be able to jump up a mountain on a pogo stick to prove their worth, but I see life very differently, lady. Strength is taking care of the people you love, forging lifelong ties, doing whatever you do well, and that includes laundry on a regular basis.

You know what I don't hear from you, Diane? I don't hear a word about your family.

Kris: You don't have kids, do you Diane? That would be so irresponsible.

Frank: No, people in a risky business like Diane's have to fight their basic instincts.

Kevin: Ten to one odds she never even married.

Grace: You're so pro-Lindy because you're enjoying all this. You haven't got much else going in your own life.

Diane: I do have family. And I have resolved my issues about what I do already, so please, how about the rest of you get over it, and get back to the case?

Now, Grace, you talked earlier about Lindy Markov's loyalty, about her deserving something in compensation. That isn't a legal argument, it's a moral one. The proper thing to do is not always the right thing. I think Ignacio said that, too.

Ignacio: Yes, I agree.

Diane: Married or not, explicit promises or not, doesn't she deserve some percentage, even a small one, of their total assets after twenty years? She doesn't even own her own home! He's out there living in a mansion with his new tootsie, and she's left with nothing.

Grace: Well, not everybody gets to own a house. I rent.

Bob: Me, too.

Diane: He violated her faith. He took a new partner, in essence. She never did.

Grace: I do think well of her for that. I do.

Kevin: We all do, I think. She's a personable girl, Lindy Markov. And she's been real successful. Don't you think we aren't giving her enough credit? She pulled herself up from nothing. If she did it once, she can do it again.

Diane: Why should she? Is Mike Markov going to do that? And aren't you admitting she was the driving force behind their business success?

Mrs. Lim: I want to say something, but first, I'm not comfortable with Diane characterizing this as a moral choice rather than a legal one. I believe Lindy and Mike had an oral contract, as valid and binding as anything written. I believe that business is, at minimum, half hers. It's not a matter of him giving her money. It's a matter of us insuring that she gets what is already hers.

I'm a businesswoman myself, and I can only marvel at their success. I'm envious, too, and I don't think I'm the only one here. But to be fair to this situation, I'm trying to put my petty side behind me and give this case the serious concern it deserves.

Grace: Well, we are all doing that.

Mrs. Lim: I hope we are all trying to do that, as best we can. Now, here's another point I wanted to make. Did anyone notice Lindy hardly paid attention when the receiver testified? Didn't seem to care about the numbers. Her eyes just glazed over.

Kevin: I thought we discussed this. She was getting her revenge by hitting Mike where he lives, in the pocketbook. The amount of damage probably doesn't matter too much.

Mrs. Lim: No. The amount is not important to her, but for another reason. She's suing on principle. We have to consider the principles here. She owns half that company. And even if what she really wants is Mike back, we can give her her share.

Grace: Whatever we decide, she loses. She'll never get him back, and dividing up the company's gonna kill anything they had going. Wouldn't it be nice if we could force Mike to go back to her? That's what she wants.

Courtney: I wanted to hate him but I never did. I just think what's happening between them is so tragic.

Cliff: Yes, it is sad. Maybe that's why we're having trouble ending this discussion and getting out of here. The money isn't really going to help her anyway.

Diane: Let's drop the melodrama. Nina Reilly said several times that the only compensation available in this case is financial. That's the way the law works.

Grace: I'm so tired of talking about this. It's hard to stay worked up about Lindy's problems after talking about them for nearly two days, although I've stuck to my original position because I definitely feel some sympathy.

Cliff: Remember the judge's instructions? You can't let sympathy influence you. As I said, that's been a problem for me, too.

Diane: We may be bored but we are right, Grace. That's worth a lot.

Grace: I don't know about that. Maybe Kevin's right, just because there's money, it doesn't mean she should have some.

Diane: It isn't just because there's money. It's because, as Mrs. Lim said just moments ago, that money belongs to both of them!

Kevin: Show us a paper, any paper, that proves it.

Cliff: Is everyone ready for a vote? It's four-fifteen, a good time to check out where we are.

Kris: Yes! Maybe we can tell the judge to convene everyone tomorrow morning. Maybe this time, we'll have a verdict!

They vote. It's five for Lindy, seven against. There's another hour of bickering but no change in the vote before they quit for the day.

>Click<

27

>CLICK<

Jury, Day Three, Morning:

Cliff: I have a good feeling about today! I bet we get to our verdict!

This has been really something. We started off eight to four in favor of Lindy Markov, and now we're seven to five against her claim. I have a feeling as we discuss the case and apply the hard test of reason, logic is telling people the law in this case should protect Mike Markov.

Diane: Not logic, Cliff. You.

Mrs. Lim: Once again, Mr. Wright, I must object to your language. You twist the truth by suggesting that those who do not agree with you are illogical. I've said all along, I'm looking at the evidence. I'm not being pushed around by my feelings either way.

Cliff: Mrs. Lim, is English your second language? I think you read nuances into very simple statements of mine that are not there.

To continue. Yesterday, Ignacio cornered me at the end of the day and asked if we couldn't discuss the church ceremony.

Ignacio: That day those two people knelt down before God and made their promises, that day they were married. They are married in the eyes of God.

Kris: Do they allow God in the courtroom these days? They don't let much else in.

Kevin: God or not, this is a legal case, Ignacio.

Ignacio: Of course.

Kevin: You have this picture in your mind of this woman in a wedding dress and this man in a tux going off to church one fine day. Here's the reality. One afternoon, maybe they have a couple of drinks. And he goes to the church to please her, and that night they hit the sack happy. If God was there, he was shaking his head in dismay.

Courtney: You are disgusting! I don't think it was that way at all.

Cliff: Now Courtney, no need to hurt Kevin's feelings. But you are awfully young, aren't you? You said yourself, you can't know what goes on between two people, didn't you?

Courtney: Yes, but . . .

Cliff: I see you have youthful skepticism. That's healthy. I also see that, although you've supported Lindy so far, you have a lot of doubts, don't you?

Courtney: A few.

Diane: Hold on. Just stop right there. This marriage thing. To get Ignacio to switch his vote, Kevin makes Mike and Lindy sound like two drunks stumbling into a church prior to a sleazy one-night stand. That accomplished to your satisfaction for the moment, you go to work on Courtney. But everybody, listen. How many people do you know who celebrate a night like that as an anniversary for twenty years? They both admitted they did. That was a solemn, honest, and heartfelt occasion.

Cliff: When was the last time you went to church on Sunday, Ms. Miklos?

Diane: Huh? What does that have to do with—

Cliff: You pose as someone who agrees with Ignacio, but you really don't at all.

Diane: I'm not posing as anything.

Cliff: C'mon, when? Six years old, Easter, yanked in there by Grandma?

Diane: Now, hold on!

Cliff: You don't believe they were married in the eyes of God or anyone else, do you?

Diane: Why are you attacking me?

Cliff: You don't answer my questions. And why is that? It's because you know Ignacio is about to realize that wedding was not important to this case. You're trying to mislead and confuse him by contradicting everything we say in support of Mike, no matter how much logic, reason and evidence we have to support our arguments.

Diane: It's true, I'm not a follower of organized religion, but I have my own beliefs.

Cliff: Something you picked up in Tibet, no doubt, after forking over sixty-five thousand dollars for the privilege of being lugged up Mount Everest by a Sherpa.

Diane: I've never been to Tibet.

Bob: Jesus. You have to pay that much to climb a mountain?

Cliff: That's right. It's a sport for the elite of the world.

Diane: I fight for every penny! I work very, very hard to earn the respect and support of my sponsors and friends!

Bob: Making slide shows and going on hikes. Whew. It's a tough job, but someone's got to—

Courtney: Stop picking on her!

Cliff: She makes it our business by bringing it into an argument. We're just trying to be rational here, trying to examine the evidence like Mrs. Lim says.

Mrs. Lim: Don't you dare quote me! I have never seen such a blatant prejudice and such underhanded exploitation and maneuvering in my life, and I see plenty of it in my business! You go too far!

Kevin: Break time! We're out of coffee. Now, that's unconscionable. I'm getting the bailiff.

They break.

Cliff: First I want to apologize if I got a little overheated in my arguments. You put your faith in me as a leader, and I take that duty seriously, so seriously, I may go a little overboard in trying to help us get closer to a verdict.

Courtney: But Cliff, it's getting obvious the only verdict you want from us is against Lindy.

Cliff: I never meant to give that impression. If the majority had gone for Lindy, I would accept that. It's just that after airing our views, we seem to be going the other way.

Bob: There is one point I'd like further discussion about. That's Ignacio's view that Lindy and Mike were married because they stepped inside a church once and made some promises to each other.

The point I'd like to make is this: our country is founded on the notion of a separation between church and state. That was so people could practice religion as they pleased, but the state could develop its own set of rules aimed at the common good.

Ignacio, is it right for you to base your decision in this case on your religious beliefs? This is a case brought before the state. Shouldn't state law be our guide?

Ignacio: *(heavy sigh)* That is something to think about.

Cliff: Of course, you have to feel good in your conscience about how you vote. But look at it this way, you can believe they were married, without necessarily voting to give Lindy anything.

Ignacio: What do you mean?

Cliff: Well, you say they were married in the eyes of God. But we all agree they weren't married according to the laws of this state. Logically, then, when it comes time for them to split up, the state's usual community property laws should not apply.

Mrs. Lim: But this analysis is incorrect. If he believes they agreed to marriage, then he must realize they assumed certain obligations under that agreement, mutually agreed-upon obligations. Remember, if there's a contract, and Ignacio is saying he believes there was from that moment, the judge said we can infer its existence and terms from the conduct of the parties. They certainly acted married. Why shouldn't they be held to the normal terms of that contract?

Cliff: Mrs. Lim, there was no written agreement, and—

Mrs. Lim: There's one interpretation for marriage, whether it happened under the eyes of God or in the eyes of the State of California.

Cliff: A case could be made that she read much more into that moment than he ever intended.

Mrs. Lim: He introduced her as his wife!

Cliff: And how can we know his intention, except as he explained it in court? He did it to please her. There was no hidden understanding that they were married. Why else would she say she was ashamed not to be married? She knew they weren't! So did he!

Diane: *(screams)*

Courtney: Diane! What is it?

Bob: What's the matter with her?

Kevin: Someone shut that crazy woman up!

The door opens.

Deputy Kimura: Everything okay in here? I thought I heard something.

Diane: Everything's fine. I just had a . . . nightmare.

Deputy: A nightmare? Um. Do we need a doctor?

Cliff: No, no. I think the lady was just trying to make a point. A loud one.

Deputy: Is that so?

Diane: Yeah, I'm okay now.

Deputy: If you're sure . . .

Door closes.

Cliff: And now I guess you'll insist on telling us all about why you just about scared everybody to death.

Diane: It was a symbolic gesture of my despair, Cliff. Nobody can follow the fancies you call logic, and you don't care anyway. You're just going to keep us here listening to your fascinating mind games until we're all hypnotized and vote however you want.

Courtney: *(giggling)* I wish I had screamed. I sure felt like it.

Cliff: Don't you guys think there should be a requirement that people on juries be mature and intelligent enough so they can follow along with the rest of the grown-ups?

Courtney: Why, you . . . I'm in college you know.

Cliff: Yes, that gives me pause. I had heard that any fool could get into college these days.

Courtney: No wonder your wife left you.

Sonny: *(shouts)* Everybody just shut the fuck up!

Silence. The clock on the wall ticks.

Bob: What do you know? He can talk!

Sonny: You want to hear more?

Bob: Not really.

Cliff: I think maybe it's time for a vote. What do you think, Ignacio. Did we get through that issue of yours okay?

Ignacio: Yes, I've given it a lot of thought.

They vote. It is eight to four against Lindy.

Courtney: Ignacio, you didn't!

Ignacio: I'm sorry, Courtney. But I wasn't voting the law before. I was voting my beliefs.

Courtney: If you can't stick to your beliefs here, when can you?

Cliff: Well, let's see. That leaves Diane, Mrs. Lim, Courtney, and, I presume, Mr. Ball, still for Lindy. I think it's about time we heard something about your views on the matter, Mr. Ball.

Sonny: Sonny.

Cliff: Sure. Sonny.

Sonny: I'm on her side.

Cliff: *(after a pause)* And?

Sonny: That's it.

Cliff: Well, can you tell us why?

Diane: He needs to know your reasoning, Sonny, so that he can substitute his reasoning. . . .

Sonny: C'mon. All that dough. She was loyal. Never fucked around on him. If he's any kind of man at all, he's got to be fair to her.

Cliff: How would you feel if I told you she did fuck around? She lied up there. We've proven that.

Sonny: How do you know?

Cliff: That's it, isn't it? We don't. How can we hand over this man's hard earned money to a woman that might not even have been faithful to him? Probably wasn't, in fact.

Diane: There's absolutely no proof of that. Not one thing was said. . . .

Cliff: My feeling is, and I think most of the guys here will agree, this whole deal is about revenge. He has a new girlfriend. He's moving on. Why is the law involved in this at all?

Sonny: Now there's a good question.

Cliff: Why should she get one thin dime?

Diane: Cliff, the only compensation available in this case is financial. We're just deciding the facts and evidence. Such as, did they have a contract—

Cliff: She's a liar and quite likely a cheat. I mean, did you see him up there? He's much older than her. Looks like a little roll in the hay's going to take some doing.

Mrs. Lim: You are shameless, Mr. Wright.

Diane: I really think—

Cliff: I believe I was talking to Sonny. Please have the courtesy to let me finish. So, here she is stuck with him. She probably had some on the side. You almost can't hold that against her. But then, he found out and left her, and then she went whoops, there goes my meal ticket.

Does she try to work it out with him? No, she runs off and hires a lawyer, gets the law involved.

Diane: Cliff, why you talk with the passion of a man with firsthand experience.

Cliff: Now, Sonny, was that right? I mean, who wants to get mixed up with the law? Who needs that involvement?

Sonny: Nobody. That's for damn sure.

Cliff: You'll forgive me for asking, but, who makes the financial decisions in your family?

Sonny: Who do you think?

Cliff: You, of course. And why is that?

Sonny: Any big decisions, I make.

Cliff: You remind me so much of Mike Markov. Obviously, you don't look alike. He's kind of a ruin, now. But once he was a strong man like you, Sonny. A boxer. He's an old-fashioned guy. He makes the big decisions, because he knows he's the right man for the job. Do you remember in court when he promised to take care of Lindy Markov? He said he would. And nothing in his past suggests otherwise. I mean, they live in a huge mansion that he's paid for for all these years.

Diane: With profits from the company they both own.

Cliff: Maybe he knows something we don't. Maybe he knows how she fritters money away on clothes and new cars. Maybe she gambles. Maybe he has very good reasons for wanting to keep control of his business, because he's terrified she'll run it straight into the ground!

Mrs. Lim: I must protest. These are speculations about issues that were never even mentioned in court. Maybe she is a financial wizard! We don't know.

Sonny: Enough. I want to vote.

Diane: Wait a minute. I have this terrible feeling about you, Sonny.

Sonny: Thanks.

Diane: You're going to change your vote just to get this over with, aren't you?

Sonny: *(doesn't answer)*

Diane: Remember in the judge's instructions? You are not supposed to decide a certain way just because other jurors favor that decision and certainly not because this jerk is trying to pull the wool over your eyes.

Sonny: Nobody is pulling any wool anywhere.

Courtney: You've stuck with Lindy all along. You know she deserves some of that money.

Sonny: Let's vote.

But the bailiff knocks. The lunch is out in the hall. Does anyone want a quick trip outside before they settle down to eat? Kris and Cliff grab their cigarettes and go, followed by a bailiff. Others hit the bathroom.

After they all come back, Cliff gets his special dish, marked vegetarian, and asks for opinions on the food. Suddenly, he makes gagging sounds.

Kevin: Slow down, there, pal. You choking? Anybody know the Heimlich maneuver?

Courtney: I do!

Bob: Sonny, help me get him standing.

Courtney tries.

Courtney: It's not helping! I don't think he's choking on anything.

Kevin: Maybe he's having a heart attack!

(Cliff's gasping and knocking things off the table.)

Cliff: *(He's talking so softly, in the commotion no one seems to hear him.)* My jacket! Get my jacket! Let go of me!

Mrs. Lim: Sonny, try to sit him up. Don't let him fall on the floor like that.

Courtney: Do you think he wants his jacket? It's probably in the anteroom.

Bob: That can't be right, or he's out of his mind. It must be eighty degrees in here.

Mrs Lim: Deputy Kimura! Get in here!

Cliff: *(This is unintelligible.)* The epi kit!

Kevin: He's trying to say something.

Mrs Lim: What is it, Cliff? What do you want us to do?

Alternate juror Damien Peck must be trying to run for help. He runs into the bailiff.

Deputy Kimura: Stay right here, please. Don't leave, anyone.

Shouting for an ambulance, he leaves.

Diane: He can't breathe! Here, you guys. Get him on the table. He needs CPR.

She works on him until Deputy Kimura returns and takes over. There's very little going on except the sound of the deputy giving CPR. A woman is crying.

Mrs. Lim: Deputy Kimura, they're here. We should get out of the way.

Frank: Look at him. He's really swelling up. Looks just like a swarm of bees went after him.

Courtney: We can't do anything more. Come on, Diane, move over.

Technician: His heart . . . Get these people out of here.

Footsteps as they scurry away.

Sonny: *(leaving)* Fight till the last gasp, dude.

Court personnel are ushering people out of the room so that emergency people can come in.

>Click<

Thursday after lunch, the court called. Nina's presence was requested at two.

"Do they have a question for the judge? Do they want some of the testimony reread?"

"No. I believe the judge needs to seat an alternate," said the clerk.

"What happened?"

"Just come on down, Nina. I believe the judge would prefer to explain."

Ringing Winston and Genevieve in their hotel rooms, where they actually were for once, Nina drove over to the courthouse with minutes to spare. She linked up with her team outside, and as a group they pushed past the curious reporters stationed outside the doors.

"What's going on?" Winston demanded, but Nina just shrugged. He looked like hell, just like the rest of them. Jeff Riesner caught up with them in the hall. His sallow face and the bags under his eyes showed he wasn't sleeping either.

"A verdict?"

"We'll know in a minute."

28

"BE SEATED," ANNOUNCED THE CLERK.

They sat while the jury filed in. Nina searched their faces. But . . . where was Clifford Wright? There were only thirteen. Judging from their troubled expressions, something major had happened.

Looking grave, Milne took the bench. "Sorry to call you all out in such haste. There has been an unfortunate event in connection with the deliberations. Apparently Mr. Wright, one of our jurors, has had an allergic reaction to something he ate. He has had to be admitted to Boulder Hospital.

"It appears unlikely that he will be released in time to resume his work on the jury. Therefore, I must seat alternate juror number thirteen. At this time, we ask if there is any objection to the seating of the alternate. Order! Order! You people in the back, be quiet or you'll be outside."

"Just a moment, Your Honor," Nina said. She tore open her juror file and Winston looked over her shoulder. Genevieve was looking at her own notes.

"Patti Zobel," Genevieve whispered. "Divorced, in her forties, works for a resort time-share company. Her husband was having an affair. Fantastic. Don't look happy. The jury won't like it."

"We're sorry to hear this, Your Honor," Nina said. "We have no objection to the substitution."

Riesner looked stunned. He conferred with Rebecca in urgent whispers. Finally he said, "We would request a recess of a day to monitor Mr. Wright's progress, Your Honor. Perhaps it's just an upset stomach, and he can resume tomorrow. Let's not be too hasty here."

The phone rang at Deputy Kimura's desk. Still standing and watching the crowd sternly, he picked up the receiver and listened. In a moment he made a sign to the clerk and began writing down something. The clerk made a sign to Milne, who said, "We will take a five minute recess. The jury will remain seated." He left the bench in a flurry of robes. The deputy and his clerk followed him.

The legal affairs reporter from the *San Francisco Chronicle,* who had arrived late in the trial, came up to Nina right away and asked, "Who's the alternate?" Nina gave him the name but little else. Patti Zobel, a plain woman in a running suit with frizzy hair, sitting in her spot with the other jurors, was trying to look calm but was obviously very excited. She had spent weeks as an understudy and had just been given a leading role.

Five minutes passed. Nina glanced at Patti Zobel. Patti Zobel looked back at her. Did she have a hint of a smile in the corner of her mouth? Could she be trying to say, I'm on your side? Nina looked away, afraid one of the other jurors would notice, intoxicated with hope.

Milne came back, his face long, and a hush fell over the courtroom.

"I regret to advise you that juror number six, Mr. Clifford Wright, passed away a few minutes ago at Boulder Hospital," he said.

Gasps and stifled cries came from the jurors. Kris Schmidt buried her face in her hands. Nina and Winston looked at each other in astonishment. Genevieve scribbled a note. *Hot dog!* it said.

Milne seemed genuinely sad. "I have never had a juror die during a trial, and I have been a judge for seventeen years," he went on. "I and the other court personnel would like to express our deep sympathy to Mr. Wright's family and friends, and to express our appreciation for the work he has done in this case."

He turned to the jury. "While I appreciate the sadness that you must feel, having worked very closely with Mr. Wright over the past weeks, I must ask you to return to your task. I believe Mr. Wright would have wanted you to do that."

Riesner asked to approach the bench, and Nina went up there with him. Out of the hearing of the jury, Riesner said, "I move for a mistrial. This jury can't carry on. It's one thing to replace a sick juror, but this is too traumatic. They can't be asked to calmly consider the evidence—"

Milne was nodding. "I agree to some extent," he said. "This can't be easy for the rest of them."

"It's not easy," Nina said, "but look at the time and resources that have gone into this trial. The jury should be allowed to reach a verdict. The whole reason for the alternate juror system is to handle just this kind of situation, to save the work that's been done. Please, Your Honor. Consider the judicial resources already expended. The parties, the attorneys—having to go through all this again is too—too awful to contemplate."

Milne waved away Riesner's next attempt to talk, and the lawyers stood there and waited while he thought. At last he said, "I would like to poll the jurors individually in my chambers to see if they feel able to continue. How does that sound?"

Nina nodded, but Riesner said, "No. It doesn't matter what they say. I request a mistrial."

"I'll take that request under submission and meanwhile talk to the jury members," Milne said. "All right, let's do it."

Another recess. The jurors returned to the jury room, waiting for their turn to be called in to see the judge. The lawyers fortified themselves with more caffeine downstairs. The reporters talked excitedly among themselves. Lindy went outside for a quick walk.

An hour passed, the most agonizing hour yet. While they drank coffee, Milne's clerk, Edith, came down and Genevieve tried to get some more information. When she came back to the table, she said, "Wow. Trouble here in River City. Edith says the doc at the hospital is pretty sure Cliff was allergic to something he ate off the lunch tray provided by the court. They ate Chinese. The rest of the jury must be shook all to pieces."

"If he told the court he was severely allergic to something and they let it be served to him anyway, his family's got a lawsuit I would love to handle," said Winston.

"That would be a first," Nina said. "Suing the county for killing a juror. Incredible. Oh, I don't even care. I'm so scared that Milne's going to call a mistrial, my hands are shaking the coffee all over my skirt."

"Me, too. I thought you just put in the next alternate if a juror got sick or died," Genevieve said. "I can't believe the judge would find it in his heart to throw away all this work."

"If we can just keep going," Winston said, "we got us a hot one in the jury room now. I saw how Patti gave you the high sign with her eyes, Nina."

"Winston, ever the optimist. This trial is it for me," Nina said. "I couldn't afford to do this again. That poor man. I feel rotten about the way I talked about him."

Deputy Kimura came through the door, pointing upward toward the court. "He's ready," he said.

Milne took the bench and the jurors came back in. "I have spoken with each of the jurors," he said. "All, including juror thirteen, have advised me that they feel able to continue; therefore, I am denying the motion for a mistrial."

Nina breathed again. She felt sad, relieved, frightened all at once. Under the table, Winston squeezed her hand.

Milne now gave the BAJI instruction to the jury covering the event that had just occurred, modifying it slightly. The jury listened intently, especially Patti Zobel, as if she wanted to demonstrate her willingness to follow the law and do a good job.

"Ladies and gentlemen of the jury," he said. "A juror has been, ah, incapacitated and replaced with an alternate juror.

"The law grants each party in this case a right to a verdict reached only after full participation of all jurors who ultimately return the verdict.

"This right may be assured in this case only if the jury begins its deliberations again from the beginning."

Oh, brother, Bob Binkley's disgusted head shake said.

"You are therefore instructed to disregard and put out of your mind all past deliberations and begin deliberating anew. This means that each remaining juror must set aside and disregard the earlier deliberations as if they had not taken place.

"You shall now retire for your deliberations in accordance with the instructions previously given."

Milne returned to his normal tone. "It is already four o'clock, and I am sure many of us are feeling upset and would like to go home to our families. Therefore the court will adjourn at this time and resume again at nine a.m. Don't forget the cautions I have given you."

"C'mon, Nina, let's go out," Genevieve said as they walked out into a cool drizzle. She reached for Winston. In response to her gesture, he put his arm tenderly around her, engulfing her in his overcoat, and Nina thought, watching Genevieve looking up at him, she acts like she owns him now. He's not going to like that. "I do believe we're all gonna get paid! Hey, Win, let's drive up to the North Shore tonight and eat at that restaurant across from the casino at Incline."

Nina made her excuses, smiling at Genevieve's boisterous confidence. "Maybe," she said. "But I'm going to meet Lindy at the office and explain what all this means to her. And remember, it's not over—"

"Till it's over," Winston said. "You go get some sleep if you can." He gently moved away from Genevieve. "Thanks for the offer, Gen, but I'm going to give those tables a chance to seduce me back, because Providence seems to be smiling on us right now, and I'm going to see if she hasn't got some extra good cheer to throw my way."

As she crawled into bed that night, Nina had a strong feeling that this would be the last night of hellish waiting. She pulled the covers up and lay on her back, thinking. If they won—oh, God, if they won—and as usual she woke up every couple of hours to lie there and fret some more, but she did have one funny dream.

She dreamed she was going to be a star, and Sophia Loren was fixing her hair. Sophia had a new pair of sunglasses for her, too.

Right. Her subconscious was apparently doing some premature celebrating with Genevieve.

Late the next morning they got the phone call: they had a verdict. Nina and Sandy drove to court together in Nina's car. Sandy peppered Nina with questions about pending cases, but Nina was useless. She could not speak. Her mind was utterly blank. She made the familiar motions, turning the wheel of the car, driving the familiar streets, but she saw nothing but disaster ahead, if . . . On the way, a naturalist on the radio ranted about the songbirds and profusion of wildflowers in Tahoe at this time of year, but he might as well have been describing life on Mars. Nina turned him off before they parked.

The whole town appeared to have come out in force to hear the verdict, a testament to the extraordinary amount of media coverage the trial was receiving. Every seat was filled. Many people stood at the back of the room.

Nina took her place next to Lindy. Sandy sat on the other side of her. Genevieve and Winston were already waiting. They nodded shortly and turned their attention to the dais. Nina crossed her fingers on her lap and also waited for Milne with an eagerness so extreme it felt painful.

The next few minutes, while the judge got settled and the jury was brought in, she passed through eternity and came out the other side. If they lost . . .

Mrs. Lim adjusted reading glasses on her nose. She cleared her throat, looked up at the court, and then back down at the paper she held in her hand. She read the verdict.

They had won.

The jury awarded Lindy Markov a total of sixty-eight point six million dollars.

Nina anchored herself to the table with her hands, suddenly unable to see through the blur of activity, or hear through the din. Dimly, she saw the judge leave, and the jury, casting smiles her way, filing out.

They had won.

The room around her rocked like a foundering ship. Nina's awareness narrowed to the whiteness of her hands and further to the sensitive tips of her fingers where they held tight to the wood as wave upon wave of elation swept over her, knocking the breath out of her.

They had won.

And she couldn't believe it. Because in spite of all the plans, in spite of the fantasies, she had never expected to win.

Her sense of unreality extended into her surroundings. The courtroom had altered, and now appeared more palatial, grander, as if the roof had opened up and sun now streamed in where dull incandescents had once prevailed.

Steadying herself, trying to control the distorting tumult of her emotions, she stood up.

Lindy had squeezed her lids down tight over her eyes. Riesner talked rapidly into Mike's ear.

Mike's face looked drawn. On the way out, he fell against a guy from CNN who was leaving one of the rows and who just managed to catch him.

"Congratulations," the crowd in the courtroom told Lindy and Nina, who fielded a dozen handshakes and high fives.

Lindy's friend Alice hugged Nina, saying, "You did it, doll. It's a left hook to the face of all those grinning baboons out there!"

Lindy grabbed Nina by the arm. "My God," she said. "If my dad could see me now!"

"Lindy, I'm so glad for you," said Nina, but the words fell flat. Nothing short of a mountain falling down could truly articulate something so huge and so fantastic.

She could feel Lindy's fingernails squeezing into her arm, could smell the excitement in the close air of the room. She could hear the voices, all merging into pandemonium. She stood still, soaking up the sweetness of the moment, thinking of Bob.

But the crowds were pushing, and Lindy's hand on her arm began to tremble.

"Let's get out of here," Nina said.

"We're trapped," Lindy whispered, looking panicked.

"We'll have more to say later when it sinks in," Nina said to the reporters, pulling Lindy away.

"Take the private hallway," she told Lindy and Alice. "Stay there until they're gone."

"Thank you for everything, Nina," Lindy said, clinging to her hand.

"It's a goddamned triumph," Alice said, pulling her away and hustling her through the door by the jury box.

And a triumph it was.

With Genevieve and Winston on one side of her and Sandy on the other, Nina gave the victory salute on the steps of the courthouse seen across California and the country on the evening news.

That evening, Matt and Andrea came over with two bottles of champagne. While the kids took pillows off the sofa and bounced down the stairs on them, the adults grabbed jackets and retired to the deck.

Matt drank one bottle entirely by himself. After several toasts, he said, "There's something I want to say to Nina."

"Sounds serious," Andrea said, filling her glass.

"It is," he said. "Nina, now I don't think it's a secret I've never liked what you do. I've never hidden my opinion of your chosen profession. You work too much. You drive yourself too hard for a bunch of troublemakers who could never be grateful enough, in my opinion."

"Oh, now, Matt," Nina said.

He put up a hand to stop her. "I never thought it was worth it. I've said it before. That shouldn't surprise you. Well," he said, "I'm going to admit something. Today proved I was wrong. Apparently, what you do has some merit after all."

"That's one way to look at it," Andrea laughed. "Now and then, three and a half million bucks worth of merit!"

"That's right," Matt said. "And I hope you know how much you deserve it, too, Nina."

"And it couldn't happen to a nicer specialist in horrible cases," Andrea said, patting Nina's hand.

"Nina, has it sunk in yet?" Matt asked, looking at her. "From now on, you can pretty much buy anything you want."

"A Roche Bobois couch," Andrea said. "Duette blinds for the front windows. Hey, Nina, you can finally break down and buy yourself a decent pair of jeans. I've been meaning to tell you that the ones you've been wearing have a couple of holes under the back pocket."

"A yacht," said Matt.

"Really? Could she buy a yacht?" Andrea asked.

"Yes, she could," Matt said. "I think. How much is a yacht anyway?"

"I have no idea," Andrea said.

"To answer your original question, Matt," Nina said. "No. It hasn't sunk in."

"Okay, here it comes," Andrea said. "Here's the question every celebrity in mourning, every landslide victim, and every lottery winner must answer at some point to satisfy the curious onlookers."

"What question is that, Andrea?" asked Nina.

"How does it feel?"

Nina lay back on the lounge chair and pulled her coat tightly around her, staring up at the sky. "It feels like one of those stars up there just fell into my backyard."

The vote had been nine to three, the minimum. Patti Zobel made it clear afterward, as she spoke to the press in the hall, that she had been the ninth vote favoring Lindy. Courtney Poole said it had been terribly close. Right before Cliff's collapse, he had just about persuaded several of the other jurors to change their minds and vote for Mike, but then the judge had said to start fresh. When they returned to their original positions, and added in Patti's emphatic arguments in favor of Lindy, Mike's support had evaporated.

For two days, Nina enjoyed her brush with fame. Interviewed by the major networks, public television, radio and even on a website Bob helped her organize, she didn't have any more time to deal with her own shock.

The attention often had a slightly hostile quality to it and generally varied according to gender. Men expressed disbelief and outrage at Lindy's success. Women called the case cataclysmic and a vindication.

Nina disliked watching the issues get melted down by the media into a gender war. She said over and over in the interviews that the truth lay somewhere in the middle. She reminded everyone that the Markov case was unique in its details because of Lindy's participation in the business. Most palimony cases had more to do with a long-term emotional connection and involved a request for support or rehabilitation. She didn't think it would advance the cause of female financial equity between couples who lived together. Several other jurors, also interviewed, seconded her guess, saying that the issue was always Lindy's work.

The jury had agreed that the separate property agreement was not a valid contract, that Lindy had signed the agreement with an understanding that there was a promise of marriage attached. They also agreed that some form of oral contract existed between the parties that promised Lindy not half of the company, but a share, which they had struggled to quantify, settling on one-third.

Susan Lim said on local television, "Anybody can come up with a good idea. Anybody can get it built. What really counts in business is marketing. If nobody buys, you make no money. Ms. Markov struck me as an intelligent person who definitely played a large part in their success. Who came up with their biggest product? She did.

That was our reasoning, based on careful and objective consideration of the evidence."

The jury had heard the evidence, and they had reached a decision for Lindy. It was the American jury system at its best.

And it was over.

BOOK FIVE
VACATIONS

Money! Money!
shrieking mad celestial
money of illusion!

Allen Ginsberg

29

PAUL FLEW BACK TO SACRAMENTO from Washington on Friday. He heard the news about Nina's verdict from a television set while biting down on a thick cheeseburger at Sam's in Placerville. Sam's was closing after thirty years and he was sure going to miss the old barn with the sawdust on the floors, and the hokey nostalgic decor.

As Nina wasn't taking his phone calls, he was going to see her personally. He had hoped to make it up there for the verdict, as she was usually at her most accessible at the moment the pressure let up, but this would have to do.

He was still angry at the way she had treated him, but he knew the stunt he had pulled had merited a slap on the wrist. However, that should not have included this telephone silence or such a prolonged lack of contact.

Still, he was not surprised by her overreaction. Big trials always brought with them a loss of control. Lawyers belted each other, clients turned to drink, witnesses left town, strong judges turned into wimps. He himself had possibly overreacted slightly to Riesner. What was the big deal? He had barely hurt the guy.

He didn't give a shit if he never worked for her again. He wanted something else from this warm female encased like Sleeping Beauty under cold glass. He wanted to break the glass and grab her, shake her back to life. But he couldn't do that. She would never forgive him for doing that. She had put up that glass to protect herself in the working world, and that was a place she had always liked too much to give up.

Until now. Now she had won her big case, the big case. She couldn't expect another with stakes like this one in her lifetime, could she? Like Sam's in Placerville, a phase in Nina's life seemed to be ending.

Barring any unforeseeable circumstances, Nina was now a millionaire. Markov still had thirty days to appeal. He would probably settle instead, and even if he did appeal, the lawyers would receive their due sooner or later.

She had been evasive with him about the details, but Paul knew a canny lady like Nina would not pass the opportunity up to make a killing on a case like this one. She had struggled along for almost a year while working the Markov case. She was on top. She had nothing more to prove.

She could even quit working.

She could move to Carmel and live with him, break open her glass coffin on her own.

A brilliant future stretched out before her. He finished his meal, quaffed a beer, and stopped to plunk a quarter into Madame Zelda's slot for what would be the last time.

The impassive, scarfed wooden gypsy shifted in her glass case, unseating a layer of dust. A ruby light lit up behind her. Her finger roved among the yellow cards laid out in front of her. The finger stopped. A card fell into the slot.

> The serpent crawls and does his harm
> The thunder raises a distant alarm
> The waters shift in restless lake
> You face great danger for her sake.
> A fool and his money are soon parted.

"Have a good retirement, you old witch," Paul murmured uneasily, and he could have sworn Madame Zelda's eyes flashed back.

———

That night, they lay together in Nina's four poster bed, having made love twice in an hour, first on a lounge pad under the moon on a private piece of deck, and again on the bed, or at any rate, partially on the bed. Bob was in Monterey with his grandfather, and would be flying out of San Francisco on a school trip to Williamsburg on Sunday. He would be gone for the next week.

Nina put a hand on Paul's cheek and rubbed.

"I love a warm welcome," Paul said lazily, his eyes closed. "We should argue frequently."

"No. Let's never argue again."

"If we got married and lived in Carmel, we would never argue." He had said what he came to say. He reached out a hand and ran it over her soft thigh.

"Why don't you move to Tahoe, Paul?" she replied, not entirely unexpectedly.

"Would you marry me if I did?"

She pushed her head into his chest sleepily, saying, "I would think about it."

"Yeah, but would you do it?"

"Don't you know you complicate everything?"

"I don't see it that way. To me, it's simple. Man, woman, desire, love, to quote the great Eric Burdon. Oh, I've thought about it. But I have a very good business down there. I've been working in Carmel longer than you've been working in Tahoe. Seriously. Come to me."

"What about your Washington job?" Her voice was very drowsy.

"I'd drop it like a hot potato for you, my love."

But Nina had stopped listening. She appeared to have fallen into a nap. Paul yawned. The big bed was a universe unto itself, the covers so thick and warm . . . he drifted off, too.

Paul woke up about one, his stomach growling. Nina still lay on her side, her long brown hair spilling onto her white shoulder. What a shame he was starving. He shook her gently and said, "Awake, my little honeybee. We skipped dinner. Let's eat."

She opened her eyes and seemed glad to see him. What more could a man ask for? Except a good meal?

"But I do have one more question about this business before we throw back the covers and you expose that enticing body of yours to the air and my worshipful gaze."

"Wha'?" she said.

"About Clifford Wright."

"What about him?"

"You sure got lucky there."

"Huh?"

"Doesn't it strike you as odd?"

She was waking up fast now. "Odd?" she said, the intelligence returning to her eyes. As he watched, absorbed by the transformation, the emphases of her face shifted from soft cheeks and full lips to jawbone and eyebrows. "There's nothing new on him. Case closed. Just a freak medical occurrence."

"Did you get a chance to look at the coroner's report on his death?"

"Why would I?"

"Monumental coincidence or act o' God?" said Paul. "Only Madame Zelda knows, and she's getting out of the business."

Her lips drew a hard line. "You smell fish everywhere you go, don't you? There's no mystery here. He died of anaphylactic shock from eating something."

"Most people with allergies find out about it before keeling over in the jury room."

"Oh, he knew he had food allergies," Nina said. "He talked about them to everyone, practically. We even knew from all those super-duper quiz sheets we got about the jurors. Didn't anyone tell you?"

"I don't remember hearing about it."

"Apparently, he had medicine that might have saved him, but nobody knew. What's it called . . ."

"You mean an adrenaline kit."

"Yes. You poke yourself in the leg with epinephrine, which

immediately stops the allergic reaction. Sandy told me about a doctor down in southern California with an allergy to shellfish who recently died from anaphylaxis. Stuck his nose over a pan of boiling seafood. He had forgotten his allergy kit."

"Why didn't Wright use his?"

"The jurors say he mumbled something about his jacket, which was right there in the closet, but they thought he was delirious. Deputy Kim found it after he was in the hospital. His breathing became blocked so quickly he never got to use it."

"So you don't plan to check further into what happened."

"Why would I? It's unfortunate, but nothing to do with me."

"No urge to examine your gift horse too closely," said Paul. "I do see your position." He hadn't meant it to sound the way it came out, but he couldn't help himself.

"Don't be ridiculous," Nina said, pushing his hand off.

"What's the matter?" he said putting it back.

She batted it firmly away. "Why can't you just accept it that I won this case, fair and square? Why can't you let me have that? You chip away at my success, hinting around that I couldn't have pulled it off if Clifford Wright hadn't died. Jesus."

Paul fell silent for a moment.

"I'm sorry," he said finally. "I never congratulated you. And you're so terrific, even out of bed. You're brilliant, beautiful, brave, bosomy . . ."

"Thank you," Nina said.

"Soon to be rich," he said.

Apparently mollified, she said, "Don't go tacky on me now."

"Okay, good. Let's turn our attention back to that very issue that's hovering around us like a swarm of starving mosquitoes. We need to talk about how this change in your financial status is going to affect our relationship. There are some things to consider."

"I thought you were starving," said Nina.

"Shhh." Turning over to face her, he put a finger over her lips. "Mail-order catalogs, for starters. You can finally afford a pair of those undies . . . you know the ones, don't you? With the missing bits here," he said, showing her where, "and right here." His hand lingered. "Let's splurge. Get two, in black silk and red. Net stockings to match and one of those things women wore back in the good old days when men ruled the universe without challenge . . ."

"A garter belt?"

"That's it! Yum. The possibilities rise up like . . . like—"

"Like wet dough!" she said.

"Like a hunk of burnin' love," said Paul, inserting his tongue into her ear.

Before she could say another thing, he jumped her.

Then they went down to the kitchen and made toast and eggs and drank all the milk.

On Saturday they rented separate paddleboats and raced each other around Zephyr Cove until the setting sun blinded them, then returned to Nina's to change into their fanciest duds for a celebration dinner Lindy was hosting at The Summit.

Nina took Paul's arm as they arrived at the restaurant on the seventeenth floor of Harrah's. Piano blues surrounded them, sensual as incense.

"I feel so grown up, suddenly," she said, enjoying the scratchiness of his jacket and happy he was here to share this night with her. "Do you remember the first time we met at that place in Carmel?" she led the way into the restaurant behind the maitre d'.

"How could I forget? A blind date. And then you went off and married Jack."

"When did we become the kind of people that go to places like this? Where's the band with the electrified hair and distortion pedal?"

"It's perfect, Nina," Paul said, reaching out to shake Winston's hand.

They sat down at a window table. Outside, way down, the lights of town twinkled. Lindy had already ordered champagne. Sandy, dressed in a shiny amethyst-colored beaded shirt over a long black skirt, argued with Nina over who could order the salmon with lemon couscous and who got the rack of lamb. They compromised by deciding to share. Next to her, Sandy's son, Wish, demonstrated how to play spoons to a Scott Joplin tune.

Wearing an emerald-green jacket over white slacks and low heels, Lindy faced the window. Nina knew she had invited her friend Alice to the celebration, but Alice couldn't make it.

After greeting Nina and Paul, she leaned forward and gazed at the lights beyond the glass, looking a little shell-shocked. "Isn't it thrilling how it's all worked out?" she told Nina. "Isn't it strange?"

Sandy offered up a toast to "The lake of the sky, Tahoe, where anything can happen and does," and they worked their way through two bottles before eating.

Throughout the meal, Nina couldn't help noticing things had somehow changed between Winston and Genevieve. Genevieve continued to tune her behavior to his mood, offering him butter, salt, whatever he seemed to need, but he seemed distracted. Nina supposed he, too, was turning his mind to the future, a future where Genevieve would figure less prominently.

"Where will you go, Genevieve?" she asked.

"Oh, I've got a million ideas! Only you know what? I can hardly think about that right now. I get so worked up during these damn things, I don't sleep. But I can't imagine going back to L.A. and starting over again, which is probably exactly what I'll be doin'." She looked and sounded tired. Underneath the gaiety, they all must be. They had crammed a couple of years' worth of work into eight months. And they had won!

They commiserated for a few minutes about the difficult transition to daily routines after the epic intensity of the past months.

"Like my mother used to say," Paul butted in. "These are good problems to have. What will you be doing next, Lindy?"

She looked startled by the sudden attention. Her plate was still full of food. Apparently, she had preferred the champagne. Her eyes had a glassy sheen. "Oh, I'll just go about the usual routines of a wealthy woman," she said. "Teas. Parties. Mansion-shopping."

"Poor you," Genevieve said, making light of her mood.

"You mean rich me," said Lindy, and everyone laughed, including Lindy.

After dinner, Nina asked Winston about his plans.

"I've got some paperwork to go through and some expenses to add up for Sandy," he said, winking at Sandy. "Then I'm planning to take a couple of days before I go back to enjoy this fine spring weather, get some exercise. I feel like I've hardly moved for months."

"Jogging every spare moment doesn't count, I suppose," said Sandy.

"Oh, and I brought a few things here. Little thank-yous for all your help." Winston reached into a bag beside his chair, bringing out a huge package for Sandy, and a tie-sized box for Wish.

"Now don't look so gloomy," he said, handing over the box to Wish. "I promise, someday soon, you'll need a tie."

"Hey, really, Mr. Reynolds. This is just great." Wish smiled feebly. He tore off the ribbon and ripped the box opening it. "Silk, right?"

"That's right."

"Great." Wish held the blue tie close to his eyes, as if the details in the pattern might cast light on what had possessed a smart guy like Winston to choose such an outlandish and inappropriate gift.

Winston broke into full-throttle laughter. "Well, glad you like it."

Sandy opened her much larger package carefully, setting the floral wrap neatly to the side of her place, untying the ribbon, and placing the interior tissue in a tidy stack until Wish looked ready to grab the box from her and tear into it himself.

Inside, nestled like an animal, was something thick and soft.

"What is it, Mom?" asked Wish impatiently. "C'mon, get it out."

"I looked at a few moth-eaten ones before I found this one. It's been well-cared-for," said Winston.

"Where did you find it?" she demanded.

"In a shop in Minden. The proprietor told me the family that owned it sold everything they had and moved to Stockton last month. They told him the man's great-grandfather made it. This was the last one he made before he died sometime in the fifties, at least that's what the dealer claimed. They had found it stored very carefully in a cedar-lined trunk. Never used it."

But Sandy stared into the box for a long time before pulling the object out to hold up. "A rabbit-skin blanket," she said. "My mother had one when I was a kid that looked like this."

"Those were big with the Washoe," Wish explained to Nina, whose puzzlement must have showed.

"That's what the dealer told me. Said they keep you so warm at night, even up in Alpine County at six thousand feet in the wintertime, you could sleep in the nude in a lean-to," Winston teased. "Of course I thought of you, Sandy."

But the joke was lost on Sandy, who stroked the blanket with a reverent hand, saying, "Each blanket lasted three years, then you made another." She scrutinized the front and back, then looked at Winston with the same intense interest. "You must have paid a lot."

"They are rare," Winston agreed.

"Used to be the Washoe hunted rabbits with nets, shooting arrows at the rabbits, who ran into the net thinking they were escaping," Sandy said. "Four or five hundred a day were killed. Then they cut the hides into strings and dried them for a day and a half. Twenty-five strings made one jackrabbit blanket for two people."

"I'm saving for a down blanket this winter," said Wish stoutly. "No animals die, and it's just as warm."

"But when this blanket was made, life was different," said Sandy, pulling the blanket up to rub against her cheek, "In those days, you survived without money. Even up here in Tahoe where it gets really cold."

The shift in atmosphere was subtle. Winston handed out more gifts, exotic flowers for Nina, Genevieve, and Lindy, a pen for Paul. Sandy put the rabbit-skin blanket across a chair.

It sat there, a reminder of times when money meant nothing. The conversation lagged.

"Oh, it is beautiful this year, isn't it?" said Nina, hoping to bring back their earlier good spirits. "More beautiful than I can ever remember. Cobalt-blue skies, cartoon clouds, a great success to celebrate . . ."

"Will you listen to this girl. She's giddy with success!" Lindy said. "Let's do one last toast, to Nina and her Irish luck."

They raised coffee cups and glasses to her, and drank.

"This had nothing to do with luck, you know," Nina said. "Without you all . . ."

"Stop her before she gushes," commanded Winston.

"And Paul here . . ." she said.

". . . whom we have forgiven for not pegging Wright as a problem," said Winston, interrupting her train of thought.

"Let's not get into that again, Winston," Genevieve said. "None of us had Wright pegged, except maybe Nina. Anyway, he's no danger to us anymore."

"According to Paul, maybe he is," said Nina. She felt a need to speak about this, even as she realized she was contributing to the erosion of good feeling they had built up.

"What do you mean?" asked Sandy.

"If you can believe this, he's hinted around that he finds the circumstances of Wright's death terribly suspicious."

"How can an allergic reaction be suspicious?" Winston asked.

"I don't know," said Nina. "Ask the expert."

Winston shifted in his chair to face Paul more directly. "What are you thinking?"

"He thinks someone spiked the food," said Nina. "Crazy, huh?"

Their waiter picked up Lindy's credit card and the bill, and walked off while the party stared at Paul, agog.

"All this commuting you have been doing between Carmel, Washington, and Tahoe has driven you completely around the bend," said Winston.

"It's just peculiar," said Paul, "him keeling over. Maybe—"

"Stop right there," Winston said. "That's useless conjecturing. Do you realize if you even hint at this notion of yours to anyone you could cause us a huge delay?" asked Winston. "An investigation by the police could hold up our money for months."

"Believe me, I never intended to hint at anything."

"He just doesn't like peculiar things," said Nina, recognizing for the first time she, too, had had too much to drink. Her head was spinning. . . .

Paul took her arm and helped her up. "I think we'll be going now," he said. "Anyone need a ride?"

No one did.

"You're not taking this further, are you?" Winston asked as the rest of them stood up to say good-bye.

"No," said Paul. "As far as I know, everyone's satisfied this was an accidental death. Nothing to worry about."

"Oh, yeah," Winston said. "Uh-huh. It always starts so innocently, but later there's running and screaming."

"What are you talking about?" asked Sandy.

"It's from a movie," Winston said, "about monsters getting loose."

30

MONDAY MORNING WHEN PAUL REACHED for Nina, he found only the indentation of her body beside him. He stretched, pulled on a pair of khaki shorts, and padded barefoot down to the kitchen, where she had left him a pot of coffee smoking and black with age. A note on the counter directed him to cereal and bananas, but he didn't want to cook. After making himself a fresh pot of coffee, he took a steaming mug out onto the deck with the morning paper, settled in, and made himself at home among the pines in Nina's backyard.

An hour later he was caffeine-boosted and ready to move. He packed up his things, throwing the comforter over Nina's messy bed. Before leaving, he called his office, directory assistance, Sandy at Nina's office, and a number down south, spending nearly an hour on the phone.

In the van, he paused for a moment to consider his options. Nina for lunch, that was a given.

He would be heading home tonight. A little Monday morning gambling? Too decadent. A run in the thin mountain air? It would be good for him, but . . . it would be more interesting to check on the silly little thing that was nagging at him.

From the bin between the two front seats, he removed a Lake Tahoe telephone directory he had permanently borrowed from a motel a couple of years before. Flipping to the county government offices pages, he browsed for El Dorado, finding the office he wanted on Johnson Boulevard.

He dialed a number, asking for directions and a fifteen minute appointment, which was, a little to his surprise, granted.

The medical examiner had his office in the same complex as the courthouse where he needed to meet Nina later. How convenient.

"Nice to have things quiet again," said Sandy when Nina finally climbed down from the Annapurna of papers on her desk for a midmorning cup of coffee. "Everyone's coming in late." She stood in the doorway of Nina's office, her own fresh coffee in hand.

"Everyone's pooped," said Nina. The last months had been hell. They deserved to sleep late. "Did I thank you for holding this place together while I was so swamped?"

"Yes, but feel free to thank me again." The long line of Sandy's lips extended slightly.

"And you're due for a big bonus when my fee comes in."

A quiver of her eyelid suggested that Sandy found this very exciting news. "Should we start looking for bigger offices?"

"No."

"Why not? You'll want to expand a little. Not enough to upset our little applecart here, of course, but a little. Since the trial ended, you look like a ghost rattling her chains. You need a project."

"There's always a letdown after a trial but I'm not sure expanding the business is what I should do."

Sandy stared at her. "You have some other plan you forgot to mention?"

"Maybe I'll take some time off. Maybe a year."

Sandy sucked in her breath. "So it comes to this," she said.

"Comes to what?"

"Money. That's what it does . . . it gets inside people. They forget who they are." She seemed to be recalling something unpleasant. "I should have known. Since the beginning of this case, you've been compromising like crazy."

Right there was a reason to close up shop and move on: Sandy's big nose. "Don't be silly," Nina said, trying to be patient. "The money only makes it possible for me to examine my options."

"You would miss work."

Nina could think of many good reasons not to work today, tomorrow, or ever again, but in the hard light of Sandy's dark eyes they appeared rather insubstantial to her at the moment. "I don't know what I'm going to do. I just don't want to make any sudden decisions."

This time, Sandy studied her without anger. "Well," she said finally, "if you're looking to keep things small and invest your windfall temporarily, say the word. I've got this ex-brother-in-law with Charles Schwab. . . ."

"When the money comes in, it will seem more real to me, Sandy. Until then, I'm just spinning spiderwebs." She looked at the papers on her desk and thought, I can't believe it really will come in. That's the trouble.

"Something else is on your mind, isn't it?" Sandy asked. "Is this about the juror that died?" She had an unerring ability to press on the sore spot, a talent she shared with Paul.

"No, there's nothing else," Nina lied. She rustled a few papers and took a final drink from her cup, setting it down on the desk ceremoniously. "I want to touch base with Lindy. We've hardly talked since the verdict. Try to reach her at her friend Alice's or at her message number, okay?"

Sandy shrugged and went back to her desk.

Nina returned to her work in a state of emotional clutter. The weekend with Paul had been good, but things were never easy with him. He was so closely tied to her in every way, physically, emotionally, and even at work. She hoped he would forget about the juror. Wright was dead and the trial was over.

She hadn't even had time to miss Bob, who had gone on a field trip financed by his grandpa to the East Coast on Sunday and would be visiting the Bureau of Engraving with his classmates sometime today. A cup of coffee gave her back the illusion of clear thinking, and she concentrated on some pending files that needed her attention. With Lake Tahoe spread-eagled out the window in front of her, she allowed herself five luxurious minutes to weave images in her mind of exotic lands and freedom from financial worry before she needed to pack her bag, resume her normal duties, and head back to the courthouse.

"You're the fellow here about Wright," said Dr. Clauson, studying Paul through Coke-bottle lenses. A skinny, balding man, he wore a wrinkled, short-sleeved shirt over trousers that were shiny at the knees.

Paul had never seen the medical examiner's office before. In his mind, Doc Clauson forever loitered in the basement morgue at Placerville, where he had first seen him.

Clauson stepped behind a battle-scarred oak desk littered with gum wrappers, wadded-up bits of trash, and a hundred file folders. "Do I know you?"

"We've met. I work with Nina Reilly."

"Her?" said Clauson, inserting a piece of Juicy Fruit into his mouth. "She gonna drag me into another mess? She send you?"

"I'm here to satisfy my own curiosity. Nothing to do with her."

Clauson liked that answer, Paul could tell. Having survived a few run-ins with Nina himself, Paul could empathize.

"Well, it's just a run-of-the-mill thing," said Clauson, pulling a file out of a stack on the floor beside his desk.

He read for a moment, then scanned further as he spoke. "One of the bailiffs dialed nine-one-one. By the time the paramedics arrived, Wright had suffocated. They tried intravenous epinephrine, but it was too late."

"Dr. Clauson," Paul began.

"Call me Doc."

"Okay, Doc. I'm curious about what it says on his death certificate."

"Anaphylactic shock"—Clauson nodded—"with an immunologic component. That means as opposed to anaphylactoid shock related to nonspecific release of mediators." He tipped back in his chair, as if relishing the chance to go over the case, and spoke in the choppy sentences Paul remembered. "Only the second case I've seen.

First one was a woman; died from kissing a man who'd just polished off a bag of chocolate-covered peanut butter candies. Dead in a couple of minutes. Killed by a kiss. Sounds incredible, I know, but it happened."

"Would you mind telling me in general terms what anaphylactic shock is?"

"Sure. Basically, you introduce a foreign agent, an antigen, into an organism, and the organism begins an all-out war against itself. Shuts down breathing or shuts down circulation, or both."

"What causes it?"

"In this case, legumes. Peanuts are the most popular legume. A peanut is not a nut, properly speaking. We think some people become allergic because they are exposed to these tricky foods before an immature system can handle it properly. Probably mothers shouldn't be eating peanuts while they nurse their babies. Kids under three shouldn't eat peanut butter."

Paul mentally totted up the thousands of peanut butter sandwiches he had eaten as a boy. "But not everyone who is exposed young develops an allergy."

"True. Most don't."

"Are there other allergies besides the one to peanuts that can be deadly?"

"Of course, in susceptible people. Spider venom, pollen, antibiotics, vitamins. Most of his life, my father couldn't eat apples. We now know that an apple reaction can be related to a birch pollen or ragweed allergic response. During pollen seasons, similar proteins in fresh fruit cause reactions in a compromised immune system. But that's an odd one. And you've heard of allergies to bee stings, right?"

"Sure."

"Can be life-threatening. Good idea to watch what you eat from the time you're very young," said Clauson, patting a stomach that had thickened slightly since the days when he sucked on Camels as if they were M&M's.

"You did an autopsy on Wright?"

"Yep."

"Mind going into detail for me?"

"Classic case of anaphylaxis. Laryngeal edema, hoarseness—he was still calling out when the medics got there, but not for long. Stridor—that's harsh breathing. Angioedema, that's a deep edematous cutaneous process. But look here, I've got a picture." He handed a large, glossy color photo over to Paul.

"Man," Paul said. "What a way to go."

Clauson laid the picture on the desk in front of him and turned toward Paul. He crooked a thin finger and pointed.

"It's the most characteristic external feature of this condition—giant hives." He looked at his report and read, rolling the medical terms officiously around in his mouth. "Cutaneous wheals with erythematous, serpiginous borders and white centers." Putting the sheet aside he said, "Discrete borders, but you can see here, so rampant he swelled up head to toe. The eyes are the worst."

"How fast could that develop?"

"In this case, minutes. In some cases, people die in seconds. If he'd lived to get treated, those big red clumps would have disappeared over the next few days."

"He say anything?"

"Throat too swollen. Now, there's two ways to die with this thing. The angioedema—which he'd feel like a lump that blocks his breathing passages—can kill by causing respiratory insufficiency. Second way is vascular collapse, which can occur with or without hypoxia. The angioedema did him in. Way I could tell was the visceral congestion without a shift in the distribution of blood volume. Also, the lungs showed hyperinflation—that's something you can see with the naked eye and with a microscope, common in fatal cases with clinical bronchial obstruction. I've got a photo here."

"If he had gotten his kit and given himself a shot, what would have happened?"

"He would have calmed down all over and gone on with the show."

"This is what I don't understand. If he knew he was so dangerously allergic to peanuts, why wasn't he more careful? Why did he eat them?"

"Obviously, he had no idea he was eating peanuts." Clauson read from his notes. "Last meal was lunch in the jury room. Vegetable chow mein, egg rolls, and fortune cookie. Didn't make it far into the cookie part. Only a trace in the stomach."

"They put peanuts in chow mein?"

"Nope."

"In the egg rolls?"

"Nope."

"The cookie?"

"Nope."

"I assume you talked to the caterer?"

"A restaurant on Ski Run Boulevard. Owner swears there were no peanuts in the food. Wright called there before to check with them and ask them particularly not to use any in his meal."

"I don't get it."

If eyes as colorless as apricot pits could be said to twinkle, Clauson's did. "I said the same thing to myself a few days ago. Then I went home. I go home at night, not much is happening. Tube, bed, let the cat out. I'm a bachelor. Women don't like my work."

"Yeah?"

"Used to smoke like a fiend. Not as good as a wife, but Mr. Butts kept me company of a sort."

Clauson chewed his gum ruminatively. Paul waited for him to get to his point.

"Took a course at the college on cooking Asian food to meet some women. Didn't find a wife, but learned to cook."

"Uh-huh."

"Decided to make myself some Szechuan chicken and home-made egg rolls."

"Yes?"

"Looked at the bottle in my hand. Peanut oil. Lots of people cooking Chinese use peanut oil when they pinch the egg rolls shut."

"But . . . isn't it the protein in the peanuts that causes the reaction?"

"Oil will do it for some people."

"Ah-hah!"

"What I said," said Clauson.

"Did you ask the cook?"

"Swears she didn't."

"You think she's lying."

Clauson's shoulders shook slightly, as if he had been tickled. "Gotta be. The food wasn't bad enough to kill otherwise." He chuckled at his joke, then looked sober. "Here's negligence that caused a death, but nobody's gonna pursue it. Guy with a time bomb in his system like that should have always brought his own lunch."

"You think they're afraid they'll be sued."

"That's right, but I'm satisfied I know what happened. Done in by egg rolls."

"You sure the cook was lying?" Paul said

Clauson sighed. Paul had apparently tried his patience just a bit. "There's no question about the cause of death. You take the history of the patient before making a diagnosis. He's been allergic since he was about three."

"But this time he died."

"That was almost a predictable outcome of another exposure. Just a couple of months ago, he took a trip to the hospital after eating ice cream that listed almonds in the ingredients, but had sneaked in peanuts as filler and flavoring without changing the labeling. Now that was a hard source to trace. This one is obvious, whether or not the restaurant takes responsibility."

Paul had had his fifteen minutes. Doc Clauson jumped up, saying he had to go.

"Enjoyed talking with you," he said. "Nobody takes much interest in death by natural causes, even interesting causes, except maybe the insurance people, and they're only interested in how much they're going to owe the grieving family."

"It's fascinating stuff, how many paths lead to death," said Paul.

"Oh, Doc," he said, as Clauson put a hand on the door, "just one more thing."

Clauson had to check his notes one last time for an address.

Nina waited for Paul on her favorite bench in the yard outside the courthouse where she could soak up sun, listening to the wind lifting the branches of the trees around her, insects buzzing, and the distant din of the highway a mile away. Closing fluorescent-scarred eyes, she drifted in dark, mindless bliss for several minutes.

"Waiting, waiting," a voice said. The teddy bear had come back, the one Paul had given her when he proposed a long time ago, the one that spoke with his voice. But how could he be here? He lived in her front closet with her ski boots, his nagging tone for the time being smothered under a down jacket. "Wake up, sleepyhead." A hand, not a furry paw, took hold of her side and shook.

"I'm not sleeping!" To her surprise, although her feet remained on the ground, her cheek had found its way to the cool, hard surface of the bench.

"If you say so, Ladyship." Paul helped her to her feet. She straightened her jacket and turned her skirt back to face front.

"I must have dozed off. And don't call me that."

"Yes, you did and I'll consider it," said Paul. "Now how about lunch? It's through the looking glass you know, napping before the meal."

"I didn't sleep much this weekend," said Nina. "Now why do you suppose?"

"Better things to do," said Paul, maneuvering himself into the driver's seat. "You've finally got your head screwed on straight."

Nina laughed at that.

"Hmmm. Exactly how hungry are you?"

"I have time for a quickie," said Nina.

"I rise to a challenge," said Paul, starting the engine to his van, whose roaring start soon settled into a purr.

"Food, I mean."

"Oh, well." He drove down the hill toward town.

"Where are we going?" asked Nina. "It's so beautiful. Let's eat outside."

"I'm thinking Chinese," said Paul.

"Anywhere with an outdoor patio?"

"I don't think so. That's not the Chinese way."

"How do you know?"

"They hardly ever have windows. Some feng shui rule, I bet."

Nina took her brush out and ran it through her tumbled hair. "You like Chinese food?" she said, wincing as she snagged a rat.

"Let's just say, this food has an unusual provenance."

"You're full of surprises, aren't you?"

"Another secret unveiled. Damn," said Paul, pulling up in front of a storefront with a large parking lot in front of it. "Next thing, you'll be finding out how many women I've loved and lost."

"How many?"

"None," he said, pausing and then adding, "so beautiful as you."

"See Paul dodge," said Nina, giving him a kiss. "But it's okay. Your two ex-wives are persecution enough for me in the dark of night."

The restaurant's low, flat building had a fire-engine-red-lacquered sign, flanked by black tiles arching over pink walls trimmed with gold paint, the whole of which somehow created the impression of a grand Oriental pavilion.

"What's this place?" asked Nina, climbing out of the van. "Looks like more than a restaurant."

"It is. They rent rooms, too. Welcome to the Inn of Five Happinesses," said Paul. He hurried ahead to pull the brass knob. The door opened, and the pleasant aromas of fresh food and spices wrapped around them.

Once seated, Nina ignored the menu. "I always have the same thing," she said. "Cashew chicken."

"Have something else if you want," said Paul. "No one's forcing you."

"No. I'm just telling you. I want cashew chicken."

"Not in an experimental mood. Got you," said Paul, looking up with interest as a smooth-faced Asian man appeared silently beside him, notepad ready. "Okay. One cashew chicken. One vegetable chow mein. A dozen egg rolls. Steamed rice. Tea for two."

The waiter dipped his head slightly and turned away.

"You must be awfully hungry," said Nina. "You plan to eat a dozen?"

"There's always a doggy bag," said Paul.

"Hitchcock won't eat that stuff."

"For your bottomless pit of a son."

"Remember? Bob's out of town this week—" Nina began.

But Paul excused himself to wash his hands. She amused herself by watching the other patrons, some of whom were picking leisurely through an array of dishes, while others, obviously office workers on a limited break, shoveled it in.

Paul wandered toward the kitchen, pushing a pair of swinging doors aside like John Wayne, feeling like an unusually large intruder invading a foreign landscape.

Painted white, with a black and white tile floor, the kitchen was on the small side, and the several people inside, wearing white aprons over jeans, whacked and clanged and moved from one end to the other with the grace of a single organism. One whole wall was absorbed by a massive silver cook top. Hanging from the ceiling, copper and stainless steel pots shone as though polished by the warm moisture suspended in the air.

"No, no!" A boy who looked about twenty waved a flat wooden spatula at Paul. "You go!"

Over a wooden chopping block, a teenaged girl ignored him, slicing away at cabbage and spring onions, her knife glinting and sharp, hair that could only be described as scarlet in color standing up in a multitude of lengths like unmowed grass. A diminutive older woman wearing a hair net opened a pan to reveal an entire fish, head and all, sweating in clouds of steam. To her left, another boy ran a

Hobart dishwasher, sliding huge trays of dirty dishes in one end and out the other.

"Smells good," Paul said.

"Kitchen," said the kid, stepping up to Paul. About a foot shorter than Paul, but tightly muscled, he stood his ground. "You leave now."

Paul saw himself in a Jackie Chan movie, about to be chopped and flipped and tossed out the swinging door. "See, I'm taking a class in Chinese cooking," said Paul as politely as he could. "And for our final we're supposed to make egg rolls. Only problem is, I'm afraid I cut most of the classes. I really have no idea what I'm doing. So I thought, well, here I am eating egg rolls for lunch. No excuse for not watching how it's done."

"No!" said the boy, but the older lady who slid the fish expertly onto a platter spoke to him in Chinese, and he stepped back, glowering. Turning his back on Paul, he hoisted the tray on one arm and glided back into the restaurant.

"We're a family business. He's my disrespectful son," she said apologetically, rinsing a massive steel strainer full of shrimp with the vigor of a triathlete. "He is very rude."

"Not at all," said Paul. "I know it's not usual to let people in the kitchen. But I'd really appreciate it. . . ."

"Sure," the girl piped in, giving Paul a smile her mother could not see. "It gets boring in here with nobody to talk to except my brothers and my mother. Come watch the expert. I bet I've made ten thousand egg rolls this year alone."

The girl's mother, who had never halted her movements for a second, tossed the shrimp, some steamed rice, and vegetables in a wok. From bottles next to the stove, she dashed a bit of this and a bit of that, watching poker-faced as Paul stepped up to stand beside the girl.

"I'm Colleen," said the girl, giving her red lawn a toss.

"I'm Paul."

"Don't shake my hand unless your girlfriend is crazy about onions." With her knife, she pushed a heap of fixings into a bowl and wiped her forehead with the back of her arm. "Nothing gets rid of this smell."

Nina had been dreaming about her fee again. She had moved on to a fantasy of buying a lakeside home with a dock and a fine boat on which she and Bob could learn to water-ski and sail. She would replace Matt's lousy boat with a new one, top of the line for him and Andrea and the cousins. Then she would buy the Starlake office building, renovate, and take over the top two floors, hiring associates and promoting Sandy to supervise people besides Nina. Paul would not bug her about marriage. Their wild fling would go on for years and years until Nina decided unexpectedly to settle down or have another child, at which time he would settle into complete fidelity and become a marvelous father.

Content to play in her imaginary landscape for a while, some time passed before she realized Paul had not returned. Puzzled, she checked the restaurant's restroom, finding it empty. As she walked back to the table she spotted him hunched over a plate of steaming noodles. The table was suddenly covered with dishes.

"Are you okay?" she asked.

"Fine, fine," he chortled. "C'mon. Dig in. They really know how to cook here. Good food."

She picked up her chopsticks and pointed them at him. "Where were you?"

"In the kitchen, learning how to assemble egg rolls," said Paul. "It's a family business. Mom supervises the kitchen. The two oldest sons, Tan-Kwo and Tan-Mo, clean up and serve. They use only the freshest cabbage in their rolls," he said, biting down on one. "Mmm."

"But you hardly ever cook. You grill. And then, only steak."

"That's true."

"So?"

"So guess what? Dad had a heart attack two years ago. They've cleaned up their act. No more greasy bad stuff. Only fresh. And only pure."

Nina tried to keep her patience. "What are you talking about?"

"Pure canola."

She threw her napkin on the table, continuing to hold her sticks aloft. "Are you going to tell me what you're talking about?" she said. "Don't force me to torture you."

"This restaurant catered Clifford Wright's last meal," said Paul. "Doc Clauson said he must have eaten peanuts in some form. They said they didn't use 'em. He thought they were lying."

"And?"

"They don't use peanut oil anymore. They don't serve anything with peanuts. They only use cashews."

Nina heard the bewilderment in her own voice. "But aren't cashews nuts?"

"He wasn't allergic to nuts. He was allergic to legumes, and that includes peanuts."

"How do you know that?"

"Various sources."

"So . . . so he accidentally ate peanuts from somewhere else. What difference does it make?"

"Nina, if he didn't have an allergic reaction to the lunch, what killed him?"

She pushed her plate away. "Paul, no. No, no, no." She put a hand to her forehead and shook her head.

"Tan-Kwo in the kitchen says Clifford called the restaurant to check about the use of peanut oil in cooking before he touched his lunch. Wright told them then how serious the allergy could be, but they already knew about it.

"In spite of sounding like he's just off the boat, that's just an act. For most of the year, Tan-Kwo is premed at UC Berkeley."

"Paul . . . you're . . . you're . . ."

"I spoke to Clifford Wright's family this morning. They're very distraught. They'd like to know more about what happened."

Nina sat very still, her thoughts beating around in her mind like Ping-Pong balls. "If someone tampered with the jury, the judge will

throw out the verdict. We'd have a mistrial. You're suggesting someone spiked his food with peanuts."

"Just considering the possibility."

"You really think there's something to find out?"

"It just doesn't feel right to me."

"Why can't you just let this alone? Paul, if this verdict is set
aside I am in so deep I might never be able to dig my way out. I bet
everything on winning. I'm in hock up to my eyeballs."

It was a plea. Paul's brow furrowed.

"So, what are you going to do?"

He took her hand. "You tell me."

31

THEY HAD AN UNCOMFORTABLE RIDE back to Nina's car at the courthouse, during which she pled exhaustion and turned the radio up and closed her eyes to drown him out both visually and aurally. She gathered her things to get out of the car and stepped out. She held the door open and leaned in.

"Okay, Paul, do it. Damn you. I won't sleep until you tell me you're wrong."

"That's my Nina," Paul said.

She slammed the door in his face.

Paul headed straight for the South Lake Tahoe police department to root out an old acquaintance, Sergeant Cheney.

Cheney welcomed him with a smile, motioning him to sit. He had a phone glued to his head, and a pen scribbling in one hand. "Uh-huh," he said. "Yep." This continued for several minutes, while Paul examined the photographs on Cheney's desk, especially the one of his wife, a lovely toasty-brown-colored woman with hair lighter than her skin, looking much younger than the overweight Cheney.

Finally, Cheney hung up. The phone rang. He ignored it.

"Haven't seen you around in a while," he said. "If you don't count the fact that you've been involved in two out of the five deaths I've investigated in the past coupla years."

"I can see you're busy," said Paul. "I appreciate you taking the time to see me. I'll keep it short."

"Let me help you along," said Cheney. He looked down at his

papers. "Clifford Wright, white male, thirty-two. Died from a severe allergic reaction called anaphylactic shock, presumably from ingesting some form of peanuts. Have I got it so far?"

"Well, yes," said Paul, utterly taken aback. "How did you know I was here about Wright?"

"I'm a detective, remember," said Cheney, "and then there was that phone call just now from Doc Clauson. He says you came nosing around the medical examiner's office this a.m. You got the Doc's curiosity bump itching. He's asked me, unofficially, to look into a couple of things."

"Such as?"

"They use peanut oil at the Five Happinesses or not?" asked Cheney. "I'll probably mosey over there this evening. I feel a hankering for kung pao prawns. They have that over there? You know?"

"I didn't notice."

Cheney clapped his hands together. "Figured you'd already been. Bet you noticed a bunch of things about peanuts."

"Like, they don't use them or peanut oil."

"Seeing you here, figured they might not."

"I guess you've already answered my question." Paul got up to leave.

"Which was?"

"How final is the medical examiner's ruling on Wright's death? Legally, I mean. The family is hiring me to find out."

"Now, how'd you hook up with them?"

"Called with my condolences and happened to mention that insurance companies don't pay as well for a natural death. They'll inherit more if somebody else hurried him along. Turns out Wright had a hefty life insurance policy. If I come up with some proof that Wright's death was less than kosher, how hard will it be to get Clauson to change his ruling on the cause of death?"

"Oh, his report's final. Unless he changes his mind."

"He can change it."

"Yep. Quick as popping one of those sticks of gum he's always got lying around these days. But the real answer is, our files on that case remain open. And now you've opened up a brand-new direction for our ongoing inquiries. Keep in touch, why don't you?"

"Be glad to," said Paul.

Back in his car, he punched numbers into his phone. "Sandy," he said. "Any idea how I could reach Wish?"

"He's right here."

"Put him on."

"Why?" asked Sandy.

"I have some work for him."

The phone must have flown to Wish, because he answered only a second later. "How," said Wish, "Chief Wish Whitefeather here," and that greeting was followed by a thumping noise, then an "Ouch." Sandy's son had a sense of humor about being Native American his mother apparently didn't appreciate.

"So you're a chief now," said Paul. "Too important for me to corner you for a couple of hours for a project I'm working on?"

"I'll check my calendar."

"I'm serious."

"So am I," said Wish, hurt. "I'm taking classes at night, you know. Police administration."

"Oh. Sorry," said Paul.

"When do you need me?"

"Today, possibly into tomorrow."

"What are we doing?"

"Interviews."

"You running the show?"

"Nope. You've been promoted from assistant to detective-in-training."

"Outstanding! But . . . how will I know what to ask? Are you going to fill me in on what's going on?"

Paul did.

"Okay, let me see if I have this straight. You think someone put something into the Chinese food this juror ate right before he tossed in his chopsticks."

"Yeah, someone out for a puff, or a stretch. Someone went out there and took care of our friend Clifford Wright."

"How do you know that's what happened?" asked Wish, sounding dubious. "I never heard anything about him being killed by someone."

"I don't know it. Yet. It's just a hunch."

"Oh," said Wish.

"I spoke very briefly with one of the jurors this morning already, Grace Whipple. She said the bailiff brought lunch in a little late, at about twelve-fifteen. They jumped on that food like prisoners of war. Said it was a real high point in a nasty morning. They had all probably been thinking about it for at least an hour. Nobody could have fiddled with anything in full view of the rest of the jury under those circumstances."

"So you think it happened when the food was out in the hall for about fifteen minutes after it arrived, before anyone ate, and all the jurors were coming and going."

"Well, it was outside the anteroom in a private hall that leads to the clerk's offices and the judge's chambers. That hall is locked. You have to have business with the court, or work there, to get in."

"So you think it was one of the jurors."

"If anyone. Only they knew what was happening in that jury room. At this point, I don't know anyone did anything. I'm just intrigued."

"Do you really think someone planned to kill this guy by giving him an allergy?"

"Not really. It's more likely, if this actually is the case, someone got angry, saw an opportunity, and grabbed it without knowing how serious the consequences might be. Maybe they just thought it would temporarily put him out of commission."

"Where would they get the peanuts?"

"Apparently, most of them brought snacks."

"I really don't get this."

"What?"

"Nina won the case. Why does she care about that juror?"

"She told me to go ahead and check it out, Wish." Paul had known she would. Ultimately, the truth was too important to Nina, even when it might work against her. "She doesn't expect us to find anything."

"But if one of the other jurors offed him, Nina's verdict will get put aside, won't it?"

"We're a long way from that happening, Wish. Right now, our role is to gather information, not to worry about what might happen."

"Okay. Who do I go see?"

Paul decided to assign Wish the bulk of the jurors, those who had supported Mike in the beginning, and those who had been persuaded by Cliff to go with Mike later, according to exit interviews conducted by the media, which had pounced on the jury after the verdict. They would have less cause to want to harm him. Paul would take the ones that opposed Wright—Diane, Mrs. Lim, Courtney, and maybe Sonny. And then he might want to talk with Lindy. She had the most to gain, although how she could know what was happening in the jury room was a problem, unless she had a confederate.

"So I need your help on two fronts. Before anything else, the first thing I want is, I need you to . . . um"—some of this was tricky; he didn't want Wish to break any ethical rules to get him what he needed, but it was the lazy way and the sensible way to keep this investigation short—"get me the jury's addresses, phone numbers, everything. Nina will cooperate on that front."

"Easy!" said Wish enthusiastically. "I'm sure we've got a list right here somewhere."

"Good, good. And then"—now here came the important part, the part Nina might not embrace so eagerly—"if you come across anything relevant, of course . . ."

"I'll keep my eyes open," said Wish. "Of course, I can't bring you anything really private."

"Of course not," said Paul, hoping nevertheless that Wish might, in his helpful innocence, stumble on something useful.

"I won't let your faith in me down," said Wish.

"Who taught you to talk like that?" Paul asked.

"That would be me," said Sandy. "Just a little motherly advice. And there's more. Find yourself another flunky."

"You just eavesdropped on a private conversation between me and your son," said Paul. "Nina won't like hearing that."

"He's underage. And I'll tell you what Nina won't like. Nina won't like you using my son to weasel your way into our private files."

"That's insulting," said Paul. "Wish would never do that and neither would I. Besides, Nina wants this investigation to be over as much as I do. She won't mind us getting what we need quickly and efficiently, and getting on with it."

"Really?" said Sandy. "Hang on while I ask her about that."

"Oh, don't bother. We can get the juror's names from public records. Now, if I promise not to ask Wish to take advantage of his position at your offices to grub through trash cans or something, can I please borrow him for a few hours?"

"For how much?" asked Sandy.

"Lindy?"

A silhouette opened the door to Lindy's trailer and stood there, irresolute.

Lindy came from the little kitchen, wiping her wet hands on a washcloth, calling, "Alice?"

"It's me." She saw Mike, the sun behind him, making a fuzzy halo of his hair.

"I, uh, hoped you'd let me come in. No phone, so I couldn't call first."

"What do you want, Mike?"

"Can I come in?"

She was so bewildered to see him that she found herself stepping aside to let him in, saying, "I can't believe you remembered the place." He followed her into the trailer and she motioned toward the table with its built-in benches. "I was just making some coffee."

"No, please. Don't bother," Mike said. He sat down and leaned on the table on his elbow and scratched his head, familiar actions.

The room felt smaller with Mike in it. She hadn't broken her solitude over the past months with any guests. A long time ago, they had lived here together for a short time. She could barely remember.

Lindy went to the window, looked out for traces of a lawyer or a sheriff or Rachel, but Mike's black Cadillac sat all alone in the turnaround. The cloud of dust he'd raised still drifted in the breeze. Besides Comanche's stall and the storage shed, the landscape, all rock and high scrub desert, was silent and shadeless at midday.

"I see you're packing up," Mike said. "You never should have come out here to this lonely old place anyway."

"Where else would I go?" Lindy said. Something in Mike's face stopped her from going on and saying what she had a right to say about that. "Dad loved it out here," she said instead. "It hasn't been so bad."

"Reminds me of when we lived out here for a while, you remember? Tumbleweed Flats, we called it. No phone, no TV. Damn, it got hot. It's sure hot out here today, isn't it?"

"Why did you come? You could see me tomorrow in your lawyer's office."

Mike looked out the window at the rolling brown flank of the mountains silently, chewing his lip.

"Did he send you all the way out here to soften me up?" She went back into the little kitchen and came back with a couple of beers. She didn't care if that was why he had come, that was how glad she was to see him, but she wasn't going to let him know that, he didn't deserve to know that, so she slapped down the beers and said, "Here. I'm having one anyway."

"You got every right to say anything you want, Lin."

Looking like a man with his head in a guillotine, his face was resigned and frightened. He'd screwed up his courage to come out here and try to tell her—what? "You look terrible," Lindy said.

"You look great. No wonder. You beat the pants off me. You did."

She had a long drink from the bottle. "I like beer out here. It cools me off better than wine."

"Seems like a long time since we talked," said Mike.

"We've had mouthpieces to do that for us."

"Yeah."

"How've you been?"

"Not good."

He didn't seem inclined to get to the point, and she didn't care. He came into the bare room and filled it up for her, completed a sketchy picture. She just wanted to sit there and enjoy his huge presence for as long as it could last.

"I've been riding Comanche all over this desert," she said after a minute. "Look." She spilled out the contents of a dirty cotton drawstring sack onto the table. White rock pieces, jagged like shark teeth on the edges, tumbled out. "Collected these a few days ago. I had to get on a ledge about fifty feet up one of those rock faces, lie on my back, and chip away with my hammer. I doubt anybody else had ever been at that particular face. I've got more of it out back in a big pail of water." Mike turned the rocks over, holding one up to the sunlight streaming onto the table.

"Beautiful. You always wanted to go out and prospect for opal."

"There is some around here. Dad looked for silver, but that was all prospected out even before he came here, and I'm sure he never thought about opal. Unfortunately, I don't think this spot is as rich as I thought it might be. I'm not finding much."

Mike nodded, looking fatigued as he had most days in court. Lindy felt the urge to apologize to him for putting him through the court case, but resisted. He'd thrown her out and chosen Rachel. What did she have to apologize for? "It's a long drive out here. Why don't you rest? You look really tired."

"Thanks. But I have to get going in a few minutes."

Yes, you need to run on home to your pretty, young lover, Lindy said to herself, using the painful thought to touch the bruises on her heart and remind her that she needed to protect herself. He had no right to hurt her anymore.

"I came to talk to you." Well, that was obvious. She saw how awkward he felt.

"One last time?" she said. "I thought we said our good-byes out by the lake that night."

"I'll be selling the business, moving on."

Guarding herself at this introduction of the business between them she said, "That's your decision, Mike, although I'm sorry to hear it. Do you want to work up some installment payment plan? If that's what you came here to talk me into, that's fine."

Mike drank most of the bottle down in one long swallow. He set the bottle down on the table with a clatter. "You haven't seen the receiver's final report. My lawyer called me just before I left. All that expansion you were working on in Europe fell apart after you left. And the bottom dropped out of the domestic spa market. A Chinese company came in and undercut us. Somehow, it didn't matter any-more to me—"

"How much did we lose?"

"We might get seventy million for it if we can sell it. Less if we liquidate and just go out of business."

"But," she could barely contain her shock, "how could that happen? I mean, at the beginning of all this, wasn't it worth at least two hundred?"

"Months of neglect," he said simply. "I let it go, along with you."

"Seventy million. Mike, that's my share. That's the judgment my lawyer's writing up right now."

"So I'm told. I didn't get it at first, but my lawyer says it's the value of the business from the time we—"

"Yes. From the time we split up. Well, that's awful news, Mike. I'm sorry." She thought. "You'll appeal the verdict then?"

"No. I'm done with courtrooms."

"Mike, why'd you have to be so pigheaded—"

"Please, Lin. Not now." Here was her chance to rub his nose in his failures, all of them, but how could she with him looking so collapsed and old in his defeat? She actually reached her hand out toward his hand, but thoughts sprang into her mind to arrest the gesture. On the witness stand he had barely admitted her role in the business. He had denigrated, insulted, cheated, and betrayed her . . . and all the while Rachel had whispered in his ear, touched his arm . . . she returned her hand to her side.

"Listen." he went on obliviously, apparently too wrapped up in his own inner struggle to admit hers to his consciousness. "You want to know the worst thing? The worst thing is I don't understand what happened to me. One day we were happy, and the next day I jumped into a bottomless pit."

She bit her tongue, going back into the kitchen to get him another beer. When she returned, he had another stone between his fingers. He turned it back and forth in the light, his face intense and absorbed.

He set the stone back into the sack. "Rachel left me this morning," he said, his eyes fixed on the sack, not her.

Lindy folded her arms. "The receiver's report."

"She read it. Then she set it down on the dining room table and she swung her purse onto her shoulder, and she said, 'Bye, Mike,' and walked out the door. Went back to handsome Harry, is my guess."

"And you came straight here to cry on my shoulder."

"No, Lin, I . . ."

"You have some nerve," Lindy said, unable to hide the anger vibrating in her voice.

"I came to tell you you were right. You're smarter than me, Lindy. You're smarter about living your life. I was too old for Rachel and she was in it for the money."

"Now you figure that out?"

"I guess I knew, Lin, but I wanted her anyway. There's no excuse, no explanation. I just lost my way." He didn't say anything more.

Lindy hadn't seen Mike as rattled as this since the old days in the ring, after a few bad thumps on the head. "Well, I guess you loved her," she said.

"For a month or two."

"Was it all because we never had kids?"

"Only a little."

"Still, too bad we didn't. Then we'd have something more important than money to fight about." She laughed slightly.

Mike was looking at her. "You let your hair go natural. And it's longer than I remember. I like it. Goes great with your suntan. You look strong again. During the trial, I was worried about you."

"Don't you sweet-talk me." She didn't tell him she had worried about him, too. What would be the point?

Mike slid out from behind the table and came around behind her. Leaning his head down, he rested it on her shoulder. He stroked her hair, pulling it gently back, running his fingers through it. "I guess that's all. I guess I should go."

"Yes, you should go now."

He pulled her up from her chair, and made her face him. He took both hands in his. "I apologize, Lin," he said, putting his cheek against her cheek, "for ruining everything."

"I don't trust you anymore," she said.

"I know."

With her eyes closed, she tasted the salt of his sweat.

32

"YOU THE PUBLIC DEFENDER?" SONNY Ball sat in the glassed-in cage at the county jail talking through a telephone. He moved fast and jerky, like a man about to jump out of his skin.

"Sorry, no. I'm from Nina Reilly's office. I'm talking with all the jurors in the Markov case."

"I don't have time for that. I've got my own trouble." Sonny twiddled the phone, nodding his head rapidly to music only he could hear.

"Looks to me like you have time to burn, Sonny," Paul said.

"Which explains why I need a lawyer."

"If your lawyer comes in, I'll leave."

"Yeah, do that. So here we are. What you want to know? Your team won, didn't it?"

"Well, we always want to do better," Paul said. "It helps to interview jurors whether you win or lose. Find out what mistakes we made or what we did well."

Sonny rolled his tongue around in his mouth. "What do I get out of it?"

"Well, I can't pay you, but—"

"Make a phone call for me?"

"Sure, I guess so."

"Here's the number."

Paul wrote it down.

"Tell him to get down here and bail me the fuck out."

"Will do."

"All right, then." Sonny assumed a hilariously serious expression, still drumming and twiddling and nodding all at once, and said, "Ain't this a laugh? I do my civic duty, and they check my name out and find this stupid drug warrant. They arrested me the minute I walked out of the jury room that day. That's the thanks I get."

"Your service on the jury was greatly appreciated."

"Think it might help get me outa here?"

"I can't make any promises."

"It's not like I got caught doing a line in the jury bathroom."

"I don't want to hear about it if you were. I'd like to talk about the last day of the deliberations."

"Sure, sure. Sure."

"You ended up voting for Lindy Markov."

"Right."

"Mind if I ask what factors influenced you most?"

"I didn't like Markov. He's the kind of guy that always takes advantage and gets all the credit. A bastard pain in the ass. Also, the girlfriend was very uppity. She never even looked at me once. And I heard so much bullshit in that jury room, my brain ached. It was time to go. And then there were issues."

Paul wrote it all down.

"Put down that I felt that an implied contract existed. And her old man made her sign that paper, so it didn't count."

"I understand that at one point, just before Mr. Wright collapsed, you were about to change your vote and vote for Mr. Markov."

"Yeah. I just about did. Then Cliff went down. You should of seen his face. I'm thinking twice before I eat Chinese again."

"Why were you about to change your vote, though?"

"Cliff went to work on me."

"His arguments convinced you?"

Sonny stopped dancing with his head long enough to let out a snort. "He caught me at the morning break, said a few things that made me reconsider. I resisted as long as I did because I thought

Markov just flat out lied on the stand. He had a shifty look I've seen a few times before. And were we supposed to believe the crud he said on the stand, about forgetting this and forgetting that?"

"What changed your mind?"

"Just before lunch Cliff started in on me in front of everybody else. Hey, he had a point about Lindy Markov. She was kinda pretty for such an old lady. Probably was messing around. He really needed my vote to win, and the three women weren't about to shift over to Mike. So, I reminded myself how a guy like Cliff might turn out to be a better friend than enemy."

"What did he say to you?"

Sonny looked irritated at the question. "Oh, maybe he'd get me a job or something."

"He said that?"

"Let's just leave it that he knew how to persuade people."

"But after he, um, collapsed, you ended up voting for Mrs. Markov."

"Well, old Cliff wasn't in any position to help out anymore, was he? So I went back around to my original vote, like the judge said to do."

"I'm curious," Paul said. "Why would Cliff pressure people into his point of view? Do you think he had some special connection with Mr. Markov?"

"No," Sonny said. "It had nothing to do with Markov. He was a power-tripper. He had to beat out the women, that was it. The mountain climber with the steel-shank shoes, the real-estate lady, and the cute little student. Courtney. He had to prove he was better than them, by winning the fight."

"But why?"

Sonny looked pityingly at Paul, saying, "You know. Sure, let 'em win, let 'em cut your balls off. That's what he said to me. Enough said?"

Paul shrugged and said, "Okay. Except you didn't feel that way yourself."

"That's because I wasn't concerned about those women doing anything I didn't want them to do with my balls," said Sonny.

"By the way, did you see the lunch as it was brought in that day?"

"We all did. We were hungry. It smelled good."

"Did anybody go out in the hall before the lunch came in?"

"We had a break and everybody ran around, smoking, drinking, snortin'." He guffawed. "What the hell do you care about our down-time?"

"Did any of the women go out in the hall before the lunch came in?" Paul asked insistently.

"I was busy, okay? Who knows and who the hell cares?"

Courtney lived with her mother in a big ranch-style family home in the Tahoe Keys. When she answered the door, Paul was surprised to see Ignacio Ybarra, another ex-juror, with her. He was holding her hand.

They talked for several minutes, but as Paul suspected, neither one shed any light on Cliff's death.

"Can you think of anyone else who might have gone out into that hallway where the food was?" Paul said, right before leaving. "Anytime in the hour, say, before you broke for lunch?"

In unison, they said, "No."

"Are you saying someone poisoned Cliff?" Courtney asked.

"Of course not. But, just for the mental exercise, if someone were going to poison him, who would it be?" Paul said.

"No one!" said Courtney.

"Diane," said Ignacio.

Paul ate his lunch at a new Mexican restaurant that had just opened up at Round Hill Mall, then drove back into town wiping chile colorado from his lips. He wondered if he would know whether Diane Miklos had dropped something peanutty into the cartons the minute he saw her. Sometimes it worked out that way.

She lived in a chalet-style home on the hill going up toward

Heavenly. Paul parked around the corner in a fine stand of ponderosa pine and reviewed his notes. Midforties, old for a climber. Genevieve had placed an article from a climbing magazine about Diane's exploits into the file. Diane had come to the mountains late, spent a couple of years getting in shape and taking mountaineering courses at Jackson Hole and North Conway, both good places to go, and then climbed several Sierra peaks. She had acquitted herself well and headed for the Alps for a year, making a winter ascent of Mont Blanc, no mean feat, and apparently there hooked up with the climber, Gus Miklos, a man from Athens with a world-class reputation. They had married a few years back, and occasionally climbed together.

She had set her sights on the Seven Summits, a goal Paul could appreciate. The idea was to climb the tallest mountain on each continent, including, of course, Everest. Besides Mt. Elbrus, the European summit, she'd managed to bag the Carstensz Pyramid in Indonesia, Aconcagua in Argentina the previous year, and Kilimanjaro the year before that. Everest and the others, Mt. McKinley in Alaska, and Mt. Vinson in Antarctica were still in the future, if she lived that long.

Paul found all this very interesting. He hoped Diane Miklos hadn't killed Wright. She must have real character to live out this particular dream.

She didn't answer the door at first, so he rang again. She finally opened it and groaned when she saw him. "I forgot you were coming," she said. "Do we have to do this?"

"I won't keep you long. We really appreciate your time."

"You may as well come on in, then. Don't mind the mess." She sat back down in the middle of the floor. The entire room was heaped with rucksacks, duffel bags, stoves, ropes, pitons and anchors and hooks, helmet, food packets, deep-loft parkas, maps, books, and boots. She picked up a piece of what looked like parachute cloth and went back to mending it. On the table lay a camcorder and boxes of film. "Well?" she said.

A small, well-built woman with narrow blue eyes and a firm mouth, she lifted her head to listen to him.

"Where are you headed?" Paul said.

"Everest." All he could see of her was a bright haystack of hair and the busy, competent hands. "They had a cancellation. I got an unexpected opening. I'm leaving tomorrow."

"Is your husband going?" Over on a buffet behind a rough oak dining room set, he saw a picture of a grinning, dark-haired man wrapped in red parka and ski glasses with nothing but blue behind him.

"He did Everest in '94. So, no. I'm on my own, so to speak."

"I'm impressed." He was. He let it show in his voice.

"Wait till I make a successful summit for that."

"I was in the Peace Corps in Nepal," Paul said, "a long time ago. Trekked up to Base Camp, went up Kala Patar to see the big mountain. The jet stream was pluming off it and had blown all the snow off the summit. Any climbers must have been blown right off, although the sun blasted down so fiercely we were wearing T-shirts. Dark-blue sky, white mountains all around, and that squat black pyramid, up so much higher even from eighteen thousand feet." He could picture it all. "You going to fly into Lukla?" he asked. "If so, I hope they've improved the airstrip since I was there."

"Don't try to scare me," she said, but she caught Paul's smile. She was thawing. "Usually the first thing people want to know is how much I am paying to have some hundred-twenty-pound Sherpa drag me up on a short rope, as if I haven't been training and climbing for years, and as if my survival won't be up to me at all."

He could guess how much she was paying. He wanted to know where she got her money. "It is expensive."

"Yes, well. I have a wealthy sponsor for this trip."

"Anyone I might know?" Paul asked. Did Lindy pay money to Diane to find out what was going on in the jury room? Did she pay her to guarantee a positive verdict?

"Nope. I have a dear ex-climbing buddy with wobbly knees who managed somehow to scrounge the money for this. She has nothing to do with the Markovs, if that's what you're suggesting." She was getting defensive again.

"Well, you know and I know you'll have to be extraordinary to

get up there. There's been so much publicity lately about the trage-
dies on Everest, but I hear you waltzed up Vinson in extreme conditions last January."

"Waltzed?" She slapped her knee, laughing. "I staggered up and
tottered down. I have never been so cold. But it was beautiful. I want
to go back and climb in the Trans-Antarctics sometime. Incredible
mountains, the bases buried in the ice sheet, whole ranges nobody's
ever set foot on."

"You're braver than me," Paul said. "Would you be the first
woman to make it up all seven?"

"No. Junko Tabei first did it in 1991."

"How did you get into climbing?"

"A friend introduced me," she said briefly. Then, as if she
couldn't resist, she added, "I used to be a professor of political science."

"I know that. From the jury questionnaire. I figured you must
have a social conscience, and that's why you decided to serve rather
than find some excuse to get out of it."

She got up with a swift, lithe movement, turned to some items
in the corner, and began sorting through them, her back to him.
"Put this down in your report, if you want. I'll never do it again. I've
never seen such a bunch of goons."

"Yeah, I've already heard a few stories."

"You mean the scream? I was driven to that. But they were so
irrational most of them, so taken in by that wolf in sheep's clothing,
Cliff Wright. I finally blew my stack. I hope the verdict stands up.
Tell Mrs. Markov it was a near thing."

· Paul nodded his head, saying, "I heard about that, too. What do
you think saved the day for us?"

Diane turned around and put her hands on her hips. "As you
have no doubt also heard, we had Rasputin running the jury. He had
them all hypnotized, all except Courtney and Mrs. Lim, and Sonny. I
felt truly sorry for our system. And then Rasputin was gone and the
alternate came in, and sanity was restored."

"Are you talking about Cliff Wright? Incredible, him getting sick."

"At such a pivotal moment, too. And I read it was peanut oil in his food. I wonder if it really was the restaurant, or if somebody didn't just put a few drops on his egg roll." A surprisingly direct person, she certainly wasn't stupid, either.

"Why, who would do a thing like that?" Paul asked.

"Wish I'd thought of it. Mrs. Lim was seething, but she didn't show it. Maybe she took him out. If so, I'll testify in her defense. There were mitigating factors."

She seemed quite matter-of-fact about these events. Sitting back down on the floor, she pulled her legs up into a full lotus. Her gray rag socks reminded Paul of his own half-forgotten days in the mountains. Noticing him watching, she said, "Suppleness is almost as important as strength."

"You seem to have it all." She really did. A woman like this didn't worry about making a living, working night and day. Her job was to live. She had even found the right man for her, a fellow traveler. Sure, she was selfish, but she wouldn't waste the best years of her life on clients that took and took and never paid on time. "But I'll tell you what I think is the most important quality for a climber. It's the ability to go one step further than anyone else would think possible. To do what has to be done in extreme conditions. To let nothing stop you. Do you think you have that ability?"

Diane smiled. "Definitely."

Paul said, "Speaking of extreme conditions, it was getting pretty extreme there in the jury room. Cliff Wright was doing his number on everyone, and you seem to have been the only one capable of stopping him."

"I'd already lost," Diane, said, watching him. "There was nothing more I could do. We were about to vote."

"And then, poof! Cliff was gone and in came the alternate with a fresh perspective, as you said."

"Just in the nick of time."

"You were out in the hall just before the food came in, weren't you?"

"I think I know what you're getting at."

"You were standing there, and—"

Diane said, "You want me to come right out and say it? Is that what you want?"

"Please," said Paul, his pulse racing.

"Okay. I'll be brutally honest. Tell Mrs. Markov she doesn't have to worry about me. I didn't see her and I couldn't testify against her. She must have done it right before I came out. Tell her—like you said, Paul. Tell her I understand it was extreme circumstances.

"Now, Paul, you tell me something. I promise I will keep it completely secret. I give you my word. I've been thinking this over and there's just the one thing I don't understand. How in the hell did she know what was going on in the jury room?"

Paul shook his head.

"Was it Courtney? Did she buy her off?"

"I don't know that it was Mrs. Markov," Paul said, finally finding his voice.

"Who else would care enough to do that to Wright?" Diane said. "I mean, come on."

"But like you said, she'd have no way of knowing how much trouble her case was in."

"It sure was a strange coincidence, then."

"You knew, you cared, and you were outside."

She laughed again. "I have better things to do with my life. I wouldn't really hurt somebody to win. Even in extreme conditions. How old are you, Paul?"

"Me? Forty. And a half."

"I was the same age, forty, when I started climbing, and these have been the best years of my life. I wouldn't jeopardize that, even for Lindy Markov's millions."

"I admire what you're doing. It's the sort of thing most people don't even dare dream about." He thought for a minute and said, "What do you think? Did somebody kill him?"

"No," Diane said. "It's going to be the restaurant. It's going to be the prosaic explanation." But she stopped him at the door, saying, "What do you think? Really."

"I thought it was you, Diane," Paul said.

He stopped briefly at the courthouse for a chat with Deputy Kimura, who assured him that no one except court personnel were allowed into the private hallway. And then admitted that yes, there were exceptions here and there.

Almost everyone remotely connected with the case seemed to have passed through at some point, including Lindy's friend, Alice, but Kimura did not recall seeing her or Lindy there on the day Wright died. "I watch for outsiders," he had said. "I didn't see anyone that day who didn't belong."

Alice looked at him through a peephole in the door. "Yes?" she said.

"I'm here to see Lindy Markov," Paul said.

"Really." She opened the door. In leopard-skin tights, a long yellow jersey, gold sandals, and disheveled blond hair, she had a gloss of perspiration on her brow that she wiped away with a kerchief. He recognized her from Mike's birthday party.

She looked him over. "She's just full of surprises these days." She was out of breath. She must have been exercising. He heard music playing in the background, but it didn't sound like exercise music.

"I work with Nina Reilly," Paul said. "Paul Van Wagoner." Lucky to run into Alice. She had reasons for wanting Lindy to win.

"Alice Boyd." She shook his hand briefly. "I'm sorry but Lindy isn't here at the moment. Mind telling me what this is about?"

"Just winding up loose ends." Actually, he found himself listening to the sultry singer in the background, the way she stretched out a syllable over several notes in the scratchy recording. He recognized the song as one from the forties, "My Old Flame." Give Alice one credit for good taste in music.

"Everything's okay, isn't it? I mean, she's going to get her money, isn't she?"

"Well . . ." Paul said, focusing once more on Alice, interested in her concern. "You know how it is when it comes to this much money."

"Shit. He's appealing isn't he?"

"He stands to lose a lot if he doesn't."

"I knew it. That bastard. He'll drag this thing out until we . . . Lindy's ruined! What's her lawyer want? More money? Because, sweetie, until we get a big check out of Markov Enterprises, there is no money." She must have heard herself ranting, because she stopped.

"I really need to talk to her for a couple of minutes."

"Ah," she said. Light seemed to dawn. "You just have some paperwork for her to sign or something like that? And this is not specifically about an appeal?" She tried to read his face. "Help me out here. Has he appealed?"

"Not that I know of."

She laughed with relief. "Jesus, you had me going there. I mean, she is my dearest friend. And she really needs that money."

And sweetie, she's not the only one, Paul thought. "Any idea where to find her?"

"She doesn't like me giving out her whereabouts."

He sighed and turned toward the door. "Too bad. Ms. Reilly's going to be disappointed. This will cause a delay."

"But you're from her lawyer, right? So I can tell you," Alice said. "She left right after the verdict. Headed for her shanty out there in the boondocks in the Carson Range outside of Reno."

"By the way, Ms. Boyd. If you don't mind my asking, where were you when Clifford Wright died?"

Alice pulled a handkerchief out and wiped moisture off her face. "While we waited for the verdict, I worked at the shop. We do a lot of impromptu weddings. It's one of the ironies of my life that I spend most of my day putting together bouquets and corsages for weddings.

My assistant will confirm that I was there that morning, until we got called in for a verdict in the afternoon. Why do you ask?"

"Ever been in the hallway outside the jury room? Where the clerks' offices are?"

"Why, yes," she said.

"Mind if I ask if there's another reason you care so much if Lindy Markov gets her money?"

"She supported me for years," said Alice simply. "That's God's truth. I'd do anything for her, and I'm not the only one. Mind telling me what this is all about?"

"Some of the circumstances to do with Clifford Wright's death are in question."

"You mean . . . someone hurt him intentionally?" The thought agitated her. "Goddamn it! I see what's going on here. This is some plan to get the verdict changed, isn't it? This is Mike's doing. He'll do anything to win! I knew it!"

He left her to her tantrum.

By the time Paul reached Lindy's trailer, his van had been complaining for twenty miles.

Lindy must have heard it, too, because she stood in front with her arms folded, apparently awaiting his arrival, in a square of yellow light from her doorway that made the only illumination for miles.

"Brrr," he said getting out, stepping directly into a puddle.

A low, foggy dusk had spread around the mountains like a silver belt. Lindy wore jeans and a thick ski sweater but he could see that she was shivering. "Come inside," she said, motioning him in.

She poured him a cup of coffee she already had made, then sat down across from him at a fold-down table. "What are you doing here, Paul? Is everything okay? I talked to Nina this afternoon and she didn't mention you were coming."

She would be his hardest interview. He couldn't think of any reason to have come other than the one that had brought him. "Some questions have come up."

"What questions?"

"You may not realize it, but the police have not closed the book on Cliff Wright's death."

She drummed nicely manicured fingernails on the table. "I didn't know that," she said. "Why haven't they? I thought he had some kind of allergic reaction. I thought they knew that for sure."

"That's true. But what they are trying to find out is exactly what caused the allergic reaction."

"How will they do that? Someone told me he was allergic to a bunch of things."

"Who told you?"

"I don't know. Seems like we were going over the jury members once and someone mentioned it."

So she knew about the allergies. That was key. "I think they are trying to narrow down the possibilities," he said. "What they think happened is that someone may have put something in his lunch."

She looked at him with a face that was perfectly incredulous. "Are they crazy? They think someone made him have an allergy attack?"

"Something like that, yes."

"Why?"

"Well, that's just it. Cliff Wright was a real leader of the jury. Did you hear the interviews with your jury after they came out? He was really pushing for Mike, and had most of them coaxed around."

"So?"

"So, the police seem to think there might be a motive in that."

She shook her head back and forth. "This is unbelievable. Are you saying they think I might have had something to do with harming this man because I knew he was on Mike's side?"

"Wright had turned almost the entire jury against you. You would have lost everything. So you see, you had good reason to worry about what this man was doing to your jury."

"But Paul . . . how could I know what was going on in the jury room?"

"You know what, Lindy? From everything I've heard, you're a smart woman. You hired Nina because you saw she'd kill herself to represent you. You built a huge business out of nothing with Mike. You know you can buy some people. I think, if you wanted to know what was going on in the jury room, you would figure out a way to find out."

She stood up. "Get out of here."

"Who told you about Wright, Lindy? Was it Mrs. Lim? She used the telephone frequently. She could have been calling you with updates on the situation. Did she tell you what a threat he was? And then . . . you passed through that hallway a few times before. Maybe you were passing through that day, worrying about him and then, there it was, his meal, specially marked for a vegetarian. Maybe you never meant to kill him. Maybe you were just angry, and you acted without thinking. Because, Lindy, if you did, it's only second degree—"

She yanked on his arm. "On your feet. I said go!"

He stood up. She reached past him and threw open the door.

"Or was it Diane?" he went on standing with his two hands wedged firmly on the doorjambs. "She needed big money the most, and she really believed in your cause. I honestly don't think she would have a problem accepting money in return for helping you out a little. Why she practically admitted she knew you did it—"

She pushed him. He held firm.

"Look, I'll make a deal with you," she said angrily. "I'm going to tell you what you want to know, and then you'll get off of my property. Do we have a deal?"

He nodded.

"I did not bribe a juror."

"Then how did you know about Wright?"

She struck him on the shoulder. "What kind of a person are you?" she cried as he made no move to leave. "Don't you know most people don't have murder on the brain and wouldn't consider such a thing for any amount of money? Or have you been so jaded by your work you can't understand that most people don't kill?"

"I'm a realist, Lindy. Just like you."

And then, in the swing of her arm, a gun found its way into her hand. It must have come from the cookie jar on the counter. Pointing it at him she said, "If that's the case, maybe this will help you understand that I mean it when I tell you to get the hell out of here."

Staggered as always at the inconsistencies and idiosyncrasies of human behavior, Paul stepped outside, backing away from her until she closed the door in his face.

33

NINA ALLOWED HERSELF A LONG walk with Hitchcock on Friday morning before getting into her work clothes. They found a field of buttercups for him to romp in, and rainbows in the dew on the bright-yellow blossoms of the Sierra Wallflower. She took in the heady smell of them, as rich and thick as something tropical, and went back home feeling forlorn. Today, Winston and Genevieve would be moving out of their offices. They would all three go their separate ways. And like the last day of school when she was very young, the day already had a bittersweet flavor.

By the time she arrived at the office, a yellow truck with a ramp stood parked on the street near the front door of the building. Wish and a friend were tipping Genevieve's desk onto a dolly.

"Have you got a pad or something to protect that?" asked Nina. "The rental place will charge me for every scratch."

"Sure, we do, Ms. Reilly," said Wish. He raised a hand to wave at her, lost his balance, and dropped the handle of the dolly. His friend yelped, but held on to the desk with both arms. Leaping back into his place, Wish bumped him, floundered, and caught himself again. "I'll just go get it."

"Never mind," said Nina hastily, scurrying into the building, unwilling to set off any further chains of events. She didn't get far. The hallway was in shambles. Boxes of files and trash bags narrowed the aisle to allow only one person to pass at a time.

"Incredible how much accumulates during the course of a trial," she said to Sandy as she entered the reception area.

"Some of the files we need to keep here, others can be stored in our storage area."

"What storage area?"

"The one we just rented," said Sandy. "You're starting to pile up dead files. Until we rent more space, we need to be able to move around."

"Sandy . . ."

"What?"

"Is . . . I mean. You seem . . ."

"What."

"Kind of down."

Sandy lifted her shoulders and began typing from a yellow legal pad.

Nina found Winston squatting on the floor in his sweats, in front of a tower of files in his office. "I think I've got this thing licked," he said. "This pile here is stuff I take. This one," he patted a stack, "is to stow somewhere. This is garbage. Where are the trash bags?"

"Sorry, I have no idea," said Nina.

"Wish!" he hollered.

Genevieve, who had already packed, stood with her arms crossed, leaning against the wall watching him. "Winston, at this rate you're never going to finish. Didn't you have some kind of appointment this afternoon?"

"Trial over. Good-bye and good riddance?" he said.

"Of course not," Genevieve said. "Just don't drag it out. Packing's a real pain, but I know how you feel. It's like when you're going to catch a plane. You fear you're gonna end up at the counter without your passport."

"There's nothing really pressing. I just have better things to do than pile old papers." Winston said.

"Just remember, Sandy will send anything along that you forget," Genevieve said.

"I don't like this," said Nina.

"You don't like what?" Winston asked.

"Everyone leaving," Nina said. "This." She waved her arms at the mess. "I got used to having company for lunch. I got used to you knowing better than me the things I knew perfectly well before you two came."

"You're a sociable critter, Nina," Genevieve said. "You just don't pander to that side of yourself enough. Now, Winston," she said. "Move over and let me help you toss files haphazardly into that box. I can do that as well as you can." Sidling over, she nudged him with her hip, but Nina thought Genevieve looked as upset as Nina felt.

Back in her own office, Nina closed the door and sat with her back to the window, thinking about how quiet it would be and wondering if she liked that. Rather than decide, she picked up her phone messages and began to return calls.

The morning passed quickly. By eleven, the yellow truck was on its way to return the furniture. Winston and Genevieve had relocated to the conference room next to Nina's office, where there were still chairs. Sandy had ordered sushi and salad for an early lunch.

Winston ate quickly. "You know that island you told me about?" he asked Nina, wiping his mouth with a napkin.

It took her a minute to recall what he must mean. "The tiny one in Emerald Bay? Fannette?"

"That's the one. Any idea where I could rent a kayak to get there?"

"Well, sure. Richardson's Resort. Head west on the highway. Turn right at the 'Y.' It's just a couple miles up on your right. They have a marina and dock. Call first to make sure you can get one, though. It's still early in the season."

He called, and they listened while he arranged to rent one for the afternoon.

"That sounds like fun!" said Genevieve. "I've always wanted to learn to kayak."

"I'm doing this for some upper-body exercise. I need to go fast. Maybe I can take you out another time," Winston said.

Genevieve's mouth turned down. "Okay."

"Are you going to hike to the teahouse?" Nina asked.

"Maybe," he said. "I'll check it out and decide when I get there."

Everyone helped clear away the trash. In deference to Sandy's forbidding nature, Winston shook her hand. She thanked him again for the rabbit-skin blanket. Nina and Genevieve also came in for a final handshake. There seemed nothing left to say.

"I'll be in touch, Nina," Winston said, pulling away.

"You better be," she said.

He saw her mood and gave her arm a squeeze. "Hey, we'll do another trial again sometime. I feel it. Meanwhile, stay out of trouble. I mean it!" he said when they laughed at the thought. "Don't you ladies do anything I wouldn't do," he said as he went out the door.

"Winston that's just not a possibility," Genevieve called after him. "I can't think of a thing he wouldn't do," she said to Nina with a mischievous smile.

Susan Lim lived in a large, two-story home in Montgomery Estates. Paul always felt this particular development had a slight unreality to it, like a Twilight Zone of complete suburban normality on the cusp of the wild kingdom. Its landscaped yards fended off the wilderness, and the forest skulked just beyond its borders, threatening to engulf it again if the mowers ever stopped.

She answered the door. He introduced himself, giving the usual explanation for his questions, and she agreed to give him five minutes. She liked to be into work by ten in the morning, when the realty office opened, and was already running late.

They sat in two chairs on the porch at the front of the house. The lawn and flowers reflected the touch of a precise, artistic hand.

"First, I'd love your impressions of the mood of this jury as a whole, how they reacted to the testimony," he said, notepad in hand.

A plain-featured woman with a helmet of shining dark hair,

Mrs. Lim wore a hint of pink lipstick that matched her jacket and brightened her face. Sighing, she shook her head. "I found the process really grueling, since you ask. It seems like such a simple thing, to ask people to listen to some information, synthesize it, and decide the facts and evidence support one side or the other. Instead, what we had in the jury room was more of a free-for-all."

"In what sense?"

"Everybody's got an agenda," she said. "I'm sure you know that. Usually, it's not so obvious. We got in there and reason just flew out the window. Not that there was a window. That might have helped."

"If you don't mind my asking, what was your position?"

"I favored Lindy Markov. From the beginning, I thought it was obvious they had some arrangements they didn't have in writing. They must have informally agreed to share things. She was too bright not to have at the very least squeezed some promises out of him. And people agreed with me, at least at first."

"I understand on the first vote of the original jury, eight people supported her."

"That's right. Then Cliff brought out his presents and threats. . . ."

"Threats?"

"Oh, yes. I believe he threatened Sonny Ball with prison. He'd found some evidence of drugs in the bathroom at one point. I believe he seduced Kris Schmidt. I suspect they slept together after that first day," she said, clearly disgusted.

"Maribel craved attention, and he gave it to her. Ignacio, well that was a shame. He's a good person with good instincts, but not someone who is used to argument on the level Cliff inhabited. Cliff dumped him in a maze and walked circles around him, all the time posing as the logician.

"Grace just needed some sympathy and he came along, the Good Samaritan giving her what she needed."

"So Frank, Bob, and Kevin already favored Mike," Paul said.

"Yes. They didn't allow anything as messy as logic to sway

them. They had picked a position and stuck with it, by God," she said, with a tinge of sarcasm. "All Cliff had to do was insure they knew how welcome they were in the anti-Lindy club with him."

"You didn't like Cliff Wright."

"I have nothing but contempt for men like him. I despised his manipulations of weaker personalities."

"Why do you think he was so opposed to Lindy?"

"I think Diane had that figured out. It had to be personal. He said he had recently separated from his wife. Maybe he was really suffering, who knows with a man like that? But he was so underhanded and angry, and so persuasive and determined in there. I'm guessing that Mrs. Markov looked like his worst nightmare come true, a woman ruining a man's bright future because of a breakup."

"I guess you're glad things happened the way they did."

She stared at him. "You mean, Cliff dying?"

"Well, with the alternate installed, the jury came back around to Lindy, didn't they?"

"That's true."

"I understand most of the jurors brought snacks along during the deliberations," he said.

"Yes."

"Anybody eat peanuts?"

"Not that I noticed."

"Anything with peanuts? Candy?"

She began to laugh. "Snickers. Butterfingers. Nutty granola bars. Peanut M&M's. Mr. Van Wagoner, is this a joke? Are you implying that someone, that I—"

"Look, I'm just saying things worked out the way you wanted them to."

"I wish my husband could hear you. He thinks I'm not aggressive enough. And here you are suggesting I . . . correct me if I'm wrong, but aren't you suggesting that I planted a peanut butter cup in his eggroll because I was so mad at him?"

"Stranger things have happened, Mrs. Lim. Did you or anyone else leave the room before lunch was served that day?"

"There were a few minutes before the lunch was brought in. Most of us left the room. I made a phone call. Some smoked, some stretched, some used the bathrooms." She shrugged her shoulders. "Everyone was really looking forward to that lunch. I even saw Diane lifting the aluminum foil and peeking at the cartons."

The implication of what she had said struck her so forcefully, her cheeks flamed. "The food smelled very good. We all thought so," she said, trying to regain her composure.

He persisted with her, but after that, she refused to answer another question.

Back in his van, Paul looked around feeling discontented. Things were looking shabby in the old vehicle. Somehow, the leopard-skin cover in back had picked up some mildew, probably from sitting in airport parking lots for days. Like it or not, his car was an extension of himself, and it was dying of neglect. He started the engine up. The people in Washington were after him for a final decision by next week. He didn't know what to say.

He had to finish up this investigation. He needed to think about Nina.

34

PROMPTLY AT NOON, PAUL ARRIVED at Bizzbees on the highway. He and Wish were ready to swap notes on their interviews. Paul found himself instead being beaten to a pulp at darts.

"So Kevin Dowd and Frank Lister stuck by Mike from the beginning. They basically loved Cliff Wright. Grace Whipple came to her door in a housecoat, and this was at about two o'clock yesterday afternoon. She takes care of someone, said he'd been having some trouble. She only talked to me through the grill in the door. She was so distracted," Wish said, pulling his arm back, and with a *thwack*, another dart met the bull's-eye at dead center.

"What did she think of Cliff Wright?"

" 'Charming,' she called him. And Maribel what's-her-name . . ."

"Grzegorek."

"She was at work over at Mikasa, but they were having a slow day. She told me she had liked Cliff, but got disappointed in him at some point."

"Oh?" Paul said, interested, taking his turn.

"Yeah. She's a real fun person. Said Kris Schmidt had already snapped him up by the time she noticed how handsome he was. Kevin told me she asked him out and he turned her down."

"So her disappointment had more to do with romance than the case." Paul tossed his last dart to the outside.

"Yep."

"You didn't tell me you were league champ at the rec center when you challenged me to a game," said Paul. "You've got an unfair advantage here."

"That's why," said Wish, selecting another dart, eyeing it closely for shape, whipping around and tossing it lightly to land beside the one already stuck in the board, "I only bet you ten bucks."

His third dart flew to keep close company with the other two.

"I don't want to play anymore," said Paul. "I came here to talk."

"Oh, come on," said Wish. "Don't be a sore loser."

With a deep breath, Paul positioned himself, dart in hand. The bull's-eye, so close from some angles, suddenly appeared quite far away. He threw. "Twenty," said Wish, marking a chalkboard beside the dartboard. "That's nice."

Paul gritted his teeth, aimed, and threw dart number two.

"On the line," pronounced Wish. He examined the board. "On the two side. Sorry."

"Thanks one whole helluva lot," said Paul. Here was one game he couldn't win. Might as well quit now. Without aiming, just to get the throw over, he hurled his last dart.

"Bull's-eye!" marveled Wish. He wiped Paul out with a few more well-placed darts, then said, "Okay, game two. Let's up it to twenty."

But Paul refused. He ordered another soda. Wish, who was on his lunch break, ate a sub. They settled near the pool table, where a slender man and a large woman were locked in combat and the room had the hush of church over it.

"Okay, let's go over what we've found out," said Paul, keeping his voice low.

They hashed out what they had heard about the events leading up to Wright's death. "Just to be thorough, I looked into some other possibilities besides the jurors," Paul said. "Rachel's ex, Harry. He might want to sabotage Mike. But Harry was at a photo shoot at an automobile dealership all that morning according to his coworkers, and anyway would have trouble getting into that hall without a hassle

from Deputy Kimura. Then there's this other guy, George Demetrios, apparently a loyal fan of Lindy's. Same problems except for a
slightly weaker alibi provided by his brother.

"Then I looked at Alice, Lindy's friend. Her alibi checked out,
but again, we're talking an employee. Nobody's alibi is airtight. But
with all three of these people, we return to a central problem: how
could these people know what was going on in the jury room? How
could they get to the food? Alice used the hall occasionally during
the trial. Kimura said he'd seen her in there. But she would have no
business there while the jury was deliberating. Someone would have
noticed her that day."

He took a long drink. "Here's a thought," he said. "The three
women jurors were in cahoots. They spiked his food together."

"Didn't someone write that in a story once?" asked Wish.
"Neat idea."

"But there isn't enough passion here for a conspiracy. He didn't
kill someone's friend or murder anyone's father. He just played with
their heads," Paul said, dismantling his own suggestion.

Wish winced as the slender man scraped his cue on the felt of
the pool table. Three balls dropped into sockets. "Yeah, people don't
kill people over being on a jury together. They just want to."

"People kill people over a pair of shoes these days, Wish!"

"Not with peanuts they don't."

"You have to admit, with this much dough floating around,
someone's easily going to want some enough to harm Cliff Wright, if
it would do any good. Lindy Markov had the biggest motive. But
that theory has a major flaw because how could she know what went
on in that jury room? How could she know Wright was turning
everyone against her? We didn't know until those jurors came out
and gave all those interviews."

"A friend on the inside?" Wish said.

"That's what I finally decided. Maybe she bribed someone.
Promised one of the jurors a lot of money to do their damnedest to
make sure that jury went her way. What if that person saw Cliff

turning everyone against Lindy and had this ingenious idea on how to stop him?"

"Which juror?"

"I don't know. Diane Miklos is the most likely candidate in that case. Mrs. Lim even saw her lifting the lids off of the lunch that day. Her lifestyle requires major injections of moolah. But she's off on a climb. That means she's already got her money in the bag, when Lindy doesn't yet. And then there is the fact that Lindy swears she didn't bribe anyone and seemed awfully credible to me."

"What about her friend Alice?" Wish asked.

"Oh, I looked into that. Lindy helped her buy a house after her divorce. She had a breakdown, and that's where most of Lindy's salary went over the past few years, to supporting her old friend."

"Lindy sounds nice," Wish said.

"Or you could see her as the type of person who needs that money so that she can keep playing the big shot with her friends and favorite charities." Feeling frustrated, Paul pounded a fist on the table, accidentally knocking his Coke to the floor. The brawny woman at the pool table missed her shot and turned eyes filled with hatred on him. She whispered to a few menacing-looking friends.

"You know I've got fifty bucks riding on this," said the nearest one, the venality in his tone a warning. He puffed out his chest and stood close enough to violate Paul's personal space.

"No, I sure didn't," said Paul. Swooping down, he picked up his cup and headed for the nearest exit, followed quickly by Wish.

"Maybe it was an accident after all," Wish said.

Paul walked more slowly. He had decided not to push back in there because after all, fifty bucks was fifty bucks. Paul could see the guy's point. "But did you see what just happened? That guy looked mad enough to deck me, maybe kill me over fifty bucks, and there was a lot more money involved in the Markov trial." Paul stopped beside the van and took a good look at his raw recruit. "I don't know where all this discussion leaves us. I'm afraid we've hit the end of the line."

"This is such a bizarre job," said Wish. "I don't know another single soul who gets to have so much fun around people dying."

After Winston left, the law offices of Nina Reilly had fallen into quiet. Because of the furniture removal, Sandy had not scheduled any clients. In the reception room, Sandy's fingers clicked across her keyboard. In the conference room, having made several passes through the place to collect her things, Genevieve scratched out a list of expenses for Sandy. In her office, Nina sat, unable to work.

Bob would be flying in from his school trip back East late tonight into San Francisco. Nina's father had offered to pick him up at the airport. They would drive up Saturday morning. She couldn't wait. She missed him, particularly today, with everyone leaving.

The phone rang to interrupt these dark thoughts. The caller was Jeffrey Riesner, who if the legal grapevine could be believed, had just lost Rebecca Casey to a big firm in Reno. Nina assumed he couldn't afford to keep her on after the Markov loss.

"You know why I'm calling, don't you?" he said, without introducing himself.

"Who's calling?" asked Nina perversely.

"Don't start," he said. "Let's attempt to talk."

"I assume this is about Markov's appeal."

"Well, not exactly," he said, hedging. "Didn't you get a copy of the final receiver's report?"

"It's here somewhere," Nina said. "I haven't really studied it." She patted around on her desk, picking up papers, looking for it.

"Find it and call me right back," he said. And bang, down went his phone.

Wondering what in the world had put him into such a snit, Nina groped around, finally locating it in a pile on the floor beside her. She read it and called Riesner back.

"This is an amazing document," she said, "if I read it right."

"You do," he said shortly. "And now I'm going to level with you, Nina."

"I'm astonished and delighted to hear that . . . Jeff."

"You can see the immediate problem. If we pay the claim, Mike's flat broke. Plus, I'm in a bind. Mike . . . has decided not to appeal the award. Naturally, he made his decision against my advice. I can cite a million errors that make this eminently suitable for an appeal, even a reversal. But he's made up his mind."

Nina almost fell off her chair. This she had never foreseen.

"I wondered if you would talk to your client about this."

"What would I say?"

"I think I saw a little sympathy up there on the stand from her. She'll realize he's gone completely off his rocker. Maybe she'll give him a break and open up negotiations for a reasonable compromise."

"We've always been open to negotiating, Jeff. I've said so many times. But we no longer have to do that. We've won our case."

"Would you just check with her? See if she's seen the report. See what she thinks. Maybe she'll want to do something for him," he said.

It was incredible. He was groveling.

"I'll do that," she said. "But don't expect anything." She tried to sound courteous and keep the triumph out of her voice. Riesner's plum of a case had turned rotten on him. His client had quit cooperating. There was no more money to be squeezed out. And she knew the worst of it for Riesner.

Losing. This public brawl had been won by a woman, by her, Nina Reilly. Not by Riesner, the good old boy.

And Mike Markov would be broke. She had better get Lindy on the phone soon to stanch any outbreak of pity.

Paul appeared in her doorway. "Looking for me?" he asked.

"Always. What's up?" she said.

"Not much." He took her up for a long kiss. "I just wanted to talk to you."

With a word to Sandy, they moved outside, walking along a road that led to the lake. "I've got a business hanging on by a thread back home," Paul said. "Just gave Wright's family the news that I haven't come up with diddly to prove his death was anything but

natural. Talked with Cheney, too. The local police haven't got anything either. They're closing the file on his death."

"No juror involvement?" asked Nina hopefully.

"Nothing I found."

"That's great!"

"Yeah."

"There's a 'but' in your voice."

"I hate the feeling there's something I've missed. Nina . . ."

"Yes?"

"You don't know anything you aren't telling me, do you?"

"No."

"I know this case is important to you, and I know my talking
with the jurors really made you nervous. But I never meant to bring
you down. I just couldn't let this pass by me without a second look."

"I'm glad it's over," said Nina.

They reached the lake and watched kids nearby throwing a ball
back and forth, and a dog running through the water after a stick.

"I assume you talked with the jurors about Wright's position on
our case," said Nina.

"Yes."

"What was it?"

"It was eight to five in favor of Mike at lunchtime. You were
about to lose."

"Remarkable timing, then," she said. "Apparently, the replacement juror favored Lindy and they all swung back around."

"Remarkable, yes."

"Well, don't look at me. I didn't do it."

"I know. Maybe Lindy Markov did, but if she did, I can't find
any proof."

"So that's it?"

"Met by a rock wall, most people stop."

"You're leaving?"

"Back to Carmel. Then D.C."

"You're going back?" she asked, and something about his demeanor suddenly made her very apprehensive. "I thought that job would be over by now."

"Nina, I have something to tell you and it's not going to be easy. Now my pattern in the past under similar circumstances has always been to be noble and blame myself for everything. That way, I get what I want and we both go away feeling good, but rather than lie to you and make it easy, I've decided to tell you the truth. You deserve that much from me. And I know you can take it."

"Fire away," she said gamely. She did not wish to hear whatever he wanted to say to her at that moment but short of running away, she knew she could not escape.

"You are a selfish woman. You want what you want when you want it. Okay, fine. That's modern, even cool. Sometimes it's even attractive. Except when it comes to me."

She absorbed the blow. "It's possible you have a point. . . ."

"And this case has changed you."

"What do you mean?"

"You've done things that surprised me."

"Such as?"

"You choose your work over your friends. Your moral gray area expands directly in proportion to the size of the pot."

"I can't believe you of all people are criticizing the way I do my job! You never followed a rule in your life!"

"That's me," said Paul. "We're talking about you."

"Let's leave my work out of this discussion."

"But we can't. You're such a lawyer, always organizing and pigeonholing like mad. Here's Paul over here, in love with me, wishing he could marry me. I'm a busy woman. I'll give him forty-nine percent. Well, I don't give fifty-one percent to your forty-nine. We both give one hundred percent, otherwise it's a waste of time."

"Paul—"

"Now hang on, let me finish. I'm taking the security job in Washington, D.C."

"What? No!" Now this she had never expected! She felt like he'd taken her by the ankles and flipped her overboard as Lindy had done with Mike on the boat. "Have you lost your mind? You don't want that job!"

"I do want that job."

"I don't understand. Things have been going so well. I thought we were happy together."

"We are, Nina, on the rare occasion we're together," Paul said. "But it's not enough for me to flit in and out of your life like I do."

"But that suits us!"

"It suits you. You need someone who wants you less than I do. You need someone available only when you're hungry, who just simmers patiently the rest of the time. I am not a back burner type of guy."

"I don't want you to go," she said.

"No, you don't," Paul said, "because I'm handy. But I'm going."

"You can't," she said, casting about in her mind for the right thing to say and coming up blank. What right did she have to keep him here? He was a passionate man, and he deserved his match in a woman. "I have lots of work for you here!" she said, knowing how weak it sounded.

"Nina. Don't pretend you miss the point."

"I need you."

"Yes, you do, much more than you realize. But remember, we're friends for life. Anybody's legs need breaking, you know who to call."

"You'll be three thousand miles away."

"A hop, skip, and a jump," he said.

He might as well be in Antarctica. The cold Atlantic was a long, long way from these western mountains. "You're leaving for good?"

"For a year, Nina."

"How can you leave California? What about your business in Carmel? You can't go."

"Yeah, I knew it would surprise you."

"Look, I am selfish. And I know I'm high-maintenance. But— maybe I'm worth it!"

"You are, sweetheart. And I know there are plenty of guys who'll be happy to pick up the slack when I let go." He looked at his watch. "Phew. It's already two o'clock. Now that's off my chest, I've got to hit the road. But you know what would be good?"

She had no idea what would ever be good again.

"A last little taste of that tempura at Sato's would really hit the spot on the way out of town. . . ."

"Wait a minute. I have more to say," Nina said.

"You can't change my mind, so don't waste your breath. Want to go get a bite with me?"

"No. I don't have time," Nina said.

Paul put his head back and laughed.

"How can you be so casual about this!" she cried. "We're breaking up!"

"And I feel like shit about it, too. Now, c'mon. Give me another half an hour of your precious time so that we can do this thing properly. You can get on my case all you want. My treat."

"I really can't. Genevieve hasn't left yet. I have to say good-bye to her."

They walked back to her office in silence, holding hands. Nina could not speak, and Paul seemed as usual. An earthquake had shaken the world, but everything looked the same, and even sounded the same. He whistled through most of the walk back.

When they got there, Paul said, " 'Bye, then." He kissed her gently, walked over to his van, waved, and drove away.

As she walked down the hall to her office, she didn't think about him leaving, but flashed back instead on the rough texture of the hair on his arms, and how poorly matched the two of them were physically, with him so large and her so small—how was it they had ever fit so well? She thought about his long thighs rubbing against her and the curve of his arm, enveloping her in his scent.

Damn him for those things he said! Damn him for giving up on her!

Sandy had deserted her desk. Nina found her with Wish, who had returned from his lunch. Holding a big green trash bag, he picked up loose bits of paper, rubber bands, and paper clips from the hallway.

"I'm going to miss them," said Nina, crossing her arms and watching. After a minute contemplating the wreckage, she pitched in. They wandered into the empty rooms, picking things up in preparation for vacuuming. Where Genevieve's desk had been, a silver chain twinkled on the floor beside a forgotten earring. In Winston's office, wadded up candy wrappers revealed a secret love of licorice, and empty cola cans had been neatly stacked for recycling in one corner.

"Uh-oh," Nina said. A piece of baseboard had dislodged where Winston's desk had been. Moving day had been rough on this office. She knelt to try to push it back into place, and caught sight of something no bigger than a spider in one corner that looked like it had fallen behind the baseboard. Leaning over to examine the area, she picked up a small metal disk. "Some kind of battery." Maybe for that little radio he always wore when he jogged? Or a watch? "He has all kinds of watches. Sandy, why don't you pop this in the mail to him. It's unusual. Maybe hard to replace." She held it for them both to admire. "It's terrific how minuscule they can make those things."

Wish took it from her. Setting the bag down, he walked over to the window and took a closer look. "That's not a battery. Look at these little holes here."

Nina peered over his shoulder. "Well, what is it?"

"Hmmm," said Wish. "A microphone?" He twisted the tiny thing between huge fingers.

"What?"

"Well, it looks a little like a bug . . . but . . ." He put the object very close to his eyes and studied it.

"You've been filling your head up with junk, reading those spy magazines," Sandy said. "I told you that was a waste of time."

"Well, maybe so," Wish said. He set the disk down on the windowsill. "I'm probably wrong."

"Oh, my God, you had me going there. I had the strangest

idea," said Nina, putting a hand to her pounding chest. "I thought maybe, I don't know what I thought . . ."

Wish left Nina and Sandy for a moment, trotting swiftly into Sandy's office and back, while they stared at the tiny thing on the ledge.

When he came back, he was holding one of those spy magazines that caters to teenagers. "See this?" he said, pointing excitedly at a quarter page advertisement near the last page. "Same thing."

The women continued to stare, only now they stared at the page. SLY BOY! trumpeted the boldface. THE WORLD'S TINIEST BUG!

"Told you," said Wish.

Sandy opened her mouth, then closed it. She folded her arms.

"But . . . how could Winston get a bug?" Nina asked.

"Anybody can buy surveillance equipment," Wish said. "Really. There are spy catalogs on-line from all over the world. Haven't you ever checked it out on the Internet? You can buy neat stuff. I wrote a paper on state-of-the-art technology for one of my classes.

"In the 1950s the Soviets bugged the American embassy in Moscow by hiding a little round thing like this behind a wooden carving of the Great Seal of the U.S., a gift from them that hung above the ambassador's desks. Whoever said the Slavs have no sense of humor, huh? That was a different device."

"How does this one work?"

"It's a simple radio transmitter. There's a range, like maybe eighty to a hundred megahertz, where you can tune in to hear it."

"How far away can you be for something like that to work? I mean, could I go home and listen in?" Nina asked, gripping the windowsill.

"You'd need a receiver. Of course those can be very tiny, too, but the quality isn't very good unless you've got something, say the size of a transistor radio, to collect and amplify the sound. Maybe two hundred meters? It varies. This is pretty sophisticated stuff."

Nina and Sandy couldn't seem to think of another thing to say.

"So someone bugged Winston's office," Wish said. "Who do

you suppose was interested in listening in on Winston's conversations? Hey, Nina. Do you think Riesner and Casey bugged his office to find out what you guys were up to before the trial?"

"No," said Nina. "I don't."

"It is terrific how small they can make those things," said Sandy, taking the object from her son. "Now, Wish, you take that trash out to the Dumpster. There's a couple of chairs left in the reception area you forgot. They need to go, too. I'm not paying for any damages, so you'll want to be very careful."

"But . . ."

"Move it."

Grumbling at being ordered around, Wish left.

"You don't think someone was bugging Winston," Sandy said.

Nina sat down on the floor. "No. Nobody planted that thing behind the baseboard. It was lying there, loose. I think the bug is his. God, what was he doing with that thing? I knew how desperate Winston was to win the case but . . ." She sniffed. Sandy handed her a tissue, and she blew her nose. "He was not around during those couple of days the jury deliberated. He did a lot of jogging."

"With that disc player–radio thing he always wears," said Sandy, frowning.

"Could he have been listening in? Or maybe he had a receiver hooked up to a recorder in his car, and just listened later, some of the time. All he would have to do was park his car somewhere near the courthouse."

"But, Nina. It doesn't make sense. What's the use of bugging the jury room? At that point, you can't control the outcome of the case."

"My God. Maybe Paul was right. Maybe he . . . did something to Clifford Wright's food, to stop him. He might not have realized how serious it could be."

"But, Nina, they always leave the jury's food in the private hallway outside the judge's chambers until it's served, right? And the door to that hallway is locked."

"Nobody bothers the lawyers if they pass through that hallway, and you can go straight through from the courtroom. I've done it myself. And Winston had a thing going with one of the clerks back there . . . He knew all about the allergy from our jury files, I'm sure. He knew about the vegetarianism. Cliff's food was probably specially marked. He could have put something in the food."

"Why leave the bug here?"

"I don't know! I can only imagine. It's very small. It must have fallen during the shuffle of moving. Either he didn't notice, or couldn't find it."

"He's got a good reputation, lots of clients. Why would he do this?"

"He lost his last case. He was desperate to win this one. His professional success really depended on that. And he knew he had a huge payoff coming if we won big enough to help him get out from under some heavy debts. Oh, Sandy." She dropped to the floor like a sack of flour and hugged herself. "Oh, my God. My case."

"You better call Paul."

She couldn't move. Reality had caught up with her, and she didn't know what to do. "Paul's gone, Sandy. I can't call him."

Genevieve appeared in the doorway, a leather bag dangling from her shoulder. "Everything okay in here?" she said. "I never saw two such blue faces in my life. What's that thing you've got there?"

"Nothing," said Nina, tucking the mike into her pocket. She stood up, dusting her hands off. She had to think more. No sense involving anyone else.

"Well, ladies," Genevieve said, looking a little sad, "the much-anticipated, awful moment has arrived. Genevieve Suchat is leaving the building."

They said their good-byes. "Don't let her work you too hard, Sandy," Genevieve said. "And, Nina, don't you let Sandy drive you to an early grave. Oh, I'm gonna miss you two."

When she left, gloom descended on them, as thick as dust.

35

"Where's Paul, Nina?" Sandy said as they walked slowly back into Nina's office.

"Going to Washington. For good."

Sandy's lips tightened. "Why that little . . . Where is he right now?"

"He might still be having lunch at Sato's. He was going to stop on his way out of town."

"Call him. He'll know what to do about this thing. He'll have some ideas."

"No."

"Okay, then. I will. We need him. He's not getting out of this."

"Don't. I'll figure this out myself." Nina went into her office, shut the door, put her hands down on the table, and placed her head over them. She stayed that way for five minutes, then called Paul.

He didn't answer his cell phone. Nina listened partway through "Announcement One. Your call cannot be completed at this time. The cellular customer you have called may have reached his destination or . . ." and hung up. "This is never going to work," she said. The Sly Boy felt hot as a live grenade in her pocket.

At Sato's restaurant, the phone was busy. She tried again and again for nearly forty-five minutes, but the phone continued beeping rapidly. Paul would be out of there any minute. Nina made up her mind. Grabbing her jacket, she went back into the reception room. "Sandy, cancel anything I have left this afternoon. I don't have court and tomorrow's Saturday. I'm going to see if I can catch up with him."

"You do that."

"Meanwhile, keep trying the restaurant just in case you can get through. Tell him to wait for me there. I'll keep my phone handy. Call me if you get through."

Fortunately, the Bronco was gassed up. Pulling up to the front door of Sato's, about to pull her parking brake, she spotted Paul heading for his van, which was parked across the street about a block behind her. Reversing quickly, she turned around and passed his van, backing up to parallel park smoothly in the slot behind him.

"Nina?" He got out of his car to meet her at her door.

"Who else, Paul?" she said, flooded with the emotion she hadn't been able to express earlier, and with relief at finding him.

"To say that I didn't expect you is an understatement. . . . unless you caved in to a sudden uncontrollable yen for sushi?"

"Paul, just listen to me," said Nina, shutting her car door. They moved to the sidewalk in front of the restaurant while she gave him an abbreviated version of the events of the morning, handing him the Sly Boy to examine. "What I want to know is, am I crazy to think this means anything? I like Winston. I don't want him to be a bad guy."

"Then why don't you just call him and ask him to explain?" he said. "Don't you trust him?"

"It's awkward," she said. "Me asking him, hey, did you plant a microphone in the jury room? Did you listen to the proceedings? Of course he'll say no. It's illegal for starters. And it's not like he necessarily used the information to win our case. Maybe he just listened. Maybe he didn't use it for that at all. I can't believe he would hurt me like this, destroy me. . . ."

But Paul was lost in thought. "What are you going to do?" he asked finally. "If he bugged that jury room, this may go beyond jury tampering. He would know Wright basically sabotaged Lindy Markov's case. Did you find any peanuts?"

For a split second, it was almost funny. Then she remembered what it could mean. "If he did anything to Wright, I'll kill him! The case . . . my God, Lindy's verdict will be in question. All the months of hell with this trial . . . Riesner! How he'll crow! And oh, Paul . . ."

"The money," he said.

"My money!"

"If you don't mind," said Paul, "I'd like to talk to Winston with you. Is that okay?"

She nodded. "Thanks. I didn't feel I had the right to ask you. But . . . didn't you say you had to get to Carmel?"

"I can leave for Washington from Sacramento tomorrow. Skip the stop in Carmel. Where is Winston?"

"I think he's out on the lake somewhere." She called Sandy on her car phone. "I've got Paul." She hung up.

"Does Genevieve know about this?"

"I don't know," said Nina. "She came in and saw me holding the microphone. I wasn't paying attention to her, I was so freaked out at what I was holding. And Winston's too smart and too proud to tell her something like this."

A new implication hit her. She sighed unhappily. "Maybe she suspected something. It's possible she recognized the microphone, come to think of it. She did look upset when she came in to say good-bye. I put that down to it being her last day."

Playing with the plastic lid on a Styrofoam cup in his hand, Paul digested this information. "Where's Genevieve now?"

"Why do you want to know that?"

"Does it make sense to you like it makes sense to me that Genevieve might just run off and warn Winston that you found the bug? What if she did recognize it, Nina?"

"She might."

"And how do you think Winston's going to react to the information if she is reporting to him right now?"

"Mad?" said Nina, light beginning to glimmer on the edge of her consciousness. "Threatened?"

"Threatened enough to want to shut her up? He probably figures he could convince you of anything. He's got to know you're dying to be convinced. You've got a fortune at stake. But he knows she of all people can nail him good. She probably knows more than she thinks she does, and it's all beginning to make sense to her."

"But," said Nina, "even granting that Winston isn't who I always thought he was, granting he might even be dangerous," she thought out loud, "how could she catch up with him today if he's on an island in the middle of Emerald Bay?"

"Same way we can," he said, picking up her sunglasses from the backseat, pulling her by the hand, opening the passenger-side door on his van, and pushing her in. "Motorboat, motorboat, go so fast . . ."

Nina got into the van with him and made some quick phone calls. "Okay, head for Meek's Bay. I called Richardson's Resort. They refused to rent us a boat. It's too late in the day, and the wind's up, they say. The bad news is, they rented the last one of the day to Genevieve, so we know she probably followed Winston. Oh, God, Paul. By now she's a good hour ahead of us."

"Why should we go to Meek's Bay?"

"Matt offered us his boat, and that's where it's docked."

"You've had some unkind things to say about that boat."

"Last time it went dead out in the middle of the lake I swore I would never ride in it again, but it's our only option. He gave me some tips about starting her up." They pulled into the parking lot. "Look for the one called the *Andreadore*."

"Catchy name. Didn't another ship ram that boat?"

"You're thinking of the *Andrea Doria*."

"Your brother has a strange sense of humor."

"Tell me about it. Usually he's docked down by Heavenly, but luckily for us, a friend was working to get it ready for the summer season. Some kind of trade. Meek's is closer to Emerald Bay."

They found the scarred twenty-two-footer easily. "Nina," Paul said, untying the ropes that held it to the dock. "I know you don't really think Winston killed Clifford Wright . . . but let's just admit the possibility." He jumped in, fiddled with the ignition, and started the boat.

"I just can't."

"But if he did . . . he's not just dangerous to Genevieve, Nina."

"There's an explanation. There has to be."

"Just don't let friendship blind you. Watch yourself, okay?"

His words evaporated behind the rattle and roar of the *Andreadore* as she set off for Emerald Bay.

Paul ran the engine at full throttle for about ten minutes. Immediately, the cool wind of late May gusted inside Nina's clothes to chill her limbs and bite at her neck.

A heavy spray flew off the choppy water below. "Would he swim to Fannette in this weather?" she said.

"I believe Matt told me once you can pull up to the rocks in a kayak," Paul said. "You might be able to get there without even wetting your feet."

"I wish we weren't doing this," said Nina. "I'm freezing already. The lake is getting really wild. And look at those clouds coming in."

Paul didn't reply, seeming lost in his own thoughts.

The wind rushed by. Ten thousand white caps adorned the vast expanse of lake. "And I'm scared," she shouted over the motor and the wind. "Slow down."

"We're in a hurry, remember?"

She remembered. She remembered that she should be sitting at a safe desk somewhere, in a warm room, with everything in control, not out here on the lake with the afternoon wind coming up, in control of nothing, with Paul, who was supposed to be gone. . . .

"What's this?" she said, stopping a leather case that was rolling across the deck. "Oh, good, Matt's binoculars."

"Here," Paul said. "Wrap yourself in the blanket." He threw a picnic tablecloth to her and she put it around herself.

She pulled out the binoculars and adjusted them to her eyes. For several minutes, she scanned Lake Tahoe for as far as she could see, almost across its entire twelve miles to the eastern shore. "Anybody who was out here today was smart enough to dock before now. There's nothing out there, not even the ghost of the drowned sailor."

"What drowned sailor?"

She told Paul the story Andrea had told her about the sailor who ended up at the bottom of Lake Tahoe instead of in the tomb he had built on the island.

Something she said must have verified something he was already thinking. "This damn lake. This whole place. It's so beautiful on the surface." He looked out at the uneven waves, and hung on to the wheel with fingers so tightly clenched they had turned white. "But underneath . . ." As if to help him make a point, the engine sputtered, then reengaged.

Before Nina could ask if the comment had some hidden double meaning only a literature major could figure out, he said, "We're almost at the entrance to the Bay. Get those binocs up."

And there it was, a boat with the figure of a woman at the helm. "It's Genevieve," she said, handing over the binoculars so Paul could look.

"What's she doing over there? That's not the way into Emerald Bay," he said, and for the first time Nina realized that the irritation in his voice, his absorption, probably masked a certain amount of fear. Paul didn't spend all his time messing with boats either, she reminded herself. An equivalent to her five-minute lesson with Matt probably constituted the bulk of his boat lore.

But he had never failed her, had he?

They tried to hail Genevieve, but in the wind, she could not hear them.

"Damn and blast!" said Paul. "She didn't even look this way. She's headed straight out to the middle of the lake. Is she trying to get to the other side? Where on God's blue water is she going so fast?"

"We can't catch up to her, now. Her boat's in better shape than this old rattletrap. Anyway, she's alone, Paul. She's okay. I don't even see Winston."

"Don't knock Matt's boat. You don't want her taking offense. We've got a long way to go. And we don't know what's going on. It's possible Winston's in that boat somewhere. Now let's just give her a little gas"—he pushed the throttle—"and we'll just see who's a rattletrap."

He got the boat up to top speed, which wasn't fast enough to overtake Genevieve, but felt very fast to Nina. Holding on to the windscreen with one hand, she stood up and waved the paper bag in the wind. Genevieve's boat rumbled purposefully ahead, jumping and dipping in the waves, sometimes heaving to one side or the other, looking dangerously unstable. At one point she turned her head, and Nina saw her lips moving, as if she was saying something, but she continued at full speed, apparently blinded by her resolve. Then, suddenly, about four miles out from land, she shut the engine off and bent over out of sight.

"What's she doing?" Paul said, adjusting the motor down, trying to close the gap between them without running into the other boat.

"I can't see her."

When they were as close as possible, he cut the engine down to low. The noise made no impression in the wind, apparently, because the next thing they knew, a startled Genevieve almost fell over at the sight of them.

"What the hell!" she called to them. "Where'd you come from?" She had a somnolent Winston caught by the arm, and as they watched, she propped him against one of the seats. He was sitting on the deck of the boat, eyes closed.

They pulled in next to Genevieve, and Paul kept the engine running, so that he could move away quickly if the wind pushed them in too close.

"We need to talk to you, Genevieve," said Nina.

"You followed me out here to talk to me? Must be awfully important. What's happened?"

"What's the matter with Winston?" Paul said.

"Oh, man," Genevieve said. "Winston. He's drunk. God. He's

a maniac. He took it in mind to drive this dang boat all the way across the lake! I told him it was too late in the day, but he was beyond listening."

"But you're driving," Nina said.

"Just for the past few minutes. He was so determined. Shouting at me. Jesus, I never saw him like this before," she said. "He just now passed out."

"What are you doing here with him?"

"After I finished up at work, I realized I had some time before I had to leave. You probably noticed Winston and I . . ." She flushed. "Well, we didn't agree about how things ought to be between us. I wanted to keep seeing him . . . he thought we needed to make a clean break. So I wanted to talk to him. It seemed like a perfect, intimate little opportunity. I knew he was kayaking so I rented this boat, and surprised him on the island with a picnic I picked up at Cecil's on the way out of town.

"We laid out a blanket on the island. We were celebrating with champagne, but I hardly drank anything. Turns out, he's a mean drunk," Genevieve said, and she started to dab at her face with her sleeve. Her light hair streamed out behind her in lank strips. "You can't tell someone like that what to do. I guess he was drinking before I arrived. A little of the champagne and he was over the top. Then he practically forced me. We got on the boat. I wanted to go back, but he had this cockeyed idea . . . it was easier to give in. And then, just a minute ago, he finally passed out. I was just going to sit him up so he wouldn't vomit and choke on it or something. Then I figured I'd head back."

"Genevieve," Paul said. "Would you toss the floats onto the side of your boat? You know, the ones you put down to protect the boat when you dock."

"Why?"

"Did Winston say why he wanted to go out into the middle of the lake?" Nina asked. Winston was completely passed out, obviously not a danger at the moment.

"No," said Genevieve. "He was way beyond reason, just pushing and demanding. I was afraid. . . ." She was half-shouting over the wind.

"Genevieve, listen," Nina said. She explained as quickly as she could what they thought the microphone they had found in Winston's office meant. "It's just possible he wanted you out here where no one would find you. If there was an accident." The *Andreadore* pitched, and Nina reached for the windshield to prevent herself from falling.

"That's ridiculous!" Genevieve said. "You've lost your marbles! How can you think that of him?"

"There may be an explanation. But you have to look at the facts. If Winston eavesdropped on the jury, there's also the possibility . . . the remote possibility he has something to do with the death of Clifford Wright."

"I . . . I don't know what to say. I'm just flabbergasted. After all he did for you! And he would never intentionally hurt me. He cares about me."

"Nevertheless," said Paul implacably. "Why don't you ride back with Nina. I'll take Winston."

"No," said Genevieve. "I'll take him back. He's out cold. Even if what you've said is true, and I think it's the biggest hunk of wet cow dung I ever met, I'm in no danger now. Tell you what. I'll head back to the dock. You two could help me by goin' back for his kayak."

"Forget the kayak!" Paul exploded.

They argued back and forth for a few minutes as the sky continued to lower until the clouds nearly touched Nina's shoulders, and the fading afternoon was darkening by the minute.

Genevieve finally clinched it. "How are you going to feel when he wakes up, huh? He'll have a perfectly reasonable explanation for everything, and then he's going to want to snatch you bald-headed for leaving his kayak behind!" She was very upset, and had slipped into her most exaggerated Southern accent.

"Paul, the island is only a few minutes out of the way. We could get his kayak," Nina said.

Paul quit haggling. Pulling the *Andreadore* swiftly up beside Genevieve's speedboat, he motioned to Nina to take over the helm, perched on the edge of the boat, and leaped before Genevieve had time to react, arms akimbo and legs flailing over a five foot stretch of lake, landing with a curse inside the other boat. He stood up and took Genevieve's arm. "You be a good girl and get the hell out of this boat," he said, guiding her over to the edge. "Nina, come in closer."

Nina obeyed, moving gingerly in. Ignoring her noisy protests, Paul lifted Genevieve neatly into the *Andreadore*.

"I'll go back for the kayak. We'll meet you two at Richardson's landing in twenty minutes. You two start back. Meanwhile, Genevieve, got any rope on this rig?"

Genevieve stood next to Nina, watching Paul and Winston recede as Nina steered Matt's boat away. "You're going to tie him up?" she said.

"Just maintaining the peace," said Paul. "You said he was upset."

"I don't believe this."

"Tell me," Paul said sternly, "where the goddamned rope is."

Looking unhappy or uncertain or both, Genevieve finally said, "I think there's some inside that hatch Win's lying on."

"Paul, be careful," said Nina, waving and steering the *Andreadore* to the southwest. She waited until they were far enough away not to cause a wake and swamp the other boat before accelerating away.

She could see that he was trying to move Winston's dead weight to one side, but the big man flopped around, ungainly as a marlin.

Nina and Genevieve covered a couple of miles in blessed silence, Nina just delighted to be going home and feeling tremendously relieved. They had Winston. Now he could explain. He could dispel this cloud of doubt about her case. They were about halfway to the resort before Genevieve said, "Oh, damn. Damn, damn, damn!"

"What is it?"

"I forgot to tell him to pick up the picnic basket," she said.

"That's no problem," Nina said. "I promise I'll get my brother to rescue it for you tomorrow."

"You don't understand!" she cried. "I took off my rings and put them in it. My mother's wedding ring is in there. I can't leave it. Someone might get there first!"

What the heck. She would rather be near Paul anyway. Paul had Winston, so they had nothing to worry about on that front. The island wasn't far off their route.

"Calm down," said Nina. "Let's go get it." She turned the *Andreadore* north and aimed for the narrow sliver of green lake in the distance that heralded the opening to Emerald Bay.

36

Rising about a hundred and fifty feet above the lake's surface, Fannette Island sat in the middle of Emerald Bay like the important central jewel in an exquisite pendant. On the first visible piece of it, on the northeastern end, heaps of granite boulders were topped by the stone teahouse. The descending clouds had leached the color out of the pines. The landscape, always rugged but usually softened by sparkling waters and sunlight, held a different beauty in the blues and grays of late afternoon, brooding in its solitude out there in the middle of the swirling waters.

Nina had decided to relax into the event, let things take their course. They had nothing to fear except perhaps Matt's unreliable boat, which had behaved admirably so far, and the unpredictable weather, which threatened, but did not deliver, rain. The island must be magnetic, she thought, because even out here, in this disquieting atmosphere, she could feel its tug. She wanted very much to hop right out of the boat and climb to the top of the little hill, to sit in the teahouse and take in the view from the top. However, the cold lake below, deep with melted snow, frightened her a little. She would come back on a sunny day later in the season when the lake had heated up, with Matt and Andrea and the kids. Bob would love finding the way up the ridge to the teahouse.

"We have to go around to the other side," Genevieve said. "To the cove. Here, why don't you let me steer? I know the way better."

"No, thanks," Nina said. She felt responsible for Matt's boat, and she knew pulling in close to the rocks in the cove in this kind of wind might be nasty.

Rocking and rolling against the stiff waves of an unruly lake, the *Andreadore* was taking a beating. Genevieve would not shut up, and kept up a nonstop stream of chatter that had the effect of making Nina very nervous.

Within a minute, they caught sight of the tiny cove that offered the only safe harbor for a boat.

"We can't get in, Genevieve," Nina said. "See that?" She pointed to the twisted tree that marked the island's most southern point. "I'm sure there are rocks jutting under the water there. The wind's up too much. It's just gotten too choppy."

"Just get in a little closer, Nina," Genevieve said, practically hopping with impatience. "I'll jump in and swim. I did it once already, you know."

Nina stared at her. "But the weather is really getting bad now, Genevieve. No, it's not worth risking Matt's boat." She scanned the bay. "Where the hell is Paul?"

Gusts of strong wind battered the little boat, and they rocked like kids on a wooden horse, holding on wherever they could.

Mist had settled over the island and over the two women, and the constant drone of the motor had by now numbed Nina to the point where she could barely hear Genevieve, even when she shouted.

"If you're so nervous, let me take the boat in closer, Nina," Genevieve said. As Nina's nerves went, so their voices had risen. Genevieve grabbed the wheel, nudging Nina out of the way with a heavy swing of her hip. "I grew up with boats."

Nina, taken off guard by Genevieve's vehemence but unable to decide how to bring order to this unbalanced state of affairs, stepped away from the wheel. "You're going to sink us," Nina said, watching as the boat moved wildly in, heading for rocks. "Watch out to the left! Ahhh . . . !"

No more than ten feet away from the edge of the island, near where the yellow kayak had been pulled over the rocks and onto the sand, Genevieve slowed the engine to its lowest speed and turned to face Nina.

"You calm down," she said. She had to shout to be heard above a sudden gust of wind that now howled around them. "Everything's going just fine."

Nina lunged for the wheel. Any control she had had long since jumped ship. "I'm getting us out of here."

Genevieve kept her hand clamped down. "No, you're not. Don't be such a chicken. Let's stick to the plan. I'm going in." She steered with one hand "I'm going to freeze unless I've got something dry," she said, and while Nina watched, she bundled a sweater with a towel and tossed them onto the sandy beach just beyond the edge of the cove. Her hair blew back from her face. She was wearing a T-shirt and shorts, and absolutely nothing else.

"There's one other thing," Genevieve said.

But Nina had a question first. "Genevieve?" she said, and for just a moment, the wind let up and she achieved a kind of passionate clarity of concentration. "Genevieve, where's your hearing aid?"

The rope had not been in the hatch under Winston at all. After conducting an intensive search, Paul located it bundled amid the life jackets, under the plastic cushions on the seats at the front of the boat.

Feeling only a little foolish, he tied Winston's slack hands in front of him. Then he tied his feet to one of the seats, tight enough so that he was satisfied Winston would go nowhere without his help. The big guy wasn't playing possum. He was unconscious.

Fleetingly reminded of his days as a cop, where taking prisoners was an ordinary event, and everyone was dangerous until proven otherwise, Paul reached for the starter. Where was the key? It didn't take him long to remember how quick he had been to rush Genevieve off the boat. She must have had the key in her hand, or in a pocket.

He would call for help, he thought, then moved on to the picture of his and Nina's cell phones tucked neatly away in the glove compartment of his car.

Cursing, he looked for a manual. Of course, rental boats had radios. But that would have been too easy. The radio sputtered, offered a short pessimistic weather report, and before Paul could figure out exactly how to dial out, died with a whimper.

Well, if you could jump a car, he thought, a boat ought to be a snap. He hadn't entirely wasted his years as a cop in San Francisco. He set about managing it.

Within five minutes, they were on their way and just in time, too. The sky had darkened slightly. They should have gotten off the lake right away, he groused silently, wanting to kick the dormant and unconcerned-looking man at his feet, but too civilized to do it.

He took it slowly, having expended all his vitality on the hurried trip out. The jolt he had felt on seeing Nina outside the restaurant had disturbed him, and it was taking him some time to recover. He had said good-bye, and there she was again to tantalize him and make him deal with his regrets.

But it didn't change anything except the cleanness of his departure. He would leave Monday, as planned. Seeing her once more was enough to convince him, if he had in fact harbored any doubts in the matter. He was putty in her hands, and the least threat to her cut through him like acid. They were too connected, and going nowhere fast.

He gunned the motor slightly. He liked speed, but Winston would get batted around. Paul would get batted around, too, so he kept his speed modest. With just a minute to tie the kayak to the boat, they'd be back on land before dark without undue haste.

They had a good ten minutes at a steady clip before they would reach the entrance to the bay. Within moments of their starting out, one of the ferries that plied these waters passed by, passengers waving merrily. Paul waved back. Left alone again, he tried singing, but in the windy dusk even the snappiest tune hung too long in the air, lingering like a dirge. He switched to whistling through his teeth.

"Jesus H. Christ," a thick voice came up from down around his feet. " 'Dixie'? Please don't tell me you're whistling 'Dixie'?"

Paul shut up.

"Mind telling me," Winston said very slowly, and although he was enunciating carefully, his words slurred, "what this rope's all about? That in combination with your choice in music is . . ." There was a long pause while Winston shaped his uncooperative mouth around the cumbersome words, "unpleasantly suggestive." He struggled to pull himself up. Paul reached over to help him to the seat beside him.

"Well, good buddy," began Paul, figuring there was no time like the present to clear the air. "You've got some explaining to do." They had reached the narrow aisle of water between two jutting peninsulas that led into Emerald Bay. Paul maneuvered into the middle and headed in.

"Without a jury out and needing my attention, I hear well enough," said Genevieve. Apparently reluctant to discuss further her miraculously restored hearing, Genevieve, scrawny but muscular under her clothing, balled up a fist, and slammed Nina in the face.

Nina fell down. Trying to catch herself on one of the seats, she put out a hand, but she was falling too hard. She heard more than felt her wrist crack. She tried to recall moves from her martial-arts courses, but her mind was filled by the growing darkness and Genevieve's astonishing transformation from colleague to deadly foe. She jumped up as fast as she could, trying to regain some footing on the slippery deck, but Genevieve was ready for her. In a fast movement, all too spookily familiar, just like the night that had sent Rachel and Mike over the side of the *Dixie Queen,* she took hold of Nina's ankles and lifted her over.

"You should have let me knock you out," she said, unaccountably holding tightly on to Nina's ankles. "But it's not that easy to do, you know. Damn. I knew I must have dropped that bug in Winston's office when we knocked my purse over during one last, very memorable lunch. Too bad you found it before I did."

Nina's face went straight into the icy blue. The shock . . . She bent her neck back to clear the water, pushing with all her might against the side of the boat with her good hand, trying to scramble her way back up into the boat, but she could feel the groaning of her backbone. Chunky waves rushed up to greet her, blurring her eyes and washing into her mouth and nose. "Genevieve, let go!" she said, spitting water.

As Nina lurched and lunged, Genevieve's grip on her ankles tightened. "If you had just arrived ten minutes later, given me time to drown Winston, you'd be cruising along in the other boat with your boyfriend, having a grand time. Doesn't that just stink? Shoot, Nina. I didn't want to have to kill you. It's just a total pisser." Out of breath with her exertions, she proceeded to push Nina down deeper, until Nina thought her back would crack. She intended to drown her, Nina realized, numb with cold and already exhausted. Then Paul would find Genevieve alone, with some neat excuse about Nina's disappearance. By the time Paul could check her story, Nina would be dead, her body gone to rest with the drowned sailor's.

"This is exactly what happens when you can't plan in advance. Otherwise, I'd have made it easier on you," Genevieve said in a feat of almost superhuman determination, shoving Nina down hard. Nina clung to the side, raising her head above the water, and when Genevieve realized she couldn't just drown her by hanging her over the side, she tried lifting Nina's limp body up and down against the boat to knock the fight out of her. Waves of unconsciousness swept over Nina. She was tiring fast. . . .

"Winston was so easy," Genevieve continued, and it was so strange, the way she wanted to explain, as if she still considered Nina a friend, and stranger still that Nina had the sense left in her bruised skull to follow her words. "Not that I wanted to hurt him. I've had so much fun with Winston," she said wistfully. "I just love that big guy. And he's been great to me. But, unfortunately, once you found that bug, Winston posed an unacceptable threat. He loves champagne, and what the hell, it seemed fitting, so I spiked it. We drank a couple of toasts. . . ."

She was thoughtful. "Even that other guy died pretty quick. There was all that catered food in the hallway outside the clerk's office, just waiting for a little Southern spice, a dose of peanut for his very special meal before it went into the jury room. His even had a vegetarian label on it. And there I was passing by with my comfort food, peanut butter sandwich in hand. It was made to order. Don't you just hate picky people," she said. "Don't you just despise them?"

"Weren't you afraid you'd be seen?" Nina gasped.

"I'd been in that hall a half dozen times during the trial avoiding the press or following that flirt Winston around. Nobody took any notice of me at all."

Nina was out of time. One more thump against the side would be the end of her. Catching Genevieve during a lifting motion, using both hands, even the one she now thought might be broken, howling with pain, she pushed off the boat straight into the lake. Genevieve, hunched over the side and caught by surprise by Nina's choice of direction, lost her footing and tumbled into the water right behind Nina.

Nina opened her eyes and saw that she was underwater, sinking like a stone into the black depths of Lake Tahoe. Maybe from the time she came up here the lake had been waiting to take her, as it had others in the past, that sailor, the victim in her first murder trial. She kicked hard against the suction, wondering how deep she was, wondering how long her stretched lungs would hold out before they spewed out air and replaced it with water. Exhausted, pierced by pain in one arm, with no idea how far she had to go, she began paddling frantically and struck something. A boulder. She followed it up and burst through the membrane between water and air. Although the boulder was completely submerged, she could stand on it and get at least part of her body out of the water.

The wind hurt worse than the water. She had to get back to land, had to. The island was fewer than a hundred feet away. She should be able to swim that in a few minutes. . . . Her body could not handle the searing cold. Goose bumps patterned like a relief map rose to different levels on every surface of her skin and she was shivering until her teeth rattled.

Completely drained of energy, panting, she examined the cove for Genevieve, spotting her instantly on the sand nearly hidden behind a bush. Genevieve had gone for the kayak. She would take the boat and get away. Nina watched, impotent, sucking in great gulps of the thin cold air, as Genevieve bent over to untie the yellow kayak, dragged it to the water, and jumped in, pushing off with a paddle. Galvanized, Nina went after her.

Swimming silently near the surface of the rough water, with one arm dragging at her side, trying to stay submerged, Nina came up along one side of the boat and heaved, using both arms, even the injured one, screaming to relieve the pain she felt. Genevieve went over. Without waiting for Genevieve's next spontaneous act, Nina yanked her off the kayak. When they reached the surface simultaneously, she balled her fist up tightly, as Genevieve had, and walloped Genevieve on the chin as hard as she could.

Genevieve's eyes shut. She sank, but Nina took hold of her hair and hauled her back up. Nina had done it. A knockout punch, one that would have done Mike Markov proud . . .

Nina tried to hold on to the kayak and use it as a float, but she couldn't hold Genevieve and the kayak. For a long moment, she allowed herself to consider letting Genevieve go. She couldn't do it. She just couldn't. With a groan of resignation, she let the boat float away.

Kicking them both back to the island without using her hurt arm proved difficult but not impossible. By the time she dragged Genevieve up onto the rocks by the cove, both Matt's boat and the yellow kayak were bobbing merrily hundreds of yards away, completely out of reach. She fell beside Genevieve on the sand, half dead from the cold, stretched out, and lapsed into a stupor of exhaustion.

No more than a few moments passed before she forced herself to stir, telling herself to keep at least one eye open. But her caution came too late. A fine drizzle of rain falling from the sky was interrupted by the shadow standing over her wielding a long, sharp blade.

Genevieve had found her picnic basket.

37

As EVENING APPROACHED THE LAKE turned to a velvety midnight-blue. The necklace of mountains surrounding the bay, shadowy outlines, piled upon each other in layers of paling grays. The wind that often came up at the end of the day kept the waves busy, lapping noisily against the shores. Swinging rapidly into the bay, moving as cautiously as he could in the deepening darkness, Paul felt they were edging toward the end of the world, and at any moment might fall off.

Winston's moment of coherence had passed, and he had settled back down and begun to snore heavily, not a healthy kind of snoring, but Paul didn't have time to worry about that.

He angled toward the empty, floating speedboat, reached over, and snagged the trailing line. With a little difficulty, he tied it to drag safely behind. The lighter kayak was floating much farther out, away from the island. But he had a more pressing question. Where were the women?

The question demanded an immediate answer. He headed for Fannette, figuring out that they must have gone back there for something Genevieve wanted. Maybe the boat had simply come loose. The kayak, too. Unwilling to imagine an alternate scenario, he let that straightforward explanation console him until he got to the cove.

No sign of anyone.

"The hell," Winston said clearly. "What kind of champagne was that?" He tried to raise his tied hands to his head, and failed.

Paul pulled away, and began to circle the island, starting around the southwestern tip.

"Genny?" said Winston, head lolling, eyes nearly rolled back into his head. "I know you don't really want to hurt me. Let's talk, honey. . . ."

"Winston!" Paul commanded. "What are you talking about?"

But the other man's eyes closed, and his head lolled back.

Popping up sudden as toast, Nina swung with her right arm, connecting with Genevieve's wrist, but she didn't go far. Genevieve took her down and sat on her.

"Don't do this!" Nina screamed. "I won't press charges!"

The strangeness of this statement was not lost on Genevieve, who half-chuckled as she pressed down with her weight, trying to still a crazed, wiggling Nina. "Jesus, Nina, you're gonna go to your grave jabbering like a lawyer." She had Nina pinned. She raised the knife, trying to jab it into Nina's throat, but Nina took hold of her wrist, and using the force of Genevieve's thrust turned the hand so that the knife faced away, but the wrist came into close contact with Nina's teeth.

"Ow!" Genevieve screeched, dropping the knife.

Rolling away from her, Nina jumped and took off.

"Now where are you gonna go?" she heard Genevieve saying behind her. "There's nowhere to hide on this little bitty island."

Nina found the rock stairs that led up to the teahouse hidden by the brush nearby. Scraped and gouged by the thorny bushes, she ignored the lacerating of her feet and the sharp twinge of her weak ankle and moved at top speed up, up, up, thinking, where could she turn off, where could she get away, buy herself some time. . . .

"Nina?"

The voice behind her was too near. Her fear at that moment equaled the terror she had felt at the sight of the knife, an icy hollowness, like she'd been invaded by ghosts and would freeze up and die from the inside out.

"Let's work this thing out, okay?" Genevieve panted. "You want your money, too, don't you?"

Because there seemed nowhere else to go, Nina ran all the way up the hill toward the teahouse, too frightened to think or even to worry about breathing. Once inside, choking back all fear, she ran over the stone floor to the open window on the northeastern tip at the highest point on the island, leaned out, took a deep breath, and screamed the highest, most piercing, shrieking, fearsome scream she could muster. "Help! Help! Help!" Three cries, like the three trips to the surface a drowning person has before dying. She knew Genevieve could hear.

Down below, she spotted Matt's boat. She jumped up and down, shouting and waving her arm.

Paul waved back.

"This hasn't been easy for me, you know. I never knew things would get this bad," Genevieve said, ducking through the low door and coming at her.

Paul whirled around the northeast tip of Fannette, going for the cove, all worries about the kayak gone, determined to get onto that island if he had to swim there.

Once nestled in, he looped extra rope to the boat, taking the end in his teeth, and dove into the black water; then he swam like hell. Almost immediately, he felt extremely winded. The altitude. He wasn't used to the altitude. He treaded water, trying to catch his breath, then continued on, using a strong, easy stroke, counting to himself to keep the beat going, the image of Nina in that window indelibly printed on his imagination; the sight of her against that black sky, her clothing tattered and flying in the wind around her.

Nina jumped out the teahouse window, landing hard on the rock below, barely catching herself before falling headlong down a hill of solid rock that would surely, surely have ended her days as a jabbering lawyer.

She stumbled to her left, but realizing whatever way she went

Genevieve waited, she climbed down the rocks for a ways, listening intently for the other woman but hearing nothing. When she fell again, straight into a prickle bush, she took it for a message from whatever spirit had kept her alive so far. Pulling her torn limbs away from the punishing thorns, she continued down a rocky slope made up of huge boulders, some cracked by weather, others huge slabs of roughness.

There must be somewhere to hide. There must be.

There was. Nina leaned her hand against a particularly sturdy-looking piece of brush and fell in.

She found herself inside a ruined pile of rocks which screened a small, dry, squarish cave, barely large enough to contain her, but very well hidden from view. Panting, almost crying with relief, trying to keep herself from making any noise, she sat down in the dirt, put her arms around her knees and shivered, burying her face into her arms.

Her eyes adjusted slowly to the darkness. When she finally looked around, she realized this was no natural formation. The walls formed a pattern, with larger boulders forming the base that gradually shrunk in size as they approached the top. The ceiling consisted of one huge slab. An intricate entryway, now collapsed, but with enough remnants to be discernible, had once lovingly described an arch.

Nina had fallen into what must once long ago have been the sailor's tomb.

"Come out, Nina," Genevieve said from somewhere above. "Don't force me to come after you. . . ."

Trying desperately to be silent, but sucking air in great gulps, Nina leaned back into the spidery walls of her cave, listening for sounds.

Wind. Rain.

And then, footfalls.

She got down on her hands and knees, reaching for something she could use for a weapon. Her hand landed on a loose rock, heavy, jagged. She held it aloft.

Only a few feet away now. The sounds came closer, closer . . .

And then, with a swiftness and noise that had abandoned stealth, they moved away.

Nina breathed out a sob. And the next thing she heard was Paul's voice.

"Nina!" His voice rumbled, deep and full and desperate, traveling across the distance like a lion's roar. "Nina!"

"Here!" she said, trying to stand up, whacking herself on the head. "I'm right here!"

She heard rocks falling around her, then the thump of heavy steps.

"Where?"

Paul's voice sounded right beside her. She pushed a loose pile of rock away and stepped out into his arms, covered head to toe with dirt and dust. After a short moment, all too short, he stepped back.

"What the hell is going on?" he asked.

"Where is Genevieve?"

"I think I heard a splash back there. Someone dove off a rock near the cove," he said.

"Her hearing aid. It wasn't real."

Paul seemed to understand immediately.

"Where are the boats?"

"Tied together in the cove."

"She'll take them both."

"Let her, Nina," Paul said, pushing the mop of her hair away from her eyes. "We can wait here. We'll keep each other warm. I told Matt where we were going. He'll find us."

"What about Winston?"

"Oh, shit!"

"You left him tied up?"

The expression on his face gave her her answer.

"She'll kill him!" Nina said.

"Why is she trying to kill Winston?"

"He knows more than we do about her. Maybe she knew when we found the bug he would connect her to Wright's death."

They tore back over the hump of hill to the pathway and ran down to the cove.

When they reached the small sandy beach, Genevieve had already unhitched the rental boat from its mooring on a rock and was climbing in. Banging against some rocks, the *Andreadore* bobbed behind. The kayak was by now a small yellow sliver on the horizon, heading toward the main body of the lake to the east.

"Where's Winston?" Paul yelled.

"There!" Nina shouted. "She dumped him! He must have been trying to swim away from her and got caught in the current." Out beyond the cove, also caught in the drifting waters they saw him flailing, the dark orb of his head dipping below the surface.

"I'll go after her," she told Paul. "I'm not strong enough to lug Winston back. You get him." She started to jump into the water, but he held her back.

"Let her go," he said.

Nina looked at Genevieve in the boat, and back at Paul. "We can't leave Winston out there."

"I'll get Winston." He held on to her.

"You're no good to me or anyone else dead!" Nina cried. "She'll run you both down if I don't stop her!"

With a look of agonized indecision, he let go.

Nina dove, swimming as fast as she could to cover the few short yards between her and the speedboat. In spite of the pain, she ordered her injured wrist into action, kicking furiously to make up for the weakness in her stroke. Behind her, she dimly noted splashing as Paul set off to rescue Winston.

Rain broke from the sky, battering the water below and the people in it. Wet already, Nina hardly noticed. Within seconds, she reached the boat. Genevieve was searching frantically for something. Alternately kicking, cursing, and screaming at the boat, she lurched from side to side and front to back. Within a few moments, she stood up, triumphant, key in hand.

Meanwhile, Nina pulled down the ladder by the propeller, straightened up, and hauled her dripping body into the boat, into air as wet as the lake, her injuries forgotten, feeling like a monster rising from the deep, larger and more powerful than the disheveled person facing her now.

In the fleeting seconds when they faced off, Nina could find not even a hint of the youth and charm and personality that was Genevieve. She faced a stranger.

"Genevieve, why?" she asked, rain running down her face, trying to give herself a moment to assess the situation so that she could decide what to do next to stall Genevieve and give Paul time to get Winston to safety. "The tension. You're not well—"

"Remember that little private meeting we had way back when? She promised me three million dollars," said Genevieve, twisting the boat key savagely.

"Who?" asked Nina, looking around for a weapon and discovering only one, the knife held fast in Genevieve's free hand.

"Lindy."

"Lindy bribed you to bug the jury room?"

"Of course not. She offered me a bonus if we won. That's a perfectly legitimate incentive in the business world. Too bad I had to open my big mouth and go bragging to Winston about it before I knew Wright was going to cause me such trouble. Even then, Winston never would have figured out what I had done if you hadn't found that damn bug."

"Lindy knew about Wright?"

"She didn't want details. She wanted to win. And she did, didn't she? I won it for her and by God, I'm going to get my money out of the deal." The engine started up. "You know I always thought I'd do like the other ants because that's what I was raised to do. But I am my father's daughter. I just couldn't resist the opportunity when it came along."

While Genevieve talked, Nina edged in closer. "What are you going to do now?"

"Take care of Paul and Winston first, then you."

"I thought you cared about Winston. And even me, a little."

"Stay back," Genevieve commanded, stabbing the knife in the air toward Nina.

Nina backed up quickly.

"You've got to go, Nina. I was stupid, losing track of that microphone. But I can fix everything right here in the tragic boating accident that's just about to happen. You accidentally run down your friends and take your own life. It's feeble, but the only witness will add substantiating details."

"The attack on Rachel Pembroke?"

"She was Mike Markov's muse, and way too influential. Without her pushing him to fight hard against Lindy we'd have had a much better chance to win the trial. And of course, she was a crucial witness. I hid in the backseat of her car, thinking I'd get her alone and stage a suicide. But she spotted me and cracked up the car before I could do anything. Then Lindy showed up out of nowhere, so I never finished the job. So I decided to trust my usual research method, listening in on the jury. This was the first time I've had to intervene to such an extent. I really am very good at my job. No one could have predicted Wright's change in attitude. It wasn't my fault."

She wouldn't look at Nina, although she still held the knife poised in one hand. With her light hair pasted to her head and water streaming down her face, she looked half drowned, half something supernatural. Moving the boat around in a circle, she searched for Paul and Winston.

Nina couldn't see them anywhere. Where were they?

"You know there are all kinds of old shipwrecks out there," Genevieve said, "bits of flotsam from Vikingsholm on the bottom of the bay around here."

"Please, Genevieve," Nina said, eyes straining out into the rain, her fright reaching fever pitch.

"Maybe, if you aren't drowned already, when you get to the bottom you'll see something down there." As Genevieve reached the end of the cove and open water, she said, almost to herself, "How did everything get so out of hand?"

Nina pounced, silently invoking God, ghosts in the lake, and anyone else who might take an interest, to help her shove Genevieve away from the wheel. Genevieve took the onslaught like a redwood, without budging. Swiping the knife efficiently, she slashed deeply into Nina's arm. "Stay back," she said, angling the boat out of the cove, "or I'll cut your throat. There's a perfect cemetery down there, one that never, ever reveals its secrets."

Fighting tears brought on by the pain in her arm, Nina turned her back to Genevieve and took hold of the rope that still held Matt's boat attached to the marina boat. The *Andreadore* bounced behind like a child's sled on a suicide run down a mountain. She untied it awkwardly, using her slashed right arm since the left remained almost out of commission. Then, lifting herself to the edge of the seats, she jumped for it. One knee slammed into a bench, and the other collapsed under her as she came in for a landing.

Watching Nina get away, Genevieve cried out with frustration.

Amazingly, the key remained in the ignition of Matt's boat. Fighting lances of pain in her arm, Nina turned the key and took hold of the wheel.

Nothing happened. The *Andreadore* had died without even offering up its usual nose-thumbing, the smell in the air of gasoline. Matt's boat began to drift east, following the route of the kayak, going out to the big lake beyond.

But maybe it was okay, Nina thought. Maybe Genevieve would forget about hurting any of them, dock on land near Vikingsholm, and climb to the highway. Maybe she had a car stashed up there. She could be in L.A. by evening, gone from their lives forever, buried in its anonymous millions.

But even while she told herself this story with a happy ending, Nina didn't believe it. Genevieve had come too far. She had listened in on the jury. She had already killed. Now she would collect her pay.

The same thought must have occurred to Genevieve because she turned the boat back toward the island.

———

Paul saw Nina reach the boat and heard voices, but he had no further attention to spare on Nina's troubles. The cove was tiny, but once he reached the deeper waters beyond where he had seen Winston, he had to concentrate on locating the head that had resurfaced once already. Stroke, stroke, steady.

Out of breath, and so cold he had to remove himself mentally from his body to go on, he finally reached him.

Grabbing first by the hair, then by the shirt Winston still wore, Paul began to tow the other man. "Winston," he said, gasping for air. "Can you help me at all?"

A gurgle, then a strangled voice. "My hands are literally tied, man!"

Genevieve had removed the ropes around Winston's ankles but she had left the ropes Paul had tied around his wrists. Paul tried but could not remove them. He had done a very good job tying them. "I'm just going to have to drag you in," he said.

"Get these ropes off!" Winston pleaded, frenzied. "I'm drowning! Get them off!"

"Hang on," Paul said. He had no energy left, not enough to argue, and certainly not enough to lug a football player across this melted continent to safety. He began to kick his feet, trying to paddle with one arm.

"You're going to kill me!" Winston sputtered, as his head dipped into the churning lake.

They had gone no more than fifty feet before Paul heard it: the motorboat returning.

Well, dark or not, Genevieve could see them easily. The moon had risen, and above the silvery water and raindrops he imagined his head as the light side of the moon, to Winston's dark.

"We're going down," he said, "out of sight."

Winston struggled violently until he was out of Paul's grasp. Held aloft by sheer will, unable even to paddle, he faced the boat that was coming at them. "Augh! Augh! Genevieve stop!" he shouted. "No!"

Rushing at them like a locomotive, big as an ocean liner, the immensity of death obliterated their small horizon.

Nina watched in horror as Genevieve plowed straight into Paul and Winston. So immersed in emotion she felt she, too, had been hit by Genevieve's boat, she twisted the starter on Matt's boat like a crazy person who had only one obsessive task to attempt and never complete. After inspecting the water for the reemergence of Paul and Winston, Genevieve brought the boat around swiftly and started back for Nina. She planned to crash her speedboat into the *Andreadore*.

"Start, damn you!" Nina jammed the key into the ignition once again and twisted, but the boat did not start.

What had Matt said on their last trip out, while she squawked and complained and swore she would never get it? The boat will start. What starts the boat is not technique, it is confidence. Here's confidence right here, see it? The black lever to the right of the wheel. Now take that confidence and mess with it. Give it a sip of gas. Move it here . . . She moved it, swiveling the key back and forth with her other hand. Nothing. Put it here, more toward the middle of the slot. . . .

Genevieve was so close, Nina could see into her eyes. What she saw there moved through Nina's body, making her tremble. She saw total concentration, pure violence coming at her. Why, those merciless eyes practically glittered with it. . . .

The engine caught.

Swinging the wheel wildly to the left, Nina thought she could feel Genevieve's cold breath as she passed, missing the *Andreadore* by inches.

With a few seconds' grace, Nina turned to look at the cove. There, on the far edge, she saw two heads popping up with a huge splash. Paul and Winston. They had somehow managed to duck under the boat. They were still alive.

Crying out in pain, she swung the boat around, pitching in the wind and tipping way to the right, so close to going over she could count the foam bubbles forming around the raindrops on the surface of the water. She would get there first. She would save them all somehow.

Behind her, Genevieve advanced.

"It's Nina!" Paul cried out. "She's coming this way."

"Nina?" Winston coughed. "She's after us, too?"

"No!" Paul said. "She's trying to lure Genevieve away from us." The muscles of his arms were wired so tight to keep him and Winston aloft, he thought they might snap. "Genevieve's not taking the bait. We're finished," Paul said. "Jesus Christ, kick your feet, Winston. Help me!"

But Winston, who had taken in a good gallon of water during their most recent underwater struggle, was far too busy trying to expel it to answer.

"We gotta go down again!" Paul said quickly. "Ready?"

"I can't!" Winston spat. "No!" and in his panic he managed to extricate himself from Paul long enough to sink from sight.

Down under he went.

Genevieve bore down on them.

Paul floundered around hopelessly for the other man's shirt, found it, and aimed for shore, flapping like a fish already dying on the hook. He pushed, he shoved, he tried his best to keep Winston above water and breathing, but all his awareness was in fact acutely focused on the sound of motors getting louder and louder. . . .

The *Andreadore* passed, giving them wide berth. He saw Nina, intent at the wheel, her long hair tangled and flying out behind her, a flag of faith. But Genevieve wanted them dead. She would mow them down first, and then go after Nina. She was close, so damn close. . . .

He touched an underwater rock with his toe. Hurling Winston violently to one side, he fixed his last hope on the rock jutting around the left end of the cove. He sprinted for it and lifted the dormant, waterlogged body of Winston behind him.

Genevieve's boat cut so close it whistled by, sloshing a great whale fluke of water to douse them. Then, robotlike, as if totally undeterred by the minor setback of failing to kill them yet again, it swung back in line to renew its inhumanly unemotional pursuit of Nina.

Genevieve knew they were safely trapped on the island. Paul watched helplessly as Nina headed for the beach by Vikingsholm. She had a hundred yard lead on Genevieve by now. She could get in close, jump out, and hide somewhere in the woods or climb the hill up to the road. She could go for help. . . .

But as he watched, the *Andreadore* pulled up short and swung around, heading back to the island.

What was Nina doing? She couldn't rescue them, could she? he thought, confused. Why come back?

She was heading for these rocks, he thought. Had the rain blinded her to the rocks and shallow water here?

She would die! He tightened his grip on Winston. Should he wave her off?

Maybe she would turn away at the last minute. But then he saw Genevieve's boat cut the same wide arc. Without Paul and Winston in the water to distract her, Genevieve quickly narrowed the space that separated the two boats.

Thirty, twenty, ten yards from the rocks, Nina closed the distance between her and the rocky peninsula of the islet where Paul and Winston lay, the *Andreadore* chugging steadily along.

Gripping the droopy lawyer at his side, Paul hauled him— bumping, grinding, and screaming—up and over the rocky tip onto the beach at the far end of the cove, then dropped him with a *thump*. He ran up a steep rock a safe distance from the point, and held up a hand to his forehead to keep the rain from streaming into his eyes.

He tried to see into Nina's mind as she flew into the wind toward him, but her fixation on her target left no room for anything except determination.

The rain pounded down hard now, and Paul no longer knew to trust his eyes.

He thought he saw the small figure of Nina stand erect on the edge of the *Andreadore* and then soar like an angel out into the deep water beyond the point just as Genevieve's boat, directly behind, connected.

He thought he saw Genevieve's terrified face.

He felt rather than saw the tremendous crash as she struck rock with an explosion so violent it stopped time.

And then, almost leisurely, he saw the rest in detail, slowed like animation examined frame by frame: Genevieve's boat flipping, coming to rest upside down, whomping down crossways over the *Andreadore*. The infinity of splintered wood sailing into the air. Fire where boats had been. Heat and light where dark had been.

Amid the splinters, aglow in the glare of ignited gasoline, the silhouette of a woman boneless as a rag doll coming to rest in the lake, poising on the surface, and sinking into its depths.

38

SUMMERTIME IN TAHOE. KELLY GREENS and chartreuses mixed with green as dark as charcoal. The forests had soaked up the melted snow that rolled off the mountains. Memorial Day came. The tourists arrived for vacation fun and did not leave.

Nina didn't notice. She came into the office that Tuesday morning in June and closed her door to everything. She did not answer the phone when it rang. She did not touch the papers that were already beginning to look musty, like something from her past. In jeans and a sweatshirt, she propped her bare feet on her desk and looked out the window toward the lake, but the picture window insisted on acting like a projection screen and the events of the past seven months imposed themselves again to interrupt her line of vision.

Sandy, parked at her own desk outside her door, did not disturb her. She knew that even on a summer morning you could have a dark night of the soul.

Genevieve had advanced through their lives like a landslide, destroying everything.

Paul had helped Nina get out of the water and climb onto the islet. There, they had waited, watching the speedboats burn. Winston woke up in time to observe with them as the burning embers of the boats sizzled in the rain, sinking into the lake in eerie silence. The kayak had floated away. It was hours before Matt notified the Coast Guard and they were rescued.

Paul and Winston had taken their stories to the police. Jeffrey Riesner had requested that the verdict favoring Lindy be vacated based on "irregularities" in the proceedings, and Judge Milne granted the request, ordering a new trial. Removing Jim Colby as receiver, he placed all assets and business management back in Mike Markov's hands.

The catastrophic outcome of the trial, since it was caused by a member of Lindy's legal team, exposed Lindy to judicial sanctions. At least she should have been ordered to pay Mike's legal fees. Instead, Judge Milne delivered a stinging lecture to Nina in open court, widely quoted in the media, that made her red to the roots of her hair, beamed Jeffrey Riesner up to the moon, and yanked out the last shreds of her self-confidence.

Mike had most of his money. Lindy had nothing.

Nina had less than nothing.

A year of her life had been completely blasted into oblivion along with Genevieve's boat.

What was left of Markov Enterprises after Mike's neglect was now his to run again until a new trial went one way or another.

Whatever happened, Nina was no longer in the picture. Her business had been shattered by the Markov case. Clients had drifted away to lawyers who had more time to return their calls. Her checkbook featured a negative balance. She could not begin to afford to represent Lindy in a retrial. She could not even pay her rent. According to her contract with Lindy, Lindy had agreed to pay at least her basic attorney's fees and costs. Even at a discounted rate, that came to over a hundred thousand dollars. Maybe someday Lindy would be able to pay the bill, but it didn't look like anytime soon.

Or maybe Lindy would just file bankruptcy and move on.

Nina borrowed more money to buy Matt a new boat since Matt hadn't kept up the insurance on the *Andreadore*. She borrowed money to pay Winston for his time in the last few months of the case. That money wasn't enough to save Winston, however. The IRS came after him for tax evasion. He was countersuing for harassment, but everyone knew how difficult it was to get out from under once the government had turned its red eye your way.

They would not be upgrading their offices. They would not be hiring new people. The complete exploitation of every financial resource available to her to get through this case had wiped her out. The boat loan was the last loan the bank would float for her, the bank had said. She needed to start regular payments on her massive outstanding debts.

Without the fee from Lindy, she couldn't. Instead, she piled the bills in a corner of the office, and watched them mounting day by day.

Genevieve had disappeared, either into the lake, as Paul seemed to think, or into the vast land of California, and the story of her disappearance and her attacks on Paul, Winston and Nina made front page news all over the state. In case by some miracle she had survived the explosion, the police charged her in absentia with murder in the second degree for Clifford Wright's death, and three additional counts of attempted murder for Paul, Winston, and Nina.

Nina did not choose to think about Genevieve any longer. She was done with her, just like everything else.

Paul delayed his trip to Washington for a week, but she was too down to talk to him. Finally, he left town quietly, without calling to say good-bye.

Nina had risked everything, and lost.

Leaving Comanche safely stabled with friends outside Reno, Lindy moved back to town temporarily to wrap up loose ends. She had decided to leave town. Some old friends had a gold mine they worked in Idaho. She wanted to go up there and soak up what they knew, plus she just needed to get away from Tahoe. It sounded like the perfect getaway for her right now.

The news about Genevieve had been devastating. It had taken her several days to recover from the shock of what had happened. Her own offer of money had somehow triggered the murder of a juror and attacks on her lawyers. She had been criminally obtuse. She was lucky they weren't charging her with conspiracy or something. Guilt overwhelmed her.

Along with the news of Genevieve came the news that a new trial had been ordered.

And so, even though Nina had advised against it because Lindy would probably get stuck with Mike's court costs, Lindy had decided to walk away from the case. She felt terrible about what she had put Nina through for nothing, but she didn't feel strong enough to continue fighting Mike.

She wished she could pay Nina, but lawyers always seemed to have plenty of resources. Nina probably had lots of money tucked away. She wouldn't have taken the case without a major bankroll, because that would be stupid. Nina would be okay, and Winston would make up his loss in a year.

Her thoughts went back to that poor man. The whole world seemed to feel that Cliff Wright had died because of her, and maybe they were right. She no longer wanted the money, the business or anything else. She had heard from Alice that Rachel had gone back to Mike begging for forgiveness. So Mike would be fine.

As for herself—she'd finally accepted that her life here, the life she had led for twenty years, had come to a close. She wasn't exactly young, but she was tough as boiled octopus.

The second week in June she called Mike's secretary and arranged to come by the house to get the rest of her things. She wanted to warn him ahead of time. She asked him to please get Rachel out of the house as a final favor to her, just for a couple of hours. Then she would go, and they would never need to talk again.

She drove the Jeep down the familiar dusty road off the highway, along the lakeside to the gate of the house. The gates were open. He was expecting her.

Her flowerbeds, in full spring bloom, sprawled with neglect. Fully half the blooms were dead and unpicked. She liked to think Rachel would love them as much as she had, and would soon have things back in order.

Sammy loped up and over her, and she spent a few minutes

petting him, saying all the things he liked to hear. From her pocket, she pulled a piece of the beef jerky he loved for a treat, and she left him to eat it on the gravel path.

Mike stood in the doorway, hands in his pockets. "Hi," he said.

"Hi." She walked up the stairs, and he let her by. "Do you have some boxes for me?"

Florencia had stacked dozens upstairs, and dozens downstairs, along with thick stacks of paper for wrapping.

"I won't need all these." She planned to take only the most special things, the carved wooden box her dad left her, a blue glass paperweight that belonged to her mother. She would box the photographs up to look at someday when the poison had drained out of them and they could no longer hurt her.

She started with the upstairs. Mike stood on the landing leaning against the banister, hands still in his pockets as she moved from room to room. When she ran out of boxes, he helped her fold and tape up some more. He never objected to one single thing, although he watched her intently the whole time.

The only place she did not go was into the bedroom closet. She couldn't stand to see Rachel's things hanging there. She decided to ask Florencia to ship anything on to her if she had left anything important in there.

She felt very tired when the time came to start on the downstairs, but there would be less down there. Those rooms were public, and except for her desk, she didn't think she'd find much.

"Want something to drink?" Mike asked, following her down the stairs.

She ran her hand over the railing one last time. "No, thanks. I want to finish up." Strange. For almost the first time since she had met him, she couldn't read the look in his eyes. He had changed. She almost wished he would complain or get angry, anything to break the tension between them.

She made short work of the desk, shoveling her paperwork into two boxes, swiftly striping them with tape. Mike helped her stack the boxes by the front door.

Giving herself a few seconds to catch her breath, she looked around one last time. Then she opened the front door and faced Mike. Wiping her hands on a piece of wrapping paper, she held out her right hand. "We had a good long run," she said. "See you around sometime."

He was hesitating, as if he was making up his mind about something but couldn't spit it out. She wanted to hear it, hear him say something she could carry away that meant he understood how good a run it had really been.

So she stood there like a fool, her hand out, when she should have turned around with whatever dignity she had left, and the tension grew unbearable.

He took her hand. And then he pulled her toward him and kissed her on the lips.

She jumped back. "Just what do you think you're doing?" she cried.

"I'm trying to kiss you, to make it better."

"You're making it harder!"

She started past him, but he blocked the way. "Will you listen to me?," he said. "Rachel's gone," he said, and suddenly he looked like the old Mike, a little shamefaced, but secretly pleased with himself.

"Don't lie. I know she came back to you."

"She did, and I'm a big dumb ox, but I'm not as dumb as I used to be." He gave her a tentative grin.

"She's not coming back?"

"I had to write her a hell of a check," he said. "It was always business with her. And I was vain and confused, an easy mark. She's gone, Lindy. And I—"

She shook her head. "Mike, don't do this."

"We could . . . let's sit down here on the steps and talk."

"After all that's happened? I don't think so."

"Just give me a minute, then, and I'll talk. Though I'm as lousy at that as I am at everything else I do without you."

Away in the distance, Tahoe gleamed.

"Let's dump last year in the lake," Mike said.

Sandy brought lunch in, two salads. She set them down on Nina's desk.

"I'm not hungry," Nina said.

"Fine. Don't eat," said Sandy. "Now what?" she asked, taking the plastic lid off and pouring dressing.

"Now nothing," said Nina.

"Is she going to pay us anything?"

"No, and I don't even have the money to cover the office rent this month. We're lucky the judge didn't order Lindy to pay Mike's attorney fees. She's already trying to come up with thirty thousand to pay for Mike's trial costs so that she can drop the complaint. She can't help."

"The landlord will carry us for a couple of months. You've made the Starlake building famous. He's got a waiting list of tenants. Here." She handed Nina a check.

Sandy's personal check was made out to Nina for ten thousand dollars. How she could have put together that kind of money Nina couldn't imagine. And here she was offering it to her boss.

"You are the best," Nina said, trying not to show her emotion. "No way. But thanks for the offer." She handed it back.

"We'll start fresh. Work twice as hard," said Sandy. "You can just use that money to get us out of the crunch." As if to illustrate this statement, she crunched thoughtfully on her crouton.

"Forget it!"

"You telling me I work for a quitter? You've still got a blanket to keep you warm at night, don't you?" Sandy turned her pebble eyes directly toward Nina's.

Nina looked back into their blackness, as if she might find in there the mysterious source of Sandy's power. She saw only a dark-haired, round-faced, Native-American woman looking back at her, no more comprehensible than she had ever been.

And at that moment, looking at Sandy's eyes, she felt the full cost of her gamble. She had risked Sandy's job, Bob's future here, their home, the work she was cut out to do in life. She had lost Paul. . . .

Because Lindy refused to go to the bed upstairs, the one she had seen him in with Rachel, they had found their way to the boat and made up the bed in the cruiser with fresh sheets. Sunlight poured through the skylight into the cabin.

Later, they found some beer and crackers in the galley. They brought the platter up to a table on the deck, and found a spot in the sun to enjoy the lazy, warm afternoon. A few boats floated in the distance, rocking like lovers with the rhythm of the lake. Distant music drifted toward them.

"I'll go see Riesner tomorrow," Mike said. "Tell him to cooperate with the dismissal."

There was no doubt in him. He sounded like a man fighting for his life. He wanted her back. But she didn't believe in miracles. Things were far from perfect. She could never trust him as she once had. "I love you, Mike, but I won't go on with things the way they have been."

Mike said, "I know. So we won't. We'll get married on Sunday."

There was a very long silence.

"Lindy. Marry me. Please," Mike said urgently. "Any day you want, if Sunday's not convenient."

Another silence.

"Lindy?" he said, sounding very anxious.

"Oh, sure, Mike."

"Please?"

"Why should I believe this?"

"I mean it. I love you more than ever. I need you back in my life. This time for good, Lindy."

For a long time she looked out across the water, remembering the last time they had been together on this lake, in a boat. The spring wind fluttered through his hair as he stood waiting for her to say something, so very different than he had been that night, a different person, as she was.

He wanted to marry her at last. Here it was, big as Lake Tahoe and just as full of mystery, the happy ending, nothing like she had ever imagined. Underneath the ridiculous, persistent, flickering hope that this time would be for good and forever, doubt and fear had taken the place of faith. She had never known how fragile it all was. She had never known how your hopes could collapse on you, and destroy you. How hard it was to go on, knowing that.

"I'll promise to marry you. . . ." she began.

"Ah, Lindy." His face creased into a deep smile.

"If you promise not to wiggle out of it this time," she finished.

"No more wiggling."

"I'll believe that when I see the preacher here on Sunday," she said.

They kissed, and then sat down on the built-in benches that lined the stern, touching shoulders. "I'm taking you on a real honeymoon," Mike said. "I know just the place."

"You want to leave right now? With the business in so much trouble?"

"The question is, what do *we* want to do? I have a suggestion. I'm thinking we might want to sell out, go somewhere brand-new. I hear there's a big opal mine in Australia for sale. . . ."

"A new start," she said. She ran a finger along his chin, refreshing her memory of its shape.

"Just sell out and go."

"I'm already packed," Lindy said, and as she said it, words from Corinthians her father used to quote came into her mind. "Love is patient. Love is kind. It is not easily angered. It keeps no record of wrongs."

She realized she would never know why it all happened, why he fell in love with Rachel, or why she forgave him. Why they had ended up in court. She did not have a clue. You just never knew about people. There were so many things going on inside them all the time, waves of memories and events, influences you could never fathom. She thought again, sadly, of Clifford Wright.

"Speaking of business," she said, "I'm going to have Nina draw up some papers for us to sign, Mike. Things are going to be different between us, marriage or no."

"Sure," he said. "Let's make it plain and simple, in writing. That ought to satisfy even ol' Jeff Riesner."

A speedboat went by, and its wake made the cruiser pitch and sway. "By the way," he said, holding her tightly, "how much is the damage so far in the legal department?"

"A lot, but Nina worked very hard for me. I wish I had something personal to give her, something really special, besides money," she said, thinking of Genevieve. "I'd like to show her how much I appreciate . . . Oh! I know. How about this for a bonus? I'll pass along my dad's claim. It's not worth anything, but it's a place to go besides her office. Maybe she would like that. I don't think I'll ever go back there now. Too many memories."

"Great idea."

"Her costs and hourly fees ran to about a hundred thousand total. Isn't it awful? What an expensive lesson. She won't get the percentage, of course."

He turned her so that the sun warmed her back and began massaging with the art of an ex-boxer who really knew what felt good. "Your legal fees are a hundred grand?" he said, moving his fingers soothingly over the knobs in the center of her back, working slowly, kneading the sore spots he knew so well.

With the tenderest possible touch of his callused hands, he was trying in the best way he knew how to erase some of the injury of the past year.

"You got a bargain," he said, and laughed. "My lawyer charged twice that."

"Moan and whine for the rest of today if you have to," Sandy was telling Nina across town, "but that's all the time you get. You have an appointment tomorrow at ten."

"Oh?" Nina had started to pick at her salad. The afternoon sun, reflecting off the lake outside, blazed into the office, warming her face. She tried to yawn, wishing she could nap for just a few minutes and forget the mountain of financial trouble she was in, but exhausted and tired were two different things. She felt exhausted but wired.

"New business," Sandy said.

"Sandy, no . . ."

"Something big." She was sitting very still, wearing her most deadpan expression.

She was up to something.

"Sandy, tomorrow's a long way away to me right now. I have a lot of decisions to make. Even if I could afford it, I can't consider getting all wrapped up in another horrible case. . . ."

"You're going to love it," she said.

And as she spoke, something stirred inside Nina, a familiar feeling, that little thrill.

What the hell, she thought.

She took her feet off the desk, straightened up, and picked up a yellow pad.

"Lay it on me, Sandy."